PENGUIN BOOKS

Fight Me

Austin Grossman is a novelist and interactive storyteller. His novels include *Soon I Will Be Invincible*, *YOU: a novel* and *Crooked*. *Soon I Will Be Invincible* was nominated for the 2007 John Sargent Sr First Novel Prize. His writing has also appeared in *Granta*, the *Wall Street Journal* and the *New York Times*. His game credits include *System Shock*, *Deus Ex* and *Dishonored*, which received the 2012 BAFTA award for Best Game. He has an MA in Performance Studies from NYU and is ABD in English Literature at the University of California, Berkeley. He currently teaches narrative design at NYU, and works as a consultant in game and XR experience design.

Fight Me

AUSTIN GROSSMAN

PENGUIN BOOKS

PENGUIN BOOKS

UK | USA | Canada | Ireland | Australia
India | New Zealand | South Africa

Penguin Books is part of the Penguin Random House group of companies
whose addresses can be found at global.penguinrandomhouse.com

Penguin Random House UK,
One Embassy Gardens, 8 Viaduct Gardens, London SW11 7BW

penguin.co.uk

First published by Penguin Michael Joseph 2024
Published in Penguin Books 2025

001

Copyright © Austin Grossman, 2024

The moral right of the author has been asserted

Penguin Random House values and supports copyright.
Copyright fuels creativity, encourages diverse voices, promotes freedom
of expression and supports a vibrant culture. Thank you for purchasing
an authorized edition of this book and for respecting intellectual property
laws by not reproducing, scanning or distributing any part of it by any
means without permission. You are supporting authors and enabling
Penguin Random House to continue to publish books for everyone.
No part of this book may be used or reproduced in any manner for the
purpose of training artificial intelligence technologies or systems. In accordance
with Article 4(3) of the DSM Directive 2019/790, Penguin Random House
expressly reserves this work from the text and data mining exception

Typeset by Jouve (UK), Milton Keynes
Printed and bound in Great Britain by Clays Ltd, Elcograf S.p.A.

The authorized representative in the EEA is Penguin Random House Ireland,
Morrison Chambers, 32 Nassau Street, Dublin D02 YH68

A CIP catalogue record for this book is available from the British Library

ISBN: 978–1–405–95187–6

Penguin Random House is committed to a sustainable future
for our business, our readers and our planet. This book is made from
Forest Stewardship Council® certified paper.

Tell me how all this, and love too, will ruin us.
These, our bodies, possessed by light.
Tell me we'll never get used to it.

'Scheherazade', Richard Siken

PART ONE

2015

I

Pretend it's normal. It's what they tell you at the sentencing. Pretend you were never different. It's not hard to do. Pretend that the boxes are too heavy, that the fire started by itself. Tell them, *it was just a lucky guess – it's not as if I'm a mind-reader*. Pretend you're just like all the others. Pretend you never even flew.

Let the very idea become ridiculous. Soon you'll turn thirty, thirty-five. After a while you'll forget that the world was ever anything but work and home and bed, and new friendships that are almost as good as the old. Let that earlier time fade, let it hang in the back of your mind like a fancy outfit you'll never wear again. Be a plain person in plain sight, one among millions.

And they were right, it gets easier. As you forget, the world forgets. Today's college freshmen were in second grade the last time I was in the public eye. Perhaps one in twenty would remember me in my professional guise, but nobody makes the absurd leap from there to the decent, mild-mannered Rick Tower. Dr Rick Tower, to give him his proper title, associate professor at a medium-sized New England college best not named.

What's he like, this man I became in the process of reaching forty? He is tall and slender and slightly stooped. He's charming and eccentric, kindly and ineffectual, his angular face always set in a worried frown or a wan smile. He's popular with the students, an almost too perfect match for what incoming students have been taught to expect of an English professor. To his colleagues he's a genial blur. Never married, no children ... what does he do with all that extra time? Reads, goes for walks, often at night. Drinks a bit, but hardly to excess. Even his vices are unremarkable.

Year by year he's passed over for advancement, one of those academic ghost ships sailing into early middle age, already at the level they'd be for the next thirty years. You wouldn't entrust the management of a departmental fundraiser to him, let alone the fate of the planet.

'Take thou this token,' he said. 'When evil arises, touch the amulet and speak the Sacred Word and its power shall be yours.'

He pressed the ancient bronze amulet into my palm, my future handed off to me like a tip to a doorman. It was still warm from his touch, thin and worn but bright with promise.

'Fear the Dark Adversary who will strive to defeat you,' he said. 'Strive to be just and fair, and all that is proper to a king.'

There was more, but I was having a hard time paying attention. Something about a royal bloodline? Enough politics, bring on the superpower! The clearest thing I remember is his face, his eyes shining with faith and hope, and the certainty that I was the one. I was fifteen years old.

Crossing the departmental lounge, I nod here and there and keep moving. They know by now I don't fraternize, and anyway there's Dutton who is obsessed with nineties trivia. He's given me a questioning look once or twice.

In my office I give myself the habitual once-over. Different hair, different glasses, different nose. I'm overthinking this. Nobody's looking for me. If my name came up, they'd remember it only halfway – a scandal, drugs maybe. Was he the one that died? Was he on that reality show that ran one season? (Yes.) But the Duttons of the world would know me, if they only thought to look. Safely out of view, I can lose myself, grade papers, spend an hour revising 'Doubleness in the Late Victorian Novel' for resubmission.

At five o'clock, the department holds a happy hour in the faculty lounge, celebrating an award for our resident poet, with sour wine and a tray of prosciutto-wrapped melon slices. I come in to hear the speech, standing at the back, until my phone buzzes and I take the excuse to hurry back to my office, the department ghost fading, fading again into the walls.

My phone has five missed calls, all from a self-storage facility.

'There's a beeping, sir. From your unit.'

'What? What beeping?'

'Sir, we'll have to ask you to come and open it up. Otherwise the police may be involved.'

'I'm on my way. Don't call the police. And whatever you do, please don't open it.'

Cutting across the center quadrangle dusted with early autumn leaves, I take a mental inventory of that storage unit, and all the things in it that are capable of beeping, and how much trouble I could potentially be in.

'Yo, Professor T, what's the hurry?' calls a C+ lacrosse player. The two girls with him laugh and whisper.

Professor Tower hurries on. *I hope you're happy not being enslaved by immortal time-travelers. You're welcome.* I think of Sinistro's space station burning silently as it drifts from orbit, bulbous and black against the bright curve of the Earth. It tumbles as it begins the long fall.

I walk southwards. The collegiate housing gives way to auto parts stores and warehouses. The self-storage facility rises from its acre of pavement, huge and orange and white, exhaling a chilly gloom.

It's no wonder they phoned me. I can hear it all the way

down the metal corridor, a cheap two-toned melody like the theme from an old video game. I know what it is. I knew the instant they told me. I turn the key with numb fingers.

With the door open the sound blares out loud and clear from its tiny speaker. It bounces off the metal walls, making it hard to find, spills out over cardboard boxes shiny with dried-out packing tape, stretched over mailing labels for old apartments in far-off towns I scarcely remember living in.

Deedle deedle beep, it goes. Step forward, listen again. All this junk. An old mattress, an armchair I'll never use again. A pair of rocket boots blackened from use. One half of a set of those bracelets that give you a force field when you touch them together. Why do I keep these things? Step back, step forward. Warm, cool, hot and hotter . . . and there it is, in a box marked 'Kitchen' under a red plastic colander nestled in with a bunch of expired bath products. A smooth oval, a little box the size of a lady's compact, two flat buttons, a speaker and red LEDs.

Beep beep, goes the box. *Deedle deedle*. What am I supposed to do with it? I didn't think it was even connected to anything.

I pocket it and start for home, the box beeping all the way, wailing of disasters to come or perhaps already in progress. Mutant teens on the rampage. Alien eyes looking greedily from high Earth orbit. The dead rising from their graves, demanding an explanation.

I pour a glass of wine and let the box thing chirp away beneath my couch cushions while I figure out what to do with it. Stamping on it doesn't do anything. Knives won't pry it open. There's no use waiting for it to run down. The fragment of uranium inside it will last for thousands of years, long after anyone but Sinistro will remember what it was for.

A neighbor bangs on the wall.

'Sorry! Smoke alarm! Fixing it now!'

At last I fill the sink and drop it in. It drifts to the bottom, trailing bubbles and trilling its stupid song, now successfully muted.

Are the others hearing it, from their transmitters? Stefanie in her Malibu mansion? Cat in whatever Eastern European nation she's holed up in? I text Jack but, as usual, he's nowhere to be found, probably partying with twentysomething techlords he calls friends nowadays.

I know what the box wants me to do, and it's going to keep beeping until I do it. I press *transmit* and it goes quiet.

'This is Prodigy, responding,' I say. 'Please acknowledge.' I press the receiver.

There's a buzz and hiss of static.

'It's Prodigy,' I repeat. 'Who is this? What's the emergency?'

Nothing. The beeping has stopped, although the little LEDs still flash. What is it? The world in peril? Has Doctor Optimal gone bad again? My fated adversary arriving at long last to menace the world, a peril from which only I can save us?

Every three months I report to the Department of Metahuman Affairs office for a polygraph test. They ask me if I still have it, if I've taken it out of the box, if I've worn it, if I've even thought about it. I say no, usually truthfully. The last time I took it out was three and a half years ago, a drunken night after a breakup.

I should check, shouldn't I? Just to be sure. If enemies are abroad, they might want to steal it. I used to have a safe built of lab-grown diamond to keep it in but those days are long past. I should be grateful they let me keep it at all. 'For emergencies,' they said, although none ever seem to happen.

I pull out the top drawer of my dresser and dump out the

socks and T-shirts, and a little cardboard box falls out with them. It rattles when I shake it. Right where I left it. I should look, though, shouldn't I? Just to be sure.

It looks like it always does. A metal disk two and three-quarter inches across and a quarter inch thick, pierced near the edge with a tiny hole for the chain to pass through. The material is bronze, like an ancient coin or statue, or the medal for third place. On one side there's an indistinct outline, perhaps a head in profile or the outline of a country. The other side shows a simple pentagon etched into the metal.

Now what? The communicator light is still flashing. Danger still awaits. It won't stop until I report to headquarters. *Take your time*, it says. *It's only the fate of the world.*

What if the amulet doesn't work anymore? There's that to be considered. It's what the Wizard said would happen, if I strayed from the path of justice. *Never for evil*, he said, *and only in times of greatest need, or else the power will be taken from you.*

Sure, I said. *Makes sense.* It did at the time. Over the years there emerged some gray areas. Like if I really needed to show up somewhere on time, or get into a party, and then there were other things, like do I need to meet Tom Cruise? And is that a 'greatest' need? Because it seemed pretty great at the time.

I shall be there to guide you, but the path will be dark, the wizard Michael Ferris said. *The burden will be heavy.*

That's fine, I said. *I can totally manage.* Even at that moment, I couldn't help thinking there had been a mistake on somebody's part. They were looking for another kid. A brave and true-hearted kid who would dare great things and make smart life choices.

I could have stopped the proceedings right there. The rightful owner was out there and I could have humbly stepped aside. I thought of it; I knew it.

Then I thought, *No. I don't care, just choose me. Make me*

whatever this is. Make me this prophesied thing I've never heard of. Make me anything as long as it's not fifteen-year-old Alex Beekman.

And then I was the Chosen One, the Prophesied Champion, heir of kings. It would be my task to save the world. I would fight a hundred battles and win them all, and never particularly deserve it.

I should check, right? Just to make sure? The chain slips over my head. Its trifling weight settles on my chest, where it once lay, day and night. I turn the lights out – as if that would fool any of the people capable of watching me.

Touch the amulet and speak the Sacred Word. Here, I shall whisper it to you. He put a warm finger against my lips to make sure I didn't repeat it aloud. He whispered it in my ear, the word of power, spoken key to the ancient miracle, just as I whisper it now.

'Raeclun.'

It comes out in a voice like a little boy's. Two meaningless syllables I have carried with me for decades: trigger and battle cry. I know it looks like 'nuclear' backward. It's not, and I'm tired of having that argument.

The change happens in a moment. The room seems to drop slightly. Colors grow brighter, shadows clarify. I'm seeing them from Prodigy's height, through his eyes. The floor creaks under my added weight. My great heart beats just thirty times a minute. I feel lighter, awake, free of the lingering aches and nausea I carry without thinking. Invincible again.

Prodigy. Stab it, shoot it, drop a piano on it, it's all been tried. Acid, poison, the vacuum of space, the pressure of the ocean depths, swords and knives, lasers and lava and lightning bolts. In the whole world, there is only one person and object that can damage me, and I don't expect to see either of them ever again.

The bathroom mirror shows me its face and it's better

even than I remember. God, I'm handsome. The face is still like the old one, but it never looked like this. It's how I look in daydreams, with classic cheekbones, a full expressive mouth, and the skin of a man twenty years younger, with better living habits. It's aging, yes, but like how movie stars dream of aging. Grizzled and sexy. The eyes still display an intelligence and firmness of purpose and a hint of leashed ferocity. Only the blade of a nose saves it from an overly generic handsomeness, but even that is somehow perfect. It even has a good haircut. Don't ask me how *that* works.

What exactly is it? It's supposed to be ancient, but I don't know if it's magic or alien technology or psychic powers or what. I've looked for the secret in books and manuscripts in the libraries of a dozen countries, across two decades and three graduate degrees. No clue, no record of it even exists. Maybe it doesn't matter. I lived with it for twenty-five years, knowing there's a part of me that was never weak, never tired, never broken. Even harmless, tame, educated Rick Tower knows it's still here, only a word away.

Motionless in the darkened living room, I can feel its smooth loose-limbed perfection. The night air outside has gone crystalline, every leaf in icy-sharp focus. I can hear my neighbor breathing, hear a boy laugh a block away, a delivery truck passing on the freeway a quarter of a mile away. I could tear this place apart. Let them stop me. Let them try.

Should I? More than once, Doctor Optimal asked me to turn evil. *Join me*, he used to say. *And we can rule the world.* Maybe I should have. I could have worn a black trench coat instead of the blue and white bodysuit this thing comes in. I would have looked amazing.

He's the one I miss, not the heroes and government operatives. If he were here he would understand. We'd have a drink and I'd ask him to tell me his theories about weather control, about the diabolical nature of the Gold Standard. Tell me about 1980s anime, I'd say, like you did back in high school. At least tell me how we're still not so different, you and I.

The phone rings, an unknown number.

'Is everything all right, Professor?' Soothing and friendly, my case officer from the Department of Metahuman Affairs.

'Fine, fine.' I try to sound like Rick Tower, higher and breathier, but it's hard to conceal the resonance of Prodigy's voice.

'We detected a subspace transmission from your approximate location. With whom were you communicating?'

'Oh yeah, just a glitch. Mysteries of subspace, right? Unless there's something going on?'

'Nothing's going on,' the voice says. 'There's no emergency. Go to bed, Professor Tower.'

He's right. Put it away, put it away before this goes any further. I'll think about this tomorrow, and if the world ends before then, well, problem solved.

I say the word and become the mild-mannered shell of a professor again. If you try, you can bury anything deep inside yourself, even a being of unimaginable power.

2

Newcomers Mansion is a high breaking wave of concrete and glass above the big box stores and condos, the mixed-use land at the edge of town. Empty now, since 1995 or so. We built it as a calling card to announce ourselves to the world, to stand for justice and daring and youth. It looks ridiculous.

Everybody hated it. The neighbors and the planning board tried to keep us out but we were young, with superpowers and destinies to fulfill. The Princess had endless money, and Jack could design and construct just about anything. We built it high – three stories, not counting the tower and sky lounges – with more sub-basements than anyone will ever find (I hope). Its triumphalist modernism owes (a critic noted) a certain amount to Eero Saarinen and considerably more to Mussolini.

The setting sun puts the glass facade in shadow and warms the concrete curve of the roofline, smooth and massive like a whale breaching the New England soil. I stand on the far side of the street, hidden in the shadow of a spreading oak, as a trio of German art students take selfies in front of it. I wonder if they even know what it used to be.

They wander off toward their next ironic photo op. I watch them from my concealment, feeling a bit stupid, but who knows? Evil lurks where it lurks. In the breast pocket of my blazer, the transponder blinks and blinks, silently urging me across the road, back to my absurd former life. What are you waiting for? The world is probably in peril.

Deep breath. My new shoes clatter on the marble walkway. The sun subsides behind the mansion's roofline. Step by step the narrow, stiff figure of Professor Tower is swallowed up in its shadow. What would a passing co-worker say if they spotted me, their eccentric colleague, in the act of infiltrating the former headquarters of a defunct teen crime-fighting quartet? Would they finally put two and two together, realize who and what was living in their midst? Doubtful. Rick Tower was my home for too long.

Does the system remember my voice? It does. The armored doors slide open and the twilight is reflected off a wedge of white marble floor.

I was twenty, the last time I walked through this door, then with a mild hangover, a duffle bag full of underwear and T-shirts, plus a prized Calvin Klein sport jacket pillaged from a *Sassy* photo shoot. The Newcomers were gone but the future was bright, with endorsement deals and prospective team-ups. Johnny Atomic had a place in Allston where I'd crash for a few days until I figured out a plan, and anyway I could sleep anyplace. It's not like Prodigy feels the weather.

Stefanie and I were the marquee faces (everyone thought we'd be a couple – never happened). Jack was the funny one, and Cat brought the bad-girl energy that played so well in the early nineties.

Behind me, a car revs its engine and startles me back to the present. The government's watchers? Somebody else's? I hop through into the cool darkness. Twenty years since I turned out the lights.

Jack's futuristic design for the entranceway was to give off a minimalist nineties cool, but to my eye it resembles the seat of a dystopian world government. I cross the sea of white marble to the reception desk, a long curved slab of blond wood. When I drop my weekend bag, the sound pings off the marble floor and bare walls and echoes up toward the high arched ceiling.

'Hello?'

Am I the only one who thought this thing was mandatory? I'm a little relieved, to be honest. It would be nice to have a moment to take this in before the rest of them start rummaging around in here. I find the controls that bring the great starburst chandelier to life.

The hallways are hung with awards, newspaper headlines and photos of us with politicians and celebrities. And villains. Loremonger, Martinet. We put Foulmouth away, but then who didn't? And there, grinning away, black eyes shining, is Sinistro. Barrel-chested, long hair slicked back, impeccably dressed. We all had our personal destinies and arch foes but Sinistro was our group's nemesis, a time-traveling world-conqueror, intelligent and brutal. The most implacable of our foes by far and, it has to be admitted, the sexiest.

Doors swish asunder as I approach, circling back through two living rooms and a briefing room. The gymnasium, custom-built for our altered physiques, still smells of our unnatural sweat. The laboratory is colossal, exuberant; the helicopter pad doubled as a basketball court. We spent so much money.

The headquarters itself was meant to be a beacon of hope and justice, and was in practice more of a halfway house, inhabited by four teenagers too dazzled to really address the trauma that got us here. It was a fortress against a lot of messiness we churned up in our wake; a perennial crash space for a mixed-up batch of almost-heroes at the edge of the powered spectrum, vigilante conjurers and off-brand samurai, Ivy League vampire kids, semi-deities dodging as long as possible the fates set down for them. We held extremely good parties.

'Is anybody here?'

The gas is off in the oversized kitchen where empty refrigerators stand among shoals of useless steel countertops and the beautiful stoves that we never used because none of us except Jack ever learned to cook.

What if they're not coming? What if I have to face whatever this is alone? Maybe the others threw their transmitters away, or lost them, or they just stopped working. Jack said it couldn't happen but people say a lot of things. Sinistro said he would live forever.

The electricity still works – powered by an off-the-books fusion plant which is one of many reasons we can never sell this place. I try the house computers but Jack is the only one who knows how to get them started again.

I text him. *Where are you? Are you coming? I can't get into the system.*

Are you getting these? What if there's a giant meteor?

Where is everybody? At a rough guess: Prague, Dubai and Fairland, which means it could be tomorrow or next week before they get here.

I wander for a while, down halls, past a billiards room, two swimming pools I'd forgotten about. It's still hard to believe how much money went into this place. The tower library is all blond wood, curved reading nooks nestled under high windows looking out toward Boston and the Atlantic. I was the only one who ever used it. I'd spend whole days here, reading or watching the snow or rain, more and more often, before things ended. The closest thing I had to a college education, snatched between missions and press conferences and celebrity galas.

How could I be this lucky? I thought it every day for the almost four years we lived together, traveled together, solved mysteries, fought weird implacable foes in city streets and tropical islands, and the rest of the time held marvelous parties for the bright young powered kids. We were always together. I can remember what Stefanie's lipstick tasted like and being kept awake by Jack's snoring and the solid shock of a headbutt from Cat.

What happened, exactly? It was the early nineties and the Champions couldn't keep going forever. Their boomer appeal was waning even if their powers weren't; echoing haymaker punches and boilerplate speeches, and moral codes that were growing stale like an overplayed classic rock album. We were glossy, wisecracking, edgy (although that was mostly Cat). We were talking to MTV about a *Real World* spinoff. The Web was fizzing into life. Justice belonged to the kids now – and that was us.

Only it wasn't, and I never even read the signals. Perhaps I'd misunderstood all along how important we were supposed to be, how cool we were. In the end we were there to save the world but never told how, or what ill-defined threat menaced a generation with no particular interest in being rescued. Then the lights came on and I was the last party guest, lingering by the drinks table.

Brilliant as we were, two decades later we have little to show for our early promise: a notorious lawsuit, two felony convictions, three bankruptcies, a divorce, a world of bad decision-making and a legacy that persists almost exclusively in sociology dissertations and bar trivia nights. It's no wonder none of us can stand to live here anymore.

For an hour I sit and grade just enough papers to keep Rick Tower's job going. The house is so silent I can hear it when the front doors open again and footsteps clump inside and on up the stairs. Stefanie would be in heels and I wouldn't hear Cat at all, so that only leaves one person. Who I last saw flailing at the controls of the candy-colored GalactiCar III that spun out over the Washington Mall trailing smoke and stolen documents into the wind.

I wait, not unlike a man chained to a doomsday machine, for the world's greatest inventor to arrive. I wonder what he looks like now, and I wonder if he's mad at me and if we'll fight. I wonder how he knows I'm up here, but then he's the world's fourth smartest man and knows all kinds of things. I hope he knows what to say. The footsteps stop just short of the doorway for a moment, then Jack, once known as Doctor Optimal, leaps sideways into view.

'X-ray fuckin' eyes!'

It's been six years since I last saw him. He's not in costume, thank god. He's wearing a dark turtleneck and an expensive leather jacket, styled to look like the Silicon Valley mogul he's supposed to be now. Even with his black hair going salt-and-pepper he still manages to look like Jack Angler, World's Cleverest Boy.

He's wearing a distractingly ugly pair of goggles: a pair of silver-dollar-sized lenses and the rest of it mostly wire and duct tape and what looks like a bent-up coat hanger.

'Jack! I thought you weren't coming.'

'How would I not?' he says. 'Come on, do you see these? X-ray eyeglasses!'

'Those look incredibly bad,' I say. 'Is that the new start-up?'

'Nah, Samsung bought and killed it. Still got paid.'

'What do you even see right now?'

'Bones, whatever,' he says. 'It's not that great.'

'Jesus. Take them off already.'

His face underneath looks puffy, like he's been eating lousy food and hasn't slept. But the quality of attention is there. A man thinking at twice the rate I do, or four or ten times.

'Did you hear from anybody?' I say. 'Any idea who died?'

'Nah, nobody talks to me.'

'Yeah, well.' I fake-consider the next words. 'So this whole thing isn't – you know –'

'What?'

'One of your things. Like, a trap? A diabolical plan?'

'Fuck off. No,' he says. 'Nice face, by the way. I like the nose.'

'Shut up, it's good.'

'Let's check the perimeter,' he says. 'This whole situation is weird. If somebody's been here, I want to know.'

The first stop is the War Room, massively overdesigned. A conference table with the sweeping lines of a stealth bomber, holographic display, individual cup holders. Jack built the computer system himself, the most powerful cybernetic brain of 1992. Twenty years ahead of its time, he told us. Twenty-three years ago.

Text floods the monitor, streaming past faster than I can follow, but Jack's gaze flicks up and down. There's a barely audible whirring sound that I eventually realize comes from Jack's left eye. It's been replaced by a tiny transparent sphere that shuffles between different lenses.

'Shit, what the hell happened?'

'Saudi yacht, some fucking thing. This one's better anyway,' he says.

The blue eye, I remember. The other is green.

When he bends over the keyboard his hair falls forward to show the shaved patch around a domino-sized slab of white plastic set flush with the skin. The latest version of the Thinking Cap, the onboard cybernetics he's been upgrading since he was ten years old. The earliest version looked like an upside-down colander threaded with green, red and white wires.

'I like the new Cap. Sleek.'

'Twelfth gen, best yet. The guts of it are in the cloud,' he says, still working. 'So what's the latest? Did Michael Ferris ever turn up?'

'Yeah, whatever. Heard from any alien fleets?'

'They're coming, don't worry about that. Shit, this is going to be a half-hour at least. Let's check the house.'

'If we run into anything . . .'

'You better believe it.' He opens the jacket to show the old matte-steel plasma pistol in his belt, the seams hand-welded, the aperture blackened from use.

'You really should not have that. How did you even get it here?'

'Honorary Sky Marshal.' He flashes a badge. 'Come downstairs, I want to see the lab.'

He put his laboratory in the basement. He liked to build big, and the upper stories wouldn't support the stacked data banks and generators and the other great engines of science – quiet now, but once they blinked and glowed like a carnival midway. Every flat surface is cluttered with tools and half-built scraps of genius.

'Look at this old stuff,' he says. He paws through the jumble of cables and odd bits of hardware, then plucks out a compact chunky bracelet. 'Wrist-mounted grappling hook, remember that one? Foosh!' He grins.

Moral lapses aside, you have to admit Jack has always liked being Jack. He takes a delicate metal circlet off a shelf and fits it around his wide forehead. Lights run up and down the delicate frame.

'Hey, you found your tiara,' I say.

'It's a multiphase sensor array. You are so far from

understanding what I do, you're like an ant — but like the other ants, never give him anything important to do. The worst ant.'

On the mezzanine Jack leans over a railing to scan the main dining room below, big enough to double as a ballroom.

'You learning anything?' I say.

'Nothing. It never did much inside the house — all the leftover magic is still scrambling the sensors. I wish Stefanie were here to straighten this out.'

'Really?'

'Fuck no,' Jack says. He kicks a red plastic cup across the floor from who knows what long-ago party. 'My god, look at this place.'

'I know.'

On a long-ago night we danced until we dropped, then played a make-out game with the guests on the front lawn, laughed ourselves silly, and watched the sunrise from the GalactiCar's landing pad that we used for cookouts on summer evenings. I think that was when I asked Jack whether we'd always be friends and he said he loved me. I wonder if he remembers it. Maybe the Thinking Cap does.

Upstairs, Stefanie's mysterious tower sanctum is just a circular room now, with white plaster walls, all mystery gone.

Cat's room never had furniture, just a bare mattress mounded over with a nest of skirts, underwear, T-shirts, shoes, condom wrappers, bits of make-up on the floor, bags of potato chips, vodka bottles. She barely slept at all and her metabolism was hangover-proof.

'Quit gawking. It's depressing to watch,' Jack says. 'Are you seeing anybody now?'

'Nobody much.'

'You're not still hung up on that Meg person, are you?'

'Please stop thinking about my dick.'

'Then get laid already. I'm the one who gets your sad-sack drunk texts once a year.'

Back in the entrance hall he walks in a final slow circle, letting the sensors take it in.

'Fuck it, the house is clean. Let's get a drink.'

'Doesn't the Cap hate it when you drink?'

'It's not the boss of me.'

We scrounge a pair of plastic cups and an ancient bottle of Scotch Jack stashed in a corner of the lab and wander up to one of the living rooms. After a few sips it starts to feel a little like old times, a thin skin of something like joy that I don't want to touch or even look at for fear of breaking the surface tension.

'You should have seen it after '06,' Jack is saying. 'The VCs were on their knees begging me to take a meeting. Bidding wars, private jets, London, Dubai. The *New Yorker* did a piece.'

'"A Boy Genius Arrives in Silicon Valley". I read it.'

Susan Orlean did a good job of capturing Jack's whiz-kid swagger, the one-off leaps of innovation that seemed to defy the laws of physics. She also wrote of an almost unconscious impulse to self-sabotage. The boy who wished for fewer wishes.

'Hey, is ESOC still on your ass?' he says.

'Yeah, Class C Restricted. Limited travel, surveillance, polygraphs, the works. I'll have to tell them I was here. You?'

'I do a little national defense work, and they give me a psych screening once a year.'

'That's it? Are you fucking kidding me?'

'Hold that thought,' Jack says. He claps the goggles back onto his face, stares at the wall, or through it.

'Okay, who's this now?'

The plastic strip above his ear flashes incandescent white,

then he's off the counter and across the room and out the door almost faster than I can follow, moving like a puppet yanked along by a wire. His nervous system must be jacked up even worse than last I saw it.

Footsteps, the front door slams, a cry of alarm. I've been away so long, I almost forgot what this is like.

3

'Looky what I got.'

In the front hall, Jack is gripping a man by his short blond hair. He's so tall, Jack must have had to jump to grab hold but now he has the man bent half over, his weird pistol jammed against the man's temple. I can hear the turbines inside the weapon whining, crawling up the scale.

I can't see the stranger's face, only that he has beautiful floppy hair and he's wearing a royal-blue blazer with brass buttons. He's got both his hands up in debonair surrender.

'Hello, there,' I say. 'Do we know you?'

'I'm terribly sorry,' he says. He sounds, somehow, more British than actual British people. 'I was told I would be expected.'

He doesn't sound angry. It's more of a genteel weariness. Like we're all just having one of those days.

'Hands on the wall,' Jack says as he lets go of the man's hair.

The newcomer straightens up to comply. He is in his extraordinarily handsome middle forties. Prince Charming slightly past his peak.

'Is everything quite all right?' he asks.

'How did you get the door open?' I ask.

'Stefanie gave me the bypass code,' he says over his shoulder. 'Didn't she tell you?'

Aha.

'You're Stef's husband,' I say. 'Finbar.'

The second husband, from the wedding I wasn't invited

to. I remember now, a collateral noble from the same kind of pocket kingdom as Stefanie, a literal Prince Charming. Or Duke Charming, I remember. They probably met on a dating app for fairy-tale characters. He can probably knock Jack across the room anytime he pleases.

'Call me Barry. And you must be Alex, er, Rick. The teacher. I'm sorry for your loss.'

'Professor. And thanks.'

'And this would be Jack?'

'Maybe,' Jack says. 'Maybe not.'

The gun hasn't moved.

'It's wonderful to finally meet you,' Barry says. 'I was sorry you couldn't come to the wedding. You were missed. Both of you.'

'I had a thing,' Jack mumbles. He lowers the pistol and Barry fixes his cuffs.

'Is Stefanie not coming?' I ask.

'She's on set all month, couldn't possibly get away. When she saw the alarm, she asked me to go see what's afoot.' He has a remarkable gift for getting a conversation moving again, post-gunplay.

'You mean Her Highness didn't make it a priority,' Jack says. 'Okay. Welcome, I guess.' He gives a sardonic little half-bow.

'Do you suppose one might find a drink hereabouts?'

'First living room on the left, sideboard,' I tell him, and point. 'We'll be there in just a second.'

When Barry's gone, Jack says, 'Do we have to have this guy?'

'What? He seems nice.'

'Yeah, but . . . you saw him. His stupid face.'

'It's not my fault you both married the same person.'

'I'm just saying. It's annoying.'

I get it, in a way. Certain missteps notwithstanding, people like me are on the side of rightness. We fight thieves, punish murderers and other wrongdoers. I don't use my powers to rob or harm others unprovoked. I recycle. But we're just doing our best, we're the same people we would be without powers.

Barry is different, you can tell right away. Fundamentally, instinctually decent and charming, and you can't imagine him harboring an ignoble impulse; he's heroic at the cellular level. And he smells great. Like a rose bush wearing an old leather jacket.

We find him in one of the dens, lounging in an armchair, elegant to the point of caricature, threats to life and limb forgotten. As comfortable as if he owns the place – which, given that he is married to Stefanie, it's possible he does.

'What exactly did Stefanie send you here to do?' Jack asks.

'Maybe I'd be useful in the event of a crisis. Is there one, by the way? Are we all quite doomed?'

'We don't know yet,' Jack says. 'Not unless you do.'

'Useful how?' I ask.

'Well, I fight a bit of crime myself. I called myself Gallant for a while.'

I remember. He was a kind of gentleman vigilante of the swashbuckling sort.

'What about it?' Jack asks.

'Well, I was a rather good detective, you know. I pick up on things. It's the faerie blood.'

'Uh-huh, what things?' Jack leans forward a little, a strain in his voice I recognize. He's pathologically unable to bear the idea that anybody else realized a thing before he did.

'You do know there's a fourth person in the building, don't you?'

Jack is dumbfounded for once. A voice comes from the kitchen.

'Ah, shit.'

Gathered in the kitchen, we watch Cat slowly uncoil from her perch in an upper corner of the ductwork, making a performance of it, supporting herself one-handed without a tremor of effort. She wears the same leather bodysuit she did at twenty, in defiance of the workings of time. It shows every over-amped muscle on her small frame.

She lazily grabs a pipe and swings into a somersaulting half-twist, to land soundlessly on the tile floor. A Black woman with close-cropped hair, a few years shy of forty although she still looks twenty-eight at most. Does she even get old? No one knows how she works, not even the ones who made her.

'Well. Now it's a party,' she says, smiling.

'Holy shit. Cat. Hi.' My hand checks for the amulet.

A microtremor crosses her body, the fleeting tick of a combat subroutine suppressed on the instant.

'Is that how it's going to be?' she says.

'No. It's just been a while.'

'Okay,' she says. 'Let me know if that changes.'

She holds out her arms in a half-ironic way. We hug and she's warm but still hard as rock and strung wire, like hugging an awkward fence post. She's had more work done, a line of bumps down her spine like a dragon's.

'What the fuck were you doing up there?' Jack says.

'Gathering intelligence. Assessing any collateral danger following the initial incident.'

'Learn anything?'

'That's for me to know.'

'This is Barry. Stefanie's husband.'

Barry offers his hand; she waves it off.

'I know.'

'Sorry to give away the game,' he says.

'It won't happen again,' Cat says. 'I take it the Princess can't be bothered to join us.'

'She would have loved to be here.'

'I bet.'

'Hey, Barry, maybe we ought to go, whatever, check on that computer,' Jack says to Barry. He gives me a look before they leave: *Don't be any stupider than you have to.*

'Well, Professor Tower? How are you?' Cat leans back, elbows on the counter.

'Fine.'

'Class C Restricted Status. Lost your tenure fight a few weeks ago. Really?'

This kind of dig is new for Cat, this instinct for the verbal jugular. I guess people change.

'I'm fine. What have you been doing?'

'Vengeance. Europe, mostly.'

'Right. I thought you weren't allowed back into the United States.'

'So arrest me. Again.' She pops open a beer. 'Did you have any children?'

'No, although I guess you know that. You?'

'None of us do.'

'Why are you here, Cat?' I say. 'You said you were done with all this. You were pretty direct about it.'

'It's a max priority. It might actually matter for once.'

'Well, I'm glad you're here. Just don't start in on Jack, okay? He's a lot to handle as it is.'

'Oh, I would never,' she says. Cat smiles, the hairline-cracked smile of a person you can't kid yourself is ever really going to be okay.

Jack bangs his way into the doorway, a little out of breath.

'Guys? Sorry to interrupt.'

'You're not interrupting anything,' Cat says.

'Whatever you say. Alex, you need to see this. Now.'

4

I used to think the oversized War Room made us look like teenagers playing at being grown-ups. Twenty years later, the grown-ups are here. Everyone but Cat looks a bit duller, fleshier, their faces settled into their lifelong habits. And then Jack's new eye glints as it shifts lenses. And my nose has gotten straightened into Rick Tower's, and I can't feel the tip anymore.

And there's a handsome stranger sitting in Stefanie's chair. Barry is looking around the table, avidly attentive. I wonder what Stefanie told him about us.

'Adept, Doctor Optimal, and Prodigy, ready for onsite briefing. Glamour absent, Gallant in attendance.' He used to love doing the briefings.

'Can you not?' Cat says.

'It's for the logs.'

'Jack, come on,' I say.

'You'd better show us,' Barry says, glancing at me.

The big hologram display lights up. A half-dozen narrow columns of text, each with a small head shot at the top, some black and white, some color. It's a cheap-looking layout, like from a free template.

'The AI was built to sift online sources for interesting data,' Jack says. 'That was back in '92 but the code's self-modifying. This thing figured out the Web all by itself.'

'No one cares,' Cat says.

'What are we looking at?' I ask.

'The *Pittsfield Gazette*,' Jack says. 'This week's obituaries.'

He zooms in a little. A smiling teenager killed in a car accident. A middle-aged man, two senior citizens. An unsmiling young woman who worked at a pharmacy.

'Second from the left,' he says.

A color photo of a man, maybe sixty-five. Roy Gillespie, substitute teacher in the Pittsfield school system for the last seventeen years. Well-liked, a bachelor, leaves no family. I stop again on that picture, on those wide-set eyes, thin lips in a slight smile. I've seen those eyes before.

'Well?' Jack says.

It hits me. No. The nose has broadened but the sandy hair kept its color. He shaved off the stupid Burt Reynolds mustache. He looked better with it.

'It can't be,' I say.

'It's him,' Jack says. 'It's Michael Ferris. He's dead.'

My first thought is, *But he was so young.* Idiotic. He was thirty-five when I last saw him, younger than I am now, an English teacher at Hanover High School.

Everyone is waiting for me to say something.

'Yeah, it's him,' I say quietly. 'I don't understand.'

'I looked him up. He's been there since 1997. His papers look legit. Nothing on his record. Won a teaching award in 2002.'

He would have. A cool teacher who could joke with the kids, assigned weird books, Sartre and Camus, and encouraged us to talk about them. He was a bachelor, sexy in a throwback 1970s way, and girls had crushes on him. He didn't look anything like a wizard.

He took me aside one day after class to tell me I'd qualified for a special test. That was how he started it. He put his hand on my shoulder like he was really pleased with me, a thing no teacher had ever done. He pretended he was driving me to a neighboring high school but instead he took me to a magic cave and merged my life with the big magical destiny that would take everything over for the next few decades.

Of course, I never saw him again.

He didn't show up for school the next day, or that week or ever again. Everyone assumed he'd been caught messing around with a student, but I knew that couldn't be right. I searched for him for years and all the time, he was a two-hour drive west on the Massachusetts Turnpike.

What the fuck did he think he was doing out there? He must have known where I was. Why didn't he talk to me?

'What happened?'

'According to the police report, somebody broke into his house,' Jack says. 'There was a tussle, he hit his head. They have no suspects. They're guessing it was an accident.'

'May I ask who . . . ?' Barry asks, not ungently.

'Michael Ferris. He was a wizard,' I say. 'He gave me my powers.'

'A worker of magic?' Barry says.

'Well, he said he was. I guess it didn't do him much good.'

'Ah. I'm sorry.'

'So that's all?' Cat says.

'What do you mean, that's all?' I say.

'I risked a lot coming here. I thought there would be a real crisis. I can get all the dead wizards I need back in France.'

'This is Michael Ferris we're talking about,' I said. 'The Wizard of the Cave. You've heard me talk about him a hundred times. I've been looking for him for twenty-five years, and now he's been murdered.'

'Who says?' Cat says. 'You're the one who told us the prophecy was bullshit.'

'Well, I don't know. I thought he was gone and now – whatever he warned me about, maybe it killed him.'

'Or he's an old guy who hit his head,' Cat says, pushing her chair back. 'Let me know when you figure it out.'

'You're going? Really?'

'Not my origin, not my problem,' Cat says. 'I have business elsewhere. The Prion Corporation's not going to destroy itself.'

'Evil forces are rising. That's why we're here!' Barry nods vigorously. At least he brings some more clarity to the situation.

'I'm a little evil myself lately, if you hadn't noticed.'

'That doesn't mean you're not threatened. We haven't even talked about suspects. What if it's a Prion hit team?'

'The Prion Corporation cares only for profit and control.'

'Queen Juniper.'

'It's not likely,' Barry says. 'She's not been active in the Midworld for years.'

'Aliens.'

'I watch the skies. Always,' Jack says. Then pauses, before intoning, 'It could be Sinistro.'

'I'm sorry,' Barry says, 'isn't Sinistro dead?'

'I swear to god, Jack, if you start with the "return of Sinistro" scenario again, you will beg for death,' Cat says.

'Well, it's somebody. And they could be coming for all of us. Are you telling me you haven't noticed anything strange?'

'Sweetie,' Cat says. 'Who's "us"?'

'Us. The Newcomers,' I say.

'We haven't all been in the same room for twenty years.'

'Six.'

'Fine, but that was an accident.'

'It doesn't matter. We swore a vow. Don't you remember?'

'Oh my god, the vow. Of course you'd be the one to remember that.'

In fact, I wrote it. No one else seemed to want to.

'You swore it,' I say. 'All of us did, that we'd help each

other, and do whatever was right. I fought Prion augmented security for you. I went into nineties cyberspace to fight — what was it?'

'Eviltron. That was a long time ago.'

'Fucking wireframe dragon. Mr Ferris was murdered. We can't just abandon him.'

'Like the way he abandoned you?'

When Cat's combat subroutines are running, she swaps into a whole different body language She enjoys it.

'Go ahead, Alex,' she says. 'I've kept in practice. Have you?'

'She's manipulating you,' Jack says. 'You know that. It's what they taught her.'

Her focus shifts, like a predator's at the sound of a snapped twig. 'Interesting observation, Doctor Optimal. He was your nemesis, after all. It would be just like you to lie low for years before striking back at your hated foe.'

'I don't do that anymore,' Jack says.

'I can see why,' Cat says. 'Given how many times he —'

'That's enough.' Jack's hand twitches above his blaster, and I think of how fast he went for Barry. Cat sees it, too, and we all see her seeing it, because we've all been driving each other crazy since I was sixteen years old.

'Go ahead,' Cat says. 'I know you're dying to.'

'Don't push me.'

Cat is fast as hell, newly augmented and has stayed in the field longer than any of us. Even at five foot six, she's got two inches on Jack. On the other hand, Jack's never gotten into a situation he hasn't gamed out beforehand.

'Guys?' I say.

'Shall we all settle down a bit?' Barry says. 'I believe we're all friends here.'

He looks from one to the other, hopefully, but the two are

locked in place. The room is charged with powers just aching to be used.

There's a bang of compressed air. Cat's hand flickers like a hummingbird's wing and she's holding a miniature grappling hook, still attached to the gadget on Jack's wrist. She winds the cable once around her wrist and yanks him to her. I don't see the slap, just Jack shaking his head, glaring, a red handprint forming on his cheek.

I whisper it, just a word, but the word is 'Raeclun'. A shock of air rolls through the room, and the scene stops. Prodigy is here.

Even if I don't feel it, I can see it in everyone else, the way his charisma draws every eye. Doctor Optimal, who has felt the power in these hands. Even Cat, who doesn't feel fatigue or the weather, feels this in her charged blood, and can't look away. The tension in the room dissolves, vaporized in his presence.

I can't believe I gave this up.

'Stop it!' Prodigy's voice seems designed for command.

'Whatever you want, Alex,' Jack says, sullen.

'I'll find Michael Ferris's murderer. Any of you can join me, or not, as you choose.'

'Let's call it a night, shall we?' Barry says. 'Let's all get some sleep.'

Jack slams the door on his way out.

'What a diva,' Cat says, pleased.

She's nineteen for twelve against him now, if I've counted right.

5

'Was that really necessary, Cat?'

We've adjourned to the kitchen for beer. It's the only room in the house where anything feels like a normal conversation.

'Jack needed a little shaking up. I don't trust him.'

'Is that why you were spying on us?'

'Oh, are we starting already? Are you interrogating me?' She cocks an eyebrow and her voice has a range of inflection it didn't possess back when I knew her. I wonder if it's part of her latest augmentation. It's annoying.

'It's a reasonable question.'

'I spy on a lot of people,' she says. 'I'm a spy.'

'So why did you even bother coming back? You obviously don't care about any of this.'

'Don't act like you know me, Alex. We knew each other for a couple of years, that's all.'

'Yeah, well, who's fault is that? You're the one who decided to go be a black-ops mercenary cat-burglar murderer. I hope it's as cool as you thought.'

'Thank you, it is.'

'Good.'

We clink beers.

'Still illegal, though,' I say. 'Just for the record. Speaking as a crime-fighter.'

'Don't care.'

'So why are you here? Really.'

'Okay. Okay. It wasn't actually my decision.'

She turns around and unzips her catsuit a few inches to

show a vivid red scar just below her right shoulder blade, small but deep. It looks like the entry point of a bullet or a blade. I can see the subcutaneous mesh.

'Cat.'

'This is from twenty-four hours ago.'

'What happened?'

'Somebody ratted me out to Interpol M, the metahuman enforcement goons. They're deep into battle magic now. These kids half my age with fucking animal heads chased me all over Stockholm. One of them had a spear. It went all the way through and skewered a lung. I crossed the Atlantic in the wheel bay of a 747.'

'Why didn't you tell us right away?'

'And show up to the class reunion looking like a loser?'

'Oh come on, everyone knows by now I didn't get tenure.'

'And I'm sure you're very proud in your own way,' she says. 'But this changes everything. There has to be a connection.'

'Yeah, there is. Not many people are capable of finding me. Jack, Stefanie and you are a few of them. And then your wizard dies? Now it's a shorter list. God, I hope it's Stefanie but it's probably Jack.'

'Jack would never do something like this.'

'Jack tried to sell the Earth to interdimensional bees.'

'I feel like that was different,' I say.

'Fine. You're my second choice.'

'What? Me?'

'You're the only one who cares about any of this shit anymore. All that old business. The rest of us moved on.'

'I didn't do it!'

'I know. But don't pretend it's not still a thing for you. You hated him.'

'I did, it's just that now . . .' Suddenly I can't quite get the words out.

'I know. He was your origin.'

'I shouldn't even care. Michael Ferris was an asshole. Who just takes a kid, tells them they're going to inherit the world, gives them a bunch of powers, and then disappears? Plus, the stupid mustache.'

'But they killed him.'

'Yeah.'

It's been a long time since I talked to anybody like me. We're quiet a moment, and for a moment we're just two impossible bodies in a room.

'I should go check on Jack.'

'Hey,' she says. 'Good to see you.'

We clink glasses.

'To absent friends.'

'To vengeance.'

Jack is where I expected he would be: on the roof, lying back in an old lawn chair, a handful of ice in a dish towel over his face. He's communing with the miniature dish antenna array he put up there. I sit beside him and look, too. Dust and pine needles have drifted into the corners and crevices. There are six of them, each the size of a punchbowl. One has frozen in place, and another is a bit crumpled, but the rest still sweep the skies, searching for signs of the galactic Spindrift War. Faster-than-light dreadnoughts playing hide and seek through the wormholes, one star to the next.

'Is that Scotch?' the dish towel asks.

I pass him the bottle.

'How's it going?'

'Centauri Alliance holds.'

'What exactly is it about, again?'

'The Hydrogen Throne sits empty. Has done for centuries. I'll get up there one day. That'll be my time.'

The dish antennae whir and spin in the moment's quiet. He inspects the dish towel then puts it back on his face.

'You okay?'

'She's lost about eight percent of her speed. She was micro-stuttering all over the place.'

'You let her hit you on purpose?'

'Sure. Systems check.' He nods, leans back in his chair, eyes closed. 'I get so tired of telling people I'm smart.'

'You know she almost got killed yesterday? Interpol M caught up to her. She says it was a set-up. Hard to argue the killing's not linked. Funny coincidence, anyway.'

'So I guess losing all my money in the past forty-eight hours makes it funnier,' he says.

'What? How is that possible? You have like twelve different companies. Aren't you a zillionaire?'

'Four hundred million dollars total valuation, and they went down like dominoes. They knew exactly how to do it, too. Senior research teams poached or lost their work visas. Patents got sued out of existence. I was leveraged all the way down, now my condo's gone. They even got the cryptocurrency – there's a whole subreddit trying to figure that one out. As of this morning I'm down to three Aeron chairs and a fifty-one percent stake in a Scrabble app.'

'Who could do all that?'

'I don't know. A lot of people are pissed at me but none of them are at this level.'

'You'll make a comeback.'

He sits up, shakes out the dish towel.

'Do you know how many comebacks I've had to make? How many times I escaped from jail, how many of my plans failed? It was the same in Silicon Valley. Except I'm a "toxic manager" instead of a mad tyrant.'

One of the antennae does a fluid twist to face straight upward, like a dog hearing its name called.

'Boom. There goes another heavy cruiser,' he says. He walks to the edge of the roof, peers up as if the stars look any different from there. The LEDs of the Thinking Cap stand out bright in a line above his ear. He wipes his nose.

'Stefanie and I used to come up here back when we were still a secret. Late at night. Just talked and played cards. She's really funny when it's just her and me.'

'I never got why your thing was a secret for so long.'

'She's a princess, I was a fat kid whose parents ran a liquor store. Summerdwell had to make me a duke, and I converted to their nonsense religion, but they still weren't happy. I guess it was inevitable she'd find someone like Barry instead. He seems like a nice guy.'

'Cat thinks you're pulling something here.'

'What do you think? Are you going to fight me?'

'I think you're a bit less subtle than this. You'd call it out, and I'd save the day.' I did, too, time and again. They cheered like crazy. I choke up a little and I feel Jack deciding whether to notice.

'Hey, are you okay?' he says, finally.

'Surviving.'

'Seriously.'

'I didn't know it was all going to last this long. They really hated me after that trial. I was just a kid when it happened.'

'You know, there are people I could talk to. Maybe get your sentence downgraded.'

'No, no. Forget it. It's what I agreed to.'

'If you start investigating this Ferris thing, they're going to notice.'

'I don't need to use my powers. I'll just look around a little.

Check out the scene. Maybe it was an accident after all. Not murder at all.'

'Maybe it's the Dark Adversary. Deserving of vengeance for the death of your master.'

'I didn't say that.'

'It was kind of in your tone.'

On my way to bed a clatter from the kitchen puts me into high alert for a moment but it's only Barry. He's in a royal-blue bathrobe trimmed in red and gold, eating a bowl of Captain Crunch.

'Couldn't sleep?' I say.

He nods and pours himself a little more.

'You know I never get to do this at the Malibu place? Not very princely, I'm afraid,' he says. 'I'm sorry about your friend. He must have been a great man.'

'Thanks.'

'Are you going to look into it? Find the culprits, and all that?'

'Tomorrow, I guess.'

'Well, good hunting.' He sighs and contemplates his cereal with the patience of royalty, as if it were a magic mirror laden with all the secrets of the world.

6

I lie awake and listen to the house and its late-night noises. It sounds like home. Below, the thud-thud of Cat working the heavy bag in the gym until she's tired enough to sleep her regular three hours. In the room right over my head, Jack tapping his foot, which he does when he reads. With his enhanced brain he tears through a book an hour. Textbooks mostly, unless he's depressed and then he'll reread *Dune* or *The Fountainhead*.

I shouldn't judge. I have my own stupid rituals. Internet searches for *megan price paris* and *megan price obituary* that turn up nothing new. She'll be turning forty soon, like the rest of us. November twenty-first, in fact. A stupid thing to be thinking about, given everything. How many years since I saw her? She's probably fine. Disappeared, just like Michael Ferris did.

Am I really supposed to find out who killed him? I'm not sure what I owe him after all this time. He told me to fight for justice, and I did so for a very long time, although it's not clear whether I have much standing to serve as a moral arbiter. I don't even hate crime that much, not really.

It's not as if I knew him well, or for very long. He was a good teacher, and then for a brief time he was more than that, those few pivotal hours, after which my life was unrecognizably different.

He brought me there to the tunnel winding into the New England rock, with its clean sandy floor, walls carved with prophetic images, the great throne, empty for millennia. It all disappeared without a trace. I don't know if anyone else believes it was there but I remember every detail, down to the tickle of the chain as he placed it around my neck. My last link to that moment is gone. Whoever took that away owes me an answer, even if it was just a burglar. And what if it really is some concerted assault, someone trying to take down the Newcomers?

Overhead, Jack's foot-tapping stops, then there's the half-strangled *k . . . k . . . k . . .* noise, which is the noise Jack makes when he cries. He must be rereading the letters he carries around from his future self. They started arriving when he was eight, showing up in his bed each night, scrawled in his own jagged handwriting. They told him he'd grow up to perfect the Thinking Cap, become the most important person on the planet.

The letters told him, step by step, how his perfect life would go, the exact sequence of actions that would build that timeline. Exactly what he'd invent, where he'd invest, exactly when the aliens would arrive to make him their leader so he could save the galaxy. He used to talk about it all the time. He never let me read the letters.

Whoever this is, they have the resources to find a man I spent my adult life looking for. They tracked down Cat in Stockholm, and took the smartest man I know for every cent he's got. It points to one of the big ones – a Craniac or Deep Melvin – but it's hard to see the motive. We brushed up against their schemes once or twice, but we're not in arch-enemy territory.

Sinistro is a logical culprit, maybe even the most likely. His plans played out over decades and centuries, plans with a thousand moving parts, plans that didn't even look like plans until the final domino fell. He may be dead but that doesn't mean he's not trying to kill us.

Can we really take Cat and Jack off the list? They both turned villain in the 1990s, and I can't trust them not to do it again. They were targeted, too, but we can't eliminate the idea of misdirection. Especially not with Jack.

As Doctor Optimal, Jack loved this kind of intrigue, all the moving parts, and he'd just love to put one over on the rest of us if there were any profit in it. Just because I can't see any profit in it, that doesn't mean he can't.

Cat is a proven killer, obsessive and merciless in her vendettas, and nobody truly understands how she thinks. What if she decided we were on the list? She's not usually this subtle – but she's right, I knew her a long time ago. I don't truly know who I'm dealing with now.

Stefanie is no less obsessive. Stefanie, who never thought the rules applied to her, not to a princess of Summerdwell. But she's only ever wanted one thing: the throne she lost to her stepsister, Juniper.

No one has much semblance of a motive, except maybe me. I fucking hated Michael Ferris for a long time, him and his bullshit prophecy. I've told plenty of therapists how he ruined my life.

The house goes silent, except for early morning rain and the tree branches tapping against the windows, and I start to drift off to sleep.

Maybe it will work out. Maybe we can still save the day. After all, we've been in worse scrapes than this.

PART TWO
1991

7

'Is this a thing that's going to happen again?' Mom says.

We're at a traffic light. It's seven-thirty on a Saturday morning, four months after my arrest. The first snowfall of the year is turning into freezing rain, washing the snow from the bare branches of the century-old trees that grow on our block.

'No, Mom.'

The windshield wipers are breaking up the thin skin of ice on the glass, and pushing the pieces around.

'"No Mom" what?'

'No, it's not going to happen again. I mean, I don't think so.' I didn't know I was going to do it the first time, so how should I know whether I'm going to do it again?

'Well, have you tried just not saying the magic word? I don't see why that should be so hard.'

I would pray for the car ride to be over, except that where we're going is probably worse. I will the ride to last longer, for us to hit every red light, for time itself to slow down. The street numbers climb anyway, and Hanover's restaurants and high-end clothing stores give way to diners and laundromats and shoe stores, signage gray with sleet beginning to stick, and then our tires are crunching on sandy asphalt as we turn off into the parking lot of an unmarked three-story brick building.

It's next to the community center where I spent three whole summers playing soccer, but I never even looked at it before. Today, three National Guard soldiers are waiting out front, outfitted for metahuman engagement. Their powered armor is the color of orange traffic cones except for the silvered face plates. Sleet hits and steams off the heat-dispersing fins projecting up from behind their wide, armored shoulders.

'I'll be back at noon to get you, all right?' my mother says. 'I'll be right here.'

'Okay.'

She clutches my arm awkwardly as I get out. She doesn't really know how to touch other people.

'Please don't give us anything more to worry about, all right? You won't, will you?'

'I won't.'

'I love you.'

'Love you too, Mom,' I say.

'Try to make new friends!'

The guard in mechanical armor escorts me to the door. Inside, there's a second pair of heavier doors that slide aside to admit me to a waiting room painted all in white. A woman behind a plexiglas barrier slides a clipboard at me to sign, and talks to someone briefly through an intercom, then directs me to room 311.

Inside, it looks more like a hospital than anything else. Offices and what look like medical laboratories; men and women in uniform who look at me curiously. It doesn't feel like a place a teenager should be; I don't see anyone else my age. It smells like disinfectant.

Room 311 is on the third floor, with a note taped to the wall outside that says: RESERVED, CLEO 8 A.M. – NOON. I linger a moment outside but there isn't any way to put this off. It's 7.48 a.m.

Opening the door, it looks like any classroom. There's an American flag, a whiteboard, metal storage closets. The walls are painted a soothing pale blue-gray.

A dozen desk chairs are arranged in a circle, and three kids around my age have already seated themselves at the farthest possible distance from one another.

Fat kid, Black girl, blonde girl – all kids from school. Each of them looks up just long enough to scope out the newcomer. I sit down between the fat kid and the Black girl.

The fat kid has a Rubik's cube that he regards with a blank expression. He scrambles it, solves it in four or five seconds, then scrambles it again, over and over, his stubby fingers quick and sure.

His name is Jack. He skipped two or three grades and takes math and computer classes at a local college. He's supposed to be a big deal. He won the big Harvard/MIT math competition for high schoolers, competing as an individual against teams from around the world. They sent him to the National Math Olympiad where he was disqualified for what was called 'immature behavior'. He's wearing, with defiant nonchalance, a bicycle helmet with green and red wires sticking out of it.

The Black girl is reading a paperback book, a plump worn copy of Asimov's *Foundation*. No one knows her but they know who she is – the girl who never talks. Half her courses are in special ed and she spends a lot of time in the school counselor's office. She's small and stocky, keeps her hair shaved almost to nothing, and wears the same thin army surplus jacket, summer and winter.

She can talk, of course, it's just that she doesn't like to, and no one wants to talk to her anyway. Not that I have anything to boast about in terms of social standing but I at least *try* to act normal.

The blonde girl has a book of practice SAT questions open, filling in the answers in a steady rhythm. I don't remember her name, just that she showed up in the middle of last year and joined the grove of other tall thin rich popular girls who eat lunch together.

None of us belongs in a room together. The only thing we have in common is the gray plastic ankle bracelet each of us wears that we can't take off, not even in the shower.

Jack seems to get bored of the Rubik's cube.

'So are we all just going to sit here?' Jack says. 'Door's not locked.'

No one responds. He tries the door of one of the metal cabinets, then opens drawers until he finds a wooden ruler. He snaps it in half, pulls out the thin steel strip at the edge. He picks the cabinet lock with it in one try.

'Didn't you see the guards?' the blonde girl says. She's in a white and navy Yale sweatshirt with jeans, hair worn up, but with her height and bearing she's obviously of the school aristocracy.

Jack ignores her anyway and sorts through the contents of the cabinet.

'Could you please just sit down before they get here?' the blonde girl says.

'Nah.' On a table in the back Jack's breaking an overhead projector into its component parts, using the bit of steel as a screwdriver.

'What are you doing?' I ask him.

'It's a surprise. Great lenses on these things. Underrated.'

'You're not building a weapon,' the blonde girl says.

'Just an insurance policy, Miss Concord Academy.'

'How would you know where I went to school?'

'I know many things,' he says.

'Sit down or I'll make you live your death a thousand times. You will beg for a final ending.'

'Tss!' the Black girl hisses. 'They're coming.'

Jack pockets the lens and dumps the rest in the closet, then gets to his seat just as the door opens and a man comes in.

I recognize him from when they first arrested me, although I didn't learn his name. He's in his middle forties, dressed like before, in a tweed jacket and Oxford shirt, open at the collar. A civilian but powerfully built, like a wrestler, his black hair worn shoulder-length. His thick features aren't unpleasant, with massive eyebrows above intelligent brown eyes.

'Well, hello, all of you,' he says. 'I'm sorry if I didn't introduce myself earlier. I am Dr Emil Potsworth, and this is the very first meeting of the CLEO program.'

His English sounds like that of a highly educated foreigner but I can't place the accent. When he seats himself two chairs away from me he has a clean smell: shampoo and Bay Rum aftershave.

'Shall we start by introducing ourselves?' His gaze lands on the blonde girl. 'Would you like to start us off?'

'I am Princess-in-Exile Stefanie Donata Telegander Maxima,' she says. 'But in this realm I may be called Stefanie DiDonato.'

I place the name, from academic awards lists and from a memorably vulgar conversation between two guys in gym class, regarding what somebody's cousin in college said he got her to do with him, and the relative credibility of said report.

'Thank you, Princess. Now who else? Code names allowed, if that's easier.'

'Doctor Optimal,' Jack says.

'Of course you are.'

'Alex Beekman. Prodigy.'

'Thank you. And you, miss?' He looks at the small Black girl.

'Combat Augmentation Test Fourteen.' The Black girl's

voice is low and just above a whisper. 'They called me CAT-14 at first, back when there were others. Then I was just Cat.'

'Cat, then. Welcome.'

'It was also the first thing they made me kill.'

The Princess turns a bit paler, if that's possible.

Potsworth writes the letters C L E O in a neat column. 'Does anyone know what that stands for? No? It stands for Changing Lives, Expanding Options, a pilot educational program in collaboration with Hanover High School. And what does that mean for you? I expect you're wondering.'

'It means we fucked up,' Jack says.

Potsworth nods, choosing not to register the profanity.

'The great Doctor Optimal is correct, as far as that goes. Each of you was apprehended in relation to a violation of the Metzner Act. Which means what? Yes, Jack?'

'We used our powers to harm, physically or psychologically, one or more non-powered victims, as an act of malice or else for the purposes of theft or fraud,' Jack says.

'Very good.'

'But it's bullshit. *Impkin* versus *State of Tennessee* established a different standard –'

'Metzner violations carry extreme mandatory penalties, even for juveniles. Lengthy incarceration at the very least. You lucky people are being made an exception. No need to thank me.'

'So what's going to happen?' I ask.

'You will remain under limited house arrest, and go through a course of rehabilitation, education, and training. At the end of which, you may or may not be deemed ready to rejoin society.'

'Mr Potsworth –' Stefanie says.

'Doctor.'

'Dr Potsworth, I think I'd like to leave now.'

'Interesting. Would you tell us why, Princess?'

'I think this is a really great program for people who need help, but I don't think it's for me.' She stands, already slinging her bag over her shoulder, and takes a deliberate step toward the door.

'Sit down, please,' Potsworth says, quietly, a little of the avuncular warmth gone from his voice.

Stefanie halts but doesn't go back to her seat. 'It's all right. My lawyers will be in touch,' she says.

'I already spoke to your family's lawyers. Your claims of sovereignty are not recognized by the United States, per the revised 1982 treaty signed with Queen Juniper. I expect you know that.'

'My half-sister is a foul usurper.'

'That's as may be. But for now, you're one of us. Take a seat.'

'You're being rude.'

'Four students at the Concord Academy are suffering from psychological trauma and persistent nightmares after your little tantrum last fall. Do you consider that rude?'

'I consider it a fitting consequence of their actions.'

'I could go on, Princess. You had quite a year last year. You went from being the top-ranked student in your sophomore class and field hockey co-captain to failing three classes. Your known offenses include four counts of metahuman assault, two of academic misconduct –'

'Shut up,' she says, her pale skin now a vivid pink.

'Drug possession, public disorder, solicitation . . .'

'Stop it!' she shouts. She raises a hand and a wooden desk chair twitches off the floor, yanked by invisible forces, then she slaps it into the glass mirror. The dry wood shatters and the glass cracks, shockingly loud in the small room.

We all flinch, except Potsworth.

She has a spark of pinkish light gathered in each of her fists, bright as a welding torch. I can feel the heat from ten feet away.

'How fast do you think the guards could get in here, if they had to?' she says.

'Don't be stupid,' Jack whispers.

'How fast?' she repeats. 'Fast enough to save you?'

'I doubt it,' Potsworth says, like it's an offhanded observation.

'I'm leaving,' Stefanie says. But she doesn't move. She's almost too angry to speak. It's obvious now, looking at her, that she isn't entirely human. Her eyes are too wide, her cheekbones too severe. I wonder how old she really is.

'Do it,' says Potsworth. 'Run.'

'Excuse me?'

'Run, if you think you can make it.' He points to the doorway. 'Any of you. Go. The door isn't locked, as Doctor Optimal pointed out. You're free to try.

'But the moment you step outside this room without my permission, CLEO and its generous protections are forfeit. You become an adult offender, and that means you get what the grown-ups get. Government metahuman response teams, trained to capture and kill people like you. If you think you can play at that level, go ahead. But if you lose, you take the consequences. Black sites, enhanced interrogations in deep ocean lock-up. Off-the-books laboratories. Your families won't know where you are and we'll make sure they're afraid to ask. Do we understand each other?'

Stefanie glares at him for another moment. She lets the lights in her hand flicker out.

'You'll never understand me.' She sits down at her desk, back held rigidly straight.

'Are there any further questions?' Potsworth says. 'Ask them now. I would hate to leave you under any illusions.'

'Why us?' I ask. 'Why do we get special treatment?'

'Because you're very, very lucky to be ideal candidates for this pilot program. Five metahumans in the same township is a rare thing, let alone the same high school. You present as baseline human and most of you come from stable middle-class homes and haven't killed too many people. It would be easy to argue that you are nice boys and girls who made their one little mistake. Don't all thank me at once.'

'So what do we have to do?' Jack says.

'Whatever I tell you to, Doctor Optimal. Train your abilities, train your minds. Decide who you want to be. Demonstrate that you could become productive members of society. You have eight months, extended at my discretion, followed by a final examination.'

'What do we get out of any of this?' Jack says.

'If you pass, your juvenile records will be sealed when you turn eighteen. You won't go to prison for the rest of your lives. Yes, Prodigy?'

'What about the fifth one?' I ask.

'I'm sorry?'

'There are four of us. Didn't you say there was a fifth metahuman?'

'There was,' Potsworth says, 'but she ran.'

8

The next Saturday, Potsworth bounces into the room looking as if he's been waiting all week for the privilege of lecturing four sleepy delinquents.

'Who's excited to talk about legal history?' he says. 'Don't you want to know about the Metzner Act? The entire reason you're here? No? I weep for the young.'

Potsworth, we soon learn, can talk for hours on almost any conceivable subject, with exacting detail. We get a detailed history of metahuman laws and civil rights, stretching all the way back to classified archaeological data – a set of cave paintings found in the Ural Mountains near the burial site of a very odd-looking Neanderthal skeleton.

For most of recorded history, the legal response to metahumans consisted of throwing rocks at weird people. Salic law and Anglo-Saxon and Confucian traditions offered minor improvements, until the Code Napoleon's redacted provisions brought us into the modern era of confinement and forced military service. It's no wonder so many people like us went to America, where they could disappear into cities full of immigrants or hike out past the colonial frontier.

When the United States conscripted a million soldiers to fight in World War I, a great many oddities were uncovered. The Wartime Commission on Medical Exceptions was formed. In the subsequent peace, Congress passed the Aberrance Laws of the 1920s, and the notorious redacted Amendment to the Constitution.

'So we're fucked from the start,' Jack says. 'I'm just smart, how is that a crime?'

'Technically, your crime was wire fraud, but I take your point. The state rules your kind with a heavy hand.'

'I'm not a weirdo or a mistake or whatever,' Stefanie says. 'Sorry, but I'm not. My power comes from the royal blood of Summerdwell. I'm exactly what I should be.'

'But no matter your origins, when you put your friends in McLean Hospital you became a rogue metahuman.'

'They started it,' Stefanie says. 'I'm sure they're fine.'

'I was only defending myself,' I say. 'Probably she was, too.'

'I'm only what the scientists made me,' Cat says.

'Does it help if I agree with you?' Potsworth says. 'But I'm afraid you gave them all the excuses they needed, and now you're under the jurisdiction of the Metahuman Investigation and Control Agency. It's the same elsewhere. Interpol M operates in Europe. Russia, China and North Korea make their own arrangements, and I very much advise you to avoid any contact with them.'

We all go to the bathroom at the mid-morning break. I don't want to pee next to a boy wearing an electric helmet but this is where my life choices have brought me.

'Wire fraud?' I ask him, shouldering my way into the restroom. He ducks into a stall.

'Fucking Feds,' he says. 'People are prejudiced against the hypercognitive. We're not all supervillains, you know.'

'But what actually did you do?'

'You know what an Ohio-class submarine is?'

'Not really.'

'Yeah, well. Be careful selling any of them to the Russkies, they'll fucking pussy out on you. What about you?'

'You know what happened to the school and all, right?'

'Fuckin' A! That was you?'

'Pretty much.'

'You, sir, are a hero of the people.' Jack emerges from the stall and inspects himself in the mirror. He carefully lifts the helmet a fraction, tugs gently on a green wire. I glimpse scarred corpse-white skin.

'I still got caught.'

'You know what, who cares? We beat this thing. We'll be out of here in June. You got plans?'

'Wesleyan, I guess, if I can still go.'

'Skip it. College is for suckers.'

'I thought about going to Paris.'

'That's what I'm talking about. We just tell this Potsworth guy what he wants to hear, then the world's ours for the taking. You and me.'

I flush at the sudden burst of sincerity, misguided as it is.

'Okay, so, this is kind of awkward,' I say.

'God, you're one of those. Fine, I'll go it alone.'

'What about those girls?'

'The bitch and the basket case?' he says. 'You gotta be kidding me.'

When we return, each chair has a fresh yellow legal pad and a ballpoint pen.

'I'd like each of you to take a piece of paper and write, in your own words, the sequence of events that led to your inclusion in the CLEO program.'

'That's illegal,' Jack says. 'I can't be forced to testify against myself. And I already told you, I thought it was a game. I'm the victim here.'

'Jack, it's over. We know what you did.'

'You didn't find anything real.'

'Jack. The shell companies in Hong Kong and Brussels were good, but we've seen work like that before. We found the safety deposit box in Helsinki.'

'That's a lie,' Jack manages to say.

Stefanie raises a long pale arm, even though she's only three feet away. 'Does this count toward our grade?'

'Everything counts. Sixty minutes. Begin.'

Stefanie presses her lips together and begins writing.

The girl called Cat writes bent over, nose almost touching the paper, in an upward-trending left-handed scrawl. There's a scar visible on the back of her neck, a vertical line of pale puckered skin that runs down below her collar and up under her hairline.

Jack, with slow and deliberate care, tears the first page from the pad, rips it in half, in half again, and into smaller and smaller pieces, then tosses them over one shoulder. He tears off the next one and shreds it as well, then the next. Every so often he gives a little snuffle and wipes his eyes, and tears up the next one.

I pick up my pen and I begin to lie. It turns out not to be hard. I just say what should have happened. Kindly wizard; precocious, morally resolute child; noble destiny. Unavoidable damages. Everlasting remorse. Sorry, everyone. Mostly.

The National Guard are still out front when I come down to wait for Mom to pick me up. Stefanie is waiting, too. Outside in the cold, under the gray sky, she looks smaller and fragile and far less dangerous.

'Looking good, chief,' Jack says, passing us. He sets out across the parking lot, his back bent under the weight of his overstuffed backpack.

'You're at Hanover, too?' she asks me suddenly.

'I'm in your grade.'

'Ah.'

Cat brushes past us.

I call out, 'See you next week!'

But she only walks faster. Instead of following Jack, she turns abruptly to her right and starts out across the sports fields. Jack has seated himself at the bus stop, working the Rubik's cube again.

'Are you really a princess?' I say.

'Yes. Even if you don't believe it, it's true anyway.'

'What are you princess of?'

'You've never heard of the place, so don't ask. I haven't been there since I was six. My fucking half-sister's there now.' She lights a cigarette with a monarchical scowl.

'That must be hard. I mean, to not be home or anything.'

She makes a disgusted face. 'God, don't sympathize. I'm a princess.'

At the far end of the soccer field, Cat reaches the outer fence and makes a startling upward leap, at least eight feet in the air, before she lands, balances a moment, then drops down lightly on the far side and disappears into the forest.

'I didn't know princesses had to go to high school.'

'My parents thought it would be good for me to "walk amongst the commoners". It was going to help me learn humility.'

'Oh,' I say. 'So what happened?'

'People didn't show respect.'

At last, a long black town car turns off the road and pulls up in front of us. A Rolls Royce, the first I ever saw, waxed to a glossy shine. A handsome driver bounces out and opens the door for her.

'Have a nice weekend,' she says as she ducks inside, and it sweeps her away from me, left behind like a prince on the palace steps.

9

I started the night patrols soon after I got the amulet. Opportunities for battling evil-doers were few and far between in Hanover's wealthy suburban streets but it seemed ignoble not to try. Who knows what evil might be lurking within our local radiologist's backyard gazebo, or prowling the perfectly maintained municipal tennis courts?

When Jack boasted to me that he could jam the tracking bracelets anytime he wanted, I felt duty-bound to ask for his help. I didn't realize he'd take it as an invitation to tag along, but twice a week he'd be waiting by the mailbox when I snuck out. It can't be because he objected to crime that much. I think, at first, it was because he couldn't sleep.

My nascent friendship with Jack is one of the least predictable outcomes of my cosmic superpowers. I'm not sure if we're really friends, or why. It's just that he doesn't worry about any of the things I worry about every second of my life. He walks through the walls I can't even see to punch through.

'Why is the cave the hard part of this to accept?' I ask.

'Because of science! Why do you just accept everything at face value?'

It started snowing at four this afternoon and now, at midnight, Hanover is muffled and padded and put to bed. Jack hurries along the sidewalk beside me, kicking up snow, taking almost two steps to my one.

'Because I was there, Jack,' I say. 'I was in the cave, literally. Statues, torches. It was exactly like I told you.'

'What do you think sandstone is? Just answer that.'

'I don't know. Sandy stone.'

'You see any granite down there? You want to talk about local geology?'

'I'm begging you. This is just what I remember.'

'I concede nothing, but okay,' Jack says. 'So Ferris gives you the amulet?'

'Not right away. He has a lot to say first. Be good. Defeat the Dark Adversary. He said I was the Chosen One, descendant of ancient wizard-kings. I think there was more but at that point I was just killing time until the handover part which, finally, he did, although there were a lot of caveats. Only in the hour of greatest need. And the adversary thing.'

'So, strings attached.'

'Right. Then we walked around for a while. He had all kinds of questions about my life, and smart things to say, like I was the most important kid in the world to him. And he was funny. You know, like in class. It seemed like hours, but when we came out of the cave we were near my house and it was only five-thirty.'

'What did you tell your family?'

'Are you kidding? They're, like, ordinary mortals. I acted perfectly normal and then went to bed. I woke up thinking it was a dream, but the amulet was still there and it was the greatest feeling I ever had. Everything was starting off. Then he never came to school again.'

'Yeah, that part's weird. But he could come back, right?' Jack says.

'You never had anything like the cave? Some explanation for why you are this way?'

'Dude, I just came out this way. I didn't even know I was different until I started talking and people freaked out. But it doesn't come from anywhere. It's not like my parents are smart.'

Jack hugs himself against the cold, and we walk faster. The moon is waning. Boston glows on the horizon.

We walk, side by side, not talking for a while. All of Hanover is asleep. It feels like we're the only ones in the whole town still awake. Still keeping watch.

'I'm not seeing a lot of crime around here, dude,' Jack says.

'Well, keep looking, just in case. I said I'd fight for justice.'

We walk on a little more, turn left on Grove. We go a different way each time.

'So what happened when he didn't come back?'

'I waited around. It was so cool, at first. I was secretly this enormous big deal and any day now, I'd defeat this evil – whatever it was – and the whole school would go nuts. Then some time passed but, hey, I understood, we're important people, things come up. And then some more time, and I think maybe it's a test. He's waiting to see how I handle the power.

'But after six months it didn't seem like a plan at all, it just seemed stupid. He told me this was a magic amulet and I just believed him? Why? There was no proof. I kept carrying it around but I started looking for an excuse to try it, no matter how dumb. Just to see if it worked, or if I could throw it away and forget about it. So then, of course, it was the spring dance, junior year.'

'They wouldn't stop playing "Love Shack".'

'I went and it was just like usual, I hung back with my friends, I was so pissed at myself, I didn't have the guts to ask anybody to dance.'

'You just ask them.'

'Yeah, okay, fine. Well, I left early and outside there was Chuck Dubek – you know him?'

'Yeah, I know him,' Jack says.

'Him and his friends started pushing me around, and I panicked. I said the word. I didn't know what would happen.'

'And then you . . . fucked them up?'

'Pretty much.' It was more than that, but I didn't want to say.

'Well, it doesn't sound that bad. They were assholes.'

'Thanks.'

'It kinda sounds like the best day of your life.'

'Well, that's not what metahuman enforcement said.'

'Wanna show me?' he says.

We stop. It's a long straight stretch of road, not too many houses. We haven't seen any cars for a while. Why not?

'I'm not supposed to show it off.'

'Who's going to stop you?' he says. 'Come on. I want to see what the big deal is.'

'Well, don't tell anybody.'

We walk a few more steps off the road, under the trees.

'Ready?'

'Go for it.'

'Raeclun.' I say it softly and feel the change happen. The blink, the far-off boom. I can't see it except in the way Jack is looking at me, but I know by now what he sees. A sixteen-year-old Adonis in spandex standing in the snow. I feel the lightness of my absurd musculature. I want to jump into the treetops. I want to crack open the sky and let the stars fall.

'Jesus Christ.' Jack hops backward. People do that.

'Sorry.'

'What is it? I mean, what the hell are you?'

'What he said, I guess. The Chosen One. What does it look like to you?' It comes out in Prodigy's voice – just like mine, but resonant and carrying. I know I could raise it to a shout that would shatter glass if I had to.

The LED lights on Jack's helmet cycle furiously. He shakes

his head, as if trying to clear it of a thought, or of too many thoughts at once.

'You're butchering the laws of physics and biology. Where's the conservation of mass? Where's your fucking wallet and coat right now?' he says.

'You haven't even seen what it can do.'

Hanover is full of glacial boulders, and the nearest is the size of a granite beach ball. Once I get my arms around it, I can lift it easily. Legs braced wide, I heft it in one hand, flip it, then toss it over my shoulder.

'There is no justification for this. Why should it make you handsome? Where do the clothes come from? This is making me nauseous.'

'Calm down already.'

'I can't even look at you right now.'

'Okay, okay. Jeez.'

I change back. He reaches for the amulet and I pull it back.

'Lemme see,' he says, grabbing for it. 'Come on, I won't steal it.'

He examines it, the chain still around my neck. He holds it up under a street light. He inspects one side, then the other, then digs out a single key on a faded red and blue Angler Wine and Liquors keychain and scratches at the metal with it.

'Raeclun.' He says it without warning.

'Hey, watch it. That's the secret word.'

'Relax, it only works for you. I wish I knew why.'

'Because I'm the Chosen One. It's my destiny.'

'Bullshit,' Jack says.

'It does sound a little vague.'

'Don't worry, I'll figure out what your deal is. Someday.'

10

I told Potsworth a reasonable amount of the truth, and Jack even more of it, but neither of them got everything. Jack was right, though: I fucked them up.

I turned, and Chuck was walking toward me, smiling the way bullies smile at somebody who's afraid of them, a combination of 'hey, we're all friends here, it's just a joke', and the feral glee of a starving person gazing down at a long-awaited meal.

I knew the look, I'd seen it my whole life. I was tall but thin, they could shove me in the hall and I wouldn't fight back. It wasn't personal. In fact, they barely knew my name. They certainly didn't know I was a hero of destiny.

It was a little less planned than I told Jack. I was terrified, like I always was, and I yelled the word as if calling 'time out' in a game of tag.

The change is almost instantaneous; a flash of light and a quick, seamless expansion. On camera, a bright burst of static.

Chuck blinked and shook his head. He was holding on to my arm that, confusingly, was thicker than it had been a moment ago. He tugged and found it immoveable as marble. He looked up into my new face, now an inch higher than his own.

He gave out a pointless little giggle. The smile was still on his face, frozen there, waiting for his brain to catch up. His eyes were taking on the shocked blankness of expression typical during first encounters with a metahuman. *Why can't I move Alex's arm? Why is he taller and weirdly hot?* His brain clawed at the scene for answers.

I wasn't processing it any faster than he was, but for different reasons. Superpowers are inevitably a kind of violence to the body they inhabit. They come at a cost, paid for in trauma or loss, or years of life, or however you want to figure the price of a body made profoundly alien to itself. Mine had been dimensionally grafted in unspecified fashion onto another body of unknown origin, technically without my permission (although I'm sure I would have given it, if not begged for it). But that confusion was still in my future. All I could tell at the time was that I was taller and every cell in my body wanted to sing and dance and leap as high as the sun.

But wait, here was something even more interesting than singing and dancing. I pulled free of Chuck's grip, and locked my hand around his wrist. He tried to yank his arm away but I barely noticed the attempt. It was funny, wasn't it? This was a guy who for years could do anything he wanted to me, and now he couldn't even get his arm back.

Fighting, I now saw, was way better than I thought it was. I always thought I must be a pacifist, but really, fighting is fucking great – as long as you're a hundred times stronger than your opponent. Meanwhile, Chuck's side of the scenario was going wildly off-script. He kept pulling at his arm, like a man with his sleeve caught in a piece of machinery. His face was beginning to register real distress.

There was a rustle of cloth and a weak inertia-less thud, which proved to be Chuck trying to punch me in the midriff. It was an exceptionally brave gesture, given the terror and disorientation that had to be setting in. The accident report would show that his wrist broke on impact.

I gave his chest the lightest possible push and he stumbled

backward, barely staying on his feet. I batted him open-handed across the face. It broke the skin, and blood sprayed as he pirouetted into the side of his car. He would be marked for the rest of his life.

The second kid, the luckiest of the three, was leaning on the car, being sick. Another common reaction to meta-human outbreaks. Vomit sprayed in a wide arc as I slung him upward by his belt and managed to get him stuck in a tree. The last kid, the football player, was running around the car to the driver's-side door. It was a smart move, but Prodigy runs a mile in under sixty seconds. He can certainly outpace a former high school cornerback with a smoking habit.

The boy's face was deathly white under his Red Sox cap, so I only gave him the smallest part of what he had coming – okay, a little more than that – and then I let him drop. I don't remember doing anything to the car, but I must have, because there was a smell of gasoline and then it was on its side, burning. The first shouts started coming from the school dance.

A few people had come out of the gym to see what was happening and noticed the car was burning, but hadn't spotted me yet. I could have called it a night at this point and maybe even gotten away with the whole thing. Alex Beekman beat up three hulking seniors? It would sound like a joke.

I didn't feel like calling it a night, and it seemed clear that I wouldn't have to do anything I didn't feel like, ever again. And look, here were the great big front doors of Hanover High School – the place I was afraid to go into every single morning – just waiting to be taught a good lesson.

I marched up the front steps and kicked those big double doors straight in. One went skidding along the linoleum, the other still hung on by one hinge. I tore it off and swung it straight through the glass trophy case that stood in the lobby.

In a moment, the school's storied history had turned to shards of glass and cheap plastic statuettes I crushed to powder beneath my feet.

I kicked down the wall to the principal's office and threw his desk way out into the parking lot. I tore up sinks and urinals, and a tide of water trickled down the hallways. I shattered blackboards, punched through walls. I found myself in the nurse's office, and that was when I looked in a mirror for the first time. I was beautiful. Of course I was. Everything was how it was supposed to be now.

How strong was I? There seemed to be no end to it. I kicked pieces out of the great reinforced columns in the cafeteria until the great iron reinforcements showed, then I tore those out. Beams overhead sagged encouragingly. They wouldn't be putting this back together again so easily.

What now? When you're as strong as I am, it's not that hard to tear a medium-sized suburban high school to pieces. The only real problem is stopping once you've started. Why not tear down the sun, moon and stars while I was at it? Don't blame me, blame the system. Blame Michael Ferris, who didn't show up to stop me, then or ever.

Other people did show up, however. Engine noises and sirens were accumulating outside. Voices hissed and shrilled from walkie-talkies and bullhorns.

I climbed the stub of an interior stairway to look at the parking lot. It was filling up with police cars and vans and armored personnel carriers; an ambulance was stopped where I'd deposited Chuck and his friends, lights running. I thought I'd left them in decent shape. Maybe they were just crybabies?

A helicopter hovered low, and then bounced high as four figures in powered armor dropped from it at once and crashed to the pavement. As its spotlight panned across the scene, I saw for a moment a human figure standing in the night sky, cape flapping.

I began to give a little more thought to my evening plans. Up until now, it all seemed like the most splendid outing imaginable. But as I started to think about how these things usually end, the outlook dimmed a little. I wasn't going to be cast as the god-emperor or even the hero of this narrative.

'No, no, no. Not me,' I whispered. 'Not me. Not me.'

As much as anything else, this is what makes me think I'm not cut out to be a supervillain. These people lose.

Behind the gym lay the sports fields and, past that, nothing but empty conservation land. Forest. I sprinted along the track, shattering varsity track records, leaped the fence to land awkwardly on the slope of a hill. I tumbled down it and kept going, through the trees, a fence, then leaped a suburban swimming pool. I needed Michael Ferris. He'd know what to do. At Prodigy's pace I could be at the cave inside half an hour.

A low-flying helicopter dropped to treetop level and buzzed along behind me. I stopped at the edge of a meadow, bounded by one of the low stone walls that criss-cross open land here, a hundred years old or more. I hefted a rock the size of a basketball and heaved it at the helicopter, which dodged adroitly and sped off. Soon I began to hear the thudding footsteps of powered armor on dirt, their running-lights visible through the line of trees.

I shied another stone at them, heard a solid clank, and one of them staggered. The rest halted to keep their ranks intact, but there was another line of them at the trees ahead of me and, behind them on the road, the lights of more emergency vehicles. The circle was closing. The soldiers halted in unison, as at an invisible line, to leave me at the center of a ring thirty or forty yards across.

I slowed to a stop, pinned in a helicopter's spotlight. Standing alone in my inexplicable blue and white costume, flag of an unknown country and forgotten cause, I waited for what came next.

The ring of uniformed figures around me parted to admit a black sedan that bumped slowly over the hummocks of dried grass and stopped. The door opened and a woman emerged, taking her time. She was tall, wearing a lavender coat and matching cloche hat. She would have looked absurdly out of place, if it weren't for her quiet self-possession.

The real power had arrived. I recognized her as Seraph, one of the Vigilants, known for her particularly aggressive brand of psychic abilities.

She shrugged out of the coat to reveal an elegant blue evening dress. She handed the coat to a policeman and accepted a bullhorn in return.

'Whoever you are, can you hear me well enough?' she said, her voice cool and mid-Atlantic.

I nodded.

'Good. I don't know who you are, or what your powers are, or what inspired you to interrupt my evening, but it's time to conclude this little rumpus. This area has been evacuated to allow use of the satellite-mounted weaponry currently targeting the base of your neck. If that won't do it, I will walk across this grass and disembowel your teenage psyche with my bare hands. As an alternative, you can surrender yourself. You have eight seconds. No one likes a ditherer.'

Part of me will always wish I went down fighting, sobbing and spitting defiance. I raised my hands in surrender. I whispered my magic word into the roar of helicopters, and I changed.

11

The night I was arrested, National Guard soldiers used a long metal pole to hook the amulet's chain and lift it from around my neck, then dropped it into a metal box and loaded me, stunned and unresisting, into a National Guard containment van where I was put into thickly padded metal restraints. As the van pulled away I could turn my head just enough to look through the tiny rear windows and see the wreckage of Hanover High School receding behind me.

Whether the ride passed quickly or slowly, I don't know. I was too far into shock to measure the time, or think or feel anything other than the blank sensation that my life was effectively over at the age of sixteen.

It might have been ten minutes or it might have been an hour, then the van came to a stop. I waited through a few more minutes of silence, then the doors opened. They unshackled me and I stumbled across a few yards of pavement, hurried along by two armored Guardsmen, with Seraph walking ahead. The eerie shield-and-eye symbol of the US Department of Metahuman Affairs was everywhere, on signs, on badges. Men and women saluted and rapidly let us through a set of glass doors into an inner perimeter. Here the rooms had less glass, more concrete.

I was stripped and hosed down with shockingly cold water. I think I cried out. Seraph rolled her eyes and lit a cigarette.

I was given a papery powder-blue jumpsuit and matching thin-soled slippers. I was photographed, finger-printed, measured, weighed. They photographed my retina, probed my ears, palpated my abdomen, X-rayed my skull, as if the Wizard's secret might be found in any of those places. It told them nothing. So far, no test has found me anything other than baseline human.

I was seated at a metal table in a room with cameras in each corner of the ceiling, and told to wait. After a few minutes an older woman sat down opposite, then read out yes or no questions from a binder, which I answered as best I could. I didn't have it in me to resist at that point. She asked about prescription medication, about recent physical or mental stresses. There were questions about my family, especially my father. They asked if I had offended any witches lately, been visited by gray-complexioned men with huge eyes, or peered into any mysterious ancient books. Nobody mentioned Michael Ferris.

The woman left and I sat there alone for so long I wondered if they'd forgotten about me. At some point I fell asleep and when I woke up, Potsworth was seated across the table from me, with a slim manila folder on the table in front of him. I asked if he was my lawyer.

'For now, let's say I'm a sort of civilian consultant. A specialist in cases like your own.'

'Okay.'

He studied me intently, with the same attention Mr Ferris had done, but different. Where Mr Ferris saw my potential, Dr Potsworth saw a mystery that needed solving.

'Let's start with your name,' he said, opening the folder.

'It's Alexander Beekman.'

'Any middle name?'

'Horatio. It's a family name.'

He made a note.

'Well, Alexander H. Beekman, it looks like you've had an interesting evening. Would that be fair to say?'

'Yeah.'

'Your file here says you're sixteen years old. You go to Hanover High School. You live with your mother, Shirley, and one sister, Leah, younger. Father . . . not around?'

I nodded.

'It's not a thick file.' He opened it to show a few computer printouts and handwritten references. 'Excellent grades, honors classes, no extracurriculars, no discipline record or behavioral problems. Is that really everything?'

'I guess.'

'Do you have any explanation for what happened this evening?' he asked. 'Two boys are in critical condition at Jefferson Hospital. A third medically stable but in a catatonic state. To say nothing of extensive damage to public property.'

'Sorry.'

'Alex, you're not giving me a lot to go on. Why did you do this?'

'Don't I get a lawyer?' I asked.

He sighed, and spread his hands, helpless.

'You've committed an act of metahuman terrorism. You're in the same boat with kids who breached dimensional walls, took out a Marine battalion, or that girl who cursed Allston last year. Lawyers don't come into it. We need to know what you're capable of and why.'

'Oh.'

'Alex, pretend for a second that it's only you and me in here. What's going on?'

'I really don't know.' I was afraid I might start to cry.

'The people outside this room are scared, and they have some very exhilarating countermeasures at the ready in case you're thinking of trying anything. Let's see if we can keep you around a little longer, shall we?'

'They don't have to worry,' I said. 'It doesn't work without the amulet anyway.'

'Aha!' he said, flashing very white teeth. 'Now we're getting somewhere. The amulet is interesting.' He fished in a vest pocket and brought out the amulet on its chain. He tossed it on the table between us. In the fluorescent light it looked smaller and cheaper than ever.

'Go ahead,' he said. 'Take it.'

'You're giving it to me?' I asked.

'Why not? It's yours, isn't it? Where did it come from?' he asked.

'A man gave it to me.'

'Okay, what kind of man?'

I hesitated. 'Michael Ferris.'

'Ah. The teacher, the one who left. I wondered about that. Why do you suppose he would give you an amulet?'

'It was for passing a placement test,' I said. I didn't trust this man and the shrewd way he saw into me, even if I half wanted him to. It seemed like another trap. I didn't think lying to him could get me into any more trouble than I was in already.

He looked at me carefully, then looked through the folder again, turning each page over to inspect both sides.

'I don't see any placement test scores from this year.'

'I guess it was, you know, verbal in format. Afterwards, he gave me the amulet and, I guess it gave me the powers.'

'He must have said more than that.'

'He told me to be good. Help people. That's all.' I remembered it again, the kindness in Mr Ferris's voice, the urgency. He'd believed it.

'Today was a funny start,' Potsworth said.

'Yeah, I guess it was.'

'So what is it? Where does the amulet come from? What's it for?'

'I don't know,' I said. 'I didn't know what it was going to do.'

'Witnesses say you said something to trigger it.'

'I'm not supposed to tell you. I promised. It's just nonsense, though.'

'Okay, Alex, I'm not going to press you. I'm going to tell you the truth about what we found about this object. We examined it, did a full spectrum scan, X-rays and all. Ran it past the materials experts. Showed it to an archaeologist at Brandeis and a couple of specialists. Do you want to guess what we found?'

'It's, um, magic?'

'We didn't see anything like that. And there's no tech in it either. It's solid metal, no air bubbles or hidden pockets. What else do you know about it?'

'It's old,' I said.

He shook his head. 'The metal is bronze, which means copper and tin and a little zinc. The patina was produced by the application of potassium sulfide, probably to make it look antique. It was made ten or twelve years ago at the most.'

'That's not possible. It's from before America. Before anything you know about.'

'I'm afraid not. Ferris probably bought it in a tourist shop, the kind of thing they pawn off as Celtic or Native American. You can have it, if you want.'

I almost refused. Maybe he was right, maybe it was all a lie or a trick and none of it meant anything. I didn't feel like I could just leave the amulet there.

He sat and waited until I picked it up again, then stood. He shook my hand.

'Goodbye for now, Alex,' Potsworth said. 'I hope we'll meet again.'

12

I remember the buzz and clang of the high-security checkpoints at Hayden, three or four of them, then a walkway, aluminum deck plate and a line of cells on one side. I could hear people breathing in some of them, snoring or weirder sounds. Laughing, buzzing.

The walkway looked down into an enclosed common area. The benches, tables and everything else were made of concrete and twice as thick as they needed to be.

My cell was the very last concrete box, maybe eight feet wide and twice as long. It had a toilet and a metal bed with its scratchy blanket and limp little pillow. A bit of a letdown, actually. Where were the lasers? My whole life was torn to bits and they couldn't even put in a camera.

I lay down for a while, then got up and looked out the window. It had a grating, and a very faint soap-bubble effect that turned out to be a force field. Mollified, I watched the sky get brighter, my thoughts still blank and echoing with the night's events. For long moments I'd forget why I was there, and then it would all come back. I don't remember falling asleep.

I woke up sometime in the afternoon and lay for a while listening to the unfamiliar building. Buzzers sounded and phones rang. A truck passed in the distance.

I walked a few times around the cell. By daylight the window looked down on a lawn of dead grass, surrounded by a high fence topped with concertina wire, and another fence beyond that, another lawn, and a low wall. Beyond that, far off, a busy two-lane highway passed from one side of the view to another.

I sat back down on the cot and I tried to take stock of my situation. Until yesterday I had never even skipped a class. Now I was waiting to learn whether I'd killed anybody and how many millions of dollars I'd cost the government.

Did I really throw a boulder at a helicopter? What about those other kids, were they okay? I was in so much trouble, I didn't even have a standard by which to measure it or any idea how completely fucked I was, like an ancient seagoer crossing uncharted ocean. At least I knew I wasn't going to be getting any college scholarships. Or going to any college. Possibly never even leaving this building again. Fuck. Ancient seagoers sailing their stupid wooden ships right off the edge of the fucking world.

The highway outside was getting busier, and then someone turned on their lights, and then everyone did. All those people driving home at the end of a normal day, people who still had their lives intact, who hadn't fallen off the edge. Well, nothing to do but breathe it in. Keep sinking. Feel for the bottom.

Footsteps approached down the tier. I looked through the slit in the metal door and saw three people pass, left to right. No one spoke. The door of the cell on my right squeaked open and clanged shut. Footsteps faded.

'Hello? Is somebody there?'

It was a girl's voice. I didn't want to answer. I wasn't feeling particularly social.

'I know you're there, I saw you looking,' she said.

'Fine, I'm here,' I said. 'What?'

'I don't know,' she said. 'Say something. I don't even really know what this place is.'

'It's a juvenile detention facility, I think,' I said. 'For metahumans. Weird kids.'

'It's kind of disappointing,' she said. 'I thought there would be lasers.'

'There's a force field over the window if it makes you feel any better.'

'Thanks,' she said. 'So what weird kid thing did you do?'

'I don't want to talk about it,' I said. 'It's pretty much the worst day of my life.'

Someone on another floor started screaming. More of a howling, maybe. There was a clatter of footsteps running toward the source. It started laughing.

'Is that us?' she asked. 'Are we supervillains now?'

'I don't know. Do you want to be?'

'I don't know. Maybe that's just what I am,' she said. 'I look like one now.'

'What does a supervillain look like?'

'I can't describe it. You'd have to see.'

'Anyway, I can't be a supervillain,' I said. 'I'm supposed to save the world.'

'Oh my god. One of those.'

'Well, what's so great about you? Do you have superpowers at least?' I said.

'Yeah.'

'How'd you get yours?'

'Gem,' she said. 'You?'

'Amulet.'

'Lucky us.'

'Who doesn't want superpowers?' I said. 'They're so fun.'

We both laughed at that.

'What's your name?' she said.

'It's Alex,' I said.

'Wait, do you go to Hanover?'

'Why?'

'Oh my god,' she said. 'Is that Alex Beekman?'

'Well, so what?'

She snorted.

'Oh my god, nothing,' she said. 'I just, I love it. That's perfect.'

'Wait, why is that funny?' I said. 'Is it because people think I'm not cool? Because, whatever, I'm in jail now. So.'

'Uh-huh.'

'Wait, who are you?' I said.

'Nobody. It doesn't matter.'

'Oh, come on.'

'Megan Price.'

I knew who she was, basically. We'd been in competition for the high grade in a few classes, which led to a cordially awkward dislike. She was round-faced, with long brown hair, eyes always a little impatient. She kept to herself and got good grades and that's maybe about all anyone knew about her.

'Megan? How did you get here?'

'I don't want to talk about it either.'

A half-moon was visible through the window, low in the darkening sky. I didn't see any lights on the horizon. How far were we from a city?

'Did they tell you anything?' I asked. 'Like how long we'd be here?'

'Just "stand here, breathe normally, please don't manifest the darkforce".'

'Okay,' I said, as if I understood.

'Oh, and there was the guy in the suit. No idea what he wanted.'

'Dinner,' a woman's voice said. 'Come on out.'

The locks on our doors snapped open. It was the same woman who brought me here last night: gray-haired, with heavy shoulders and hands and a metal eye.

I stepped out onto the landing. We waited, but Meg didn't come out.

'Hurry it up,' the guard said.

'I'm not hungry,' Meg's voice answered.

'Nobody stays in the cells for meals.'

'I don't care,' she said. But a moment later, she came out.

The familiar figure of Megan Price was unsettling; the utter strangeness of my surroundings kept it slightly unreal. With the sight of her came the unpleasant awareness that this was taking place in my actual life, the same one where I rode the school bus and took English exams.

It wasn't quite the normal Megan, though. She had never worn that blue jumpsuit, never shown up to school without make-up, her hair unwashed, stringy and askew.

Some of the changes made no sense, as if she too had changed when translated into this dreamworld. She was taller by at least an inch, close to my height now. Her skin wasn't just pale, it had a faint lilac tint. Surely her ears hadn't been quite so long or tapered? In the center of her forehead, there was embedded a flat, diamond-shaped purple gemstone.

'So this is me now,' she said.

I realized I was staring.

'It's nice,' I said.

'Don't be stupid.'

'No, really. It's a striking effect.'

'Oh, shut up.'

'No chatting,' the guard lady said.

The cafeteria wasn't all that different from our high school's. The tables and benches were bolted to the concrete floor but that was about it. Like ours, it was too bright and smelled like a queasy mixture of every food at once, and loud kids sat together while quiet ones sat alone.

It wasn't entirely the same. Guards stood looking down at us holding a bewildering variety of weaponry. The crowd of kids was at first a buzzing, discordant muddle of altered bodies and hypertrophied musculatures, strange clashing energies radiating from hands and eyes, fiery orange and cosmic purple.

After a moment I could focus on individuals. Unruly, thuggish-looking home-brew cyborgs with matching MIT tattoos. One end of the room was dominated by a teenage girl grown to twice normal size who crouched over her table, sullenly alone, her face the size of a big-screen TV, eating from trays held between thumb and forefinger. She bore a painful-looking black eye, just beginning to yellow at the edges.

'Can we just sit over here?' Meg said when we had our trays, pointing to a corner table where a girl sat alone, leached of color, her shape flickering like an old movie's. She gave us a mournful look, then slid down to the opposite end.

I looked down at my meatloaf and mashed potatoes. Was my family eating dinner now? Were they talking about me? Were they going to watch TV afterwards like I didn't even exist, like I wasn't sitting here looking at a guy with a wolf's head trying to drink from a milk carton?

'What are you thinking about?' Meg said.

'My family,' I said. 'Why haven't our parents come to get us?'

'Maybe they don't know where we are,' Meg said.

'My mom's a lawyer,' I said. 'She'll know what to do.'

'You can't trust parents,' Meg said. 'You can't trust anybody.'

At the end of forty-five minutes, a buzzer sounded. The giant girl was escorted out, squeezing awkwardly through the exit doors, then the rest of us followed.

*

The sun was down, the stars out. It was getting chilly in the cells and the single thin blanket wasn't much protection.

'What did you do for that World War I paper?'

'I can't remember,' she said. 'Does it matter?'

I supposed that it didn't.

'Hey, wait,' Meg said suddenly. 'Weren't the SATs tomorrow?'

'Yeah, but they might have to be rescheduled. I sort of destroyed the school.'

There was silence, then a loud burst of laughter.

'Oh my god, I can't breathe.'

'It's not that funny,' I said.

'Alex Beekman destroyed the school,' she said. 'Aren't you a good guy? Was it doing something evil?'

'Kind of sucking, I guess?'

'Oh. Well, yeah, it did,' she said. 'At least no one got hurt. Did they?'

'Yup.'

'Oh. Okay.'

'Lights out, kids,' a guard called, a man this time.

The overhead fluorescents in our cells went out. For a moment it was pitch dark, then my eyes adjusted and the moonlight painted faint outlines of bed, toilet, the armored door.

'Who got hurt?' she asked, after he was gone.

'Chuck Dubek, and some of his friends.'

'Oh, right. He had that stupid car.'

'Well, not anymore,' I said. It was funny for a second, then I remembered the blood. 'God, I messed up.'

'Trust me, you didn't mess up that bad.'

'Why, what did you do?'

'Forget it,' she whispers.

'I bet it wasn't that bad. Did you rob a bank?'

'Is that what you think supervillains do?'

'I never met one before,' I said.

'I stole from some people.'

'Okay. Well, I guess you had a good reason.'

'It sure seemed like it,' she said.

'But you got the thing? So that worked out.'

'Except for the curse, yeah.'

'Uh-oh,' I said.

'I'll figure it out later,' she said. 'I'm going to get a little sleep. I was up all last night getting arrested.'

The next day passed like the first. The rowdy cyborgs were still there; the giant girl was gone. We talked to the guy with the wolf's head; he turned out not to be a werewolf. It was just a thing that happened in his family. Meg introduced herself to another purple girl, but this one didn't seem to speak English. We guessed she was an alien. I wondered what it was she did wrong.

'Alex?'

It must have been around midnight. It was cold in the cell, and the moon was gone.

'Alex,' she repeated.

'I'm awake,' I said.

'What are you doing after this?'

'After spending my life in prison?'

'You don't know what's going to happen. We haven't even been arraigned. Anything could happen. Don't you have a mission, or a destiny?'

'The Wizard said he'd take away my powers if I did anything like this. So then I won't be a metahuman anymore. Maybe they'll let me go.'

'Then what?' she asked.

'I don't know. What do people do? I could go to school. Be a lawyer like Mom.'

'Maybe then you could get me out of here.'

'I'd do my best,' I said. 'Why, what would you do?'

'Get out of Hanover. Travel. Have adventures. Everything I ever wanted.'

'That sounds better than law school.'

'Well, you made your choice.'

There was a sound then, far off in the building, a crash of metal on metal. Shouts, then a sharp detonation, and the lights in the yard outside went off, all at once, in unison. Amber emergency lights came on outside. An alarm was ringing off someplace in the building.

'Probably those cyborgs,' I said.

'Shh. Listen.'

'What?'

'The force field is off.'

She was right. A sound long since faded from awareness had vanished.

'It'll be back in a minute,' I said.

'Then I'll have to go now.'

'Go? Like, escape?'

'That's what supervillains do, isn't it?' she said. 'They lock us up, we escape.' She tried for a devil-may-care breeziness and didn't quite get it.

'Come on, Meg. You're not an actual supervillain. You're just purple.'

A silence followed. I pictured her there in the moonlight, gathering herself for something.

'Alex, I haven't been totally honest with you.'

'Um, in what particulars?' I said.

'God, Alex. Okay. I saw you go into the cave with Mr Ferris.'

'What? What were you doing there?'

'I followed you,' she said. 'Let me just explain. I thought there was something weird about Mr Ferris. I was investigating.'

'Investigating? Like a girl detective?'

'I read a lot, don't judge me. Yes. He was weird. He let me use the phone in his office once and he had this notebook where he wrote about students. He had a list with people crossed off, but you and I were left, and Kevin Mason and Anita What's-her-name who sits in the back. He wrote down things we said, and drew little family trees. He even knew my grandparents' names. More stuff that wasn't in English.'

'So you were stalking him?'

'I was just paying attention, that's all,' she said. 'It was a mystery and, I don't know. I wanted to see if he'd pick me. Then I saw you get in his creepy car. I was weirdly disappointed.'

'He said I was taking a special test.'

'I followed and saw you go into the woods, and then I just thought there was going to be a murder so I had to see that.'

'Great.'

'You're the one who went along with it,' she said. 'Anyway, you know the rest — that crazy cave and the old guy. I was just mad he chose you instead of me. You're not even as smart as me.'

'Your GPA is like zero-point-one higher than mine. Plus, I don't know, what if I'm an extremely good person?'

'Well, you're the specialest boy now, so don't worry about it. I watched you leave — you certainly looked pleased with yourself.'

'First of all, it was the best thing that ever happened to me —'

'Shh. Then I thought, hey, I might as well look around. Those caves are a lot bigger than just the part you saw. There were galleries that went on forever, and libraries and banquet halls and a bridge over a chasm I couldn't see the bottom of. Then I found the temple.'

'What, like a synagogue?'

'More like a hotel lobby, but for an evil god? It was huge, with columns, and it was all black marble. There was a statue. With that gem on its forehead.'

'You stole an evil gem?'

'Not everything purple is evil,' she said. 'And I wasn't leaving empty-handed. I drove home, and my dad was pissed I was out late, but too drunk to do anything about it. I messed around with the gem for a while – making wishes and all – but it didn't do anything, so I left it in a drawer for a year. Then late last night it lit up, and it talked to me. Whispered.'

'You didn't find that creepy?'

'It was scary at first, but it was actually a pretty good listener, unlike some people. It asked me about myself. I told it things I've never told anyone. It seemed to go on for hours. Then it asked me what I wanted, and I told it. To get out of that house and never come back. To go where I want. I told it I wanted everything, and it told me the price.'

'You didn't.'

'Of course I did. It's not that bad. I promised to be evil and ruthless and laugh in the face of justice. And one more thing. I promised to destroy the one whose power had awakened that night.'

'Okay, wait.'

'I didn't know it was you.'

'Really, though.'

'I know! It's pretty funny, right?' she said. 'And it said I had twenty-five years to do it, so that's a ton of time. Who knows what's going to happen? Hang on.'

There was a scrape and creak of bending metal on her side; a moment later, she had my door open. She stepped inside.

'Hey,' she said.

In the darkness, I couldn't see the changes the power had made in her, and she was just Megan Price again. My nemesis.

'I'm not fighting you just because jewelry says to.'

'Relax, I'm just leaving. Once I'm through the fence, I get to the road, steal a car, drive north until I'm in Canada.'

'What's in Canada?'

'Who cares? From there I can go anywhere. I'm going to live in Paris. Learn French, wear amazing scarves. You should come with me.'

In a week of shocks, the biggest one may have been Megan Price asking me to run away with her to Paris.

'I can't do that.'

'Why not? It'll be fun.'

'I have to finish school.'

'School sucks. You destroyed it.'

Her face was close to mine. In the close air of the cell I could smell her, all the sweat and fear of the last twenty-four hours. There was a body closer to mine than anyone's had been in a long time.

'We can't. We're just kids, Meg,' I said. 'How do we pay rent?'

'Steal stuff. And I heard the big villains are always throwing parties for powered kids like us. Warehouses, mansions. It's how they get people to join them.'

'I can't,' I said. 'I'm not like you. I took a vow.'

'So did I.' She sat down on the bed. 'Well, do what you want. Just – before I go, show me this power you got, okay?'

She looked up at me expectantly, not a Megan Price look at all.

'It probably doesn't work,' I said. 'I used it for evil ends.'

'You are so boring right now. Just try it, and I'll get out of your hair.'

'Just don't be disappointed if nothing happens. Move back.' We retired to opposite corners, then I held up the amulet and whispered, 'Raeclun.'

It comes again, the sense of expansion and lightness. I'm starting to like it.

'Oh my god,' she said, in a whisper. 'Oh my god, you look beautiful. But then also like you. It's weird. Can I . . . ?'

She put out a hand. I nodded and she touched my chest, gently, feeling the preternatural power inside. I was never more aware of the mystery of this body, full of secrets it couldn't tell, saturated with them, from its invulnerable skin all the way into the magical fires of its heart.

'Come with me,' she said. 'You know you can.'

The awful thing was, I knew she was right. Maybe he didn't mean to, but Michael Ferris had given me more than an amulet – he gave me a bigger life, if I wanted it. But that wasn't our deal and, at bottom, I knew I wasn't worthy of it. But still I wanted to be.

I shook my head. 'I can't.'

'Be like that. But you're wrong, and you'll come to Paris someday. It's probably our destiny.'

'I will. I promise.'

'Now, watch this.'

She took hold of one of the bars on my window. Something like dark liquid glass was running down her arm, viscous but forming tendrils that flowed out, glossy and prehensile, to seize the window bars. The last of the moonlight glinted on its faceted surface. Meg's face went taut with concentration and the black tendrils flexed, then contracted. The bars shifted in their sockets, flexed, bent inwards, then with a grinding sound they tore from their sockets. She dropped them on the bed.

'Cool, right? I call it "the darkforce". I'm still learning how to control it.'

'I guess you're really going,' I said.

'Yup,' she said.

All of a sudden she kissed me, hard, holding my head to hers, as if clinging for one last moment to the old life, then she let go.

'Bye, Alex Beekman.'

'You'll be okay,' I said.

'No, I won't,' she said. 'See you in twenty-five years.'

She did a little wave and a crooked smile, stepped from the bed to the window, then jumped down.

I hurried to the window. She must have used the darkforce to catch herself, because she was already sprinting flat-out across the lawn. She was halfway across when the floodlights came on, blindingly bright. She stopped, seemed to dither a moment, turned to look up at my window. A bullhorn voice barked at her, the voice half command half panic.

She turned and sprinted for the fence, bullets churning the dirt behind her. She sprawled forward with a shriek of pain or anger, but the darkforce must have taken the impact. She steadied herself with one hand. I saw her other arm fly up, and then glass shattered and all the lights went out at once. She was gone.

My first kiss left a strange energy inside me, wild and new as any cosmic radiation. I sat on the bunk with my body tensed all over, trying to hold on to it as long as I possibly could.

PART THREE

2015

13

Successful team-ups are rare things. People with superpowers don't like each other. Wizards don't like technology; scientists hate anything magic. Ex-military are pompous assholes, mutants think no one understands them, aliens can't read human social cues, robots are fucking robots. And everyone, *everyone*, is the hero of their own story. The Newcomers' four years is pretty impressive when you think about it.

By the time I wake up, Cat has already gone. No note, and no reason to expect her back. Jack's hiding in his laboratory, hoping Barry will leave, which he doesn't. I know when to wait Jack out. Late that afternoon, he taps on my door.

'You got a wire stripper?' he says.

'Nope.'

'Oscilloscope? Banjo? One of those toy dogs Sony used to make?'

'The Best Buy is a quarter mile down the road.'

'I have a lifetime ban,' he says. 'Just come with me, okay?'

Jack hands me a shopping list and waits for me to assemble the parts to today's work of genius. We stop at the Whole Foods for bachelor-style snacks – chips, salsa, guacamole and a pile of frozen pizzas. I pick up a bottle of rosé, Jack snatches it away and replaces it with some Austrian stuff that costs three times as much.

'It's a bargain, if you know what you're doing,' he says, and tosses in a bottle of expensive Scotch.

'I thought you were broke.'

'Yeah, but I'm not *poor*. Yeesh.'

His card gets declined anyway but when the teenaged boy at the register looks at it he does a double take.

'Are you . . . Doctor Optimal?'

Jack nods, puts a finger to his lips.

The kid waves Jack's card away. He puts a hand to his heart and leans forward. 'We're all behind you, dude. Just give the word.'

'The time's gonna come.' He claps him on the shoulder.

The kid does the heart-with-his-hands thing as we hurry away.

'What was that?' I ask him, out on the sidewalk.

'Those 4chan guys never quit,' he says. 'I'm stuck with them for life.'

'I can't believe you're the one who still has fans. I saved school buses full of children! You stole the Golden Gate Bridge!'

'People like me,' he says. 'I have a good personality.'

'Seriously?'

'And I don't pretend to be things I'm not.'

'Ouch.'

We pass two blonde college-age girls who giggle at us, just a mismatched pair of middle-aged men. I hope they're happy attending classes and not working in a radium mine, lashed by the electro-whips of the sentient lobsters I sent back to their home dimension. Really, don't thank me. Happy to help out.

Barry's still at headquarters, not doing much other than long skincare rituals and failing to leave. That evening, I corral them into the same room, with the promise of Thai food, and pass around the wine. They both turn out to be Hitchcock fans and we turn on *The 39 Steps*. Somewhere in the middle of *Notorious* and the fourth bottle of wine I get them to agree to band together and solve crimes – or one crime, at least.

'Good,' I tell them. 'The funeral's tomorrow.'

Barry's car is almost aggressively luxurious; we drive the hundred miles west in its padded self-heating seats. I'd forgotten what superhero life was like, the standard of living I took for granted when I was twenty.

The Pittsfield cemetery is less of a premium affair, a square mile of gently rolling land, a dark green carpet frayed with unmown grass at the edges.

We watch from higher ground. Four workmen in jeans and sweatshirts who lower Michael Ferris's cheap state-provided coffin into the ground. A couple of middle-aged men and women stand clustered together against the stiff wind.

'Colleagues,' I say. 'Not much to go on.'

'Odds are it was just a burglar,' Jack says. 'The killer probably didn't even know Ferris's name.'

I scan the empty horizon in search of sentimental old enemies or guilt-ridden assassins waiting to pay their respects, but none present themselves. The mourners and workmen disperse. We meander down to his gravesite but there's nothing to see, only a square stone set in the earth.

Roy Gillespie, 1959–2015.

Barry's trench coat flaps in the wind, blown back at the perfect dramatic angle, as if it practiced in its off hours.

'Imagine it,' he says. 'Living alone for years, teaching under an assumed identity, never admitting the truth to anyone. How does someone end up like that?'

'Pathetic.'

According to the police report, Michael Ferris died of a traumatic brain injury in his home, during a routine-seeming burglary involving one or more persons, identities unknown. Normally the government might liaise with local law enforcement before sending me in, but we're entirely off the books for this one.

The home in question is a small one-story house with yellow siding, no more than sixty or seventy years old. There's a little square of untended lawn in the back, bordered by a fence of untreated wood. Police tape flutters across doors and windows. Jack, Barry and I park down the street in his car and watch for a while, but no one goes in or out. No police cars pull up. Nothing moves at all on the block except for an older man who comes out to stare at Barry's car, which probably costs more than his house did.

We pick our way past rolled-up newspapers scattered on the lawn, edge past the Honda Accord taking up the carport. The backyard slopes upward away from the house, backed by scrubby forest. Two lawn chairs rust together. We gather again at the front door.

'There aren't any wards, none that I can sense,' Barry says. 'No defenses at all.' His tone says it: *What kind of wizard was this? Was he even a wizard at all?*

'Check again,' I say. It still seems impossible that the man who gave me superpowers, the Wizard of the Cave of Wonders, didn't protect himself. In the cave his voice had the heft and thunder of occult power, and his long-fingered hands, raised, seemed poised to unleash the tempest. Maybe Ferris used up all his firepower on the intruder?

The door isn't even locked. To the right, a kitchen smelling of spoiled milk. Yellow linoleum tile is peeling up; it must have been there since the 1970s. The cabinets and drawers stand open, as if searched, but that might have been the police.

The bed rests unmade, surrounded in a desolation of gray

carpet. An Ikea dresser holds socks and underwear and T-shirts for classic rock bands. The closet holds cheap suits and a leather jacket, all still smelling of his cigarettes. A bedside bookshelf holds staples of the high school curriculum: Faulkner, Bradbury, Salinger; *The Art of Motorcycle Maintenance*. There's an anthology of American poetry, and books by de Beauvoir, Kerouac and Bukowski.

The one thing I recognize is a gold-plated cufflink left in the drawer of the nightstand, stamped with the Trans Am Firebird logo. I watched it rattle on the dashboard for the whole long car ride to the cave. It was a bachelor's car, the car of a man who owned cufflinks. The glove compartment hung open, displaying cassette tapes of bands I had never even heard of, mix tapes in feminine handwriting. It smelled amazing, spicy and musky, and I wondered if someday I could smell like that. I wondered, not daring to put it into words, if Mr Ferris and I could be friends.

Of the bathroom, the less said the better. The living room is a matching display of aging bachelor tristesse: a brick fireplace, never used. A bobblehead Red Sox figurine sits on the mantle. A worn couch and a huge flat-screen TV, the most expensive thing in the entire place. The box it came in still leans against one wall.

What the hell, Mr Ferris? What happened?

'Jack? Is the Thinking Cap giving you anything?'

'I'm not getting anything the police didn't. The intruder popped the front door lock, looked around, went into the living room. Maybe looking for that TV. Ferris woke up, tried to start something. He got knocked back, fell, hit his head on the fireplace mantle, fell here.' He points to a darker patch on the carpet. 'Burglar ran for it. The body must have lain here for two or three days.'

'That's all you found?' I say.

'What else? The whole thing happened in a couple of minutes. I bet they didn't even mean to kill him.'

'But what did they take?'

'What would this guy even have?'

I pull out all the dresser drawers, tap the back of every cabinet. No hidden compartments. No secrets at all. The couch cushions yield forty-five cents. With the power off, the house is becoming dimmer and darker.

'Come on, Alex,' Jack says. 'Maybe he was just an ordinary guy with one job. He gave you the thing and that was that.'

'Don't you have X-ray goggles?' I say. 'They must be good for something.'

He fetches them from the car. They look as dumb as they ever did, but they work. Jack scans the kitchen, living room, stops at the fireplace.

'Wait,' he says. 'That brick's looking funny.'

He pulls it out and gropes inside and pulls out a little twig.

'That remind you of anything?' he says to me.

But it doesn't look like anything. A twig.

'It's holly,' Barry says.

'So?' Jack says. 'Like Christmas?'

'It has an older meaning than that. Hope.'

'Did you learn that from a Hallmark card?'

'It matters,' Barry says. He holds it up, frowns, kneels down at the fireplace. He traces a square on the brick surface, and a pattern of lines.

Jack watches with disgust as a section of brick slides aside to reveal steep narrow stairs.

Below this house, Michael Ferris made another cave of wonders, although this one is smaller, and parts of it look like any suburban hobbyist's. One wall hung with hammers, drills, hacksaws and soldering guns. Several personal computers; a shelf stacked with engineering textbooks turns out to hold theoretical physics texts, and books on home forging. A whiteboard crammed with notes and equations, the same jagged lettering I remember from the blackboard years ago.

It contains a marvel. Or, what's left of one. He tacked an enormous blueprint on the wall. Much annotated, dappled with crossings-outs and erasures, it is a plan for a fantastical machine. In form it's a cylindrical enclosure like a small skeletal gazebo, or the scaffolding that would surround one. The framework supports racks of prisms, and dotted lines show where light from clusters of laser projectors bounces around between them in a complex web, to emerge focused inward and upward at a sphere suspended at the top like a disco ball. Scale markers show it to be about ten inches across.

The real thing must have sat in the center of the room, but no longer. The remains of it are lying in a heap of bent pipes and shattered glass.

'What the fuck . . .' Jack says from beside me. 'Who was this guy?'

He stares up at the blueprint for a long time, then back at the wrecked prototype. This is what we do. The hero business always means walking in halfway through the plan, and you're just running to catch up with the plot. His left eye, the mechanical one, shuffles its lenses. He bends to inspect a shard of broken glass.

'There's a couple of dots of blood here. Ferris must have tagged him before he went down.'

'But what was it? What was worth killing him for?'

'You really don't recognize it?' he says. 'What does it remind you of?'

'Wait.' I do remember it, I just don't have the context. A space station, a desperate fight in cramped quarters, artificial gravity skewing as the floor beneath me tilted, and a roar of anguish from our opponent as Stefanie's mystic spear struck home.

'Sinistro,' I say.

'This was an almost exact reconstruction of Sinistro's time machine,' Jack says. 'A hell of a feat. Thirtieth-century technology.'

'Would it have worked?'

Jack looks it over with a critical eye.

'Maybe. Your guy was no dummy, you know that? For a wizard he knew his way around temporal engineering. But this is thirtieth-century tech. And he's missing the thing that made it run. The ball.' He points at the sphere in the center of the diagram.

'What's that?' Barry says.

'The Time Core. It's the mainspring of the whole business, the thing that actually engages with the chronal fabric. That's what they came for. Kind of pointless, because it hasn't worked since your wife jammed a magic spear through it in 1995. Nobody from this century could have fixed it,' Jack says. 'But I think Ferris was trying.'

In the end, you find whoever's responsible and haul them off to jail and all the while they're laughing their faces off, or else they escape through a glowing portal. Half the time there's never a clear explanation. You collect the thanks of a grateful nation, sure, but you're left thinking: *Who was that guy? What was he trying to do? What were all those hats about?*

Barry and Jack begin a search but there's no point in my joining in, not with my eyes blurring the way they are. Upstairs in the bedroom I sit on the Wizard's sad old bed with the smell of his stupid old jackets around me.

The old man was building a time machine. The man who left when I needed him most was going to go back and find me.

*

Later that night, Barry is in the kitchen again, eating cereal in his fabulous pajamas. This time, it's paired with a large glass of whiskey.

'It's five o'clock somewhere,' he says, mechanically.

He's right. In Summerdwell, it's five o'clock nearly all of the time. The Summerdwellians like it that way.

He pours me my own glass.

'Thanks.'

'Do you know, the house computer keeps asking me how long I'm staying?' he says.

'I'm sorry. That must be Jack's idea. He can be kind of obnoxious sometimes.'

'He's not so bad. Stefanie speaks well of him. Of all of you, actually.'

'Really?'

'I've heard so much about you, I had to come and see for myself.'

'It's, well, it's very nice to meet you.'

'Listen.' He stops himself and starts again. 'Listen, do you suppose I could stay on here for a little while?'

He swallows nervously, waiting for the answer. I would guess he isn't accustomed to asking for help.

'Sure,' I say. 'As long as you'd like, as far as I'm concerned.'

'Thanks. Appreciate it. Maybe I could help with your mission a little more. Part of the team, as it were.' His humility is awkward, and seems to be a bit forced.

I have no idea how powerful he is – or how truly old he might be.

Some further thought is churning inside him. Brave as he is, he is palpably nerving himself as he downs more Captain Crunch. Finally, he lays down his spoon.

'Stefanie and I might be having a little trouble. She's been going through an odd patch. Truth be told, she asked me to push off for a bit.'

'I'm sorry. I hoped you two were happy together.'

'We were. I don't know what it is. Drugs, maybe. Her career has been foundering lately. Perhaps she just doesn't love me as she used to.' He looks authentically miserable at this point, although he can't help but make it picturesque.

'You're not thinking of divorce, are you?'

'She's done it before. It's not common for our sort of person. It's all happily-ever-afters. Except for us, apparently.'

I've rarely known Stefanie to be especially happy, but I don't mention it.

'We can hope for the best. You're a handsome prince, right? Don't you get a Hollywood ending?'

'Malibu, actually. It's a bit different.'

14

There are many, many gadgets that villains shouldn't be allowed to have – hyperdrive, bombs of any description, large magnets, objectionably long stilts – but time machines make up their own special class of contraband. Even good people shouldn't be allowed to have them.

The list of reasons is endless. Traveling to the future, you might not be able to help picking up knowledge that would change how you act in the present. Going backward, the implications are terrifying. In theory, most alterations of the past have only local consequences, quickly swallowed up in the larger noise of a chaotic world. Or maybe you could make a bigger change and get what you want, but there's always the possibility of unforeseen effects. You could cause a major shift entirely by accident. Maybe your memories would change so you wouldn't even know you'd done it. Maybe this has happened a hundred times already.

Driving home, the previous day, no one brought up the question of what reason anybody would have to steal a time machine in the first place. I guess because there are too many; too many regrets, too many quests unfulfilled or abandoned, too many vows we broke or never should have made in the first place, too many lessons learned too late, too many bluntly obvious stupidities we did anyway.

The past is a foreign country: they haven't fucked everything up yet there.

*

Jack loves giving a War Room briefing as much as he ever did.

'Suppose you wanted to repair a time machine. How would you go about it? Anyone know?'

I don't bother answering. Jack was inclined to monologuing even before he officially became a supervillain.

'Of course you don't! It shouldn't even be possible to build one, a device that vaults in a direction we can't see or imagine, past- or future-bound to land minutes or years away, able to strike at the root of cause and effect. Unthinkable, except to the world's most brilliant minds.

'I got a prototype engine running once, but even mine was unstable. This machine is thirtieth-century tech. I doubt if even Sinistro knows how the thing works, but with even a basic knowledge of chronophysics we begin to see what would be required to reassemble such a device. Three items, in ascending order of impossibility.

'One. Map of the local chronometric terrain. The time stream is messy as hell, it's always stretching, torquing, all kinds of four-dimensional swirly shit going on. It's insanely computationally intensive math. There's only a couple of machines out there that could do it. But it *can* be done.

'Two. Portable energy source. Time travel sucks up massive amounts of energy, and you need to be able to take your generator with you. A backpack fusion reactor could do it, so we'll want to scan the underworld chatter for anybody stockpiling protium, deuterium, tritium. But even with the right materials, plasma containment's a real bitch. Call that one nigh-impossible.'

'How many people could build such a thing?' Barry says, clearly a little smarter about Jack than I gave him credit for.

'Aside from me, you mean? A couple of people have done it. Deep Melvin, Machine Intelligence Coalition. Guys on that level.'

'So what's the last item?'

'Number three is the one that matters: a working Time Core. No way to duplicate, there's only the one Sinistro had. It's from the year 3000 AD, built out of some fancy crystal computation lattice. Even I don't know how to fix it.'

'Who does that leave us for suspects?' Barry asks.

'The good news is, not many people could pull this off. First off, we gotta talk about Sinistro.'

'Who remains, er, dead?' Barry says.

'Yes and no,' Jack says, raising a finger to forestall objection. 'Sinistro is –'

'Was –' I put in.

'Will one day be Emperor of the Earth, in the year 3000,' Jack continues. 'His ruling council revolts, global war breaks out. He loses, flees into the past as an immortal time-traveling warlord bent on world conquest. He's all over the history books if you look for him, faking his own death like a maniac. He was a Borgia, he was Mehmet the Conqueror and at least three Popes. His secret society infiltrated every government in the world.'

'But then he died,' I say. 'In 1995. We watched as his space station fell from orbit. Nobody got out.'

'This would seem to exonerate him of the current crime?' Barry says.

'So you might think!' Jack says. 'So. You. Might. Think. Alex, do you want to do this part?'

'You go ahead.'

'Fine. Sinistro died in 1995, yes, but in historical time. He spent a couple of centuries of his life zipping up and down the time stream. Plenty of moments, past and future, when there was a Sinistro alive, maybe more than one. You never know when a non-deceased Sinistro from earlier in his life is going to pop up and make trouble. And this,' he concludes, 'is why you never let a villain get hold of a time machine. So that's one option.'

'Perhaps it is the work of Queen Juniper.' Barry's regal brow furrows, his resonant voice takes on a darker tone. 'The wisest of the faerie folk know of things we might well deem impossible.'

'Huh,' Jack says. 'Yeah, I hate to say it but we can't count them out. Wish Stefanie had got the throne back.'

'What about the Prion Corporation?' I say. 'They're pretty tough.'

'They used to make an awfully good espresso machine,' Barry says. 'Back in the nineties.'

'They made Cat,' I say. And other things. I still shudder at the memory of their pale, Armani-suited Chief of Operations, no longer remotely human. I remember what we saw on their legendary Fiftieth Floor.

'Yeah, well, here's the thing. Barry and I found that little blood-spatter at the scene.' He hits a key and the monitor flicks on with a picture of the usual weird blobs you get under a microscope. 'I took it to the lab and it's pretty far from human-standard. Zoomed in with the electronic microscope and there you go.' A grainy picture of what looks like a Lego octopus. It zooms in once, and again, to show a blurry maker's mark: the infinity sign of the Prion Corporation.

The pause that comes is awkward. Barry looks particularly British.

'One hardly likes to say it,' he says.

'Okay,' I say. 'Okay, it's not conclusive, but I'll talk to Cat.'

'Alex, come on,' Jack says. 'You can't get sentimental here.'

'This doesn't prove anything.'

'It's not complicated. She hears about the time machine and breaks in. Ferris sees her, she takes him out, makes it look like an accident. She didn't expect it to set off the alarm at headquarters, so she shows up to keep an eye on us.'

'She wouldn't leave blood at the scene,' I say. 'She's too much of a professional.'

'Maybe Ferris was more than she bargained for. Maybe she's just getting sloppy. We know she's not what she used to be.'

'What does she do with it afterwards? It's still broken.'

'She must have a partner who can fix it. Maybe Sinistro? It wouldn't be the first time he got one of your girlfriends for a protégée.'

'Yeah, that was fun,' I say. 'So now what? You want to hunt her down now? Turn her in?'

'Don't ask me, Alex. This whole thing is your show. Do you want your revenge or don't you?'

A melodious trilling fills the room and we all check our phones, then realize it's my subspace communicator.

'Hey.' It's Cat.

I put her on speaker.

'How the fuck did you do that?' I ask.

'Did I not mention I'm a spy?' Cat says.

'Fair enough.'

'We need to meet.'

'Yeah. We do.'

'See you in twenty minutes. The usual place. Alone.'

She hangs up. Barry and Jack are staring at me.

'Are you two going to fight?' Jack says.

I shrug. I'm not sure we ever stopped.

15

When we dream of getting superpowers, we dream of people like Keystone, the kind who ignore clearly posted warnings – LASER BEAM HERE – and are rewarded for their fecklessness with a lifetime of swooping through the air to the cheers of millions.

Those are the lottery winners. But there are other ways into it that we don't talk about as much. People whose powers were seared into them. Strength, speed, cognition enhanced. She can sit absolutely still for hours, or flit through a crowded room like a strobe light. Situational awareness just short of clinical paranoia.

Our 'usual place' is a bar in an MIT-adjacent corner of Cambridge where we used to drink on late nights when we wanted to get away from the others. It used to be a dive bar but it's been upscaled into some kind of cocktail symposium. The grad student behind the bar gives me a tall vodka drink with leaves in it, and I sit with my back to the door. For once I'd like to see her coming.

I needn't have worried because this is late-period Cat, who I'm starting to realize I can't really stand. She stops in the doorway to pose, silhouetted in leather jacket and bodysuit, hips askew for the benefit of the nerds drinking at the bar. Cat always had her niche appeal, but in the 2000s her fandom really took off. Nerds of a certain kind, militant libertarians, off-the-grid leftists, guys who own a sword and a kilt and probably a large snake. I get it. Girl assassin but give it a nineties nostalgia spin. Daria with throwing stars.

She orders a bourbon up and doesn't even think about paying. She crosses the room to slide into my booth, eyes on me, a vampy gunslinger. I glare at the bartender until he looks away.

'What's your "libation"?' she asks.

'It's called a Day Star.'

She sips it and makes a face. 'Why does it have cilantro?'

'It had the least cilantro of anything on the menu.'

'You came alone, right?' she says. She does a little sleight-of-hand trick where she palms a knife from someplace, balances it on one finger, flicks it out of existence again.

Bartender: riveted.

'I'd hate to have to fuck Barry up.' She lights a cigarette.

The bartender gazes at her, lost in admiration.

'I have questions,' I say.

'What happens if I give the wrong answers?' The bourbon in her hand is trembling a little.

I think of what Jack said – is she losing functionality?

'I don't want to fight, Cat.'

'Don't you?' Her pupils are wide with combat endorphins. 'Not even for old times' sake?'

'Don't you ever stop trying?'

'Oh, I've got some new tricks. I could crush your trachea before you get the word out. Or cut out your tongue with the broken glass from your overpriced cocktail. I've run the scenario over a hundred times in the past few seconds and you won two of them. But please, give it your best shot.'

'Cat, what the hell is wrong with you? Why is every conversation this sexy fencing match now?'

'I had my personality modified for operational reasons,' she says.

'It's annoying.'

'Well, at least I kept my original nose.'

'That can't literally be true.'

'I mean the one I left the Academy with. Fine.' She almost manages a smile. At least she can still break character. 'So what do you want?'

'Did you kill Michael Ferris or didn't you?' I ask.

'What would you do if I did?' she asks. Her eyes flicker just a little. Checking the corners.

'Don't play around. We found your blood at the scene. Maybe it was an accident. I just want to know what happened.'

'If it were me, it wouldn't have been an accident. Alex, are you okay? Something's off about this. Have you even checked on Stefanie?'

'You think it's her?'

'God, I hope so. I'd love another shot at her.'

'What about the blood?'

'You want to know about the blood?'

'I think I have to ask, yeah.'

'Fine, finish your Day Star. I'll drive.'

The bartender stares after us as we leave, eyes brimming with longing.

We climb up Route 2 out of Cambridge until it hits the long semicircle Route 128 makes around the Boston area, to serve the technology companies that spun off from MIT and Harvard, the government-funded 'Massachusetts Miracle' of the 1970s and '80s. Those were the companies our parents had moved here for, where they busily drew up the blueprints for the Cold War, for the vast apparatus that started here and ended in B-2 bombers cocked on runways in Alabama and radar platforms in the North Atlantic and, almost incidentally, the internet.

In fact, my father helped build SAGE, the sensor network

whose job it was to detect incoming Soviet ICBMs and fire off ours in response, triggering World War III, at which point most of us would die in Dad's radioactive fires, and the rest would live on in savage tribes scavenging among the toxic ruins of our own cities. In the meantime, though, we had big houses and excellent schools.

The aerospace giants of my Cold War youth are mostly gone now, forced out of their glass-box buildings by nimble internet and biotech start-ups with names like ZappyDoo and Daddy-O. The whimsy-branded logos of the newer corporations look like giant toys left by the roadside.

Cat drives at enormous speed, steering one-handed with neat little jerks of the wheel.

'This all feels off, Alex. It's messing with your head.'

'Did they reprogram you to be all empathic and emotionally intelligent?'

'Yes,' she says. 'Doesn't mean I'm wrong.'

She pulls off the highway, veers off the surface street and onto an access road, then into the back parking lot of an office building, a black glass box. We pull in under the amber lights.

It's derelict. A few taped-up windows, and most of the grass has died. The rest is dirt and dust, compacted by the heavy treads of the backhoes and steam shovels standing empty around the perimeter. Weathered yellow police tape still hangs from the columns around the outside of the gutted building.

Over the door, a lighter patch of concrete where the infinity sign once was – the one-time logo of Prion Industries. Cat rests her arm on the steering wheel and gazes up at it.

'I can't believe Google bought my childhood.'

*

It's now possible to feel a tiny bit of nostalgia for the Prion Corporation. They had a very period-specific type of cool. They used to deal in stealth fighter planes, bioweapons, killer satellites, military robots and the like. Their buildings were towering dark monoliths that loomed above rain-slick streets in London and Tokyo. They were staffed by wolfish young men with their hair combed straight back and carefully icy women in slim-cut Armani suits. If you didn't have a steel briefcase chained to your wrist, you weren't management material. They all had a second language – Japanese or Russian – and their hobbies were chess and having impersonal sex in their minimalist corner offices decorated in rainforest woods, neon, and black lacquered furniture.

The building's lobby was once a marble-floored space the size of a Roman piazza adorned with stone monoliths, Assyrian statues and a fountain of water as deep and black as a chief executive officer's dreams. The fountain is dry now; dirt and leaves have profaned the expensive marble.

'We're trespassing, if that matters to you,' I say. 'Breaking the law.'

'Is there any possible way you can admit this is fun?'

A stairwell leads us to a basement supply room, just empty shelves now, but there's a sealed access hatch set into the floor. She fiddles with the lock then yanks it open. It yields a puff of cold musty air, and darkness behind it. She waves a flashlight, showing dirty gray tile. I'm starting to think the entirety of New England sits on top of mystical rock formations and industrial tunnel networks. Where else would suburban kids get their origins?

She lowers herself in and drops to the floor. I follow, and a motion sensor flicks on fluorescent lights, to show a wide corridor with cinder-block walls painted a pale yellow. A vault door at one end, opposite a rectangular metal grating at the other.

A sign shows an enthusiastic cartoon rabbit, with the words 'Welcome, Future Pioneers of the Broken Earth!' emerging from its mouth in jazzy pink cursive.

The grating slides up to reveal a long hallway with mirrored walls, floored with black and white tiles. Each tile is labeled with a letter and a number in orderly sequence.

'Oh dear,' a bright cartoon voice warbles through a cracked speaker. Cat says it too, in unison. 'I shall be too late!'

The floor creaks and rattles, and half the tiles flip, scrambling the pattern. A loud ticking commences, as of a titanic pocket watch.

'It's lethal but at least they tried to make it fun,' Cat says. 'Come on, let's try it.'

I've seen her original spec. Alloy-laced bones, nanoscale machinery. We've fought hand-to-hand, and possibly I've been in love with her, and I've long suspected she's smarter than any of us. It's still a little shocking when a woman on the cusp of early middle age jumps ten meters forward from a standing start. She lands, pausing only long enough to scan the next few rows, then hopscotches across the tiles according to a pattern I can't see. I can hear projectiles spatter off the wall. She combat-rolls under a swinging pylon and slides into the safe zone.

'Your turn!'

I whisper the word for Prodigy and walk through the gauntlet and feel the familiar sensation of sharp objects ticking off Prodigy's skin.

'You have been reclassified,' says an electronic voice.

'That means you're dead,' Cat says.

The hail of steel blades and poison darts intensifies, followed by a jet of toxic gas. I get reclassified eleven more times before I reach Cat's place at the far end.

'Cheap win,' she says.

She's right, and this is the fundamental unfairness of me.

Against monsters, against robots, against collapsing buildings, even against all of Jack's matchless engineering, I win anyway.

We go on. Walls try to crush us, and razors fly out to cut us. Cat dodges spectacularly, I endure.

'This was supposed to prepare us for the fall of civilization,' she says. 'You can see how regular high school was confusing at first.'

The next section is a kaleidoscopic maze of mirrors and glass. Cat presses a finger to her lips. Somewhere in the flickering darkness something moves.

Cat negotiates the labyrinth flawlessly. Behind us, a heavy, halting tread keeps pace. When we slip out the far side, an eight-foot-tall robotic rabbit in a dilapidated tuxedo is watching us from the exit. It waves one bladed hand and turns away, heading back into the shining labyrinth.

Jets of fire. Combination locks sprouting needles coated with long-expired poisons. The door springs open.

'Still got it,' Cat says.

Beyond is a wide circular room overlooked by a viewing gallery. The walls are painted in red and black diamonds, rather like a circus big-top.

'Congratulations, Candidates,' says the voice. 'Prepare for the Culling.'

'That means you fight a classmate to death or disablement.'

'Holy motherfucking fuck. That's terrifying.'

She shrugs.

'It wasn't as bad for me. I was the star of the program. Everything they tried on me worked – every implant took, every growth hormone worked like crazy. I just kept getting stronger and faster.'

'You had to do it to survive.'

'No one here thought they were going to survive,' she says. 'It's just what we did. They fed me poison and I loved it.'

'I'm sorry.'

'Funnily enough, that's what I told Meredith,' she says, but the slink has gone out of her now, whatever way it came in. The long-gone stiffness in her gait has returned, specter of the long-ago girl who wouldn't speak.

I kick down the exit door. We pass through the residential wing, just a line of cells. Cat calls out the list.

'Stony Marco. Meredith. Me. Guillaume the Psychic. Sherry the Nice One, who went back to work for them. Poison Shalom. Fast Margaret. Jeremy Brighteyes. Margaret Hook-Hands. You fought her once.'

'She's calling herself "Crescent" nowadays. Kidnapped the Trilateral Commission.'

'Same old Margaret,' Cat says. 'She has the same junk in her blood that I did. You should tell Jack. But that's only part of why we're here.'

We climb the stairs to another laboratory wing, a tech giant gone to seed. Cat puts a finger to her lips and beckons me forward. We sneak through the engineering offices, past forests of skeletal robot arms, autopsied aliens in formaldehyde, blueprints for futuristic stealth jets shaped like half-melted birds of prey.

We pass through a forest of hundreds of empty cubicles, each with a tenantless keyboard tapping and clicking by itself, lines of scrambled text and unrecognizable symbols unrolling continually on the monitors. We pass a room of thin gray alien bodies in all stages of dissection.

There's a human skeleton half sheathed in metal, gunmetal vats that emit a rotten smell. I pull Cat away and into the next stairwell.

She stops on the next landing and sniffs the air. 'Huh. Someone else was in here, and recently. I can smell them and it's familiar but not.'

We climb a cylindrical shaft crowded with bundled cables plastered with red-and-yellow warning stickers. She takes my hand and presses it to the surface. Cold.

'Coolant. This is the other reason we're here.' She hisses the words in my ear. 'They've turned Eviltron back on.'

'God, I hate that name.'

'It's what it called itself.'

Eviltron was Prion's final-generation supercomputer, parallelized and quantum-enabled. Its weird operating system included a whole simulated fantasy cyber-world we projected our minds into. I can't even remember the logic. We took on alter egos to do battle with its core memory, which took the form of a neon wireframe dragon lurking inside a glowing castle. It was an incredibly involved business. Jack was a dwarf, and he was so mad about it.

Afterwards, we all watched as Jack wiped its memory banks. That should have been the end of Eviltron.

Cat leads me through the executive wing to its refrigerated chamber and there it is – three blunt cylindrical pillars arranged in a triangle, silent and frost-rimed, each with its glowing red eye. In the center, the holographic display shows a tangled skein of thousands of red, green and blue threads, impossibly tangled, slowly rotating as we watch.

'It's the time stream,' I say. 'Somebody used Eviltron to make a map of it, exactly like Jack said.'

It's the work of a moment to unplug the power and data cables, as thick in diameter as my thigh. We listen to the room-shaking decrescendo as its systems shut down, but it's too late. The floor is coated with ice crystals that clearly show footprints entering and leaving. Somebody got what they came for.

We're both weirdly giddy as I drive us home.

'Are you and Jack and Barry a team now?'

'Hell, yes. We're called Bachelor Force One.'

'What about "The Stefanie Project"? You're all in love with her.'

'For the millionth time, I'm not. I don't think any of us have real long-term relationships, for some reason.'

'Personally, I don't fucking feel like it. What's your excuse?' she says. 'Pull over here by the bus stop.'

'You're not coming to the house?'

'I'm not dealing with Jack.'

I turn the car into a side street and park, and we sit in the darkness for a little while, letting the adrenaline wear off.

'You know, I don't even care anymore you put me in jail in '99?' she says. 'It's how I got into intelligence work.'

'Well, I'm sorry anyway.'

'Don't worry, I'm still getting revenge,' she says. 'But I didn't kill your wizard.'

'I believe you,' I say. 'We'll find whoever did it.'

'You won't find them. They'll be dead. And I'll have their time machine.'

'Rae–'

A half-second before, she was in the passenger seat, belted. Now she's straddling my lap, lips hard against mine, a cold hand on my neck, ready to tear my throat out. After a long time, she breaks the kiss.

'Did you ever think about how insufferable you are?' she says.

'What?'

'Do you know that villains call you Wizard Bitch? "Look at me, I'm the Prophesied One, I'm hitting you 'cause a magic guy said to."'

'That's not funny.'

'It's not supposed to be. The real point I was making tonight is that you have no idea what the world needs. I have as good a right to that time machine as anybody.'

'Cat, don't.'

'No, listen. I've thought it through. I don't need Jack to tell me I'm slowing down, I monitor my own systems. But if I can just go back, I can stop everything you saw tonight from happening. I can put things right.'

'I know, but Cat . . . we all promised we wouldn't do this.'

'Did we?'

She looks at me with a little smile, kisses me again, and she's gone like always, moving like the summer wind or the morning dew or anything else beautiful and mysterious that never learned to stick around and finish a conversation.

16

Here's a story I've never told anyone. Everyone thinks Cat and I didn't get along especially well, but there's a thing they don't know, which is what exactly happened during Jack's brief phase of experimenting with time machines.

He actually got one working: a jerry-built framework of PVC pipe and wires, a little tent with a silver sphere spinning in the middle. He spent a while sending test items into the past and future, then moved up to rats and mice and a very annoying monkey (which was subsequently banned from the house). Then we played around with little ten-minute jaunts back and forth, which stopped in a hurry, because when you meet yourself and see how your hair really looks, things are never quite the same.

Cat and I volunteered for a longer trip. Two hundred years, a quick look around, just the two of us. Jack assured us it was safe – and who could resist? We crouched in the apparatus and watched Jack punch in the coordinates and off we went to the future. We appeared in a sealed featureless room where two white-haired, white-clad members of the Cross-Time Diplomatic Corps welcomed us with gifts and smiles and the polite but very clear message that we were never, ever, ever to do this again. They watched us, arms folded, as we set the coordinates for our return.

It should have taken only a moment to come back. We knew it was taking too long, and when we smelled burning insulation, we unlatched the plastic door. Instead of the cigarettes and stale booze of a Friday afternoon in the old house, our next breath was of the warm wet air of Eden, giddy with the rich scents of pollen and vegetable rot and a jacked-up oxygen ratio.

The defunct time machine had set down on a hilltop overlooking a dense forest of semi-evolved pine trees, and the unique primordial silence you'll never know until you've heard it. One hundred thousand years ago is the nearest I've been able to date it – well before Sinistro was a glint in any Cro-Magnon's eye. We stood there in adrenaline shock. I put my hands on my knees; I sat down on the ground, trying to breathe. It wasn't even the right time of day.

That night we built a fire.

'It can't be that long,' I said. 'I'm sure Jack's working on it.'

'How's he going to find us?'

'Physics, time, explosions – this problem's right in his wheelhouse.'

'That machine looked pretty wrecked.'

'So it's a hard problem. He'll get it eventually.'

She stared at the fire for a bit.

'Alex, you have to face it.'

'Face what?'

'It's time travel. It doesn't matter how long it takes to solve it. If anyone were coming to fetch us, they would have come to our point of arrival. They would have been here hours ago.'

'Oh. You're right. Oh, shit,' I said. 'Oh no.'

'Yeah.'

It was too big to talk about right away, but by morning, the truth had settled in and become real. We weren't visitors here. This was home.

I spent the entire next day in a state of shock while Cat set about hunting and making a fire and keeping us alive. Of the two of us, she coped a lot better, maybe because she never expected anything else but civilization-ending disaster.

Shock and despair gave way to a kind of mad amusement at the entire thing. A whole planet where we were the only beings ever to have seen a cartoon or brushed our teeth or thrown a Frisbee.

Without any discussion of it, after the third night Cat and I were together. We built a cabin on a hillside by a river. I got to be a decent hand at chipping flint axes; Cat figured out how to brew beer. Every once in a while we bumped into some Neanderthals who were, by and large, decent people if you're not looking for witty banter. I formally retired the white costume, buried it under a cairn of rocks. It was incongruous in this green world, and there was no crime to fight. There weren't even any laws.

I exchanged it for leather breeches and a wolfskin cloak, the lord of primordial suburban Massachusetts. Cat and I fished and hunted together, noble forest citizens. We were never bored. Saber-toothed tigers are long gone now, and no one mourns the loss more than I do, but at the time they were everywhere and fucking terrifying.

We'd shown up in spring, and toward midsummer we took a few days to hike to the distant sea. It was warm and no doubt contained unspeakable primitive horrors. I wouldn't swim, but Cat went out for a bit. We watched the sun go down, drenching us with the burnt reds, yellows and saffrons of the still-youthful star. When the gigantic full moon rose, it was almost too romantic, and we were drunk, and we got married. There was no one else to do it, so we exchanged our made-up vows in front of the moon and collapsed into laughter.

Summer was tipping over into fall. One day we got back from hunting, and there was Jack, waiting for us and grinning his face off. He drank primeval ale with us and treated us to the story of how he reconstructed the path of the damaged time machine, then calculated exactly how its catastrophic failure distorted the chronometric skein, and our consequent path through time and space.

We'd traveled in time but not in space, and that helped, but no one but Jack could have done it. He boasted to us he'd managed a margin of error of three days. He never knew his math was off, and neither of us corrected him. Getting within a hundred years of arrival would have been a staggering feat. We did our best to restore the site to its pristine condition before we left, although Jack assured us the butterfly effect theory was nonsense – the forest would reclaim everything, and any trace we'd left would be lost within the probabilistic noise of it all.

We all swore off time travel after that. No one ever noticed we were four months and one week older than we were supposed to be. The one time I even mentioned it to Cat, she shook her head; she'd rather pretend it never happened. And given the temporal paradoxes involved, no one's even sure it did.

17

Rick Tower doesn't just keep on existing all by himself. He is a well-documented piece of reality, but somebody has to show up in the morning and put on his clothes once in a while, walk around and teach his classes and answer to his name, even socialize a bit.

I put in a few hours in the department, sip burnt coffee at a faculty meeting, counting the junior professors who interrupt one of the most powerful entities on the planet midway through a sentence.

My next polygraph test comes in two weeks, and what am I going to say? Interfering with a police investigation, fraternizing with metahuman associates. I could be locked up, the amulet taken away for good. I could probably give them a good fight, but I'd be on the run for the rest of my life.

Safer to be soft, privileged Rick Tower again, to sleep in Rick Tower's bed, dream his dreams, and wake up to him every morning until I die and Prodigy at last disappears without a whisper.

Or I could tell them that, last night, in the laboratory, I walked as a titan, then I kissed a demon's lips. That it was all worth it, and they can come for me and do what they will.

I stop at my apartment afterwards, for the sake of appearances, and to get a change of civilian clothes. The lobby looks like it always does – quiet except for the buzzing of fluorescent lights illuminating the corkboard and stray junk mail left on the floor.

The first sign of anything off is the scent of an exquisite

perfume hovering over the ancient dried flowers in their cracked vase, lingering by the battered mailboxes like a strayed party guest. Then, a silver thread caught on a splintered step by the second-floor landing. The door of my apartment has been left slightly ajar and now I can smell burnt jasmine and hear the subliminal hum that can only mean faerie magic.

Stefanie.

When I wasn't invited to her second wedding, I just assumed I'd never see her again. She moves in her own world now, after all, and there was only so much we ever had in common. She certainly didn't care about whoever murdered Michael Ferris – a fellow magic-worker, yes, but of a very different school.

I pause at the threshold. Is it a friendly visit? She isn't even supposed to know where I live. It would be too much to expect her to call first. In her mind, a princess is always welcome.

Her wide faerie eyes will be taking in my second-hand furniture, laundry left out, mismatched cutlery. How long has it been since she was in an apartment with only three rooms?

What fallen realm is this? she thinks. *What has Alex come to?*

I don't particularly want to see her. I can hear footsteps as she paces around inside. She huffs a sigh of royal impatience. I could walk away, kill a few hours in the hopes she'll leave, perhaps flit out the window like a moth or a trapped bat. But she won't. Princesses don't visit every day, and not without reason.

I walk in, unnerved, and stop just inside. Typical that she can make me feel like an intruder in my own apartment.

'Hello? Who's there?'

'Well, it's me, silly.' Magically chirpy and sultry at the same time.

A blonde woman, slender, with a heart-shaped face that is still beautiful to the point of cliché, on top of which she's dressed in a silver ball gown and tiara fit for a costume party. On anyone else it would look ridiculous, but she's so poised and natural in it she makes the whole world look under-dressed.

I catch my breath, and smile in spite of myself, when she steps into view.

'Alex. Hi.' She smiles, the one she constructed for the cameras. I remember the teenaged one, still not quite formed, awkward and eager to please.

'Your Highness,' I say, after a moment. 'Back from the wars.'

'I even won a few.'

'I had no idea you'd be here.'

'I was doing a shoot, out in the Berkshires, and I was on my way back to the airport and I thought, why not stop in and see an old friend?' The smile cracks just a little, and she shifts her weight. Her shoes are silver, too, their high thin heels a tiny masterpiece. Whatever magical shoemaker made them would weep to see them touching the potato chip crumbs on my fraying carpet.

'That's so nice of you.'

'Come here, won't you? It's good to see you.' She gathers me in for a hug.

One expects a kind of ethereal cloud, but she's solid flesh and blood – and strong arms, ungodly so. I mumble 'you too' into her spill of blonde hair. She hangs on for a long moment, long fingers on my back, then releases me.

'How did you know where I live?'

'Magic, stupid.'

'Do you want anything? A drink? Wait, is it "Your Grace" now? Or "Your Highness"?'

'Still "Highness", and only when it's official state business.

Like if I'm knighting you or condemning you to death. And yes to the drink. It's after noon, right? Like old times.'

I hold up my very best Scotch for approval, and she nods. I fetch two odd tumblers from the kitchen.

'Old times,' I say, and we clink glasses.

She looks with exaggerated care for a spot, before settling back on the couch.

I look for signs of age but find almost none. Of course, she's not human and never was – and if what she says is true, she might live to be two hundred years old.

'How long has it been now?' I ask.

'Since Houston in, oh no, 2009! The accidental reunion.' Her laugh is the same, at least, and there's a hint of the real smile. She takes a sip and makes the loveliest little grimace before setting it down.

'Did you hear?' I say.

'The alert? Yes. I sent Barry.'

'He's nice. Michael Ferris is dead.'

I watch for signs of feigned surprise but her look of concern is royal perfection.

'I'm so sorry. How did it happen?'

I tell her, skipping the evidence against Cat. If she wants to be part of the investigation, she can say so.

'Jack and Barry,' she says. 'How funny. Dear old Jack and his toys. But not Cat?'

'You know her. She'll do her own thing.'

'That's too bad,' she says. 'Is this about the quest? For the – thingy?' She never cared much for my origin story.

'I should have asked, what's happening in your kingdom? Are you going to get your throne?'

She shakes her head. 'Juniper still sits on the bronze throne but the people of Summerdwell remember me. Their rightful true-born princess.'

'I really hope it happens.'

'It's what I was born for.' Her phone buzzes and she ignores it, wandering over to the window. She looks down at my neighbor's yard, at the rusted outdoor grill, as if still curious about mortal ways. The moonlight takes her dress from pretty to glorious.

'You know it's a secret who I am, right?' I say.

'I know. I liked your old nose better.'

'Everyone did.'

'Do they still check on you?'

'Polygraphs once a month.'

'It's not right,' she says. 'Your having to hide like this.'

'You might have said so at the time.'

She taps one sea-green nail against the windowsill, an old habit.

'Jack and I did what we felt able to do,' she says.

'Yes, I read it. Would it hurt you to apologize?'

'The throne of Summerdwell doesn't apologize, silly.' Her faerie eyes read differently in this older face. Not so cute anymore.

'Maybe you should leave, Stef.'

'Just because we were in high school doesn't —'

'Get out.'

She's settled one delicate foot behind the other, a shoulder's width apart. 'Maybe you'd better call me Your Highness, after all.'

'Don't fight me, Stef. You won't win.'

'You know, I'm actually curious,' she says.

She crooks a finger. Distant thunder sounds, and light flares within the Summerstone mounted on her tiara, and I remember the price she paid for it.

'I wonder if your little trick still works. You always worried about that. Or if the government found some way to neuter you. Whereas the power of Summerdwell is, as we know, eternal.'

'You'll find out.' My glasses slip down my nose and I slap them to the floor.

She smiles a little more widely. A wind springs up from nowhere and scrambles xeroxed manuscripts. White petals whirl through the room, dislodged from some unseen eldritch tree. It's a pretty effect. Everything about her powers is pretty, which doesn't make her less dangerous.

'Well?' She lets the moment go on a fraction longer, then smiles and lets her hands fall.

'Look at us, two old friends,' I say. 'I apologize, formally.'

'And I accept, Alexander H. Beekman.' The heat lingers a few moments more.

'Thank you. It's Professor Tower now.'

'Your hands are shaking,' she says. 'Alex, we mustn't fight. I know we've gone different ways, but you shouldn't forget about me. We're friends.'

'I know.' *Don't tell me about being forgotten*, I want to say.

'You should come see the Malibu place, okay? I'm busy with the album launch this week, but come out later and we can spend some real time.'

'I will. Of course I will. But I'm actually a little busy this week.'

'Of course.'

In a few more minutes the conversation runs its course. We were probably the least compatible pairing in the group, except her and Cat. She does her courteous farewells, and departs. I watch as she leaves by the side exit, descending the three worn steps as if to an invisible nation's silent applause.

Stefanie's presence brings its own contact high, the buzz of her attention and celebrity status. For a moment you're in her world of luxury hotel suites, frolics and safaris, of easy three o'clock drinking, and always good news. I'd forgotten how quickly she takes it with her when she goes.

Reaching for Stefanie's lipstick-smudged tumbler of whiskey on the fireplace mantle, I stop to notice the Arthur Rackham print now sits a little to one side of its usual place lined up with a medallion in the woodwork. It's two inches to the left.

Stop, reset. Normally when I come home, if I'm alone, I do some checks. Internet searches for myself, for Cat, a few other people. I check the apartment for signs of intrusion. Pointless, as my enemies almost certainly don't know where I am. Most of them are in prison or dead anyway; almost nobody in that line of work ages well. But I'm ready anyway, just in case somebody shows up: Baron Ether or Mr Maniacal. But Stefanie, Princess of Power?

I walk slowly through the apartment to see what emerges. Books stand askew on the shelves. The closet door is closed tight and the junk drawer in the kitchen is wide open.

I picture her moving delicately through my three rooms on the third floor of a landmark building off College Avenue. Frowning a little, embarrassed to see how little space my life takes up, she rummages. She looks through drawers of flatware and kitchen things, shifts stacks of chipped dishes. With a shudder of aristocratic revulsion, she opens dresser drawers and checks the pockets of a thrift-store blazer fraying at the cuffs. Her strong beautiful hands explore the night table, the medicine cabinet.

She played this very cool. She had only a few moments from hearing me on the stairs to my coming in – not enough time to put things in order, but enough to get into character as a dear old friend on an unexpected visit. If I hadn't hesitated, I could have caught her outright.

What did she need that she couldn't ask for? A beautiful

woman, with four houses, a royal title, and the power of flight among other things. A woman with all the luck in the world.

And maybe she has too much pride to admit to needing anything, especially from me. She's sorry for me. Sorry I didn't get married, sorry I'm at a state school, an assistant professor with a four/four teaching load, failed tenure bid and not even the dignity of my own name.

But then, I'm a little sorry for her, too. She'll live a hundred more years and never know the things I know. Like the shorter poems of Milton, or how to buy a drinkable wine when you only have seven dollars, or how to ride on a bus for six hours without going crazy. She doesn't know how to sew on a button or give a decent apology or when to call someone's bluff. She doesn't even know I'm a king.

I sleep late the next day, write emails, and then late in the afternoon I walk back to headquarters. I pack a shovel and a rope and a flashlight, and borrow Barry's car. I drive northeast on the highway, to the long narrow road through the forest that leads to Michael Ferris's trailhead.

I quickly lose the path in the forest of birch and maple, just like it always happens. It's bright, a warm day for a walk. I march along, trying to relive the original time, but by now it's gotten mixed up with all the subsequent unsuccessful tries. Five minutes walking, or ten. Sometimes I find the stream, sometimes not. Then off the trail and running another five.

I stop at a clearing that looks about the right size. I find the center and probe in the soft dirt and wet leaves, looking for anything solid. There's nothing but mud, but let's dig anyway. It's wrong to dig on conservation land, but let's think of the big picture. I'm preserving the world from a looming darkness.

I dig down a foot, then fill it back in. I do the same in two more spots. I stop and smell the pleasant forest rot. A gust of wind shakes a shivery fall of raindrops, then the air is still again.

I wait for the sound of thunder, a tremor in the ground, for the great magical cave to open up again, just once more. I give it five minutes, then set out through the brush until I find another clearing. I keep doing it for another hour, and then pack it in. I do this once a year, even though it never changes things and doesn't seem proper behavior for a king.

Cat asked me what I wanted, and the more I think about it, the more I want a lot of things. Tenure, yes, but more than that. The dignity of my own name. Most of all, I want to dig a hole in the ground in this forest and find a magical labyrinth with a wizard inside. Which, of course, never happens – except for that one time when it did.

PART FOUR
1992

18

Three months ago, I thought my life was over. I'd spend the rest of my life in an enhanced-security facility, or get dissected in a government lab, maybe fired into a neutron star just to see what happens.

Now it's like nothing ever happened. The damage to school property was chalked up to an as-yet-unidentified supervillain with a cosmic grudge against upper-ranked New England high schools. The only people who know any different work for the government. Apart from Chuck Dubek and his friends, but nobody's seen them for a while.

Half the school is gone, and most of the remaining classrooms have blue emergency tarpaulins for walls and ceilings. We put up with construction noise and keep our coats on for cold days, but nothing else has changed. High school is a monster not even I could kill.

The only difference is that I'm part of the newest, most exclusive clique at Hanover High. I was never on a sports team or in the drama club but now I'm one of the CLEO kids, with a membership of four, and we're not currently accepting applications, thank you. We haven't got jackets or a table in the lunchroom. We're so elitist, we don't even talk to each other.

We share only a few things. Our ankle bracelets, and all the subterfuges we have to go through to hide them – long pants, long skirts, bandages for invented ankle injuries. Of course we have our meetings, every Saturday morning without fail.

Nobody enjoys those at all, unless you count Potsworth,

who never seems to tire of his own voice. We're given in-class writing exercises that seem pointless, and encouraged to share our thoughts and feelings, which according to an unspoken agreement we never, ever do.

The mid-morning break isn't long enough to do much of anything other than pee and walk down to the loading dock with Jack and listen to whatever he's obsessing about this week: quantum physics or geopolitics or his conspiracy theories (I learned not to ask him about the Hollow Earth). Every once in a while, Stefanie comes to smoke a cigarette and ignore us.

Until today. We're staring out at the third straight day of rain when she turns to us and actually says something.

'Jack, you go to computer classes, right?'

'They ran out of things to teach me when I was eight,' he says.

'Okay, whatever. Can I ask you to do something for me?'

'Maybe, maybe not.'

'So my dad, he's pretty good friends with Billy Weld? The governor?'

'I know who the governor is,' Jack says.

'So he has dinner at our house sometimes,' she says, tossing her hair just a little. 'I was just telling him about CLEO and how I don't belong here, which is true anyway, and how it would just be better for everybody if I didn't have to go.

'People do my father a lot of favors, you know? But Billy just kept changing the subject. After he left, my father told me he'd already asked. He called everybody in the world who owes him a favor, but the moment he brought up CLEO, they shut down. I want to find out why.'

It's the longest sustained speech I've ever seen Stefanie make to a person; I would have blushed to be the focus of all that attention, the halo of perfume, the flash and address of those blue eyes. Jack seems indifferent.

'That doesn't mean it's a conspiracy. Sounds like your dad doesn't have the kind of pull you thought he did, Princess.'

'Don't talk about my father,' she snaps. 'And you're not as smart as you think you are, you know that? How do you think we all ended up at Hanover together?'

'It's just where we ended up'

'After Concord Academy kicked me out, I tried every prep school on the east coast and none of them would take me. Or take Alex – he lives at 1410 Coolidge. Alex, where do the other kids on your street go to high school?'

'It's Dover High mostly. I never thought about it.'

'Alex isn't even in our school district,' Stefanie says. 'He's just over the line but they let him in. And Cat – nobody even knows who she is but they enrolled her. Jack, you were kicked out of Hanover, what, twice?'

'Four times. I've been taking classes there since the sixth grade.'

'They took you back every time. You see? They put us here on purpose. Long before any of us got sent to juvie.'

'Shit,' Jack says. 'They collected us.' He's so astonished, he's forgotten to be mad that he didn't see it first.

'It may not be a conspiracy but it's something. Why did they move us? What is CLEO, really? Can you find out?'

'I get you, Princess,' he says. 'I can do it.'

Jack watches her go, helmet lights pulsing and a distinct blush tinting his froggy features.

'Stuck-up bitch,' he says. 'What's so great about her?'

'Other than she's a princess and looks like a model?'

'You should go for it, then.'

'Come on.'

'You could, you're weirdly good-looking except you hunch over and act like a dork. She's just another rich kid. She acts all high and mighty but I happen to know she was the cocaine queen of the Boston club world. Anyway, I'm not superficial when it comes to my girlfriends.'

'Wait, who's your girlfriend? Girlfriends?'

'I move in more mature circles than you probably have access to, Alex,' he says. 'So you gonna ask her out?'

'No. I met a girl,' I say. 'We kind of had a thing. In jail.'

'Uh-huh. Where is she now?'

'Paris.'

'Okay,' Jack says. 'Pretty cool.'

When we get back, Potsworth is waiting at the door.

'Bring your bags, people. It's time to stretch our legs.'

He leads us to the ground floor and through corridors running further back than I expected, to a door marked TRAINING. He holds the door.

It's a gym. The sweet smell of varnish mixes with a sour cut of rubberized gymnastics pads. Potsworth strides to midcourt, carrying a mesh bag of basketballs.

'You've all been hiding those powers for too long. We're going to have a little friendly competition.'

Nobody looks terribly happy. I haven't used my powers for anything since the incident.

'Can I be excused real quick?' Jack asks.

He's probably faking a stomach problem. To see Jack attempt any sort of athletic feat is one of high school's crueler spectacles. Maybe I should fake one, too. Twice now I've used the power outside its intended purpose. How many times is too many? And is anybody counting?

The truth is, I can't help but wonder how our powers are all going to stack up, and which of us might be out of their league? And what does Cat even do? On some level, I think we've all been waiting for this since I walked into CLEO.

Then I forget about power rankings for a second when

Jack comes back. He wasn't looking for a way out. He was only changing into his costume.

How can Jack be one of the most intelligent beings on the planet, and still be able to misread a room this badly without realizing it?

A skintight silver jumpsuit pulled painfully tight at the waist by a black nylon belt hung with weighty pouches. He has used red gaffer tape to make a design on the chest, a messy circle that might either be a planet or an atom.

I can't even look at him directly, it's so much the stuff of deeply personal fantasies best left unrealized. The jumpsuit itself is apparently hand-sewn, ill-fitting and, worst of all, cheap. It slowly dawns on me what I should have realized before: Jack's family is poor.

The four of us can only watch, frozen in sympathetic embarrassment, while Doctor Potsworth bangs his hands together in a slow clap and Jack struts his way back to the lineup.

'That's what I'm talking about. Now, this is going to be easy for people with your abilities.' As he speaks, he places two basketballs at each free throw line. 'First, hit four shots from the foul line. Then fetch me just one of those balloons.'

He points upward. The gym has four thick climbing ropes, and a pale-blue helium balloon is tied to the top of each one. Jack raises his hand.

'Can we damage the ropes?' he asks.

'No.'

'Can we damage anything?'

'You may not. And don't get any paint on you.'

'I don't see any paint.'

'Then it shouldn't be a problem. Ready? Fastest time wins.'

'Wins what?' I ask.

'The contest. Jack, will you start us off?'

'I surely will.' He rubs his hands together.

'Good man,' Potsworth says. 'Ready, steady . . . go!'

He clicks the stopwatch.

Jack has never scored a point in any sporting event, as far as I know, but still he trots to the free throw line like a world champion. He picks up one of the balls and assumes a ready position. His helmet lights flash. He goes utterly still, his physique locking almost audibly into place. He stays frozen for four or five seconds, then his body smoothly launches the ball as if he'd practiced it a hundred times. The ball rises in a slow and spinless arc and falls through the precise center of the metal ring. Nothing but net. He does it three more times, each time the same, as if playing back a recording.

'Style points for Jack,' calls Potsworth. 'Now get me that balloon.'

I want to look away. I've seen Jack try to climb a rope before, and this one is six times his own height. He doesn't even try. He pulls components from several pouches and clicks them together, then flings the result upward like a falconer. It whizzes upward, a mouse-sized drone helicopter, to slice neatly through the nearest balloon's string and clamp hold of it in tiny pincers.

A percussive snap-snap-snap jerks our eyes back down. Potsworth is in a marksman's stance, repeatedly pulling the trigger of a blue pistol aimed right at Jack's chest, fifteen feet away. Pink fluid spatters everywhere. It's only a paintball gun. *Don't get any paint on you.*

Jack is grinning. The paint isn't hitting him at all, but splashing off a point a foot in front of him. He stands untouched, like a saint delivered from the consuming fire.

'Force field, bitch,' he says.

Paint drips down the invisible wall in front of him as the

little helicopter tows its blue balloon into Potsworth's waiting hands. He notes down the elapsed time.

'Well done, Jack.'

Jack gives a little bow and walks back to the line, giving us another good long look at that costume. He's blushing red. Underneath his anarchist swagger, he still wants to please the teacher.

'Next up! Cat!'

She doesn't move, just shakes her head.

'No more tricks, Cat, I promise you. It won't be like before.'

Cat waits a long moment, then lets her denim jacket slip to the floor. The plain white T-shirt underneath reveals her starkly powerful physique, a masterwork of both nature and artifice, muscles almost unnaturally distinct. Her brown skin is a moonscape of puncture marks, ragged wounds, neat surgical scars and flat burnt patches.

As she walks, Cat seems to wake from a long stupor. Her sullen shuffle dissolves into a fluid trot, her eyes brighten with intention. She doesn't break stride as she scoops up the ball and flicks it high into the air. The second and third are on their way before the first has fallen. She snatches the last ball one-handed and, with no preliminaries, leaps her full height across fifteen feet of hardwood to slam it through the hoop.

Potsworth fires before the echoes have even died away. He works the trigger as rapidly as it will go but Cat dodges each paint pellet, slipping past each one with the smallest little turns and sidesteps until the magazine is empty. She doesn't even look at him as the magazine runs out. She swarms the ropes without using her legs, snaps the string on a balloon, then drops the full distance to the floor.

'Very good, Cat. You're the time to beat. Now you, Alexander.'

For the fourth time in my life, I say the word and change. Stefanie's eyes widen; even Cat's do. I can surprise people, too.

I can smell the chemicals used to scrub the gym, the distinct smell each person in the room gives off – Potsworth's sweet tobacco contrasted with the bitter, cheap cigarette smoke that clings to Stefanie. Cat registers as earthy but not unpleasant, underpinned with a chemical edge. Jack is a tangle of junk food, body odor, and the silvery vinyl of his outfit.

The basketballs are easy; Prodigy's spatial sense is as unnaturally developed as the rest of him. I slow as I come to the last one. I've never tested myself for speed. Can I dodge a paint pellet in flight?

With the last ball in the air, I clock Potsworth getting himself into stance. I dive forward to catch the last ball before it hits the ground, roll, and heave it straight at Potsworth. The ball hits his right wrist squarely and knocks the paint gun from his hands, to skate across the polished wood floor. The rest is easy.

'Very clever, Beekman, but Cat still leads,' Potsworth says, as I hand him his balloon. 'The final challenger is Stefanie.'

Stefanie's face is carefully neutral but we can all feel it: this is a grudge match. Stefanie rolls her shoulders under her forest-green Dartmouth sweatshirt, then walks easily to the foul line. She picks up a ball and dribbles it twice, plainly the only one of us who has ever voluntarily handled one. She tenses, shoots. The ball hits the back rim, bounces, and goes in. The second is a swish, the third takes two bounces to go in. She dribbles the last one a few times, gathers herself and shoots again. Swish.

She doesn't give Potsworth even a glance. He watches her coolly, pistol at the ready.

She shakes out her arms, rubs her palms together and begins her ascent, long legs twined around the thick braided rope. She climbs slowly but with perfect competence. She slides to the floor, balloon in hand.

She still has thirty feet to cross to hand him the balloon and Potsworth has a clean shot the whole way. He cocks an eyebrow, plants his feet, and aims. Stefanie walks with a measured pace, perfectly composed. Twenty feet, then fifteen. What's he waiting for?

Potsworth frowns, shakes the gun, then aims again, grimacing with effort. His hand trembles. At ten feet away, Stefanie halts.

'The magic of Summerdwell is not yours to command,' she says. 'Do you understand?'

His hands shake. He grips the pistol hard. Now Stefanie frowns. She holds out a long arm, hand clenched.

'Stand . . . down . . . Princess,' he says, between gritted teeth.

'Do you understand?' she repeats. All the force in her carefully leashed anger directed into restraining her teacher.

An alarm sounds, shatteringly loud against the hard floors. A red light flashes above the door behind Potsworth, and the door bangs open. Three armored guards hustle in, pistols unholstered.

'Sir? Is everything all right?'

Potsworth's throat works, struggling to take a breath.

Cat, Jack and I shoot glances at each other, unsure of the right play. I step between Stefanie and the group, hands up, but the guards fan out, flanking us, weapons aimed.

'Princess DiDonato, you're engaged in metahuman assault. Cease immediately, we are cleared to fire.'

'Say it, Doctor,' she says. Her lean frame is agonizingly tense but her grin is all murderous joy.

'Come on, Stef, cut it out,' I say.

One of the guards mutters rapidly into a radio clipped to his shoulder. *Developing situation.*

'Say it.'

'Stef, fuck these guys, they're not worth it,' Jack says, almost gently. 'They're nobody.'

'Sir, can you speak? What's the order?' the same man says. He sounds frightened. He starts to raise his rifle. Stefanie's eyes flick to him just for an instant, and then Potsworth's trigger finger convulses. A bright circle of pink paint appears dead center on the pine-needle-green sweatshirt.

The guards don't move, weapons still trained on Stefanie.

'Weapons down, gentlemen,' Potsworth says, his voice clear and powerful again. 'This was merely an exercise. Nothing worthy of comment.'

The alarm stops, the guards file out again, and the red light flooding the gym returns to the pale light of morning. Stefanie walks straight to the exit and slams the door behind her.

'That will be all for the day,' Potsworth says. 'If you see her, tell her it's washable paint.'

The paint-splashed sweatshirt is in a garbage can in the hall.

Stefanie isn't hard to find. She's standing on the edge of the front parking lot, long arms wrapped around her angular form. Two of the MICA guards are watching her curiously.

Her arms are red and goose-pimpled in the cold. For once, we look the same age.

'Don't touch me,' she says, although I'm nowhere near her. She digs a cigarette out of her back pocket but it won't light.

'Are you okay?' I say.

'I want to go home.'

'Potsworth says class is over.'

'Not that home.'

'I thought you were going to –'

'My parents have given up their claim to the throne. They say we're going to live here forever. I hate this place so much.'

We both look out at the asphalt parking lot, speckled with chewing gum and rimmed with dirty plowed-up snow.

'Yeah, it's not great.'

'You'll be fine. This is your place,' she says. The cigarette finally lights and she takes a drag. 'I wasn't born for this. To be in a place like this high school, with people like you.'

'Hey, I'm the Chosen One. There's a prophecy.'

'It's not the same. You're commoners.'

'Yeah, well, I guess we are. Sorry,' I say.

'Probably not your fault.'

'Most of us kind of like you, if that helps.'

'Great. What do I do now?' she says.

'I dunno. We're mortals. Walk amongst us.'

She sighs, drops the cigarette and stamps on it, then wipes her nose. She looks beautiful and, for a moment, mortal.

19

'Try slouching,' Jack says.

'I am slouching.'

'Well, slouch worse.'

'It's not fair,' I say. 'You get to be smart in school. Stefanie gets to be beautiful. Why can't I get something out of this?'

I hunch over, try to let Prodigy's belly protrude, but it just throws his six-pack into sharper relief.

Jack shakes his head.

'You look like Rob Lowe did a lot of sit-ups. Then he entered a limbo contest.'

I stare at the image in the mirror. Even in my stupidest T-shirt and ripped jeans, Prodigy's crisp jawline and immaculately sculpted calves, his melodious yet quintessentially masculine voice, are a fantasy of what puberty should bring. His skin is radiantly clear.

'It's not like you're ugly, dude,' Jack says. 'But he's two inches taller than you are.'

'I should have done it last summer,' I say. 'Just disappear. I'll say I had a job as a longshoreman. And a growth spurt.'

'You always wanted to be a longshoreman,' Jack says. 'Your sole ambition in life. You stayed with your cousin. The noted French longshoreman.'

'It would have worked,' I say.

'But I thought you could only use your powers at your hour of need?' Jack says.

'Well, I need to be cool in high school.'

'You are,' Jack says. 'Just nobody knows it.'

He's actually right, in a way. I'm distant, arguably mysterious. I don't talk to my old friends, and there's no way to explain to them that I've fought cops and gone to jail and kissed a girl, so is it surprising that their Dungeons and Dragons game looks a bit pedestrian? Is it any wonder I'm weary of the trivialities of suburban life? 'I've been to France' is the only plausible non-supernatural explanation I can come up with for any of this.

Every day, I meet my mother at 2.55 p.m. in the school parking lot to be driven home. She's always on time, trying her best to be cheerful in the face of this daily reminder that her son is a juvenile delinquent metahuman.

She's late today, and I've barely said my hellos and closed the door when she pulls away from the curb. She turns to reply and nearly runs over Cat, who is jaywalking across the crowded intersection.

Mom brakes, horrified to be running over an entire third of her son's social circle. Cat, though, spins like a matador, and cocks her fist, ready to shatter the driver's side window.

My mother manages to perceive this as a friendly wave and pulls over.

'Isn't that one of your friends?' she says. 'Wouldn't she like a lift?'

She rolls down the window to say hello. Cat is visibly unclear on whether or not she is fighting a piloted vehicle until she sees me in the passenger seat. By then it seems too late to pretend we don't know each other. A couple of kids stare as the forest-dwelling special-needs girl hops into the back seat of my mother's car.

'Mom, this is Cat,' I say as we pull away from the curb again.

'It's nice to meet you, Cat.'

'Take Mass Ave north, please,' Cat says. It's a polite voice I've never heard from her, almost an octave up from her regular speaking voice. It sounds like she's worked on it, an adaptive mode.

It doesn't come with small talk, however.

'Do you have a lot of classes with Alexander?' Mom says, after a minute.

'No, I'm only a junior,' Cat says calmly, but out of my mother's view she's doing a strenuous finger exercise.

'You're so young. Did you skip a grade? How old are you?'

'I had a different school before this. They didn't tell us our ages.'

'Alexander is thinking of being a doctor,' my mother manages to say.

'I have literally never thought that.'

'I used to know a lot of doctors,' Cat says.

'Cat was home schooled,' I say. 'By, um, doctors.'

'They did things to my bones, then they died.'

'Ah,' my mother says. 'I suppose you're in CLEO.'

'I did a crime. If you turn right here, it will be on the right. Right here.'

She stops us in the middle of a long stretch of road, just before the bridge where a disused railway line runs overhead. It's starting to rain. My mother looks around for any sign of a house.

'Are you sure?' my mother says.

'Yes. Thank you for the ride, Mrs Beekman.'

'You should come over for dinner one of these days. We'd love –'

But Cat shuts the car door.

Mom rolls down the window. 'To see you. Do you need an umbrella?'

Cat doesn't answer, just sets off through the grass and wildflowers growing wild on the embankment.

'I didn't know there were houses back there,' Mom says. 'Are you sure she's all right?'

'I don't think anybody bothers her,' I say.

'Well, I'm glad you're making friends. You could ask her out maybe. People do that, you know.'

'Great. We could have dinner in the woods.'

'She's just going for a walk,' Mom says. 'She looks like she gets a lot of exercise.'

'Yup, she does.'

'What about that other girl? Stefanie? She seems very popular.'

'Mom!'

She falls silent. Perhaps contemplating the fact that her son only knows two girls. Aren't delinquents supposed to be, if nothing else, attractive?

Next Saturday, Stefanie stops me outside, before class.

'We need to meet. All of us,' she whispers, leaning close, enveloping me in the atmosphere of soap and scented shampoo and scentless girl-breath.

'What is it?' I say. I'd almost forgotten her ideas about CLEO, the investigation, the looming conspiracy.

'Not now. Jack says he can turn off our tracking cuffs for a few hours. I've got a plan.'

We take our seats, to sit through a morning discussing the risk factors associated with various paranormal abilities, which means several hours of bad news for each of us. Not least for Jack; it's rare for any of us to integrate well socially, but ten times more so for the cognitively enhanced like Jack.

'That's a stereotype,' Jack says.

'It's a risk factor,' Potsworth says. 'You know the statistics, especially for the cognitively enhanced.'

'Hey, some of us do our thinking for the greater good, like Logic Bomber does. Or Overclock.'

Potsworth cocks an eyebrow.

'He had "No Time for Crime".'

'Thank you, Alex.'

Potsworth raises both hands, admitting defeat.

'None of you would be here if I thought you couldn't contribute to society,' Potsworth says. 'But this isn't only about villainy. Statistically, there's a good chance that by the time you're thirty, one of you will have a drug dependency, or be homeless, or have severe mental health problems. A few of you have already gotten a head start.'

'Not me,' Jack says. 'I'm not a head case.'

'I find that interesting, coming from the one of you who's spent by far the most time in institutional care.'

'That was a bullshit misunderstanding. And that's a sealed file. I could sue you,' he answers.

'As I was saying, the most statistically likely outcome for people like you – does anyone know? Suicide, which is a more frequent outcome than the rest combined. Don't be shocked. Not everybody's journey comes to a good end.'

It's hard to pay attention, with the thought of being able to get away for a few hours after the meeting. None of us has been outside and unchaperoned for months.

We meet behind the building after class. Jack has already got Stefanie's Walkman out and he's rebuilding it with the aid of Scotch tape and a handful of paper clips, turning it into a makeshift jammer for our ankle bracelets.

Jack and I call our parents from the payphone by the bus stop. Stefanie calls her parents, an argument that escalates until she slams the phone down as the car arrives.

'Well, that was nice,' she says. We pile into the back seat of the Rolls Royce, squeezed against one another with our coats and backpacks and muddy shoes.

'Take us to the mall, Guillermo,' she tells the driver.

I've never cared one way or another about the Wessex Galleria but this afternoon the brightly lit spaces, the damp indoor air and the sharp brassy echoes above the Christmas music, the thunder of a fake waterfall, all feel like a paradise for the human spirit.

Suburban mothers shepherd toddlers through; girls in sculpted hair brush past us, glancing at our mismatched foursome.

Stefanie's tall lean elegance contrasts with Jack's defiant lack of cool and my regular plaid shirt, jeans and Baracuta jacket, uniform of teen nobodies everywhere. Cat would look halfway normal if she didn't look so jittery.

'Could you maybe stop that?' I say.

'There's too much movement,' she says. 'My combat routines keep starting and stopping.'

'It's a mall already. No one's going to kill us.'

'That's what dead people say.'

'I thought you had news,' Jack says to Stefanie.

'I just want to be normal for a second. Can you just walk around a little? Go to boy places. Cat and I will meet you at the food court in an hour.'

'Fine.' Jack's already speed-walking to the Radio Shack. His expression surveying the shelves ripe with cameras and cassette players is borderline indecent. I visit the bookstore and stake out a table in a corner of the food court until the girls arrive. Cat has emerald eye shadow and a Minor Threat T-shirt.

'I showed her Hot Topic,' Stefanie says. 'I'm so sorry.'

'It says "Minor Threat",' Cat says.

'I see that.'

'She's so much fun,' Stefanie says. 'Ask her about the Agony Maze sometime.'

Jack shows up with a tray laden with food.

'The cash machines here are just sitting ducks,' he says.

'Can we get started?' Stefanie says. 'Not that I don't love being seen with you guys.'

'So, okay,' says Jack. 'CLEO is some kind of untouchable program, we know that much. And someone pulled strings to get us all in it. Is that so bad?'

'There's more,' Stefanie says. 'Doctor Potsworth is one of the biggest people in his field. It doesn't make sense for him to spend all this time on four high school students.'

'Maybe he's actually a good person,' I say. 'Maybe he likes us.'

'God, you're naive,' Jack says. 'Think about it, how did CLEO even get authorized and funded? Politicians hate voting for anything that makes them look soft on metahuman crime.'

'So what happened?'

'There was an absolute shit-ton of lobbying and campaign donations, orchestrated by professionals. Practically untraceable, even for me – and I crack nuclear codes in study hall.'

'No part of that is good news,' Stefanie says. 'So you didn't get anything?'

'I said "practically".' Jack shakes out a long sheaf of printout. 'Traced it through about ten different offshore accounts, but the payments match up.' His stubby finger stabs at different numbers he's circled. 'Prion Enterprises.'

'Like the espresso machine?' Stefanie says.

'They make more than that, but I can't figure out what. I even called and did my Bob Dole voice. I checked with my future self and he had nothing.'

'Goddess preserve us,' Stefanie mutters.

'I know what they make,' Cat says. She's been sitting so quietly, we'd almost forgotten she was there. 'They made me.'

'Wait, wait, wait,' Jack says. 'What?'

'They wanted to build new kinds of soldiers and assassins to sell to governments. They stole kids out of the foster system and did experiments on us.'

'That can't be real,' Stefanie says. 'People would sue.'

'I don't have any money.'

'She's not a rich piece like you,' Jack says. 'She barely has a name.'

'Respect,' Stefanie says. 'I'm not going to say it again.'

'He's right,' says Cat. 'We were nobodies. I had to get a birth certificate and a Social Security card before I could even go to school.'

'So you're not actually learning disabled, are you?' Stefanie says. 'They just didn't teach you anything.'

'The Puzzle Arena took many lives.'

'CLEO still keeps us out of prison,' I say. 'We can't just blow it up.'

'Alex is right,' Jack says. 'We just have to be ready if they want to pull anything. Watch each other's backs.'

'Just don't try to sit with me at lunch,' Stefanie says.

'Like I would want to,' Jack says.

'That boy is watching us,' Cat says abruptly. She flicks her eyes at a table behind Jack.

I saw him when we came in, off by himself, a boy in a hoodie hunched over an empty table, a cane propped against it. He sees me looking.

He levers himself up with the cane and begins to thrust himself step by step toward me. His hood falls back to show his face. Chris Berkowitz. One of Chuck's friends, the athlete. His hair is longer, greasy. He trembles as he walks, hip askew. He looks like one of the kids he used to make fun of. Stupidly, I try to focus on my French fries instead of the figure looming closer in my peripheral vision. He stops and stands there until I look up at him.

'Hey, Alexander. Long time no see.'

'Umm, hey.'

'It's Chris. In case you didn't recognize me,' he says. 'Are these your friends?'

'Yeah.'

'Let's go,' Stefanie says.

I stand but he lunges to catch my arm.

'Wait,' he says. 'I want to talk to you.'

'I'm sorry, I can't.'

'What are you?'

'I don't know what you mean,' I say.

'The Feds said they'd pay for college as long as no one talks, but you know what? I don't care. Just tell me what you are.'

'I can't tell you!'

'Hey!' he shouts at the crowd of diners, pointing at me. 'This is the guy who destroyed the school! He did this to me!'

'Come on, Chris,' I say, but it comes out like a plea. 'Chill out.'

'You're going to pay for this, you little fag.'

Then Jack is standing next to me, elbowing into the conversation.

'You want to fuck with this guy?' Jack says. 'I can ruin your life from a payphone.' He flexes his fingers as if ready to start typing then and there.

Stefanie's eyes have gone a solid red. 'If you speak of this again, your nightmares will never cease.'

'Who the fuck are these people?' Chris says.

'Friends of mine,' I say. 'But not as nice. Understand?'

Chris doesn't answer.

'Let's go,' Jack says.

Chris waits a moment before finding his bullying swagger again, or maybe it's courage.

'Fuck you!' he calls after us. He grabs a paper cup of soda from a child's tray and tries to throw it at us but loses his balance and falls, scattering half-melted ice cubes.

'Did you do that to him?' Stefanie says when we reach the car.

'It was an accident,' I say. I was still trying to process the permanence of what I'd done. Why couldn't I have walked through walls, or had a magic dog?

'He was an asshole,' Jack says. 'Fuck him and his friends.'

Stefanie drives off, Cat departs at an even trot, Jack trudges to the bus stop.

A little later, my mother's car pulls up to the entrance. My mother smiles at me and the car wraps me in all the familiar cues of home – smells, the warmth, and the sound and vibration of a poorly tuned engine. We drive away into the normal world, where future selves are all silent and where office parks don't ever hide catacombs full of superpowered children.

PART FIVE

2015

20

Invisible to mortal eyes, the enchanted bridge to Summerdwell can be found at the very top of a steep hill on the edge of a forest behind the high school. On the shelf of brittle iron-banded rocks, inscribed in white spray paint, one can read a single word: 'Aerosmith'. Every year more and more scree, candy wrappers, cigarette butts and shards of brown bottle accumulate at the bottom of the hill, but the word remains.

Jack and I sit in a car at the back of the parking lot, checking our phones. I haven't told him about Stefanie's visit. I feel bad keeping it from him but I strongly suspect he'd be extra weird on the subject. If Stefanie starts to look guilty, it's better if he puts that together on his own.

'Are you sure we weren't followed?' I say.

'Ninety-nine percent.'

'If they find out, I'll be in trouble just for talking to you.'

'I'm your old enemy. They think we're in cahoots?'

'Who knows what they think cahoots is?' I say. 'But yeah, it's probably worse that I talked to Cat. Especially now.'

Cat's hard to track, but Jack has managed to eavesdrop on MICA chatter. Several unsolved, unexplained crimes have already taken place. Raids on metahuman criminals mostly, running down a list of lairs. She doesn't appear to have found anything useful.

'Did you try subspace comms?' he asks.

'She doesn't answer.'

'Maybe you should take the hint.'

The sun is almost touching the low horizon of wooded

hills. We get out of the car and find the right spot. If you stand there and face precisely the right angle, you will see a low metal gate and beyond it the bridge itself, delicate as spun sugar. Every few years a stoner kid will spot it.

'I'm not crazy about this,' he says.

'We tried Cat so we're trying your ex. Fair's fair,' I say.

He shuts his eyes for a moment as the Thinking Cap's lights cycle.

'If Stefanie's involved she'll be a lot more subtle about it.'

'I know.'

After a moment he says, 'You never, like, hooked up with Stefanie, did you?'

'What? No.'

'No judgment. Everyone knows you had a crush on her,' he says.

'Oh my god, for like a millionth of a second. Don't worry about it.'

'It would have been cool in a way. Like the Cubs winning the World Series.'

At 6.20 p.m. the bridge shimmers into being. First the base, then it shoots out over treetops on filigreed pillars looking thin as spider silk at this distance.

This is the Middlesex Bridge, one of a dozen or so crossings – there's one on a rooftop in Singapore, a forest in Vermont, a certain alleyway in Istanbul. Stefanie and her family might have come through any one of those, but they arrived here in Hanover, only minutes ahead of her stepsister Juniper's soldiers. They came with nothing but a few items of clothing and most of the royal treasury in gemstones.

Through the gate, then Jack sets one foot on the bridge's glassy paving stones. He tests his weight on it.

'I hate this,' he says.

'Will you go already?'

'Just let it fade in a little more. The Thinking Cap is yelling at me.'

'Does it still not believe in this stuff? You were married to the monarch of this place for four years.'

'You think that makes it easier? I'm having flashbacks.'

I give him a little shove and he goes. A few more steps, the land drops sharply away. The power lines that should be below you aren't there. Keep walking and you'll see the mossy banks and blood-warm water of the meandering Bellwater a hundred feet below you. You're in Summerdwell.

We take our time crossing the half-mile of bridge, stopping here and there at the glassy railing to look out at the view. There's no mistaking you're not on Earth. There's an innate sorcery that makes every night feel like a Midsummer's Feast, special and a bit sexy. It's late afternoon all of the time here, except when it's an enchanted midnight or glorious morning. Imagine having six years of Summerdwell's golden horizons, then getting stuck living in our world of plastic and apps. No wonder Stefanie wound up in CLEO.

At the bridge's midpoint we pass a pair of wardstones to either side. Ancient granite, deeply engraved. Nothing but warm air to us, but to Stefanie it's a solid wall. The bane of her existence.

'I always thought Stefanie would get this place back,' I say.

'You can't just drive a pickup truck full of C4 across the enchanted bridge. Even if you got there, you'd need a tactical nuke and then you've irradiated the Bellwater and wiped out a cohort of elite faerie guards and it's a PR nightmare.'

'Couldn't you help? I thought conquering worlds was your specialty.'

'I'm going to conquer the world I was born in. Not some faerie place.'

'"Was going to."'

'What'd I say? Anyway, I couldn't work out a way to do it.'

'I get it,' I say. 'I hate doing somebody else's adventure too.'

'Yeah, well. Try not to get married.' Jack keeps tapping the side of his head. 'I forgot there's no cell towers here,' he says.

'Can you work without it?'

'For these yokels? Please. I can handle them *au naturel*.'

'How do you want to play it?' I ask.

'Just follow my lead,' he says. 'Intrigue is like the national sport here. Just don't punch anybody.'

'That's kind of my thing, though.'

Jack hocks and spits over the side of the bridge to watch it fall through the golden light. Far off, either a very big bird or a small dragon circles lazily. Beyond it, the horizon fades into green, gold, blue.

The great bridge ends at the top of a cliff, and there stands a Gothic fairy-tale confection, the Gateway Castle. Its spires soar upward to taper into needle points lost in the deep blue of late afternoon sky. The flags they fly aren't Stefanie's green and gold, but Juniper's red and white.

A man dressed all in white is waiting for us outside the gates. Silver, not iron.

'Shit, it's Himself. I thought we'd get a flunky,' Jack says.

'He still owes us for bringing them back their unicorn. You really saved the day on that one.'

'Okay already.'

'Couldn't have done it without you.'

'Shut,' Jack says, 'your fucking mouth.'

Smug old Archduke Zoriah. He's dressed in a white uniform decorated with medals. He wears a thin dueling sword, scabbard chased in silver. It matches his mane of hair and neatly trimmed beard. He's tall like all of Stefanie's race, but muscled, and it's hard to read his exact age.

There's a spidery little table and chairs set up with fruits and cheeses of the realm, a bottle of their clear dry white wine and three tall slim glasses. He rises and grips each of our hands in turn, smiling.

'Be welcome to Summerdwell, Lord Consort Jack. And you, Honorary Count Beekman. It's been far too long, even here in Summerdwell.'

'How's it hanging, Your Grace?' Jack says.

Rather than answer, the Archduke pours us all a little wine. The taste of Summerdwell wine is what I remember: mineral and apple and something else one can never place, a happy memory just out of reach. The vintage doesn't cross worlds though; taken to Earth, it reverts to a moderately good Chardonnay.

'And how fares the Lady Stefanie?'

'Queen-in-Exile Stefanie is well,' Jack says. 'She looks forward to a renewed recognition of her royal station.'

'The Queen will consider her petition in due time. Until such a time, the wards remain in place.' He gestures to the nearest one, set into the paving stones.

Wings beat, and a wyvern passes overhead. Its iridescent green scales catch the setting sun. The rider gestures with a spear.

'And the kingdom? All is well?' Jack says.

'The people thrive. Three giants have taken up residence in the southern forest and we are making preparations, just in case. A return of the crown jewels might be appreciated.'

'The Queen-in-Exile will consider your petition in due time.'

Zoriah inclines his head in mock gratitude, then raises one hand. Whoever's watching gives an order; heavy bolts and bars slide away and then the gates swing open. We are escorted through and into the courtyard, then up the stone steps to the top of the barrier wall.

Beyond and below us is Summerdwell, the golden lands. Green and gold farmland dotted with castles, then the deep forests and borderlands, with far-off peaks and adventures untold under the ever-setting double moon. If you expect Summerdwell to make sense, you're missing the point.

Admiring the view, Archduke Zoriah speaks without looking at us.

'Listen,' he whispers. 'Quickly. The Queen's spies are everywhere. Tell Stefanie she must come home soon or not at all.'

'I will give her that message,' Jack says, giving me a sideways glance.

'I gave her messenger what she asked for, but I must know her plan before we can act.'

'All in due time,' Jack says.

'Forsooth,' I say, 'it flies upon wind. Time, that is.' The wine is getting to me.

Jack treads on my foot.

'How will she enter the kingdom?' Zoriah asks. 'She cannot pass the ancient wardstones, not with the mark of exile upon her. She must know such power is beyond her.'

'She is not known to be a fool,' Jack says, with a credible imitation of Stefanie's hauteur. 'Or a weakling.'

'So she has told me.'

'So she's really feeling this one,' Jack says.

'Much as you say, Lord Jack, but I can only risk so much. The Queen keeps me on as a sop to the old loyalists, but I can't back another losing cause.'

He beckons us, leads us back down to the table and chairs where he greeted us, speaking loudly.

'I hope one day Stefanie will change her mind and pledge fealty to her rightful Queen,' he says.

'That doesn't really sound like her,' I say.

'Until then I wish you well. And you too, Alexander.'

He clasps my hand in both of his, presses something soft into it, then folds my fingers over it. A velvet bag with something inside, hard and rectangular like a domino.

'I bid you farewell,' Jack says. 'Summerdwell is Eternal! We'll call you!' He throws an inexpert salute, turns, and stumbles down the first few steps before getting the hang of it.

'Well, bye,' I say. 'Fare thee well, I mean.'

Light-headed from alcohol and adrenaline, we wobble out onto the bridge in all its silvery Beaux Arts perfection, just as the huge lamps begin to glow. A rare night is falling.

'Ha!' Jack slaps the railing. 'I bespoke him fairly. I bespoke that motherfucker fairly.'

'Yes, you did.'

'Summerdwell day drinking's the best day drinking. Zoriah was a little pissy, though.'

A cooler wind rustles Jack's hair.

'What did he slip you?' Jack says. I shake out the bag. It's a thumb drive.

I say, 'Do I need to tell you what's on it?'

'It could be the time stream map.'

'You're putting a lot of faith in her,' I say. 'You know we have to go ask her, right?'

'Why can't Barry do it?'

'Not with the divorce and all.'

He stops walking again.

'What divorce?'

'Shit.'

'They're getting divorced. Her and Barry? What?'

'I thought he told you, or else you'd figure it out. You're smart like that,' I say.

He takes a shaky step back and bumps against the railing. I'm not sure I've ever seen him this surprised.

'Are you okay?' I ask.

'Yeah, it's fine. It just wasn't in the known scenarios.'

He doesn't look fine. Jack's bent over a little now, hands on his knees. Jack's LEDs are flashing white.

'It's the whole reason he's staying with us. I thought he was going to tell you.' I rest a hand lightly on his back, sweaty and overheated. He shrugs it off.

'I'm fine, I'm fine,' Jack says, straightening up. 'It's just weird. I thought she was happy, like she'd finally got what she wanted. I thought it was all settled.'

'Well, you seem a lot more upset about the divorce than the idea that she might be a supervillain.'

'She always had a little of that in her. She couldn't have married me otherwise.'

'I can go on my own if you need.'

'She'd eat you alive, and you know it,' Jack says. 'Let's get to the car.'

Behind us, Gateway Castle's fairy lights begin to come on, pink and blue and green. We hurry back, with our shadows long in front of us, and emerge into the New England night air. At the rate time moves, it must be early morning by now. The roads are empty.

'Hey,' Jack says, 'remember that time we were there and that old guy jumped out and asked you to bring him that stuff?'

'A dozen feathers from the Manifold Swan and he'd tell me where to find my heart's desire.'

'Did you ever get back to him?'

'Nah,' I say.

In fact, I searched every library I could find. But there's no point in admitting it now.

21

Jack conjures a pair of plane tickets out of the dozen company credit cards he swaps around like a Three-card Monte dealer. He throws in a pair of suites at the Beverly Wilshire ('money's a construct') and the limousine in which we are now traversing Wilshire Boulevard, bound for a VIP party like overage characters in a Steely Dan song.

The bleached sidewalk outside is worlds away from the rain-mopped greens of Amherst and Cambridge. I roll down the window and close my eyes and breathe in the warm smoggy air until it starts to feel right. I let it wash away whatever it was I was doing back east in the decades-long charade of Rick Tower. Did I really teach all that poetry to kids? Did I care that much about losing tenure? That wasn't me. It was never me.

Jack huddles on the far side of the back seat the whole time we're on the 405. He stares out the window when he's not texting, pre-gaming on Scotch and a pair of colorful pills.

'Dextroamphetamine,' he explains. 'I stripped out the addictive properties. You want some?'

'No, thank you. Are you taking it to market?'

'FDA fucked me. The usual.' He pops another one.

'Maybe you should take it easy with those.'

'Mind your own business. And fix your tie.'

I'm wearing the oversized black suit and black tie that Jack picked out for me. In this one I look like an extra Blues Brother.

'Is this really what people wear?'

'Trust me, you're on the cutting edge.'

'What if there's a ska band, and they think I'm in it?'

'Ska's cool again.' Jack himself is wearing his colors: a silvery gray three-piece suit with a purple tie, and a pin with the insignia of a Battle Commander of the Galactic Fleet. He copied it out of his letters from the future and had dozens made.

Stefanie's people picked out a hotel in downtown LA as the venue for her album pre-release party. I've never heard of it, but then I've led a sheltered life. Jack stops the driver a few blocks away.

'We'll walk from here,' Jack says.

But once we're out of the car he doesn't go anywhere, just leans against a wall for a bit.

He waves me off. 'Don't. I'm fine.'

'You said. You want to talk about it?'

'Did I ever tell you why I turned villain?'

'Yeah, I think you touched on it a few times in the eighty hours of speeches you made me sit through.'

'Well, I wasn't lying about any of that,' he says. 'But I was also a little mad about the divorce.'

'This is a shocking revelation.'

'I always thought if I could be with Stefanie, the Optimal Timeline mattered just a tiny bit less. After she left, I thought, fuck it, why not just go for it?'

'Plus, if you were emperor of the world that might seem kind of hot.'

'You can't rule it out.'

'You know,' I say, 'maybe I should do the talking in there.'

'Hey, I think I can talk to my ex-wife,' he says.

The hotel lobby is striped black and white across the walls and floor, oversized and shiny, and radiates a lack of welcome, not unlike a supervillain's lair, except here they make you pay for things you break.

It's also very well defended. I don't see any sign of a party but Jack makes a straight line to a young woman in fashionably chunky eyeglasses loitering near a conspicuously unmarked elevator. She tries not to make eye contact but he plants himself right in front of her.

'Jack Angler plus one.'

She mimes checking her clipboard.

'Could you spell that, please?'

I can't tell if she's a consummate professional, or doesn't even know this is Stefanie's ex because it all happened before she was born.

'Get me one of her people,' Jack says.

'I'm sorry?'

Four or five party guests are stacked up behind us. The black suit renaissance doesn't appear to have reached them.

'You're event staff. Let me talk to one of her people, and we can get this done.'

She stares him down, assessing his potential as a threat to the party vibe. It is, she surmises correctly, well off the charts.

'One moment, please.'

She looks behind her and nods to a second woman standing by the elevators. That woman, in turn, sends a text.

Ten seconds later, the elevator opens to reveal a beautifully dressed African-American man, square-faced and smiling. He beckons us over and ushers us inside.

'Thanks, Dave,' Jack says. 'I owe you one.'

'Don't even think of it,' the man says. 'Good luck with the missus.'

They fist-bump as the elevator closes.

'I got his kid into college,' Jack says.

*

The party suite is a penthouse overlooking downtown LA. The white walls have floor-to-ceiling images of the album cover, Stefanie's scowling face over the title, *Bow Down*. Ranks of monitors are playing the video to 'Once and Future', apparently their lead single, featuring Stefanie riding a winged horse over a stunning computer-generated mountain range, while her autotuned soprano punches out the melodic hook. It's not bad. Stefanie wouldn't stand for that.

The suite is packed with people dancing, and fragrant with fancy alcohol and clean rich-person sweat. They might be in their twenties or thirties, I've lost the ability to judge, and the rules are probably different here. The women wear tight party-optimized dresses in primary colors, but the guys are all in T-shirts. They all seem to have spent the same amount of time on their hair. We skulk along the edge of the dance floor, an aging nightclub host trailed by a nervous undertaker.

'Can you believe these losers?' Jack says. 'Stef's really hitting bottom.'

A black-clad waiter hands us each a fizzy signature cocktail in a plastic cup.

'It looks pretty happening to me.'

In fact, we can barely hear each other. Everyone is laughing, or loudly making some conversational point.

'Assistants and PR types. This is what happens when nobody your own age likes you.'

He shoulders straight into a roiling stew of interns and copywriters without breaking stride; I try to follow but the gap has already closed. It occurs to me, once again, that Jack's lifelong blindness to social cues is a perversely adaptive trait. His inability to perceive his uncoolness may actually make him cool.

I'm a very popular professor. I appeal to younger people. I push my way to the windows and pretend to lose myself in profound contemplation. *RAECLUN, RAECLUN.*

Jack is right about the crowd. They're not famous, just young and canny in a way I never was.

Jack pokes the small of my back. 'You look like somebody's dentist got on the list. Fix your tie.'

RAECLUN.

'Did you find Stefanie?'

'Not yet, but there's a VIP room. Come on.'

There's another security detail to pass, two enormously beefy Anglos standing out for their pale-blue suits and lack of affect. They nod to Jack. I nod to them, not that they care. I could have taken them if I had to. I can 'take' almost anyone, for what that's worth.

The VIP section looks just like the outer room, but a lot quieter. The people are older, more tanned, with more silver hair in the mix, and the men wear jackets at least. A few of them are in high-fashion peacock mode, but for the most part it seems like actual rich and famous people don't bother to look it.

'She'll be vulnerable,' Jack says. 'Her career's obviously in the toilet.'

'So's yours,' I say. 'So is all of ours.'

'Hang back,' he says. 'I'll do the approach.'

'Okay, but don't make it weird.'

'Weird how?' he says, and he's off again, crashing right through circles of conversation.

Heads turn to follow him, hoping for a scene.

I take another drink from a passing tray, then spill it when a warm, long-fingered hand clamps down on my wrist.

'OH. MY. GOD.' Stefanie's sloppy smiling face shouts straight into mine. 'How are you here?'

'Hi, Stef.'

Tonight she's out of fairy-tale garb, in a streamlined crimson sheath dress and a minimalist silver band for a tiara. Her royal hauteur is smudged only slightly by several strong cocktails.

'Come with me. This is the most perfect thing that ever happened,' she says. Her face is inches from mine.

'We should really talk,' I say, smiling into a blast of boozy breath.

'Shut up. You will not believe this.' She's pulling so hard that resisting would mean a public tug-of-war.

I can only stutter-step along behind her. 'It's important,' I say.

'Not now, darling,' she says. 'Fast, fast, fast!'

Our destination reels into view: a circle of stubbled young men in heartbreaking suits, and one woman in a neat maroon blazer holding a glass of untouched champagne.

'Well?' Stefanie says.

I look dumbly into a stranger's searching eyes, her wide mouth, black hair cut in fashionable bangs. Lilac skin, lips night-purple. My brain has turned into a blundering detective, unable to follow the evidence to its obvious conclusion.

'I didn't know you would be here,' Meg says, soberly. She has a faint lisp now. Newly pointed canines peek out from over her lower lip.

'It's Blacklight! This is the greatest thing ever! Come on, you guys, hug,' Stef says, and drapes her long arms across our shoulders and strains to push us together.

We squirm like two cats who don't want to be friends.

'Thanks . . . thanks, Stef . . .' I say.

'Why don't we go out on the patio?' Meg says to me.

Stefanie stage-whispers, '*You're welcome!*'

Outside, the heat of the LA afternoon is dissipating as the sun descends through the smog over the 1-10, turning all the neighboring skyscrapers red-gold. People are smoking on the patio, sorcerers mostly. One of them gives me a sharp look. His eyes are a solid purple. I wonder what he sees.

Meg and I lean together on the railing and look out at the carpet of Mission-style roofs and white stucco, spreading north up to the Hollywood hills.

'So,' I say.

'I guess this was inevitable,' she says.

'You look nice.'

'Your nose is different.'

'You got fangs,' I say.

'They came in last year. Maybe I used the powers too much. Or maybe I'm just getting old.'

'You're not old.'

Fangs aside, her smile looks the same.

'Are we going to fight?' I ask.

'What? No. We're not in our twenties anymore, thank God. Is that why you're seeing Stefanie?'

'No. I'm not even supposed to be here. I'm on the Restricted List, ever since the trial,' I say. 'I'm Professor Rick Tower now. I teach English at a small New England college. I like free jazz and going to art openings.'

'Was jail not an option?'

'Not this time.'

She lights a cigarette. A blinking ambulance pushes stepwise through the slow northbound traffic on the 1-10.

'Why are you here?' I ask. 'Are you friends with Stef now?'

'Like that would happen. No, my firm does contracts for the record label. I thought it would be funny to show up.'

She hands me a card: *Karen Cena, Avocat d'Affaire, Ligo & Cena. Paris, France.*

'Paris? That's great. You made it.'

'I always said I would.' *So did you*, she might have said.

'I'm happy for you.'

'So are you here on a mission?' she says. 'I thought the four of you split up for good.'

'Oh, no. Stefanie's still a friend.'

'You must be pretty good friends if you and Jack came all the way to LA.'

'She's launching an album.'

'Oh, that's right. Have you heard the album?'

'It's great,' I say.

'Really? What did you like about it?'

'It's, you know, good. Good Stefanie-type music.'

'In a way it's cute that you never changed,' she says. 'Did you ever find that dark enemy guy?'

'Adversary. No.'

'Do you still believe in the prophecy? All that stuff in the cave?'

'I don't know. If Mr Ferris knew the future, maybe he wouldn't be dead.'

'I guess you can ignore it easier than I can. I see it every time I look in the mirror.'

'Are you worried about the twenty-five years thing? Do you think it matters?'

'I don't know if it matters,' she says. 'I'm Karen Cena now, and you're "Rick Tower". How long since you were Prodigy?'

'Not that long.'

'Show me,' she says.

'Raeclun.'

She looks me over. Prodigy, the old marvel.

'There he is,' she says. 'He's got your old nose. I like it better.'

'Everyone does.'

'Now come here,' she says.

'What is it?'

'Hold still.'

She raises one finger, then holds it to my chest, just below the collar bone.

'What are you doing?' I ask.

'Wait.'

She lets the glossy darkforce flow out, to cover one fingernail with rich glossy black. She runs it down my chest, slowly, allowing it to part the fabric and lightly break the skin beneath and draw a thin red line down my chest, Prodigy's blood red as any man's. I watch, mesmerized, as the familiar shivery sting of it hits my core, followed by the cold shock that washes through me.

'I just wanted to see if it still worked,' she says. 'Is the darkforce still the only thing that hurts you?'

'Yes.'

'Lucky me,' she says. 'So, really, what are you looking for here? It wouldn't be a time machine, would it?'

'How would you know that?'

She shrugs. 'Word gets around. Sinistro always promised I could use his, then he never did.'

'Why would you want –'

A glass breaks inside the party, a woman screams, then what sounds like the whole bar tipping over.

'Oops,' Meg says. 'Now it's a party.'

The percussive whoosh of Jack's plasma pistol sounds once, twice, three times. People are backing out onto the patio.

'I should go see,' I say.

'You go,' she says. 'Look after your Newcomers.'

'You're not coming?'

'My work here is done.'

22

The last and bravest partygoers are recording, with upraised smartphones, the drama playing out in the center of the VIP room. Jack and Stefanie are crouched, circling each other through a festive debris field of plastic cups, shattered furniture, souvenir gift bags, and shoes and handbags left behind by fleeing partygoers. Pushing past the guests, I step on a tiny broken spiderbot, one of Jack's go-to devices. Where he keeps them is his business.

Jack has his old pistol drawn. His jacket is missing a sleeve, shirt stained with sweat. Stefanie's red sheath dress clings to her, soaked in sweat or booze or ectoplasm. She must have kept up her training, because no fewer than four translucent colored spheres orbit her thin frame, with only a hint of drunken wobble.

The room stinks of plasma-scorched ozone and the jasmine scent of magic. They've already gone a few rounds.

'I didn't say you were a traitor,' Jack says.

'It was implied,' Stefanie says.

'Well, what am I supposed to think?'

A greenish sphere brushes his force field, throwing off sparks. It was always the flip side of their intimacy, the way her sorcery bristles at anything high-tech, and Jack's equipment sparks and surges at the touch of magic.

'Stef, I don't want to fight you,' he says.

'Drop the gun then,' she says.

'You first.'

The green ball comes back and he fires at it, misses, and

breaks the window of the DJ booth. The glass doesn't shatter to the ground, but hangs in place, suspended. Stefanie waves it into orbit around her. She jerks her head and a piece of glass darts at Jack, only to shiver into crystalline splinters. A second one zips through, though, and draws a red line across Jack's cheek.

'First blood, darling,' she says. 'Must we take this any farther?'

'Just till you give me a straight answer.'

This, I remember, is the thing that threw them together and broke them apart, the no-brakes quality of their interactions. Long before they got together it was apparent that they were two of a kind, driven by two forms of the same relentless ambition.

'Enough!' Prodigy's voice can be as loud as I need it to be, loud enough to mark a pause in their very public Apache dance. I'm not exactly sure what happens next, or who fights who in this scenario. If it came to it, which of the three of us would come out on top? Each of us is thinking the same thing, Stefanie's sly strategic mind, Jack in a fever of calculation.

A sound enters the room, loud in the sudden silence. Jack's slow shift of stance and Stefanie's whispered incantation come to a halt. An eerie melody, whistled in a low and resonant tone. It takes me a moment to recognize the theme from 'Once and Future', rendered at half-speed, strangely beautiful.

'One of yours?' Jack whispers. He looks at Stefanie, who shakes her head.

The chorus builds to its swooping majestic sign-off, and then its source steps through the spectators into the circle, a man in a blazing white suit. The remainder of Jack's microdrones hit the floor with a sound like spilled marbles.

Broad-faced, massive nose, dark shoulder-length hair curled up at the ends like the king on a playing card, radiant as a bride in the silver-white jacket, pants, necktie, polished shoes, white cane. Sinistro, future Emperor of the Earth, looks like a comic actor in the role of God.

Sinistro. Tyrant, warrior. History's curse, who fought at Thermopylae and Shiloh, whose feet trod on the ashes of Carthage and Constantinople and Dresden. His eyes sparkle behind the diamond-shaped lenses of thousand-dollar sunglasses; laugh-lines crinkle at the edges but no more than they did twenty years ago. He does a little suggestion of a shuffle-ball-change, flourishes the cane in an unspoken *ta-dah*.

'You all got fat,' he says.

'Sinistro!' Stefanie says it like a curse.

'Greetings, Princess,' he says. 'Hello, Jack. Hello, Professor Tower. Lovely suit. Is Cat not here? Creeping through the ventilation, perhaps?' He eyes the ceiling with suspicion.

'She's not here.'

'What a shame. You used to be so close, or so they tell me.'

'What do you want here?' I ask.

'Aren't we here to celebrate the work of an artist? I've followed your work with interest, Stefanie. And yours, Jack, very fine. Even yours, Professor, although that second book is a bit of a slog. What a bunch of strivers you turned out to be.'

'Is that supposed to be an insult?' I say.

'Not as such, no. It's just too bad it didn't quite work out for any of you. Jack, you're broke as your parents now, and Stefanie, even your kind feel the bite of age eventually. And of you, Professor, we need not speak. Who'd have thought you'd end up so boring?'

'I'm not done yet,' Jack says. 'Unlike you.'

'Touché, Jack. As I've recently learned, I'm due for a sad ending in a few years of my subjective chronology. But I was diverted into your year of 2015 by a certain party, and informed of my fate. I might perhaps change the past. It's put matters into doubt again. I could have a long life ahead of me. I could still rule the thirtieth century again, or – who knows? – perhaps the twenty-first.'

'Who told you?' Jack says. 'Who's doing this?'

'Shoot him now, Jack,' Stefanie says.

'Do you really want to fight?' Sinistro says. 'From what I've been told, you barely managed to beat me before, and that was twenty years ago. None of you are looking your best. You look quite worn down, I have to tell you, while I remain – as always – in my prime.'

He picks up a last untouched glass of champagne from where it's been leaving a ring on the grand piano.

'Is that why you came here?' I say. 'To brag about being immortal?'

Sinistro holds up a hand, chugs the last of his champagne.

'Actually, it's not. I was just curious to see how you'd all turned out. And look – I didn't even have to ruin this party. You kids did it all yourselves. The Newcomers, broken at last.'

Jack draws his pistol but, fast as his CPU is, Sinistro is still faster. His cane slaps it from Jack's hand and it clatters into a corner.

'Always the guns,' Sinistro says. 'Don't worry, I'm going, but I'll be in touch, kiddies. Ciao, ciao.'

He turns his broad back on us, daring us to take a parting shot. The crowd parts for him and he's gone. The remaining Security staff rally to begin ushering slightly traumatized partygoers back to the elevator.

'Thank you for attending,' Stefanie tells the crowd. 'I hope you enjoyed this completely staged entertainment. Don't forget to pre-order and watch the videos and download the Snapchat filter, and there's a dance we made up if you want to make TikToks. Souvenir gift bags are by the door. Farewell.'

With the last of the guests gone, all the adrenaline leeches out of the room and we're just three old acquaintances covered in sweat.

'Don't touch the glass,' Jack says. 'I gotta see that DNA.'

'Was that really him?' I ask.

'Who knows? Do you think he clones himself? We don't even know what was keeping him alive in the first place,' Jack says.

'It's too weird not to be real,' says Stefanie.

She's right. The deadpan delivery, the familiar labyrinth of charm and double-bluff are more convincing than anything else.

Jack rummages for an intact bottle of vodka, soaks a napkin and swabs the cuts on his face. With the rhythm of an old married couple, he hands it off to Stefanie, who takes a swig.

'Congratulations on the album,' I say. 'I hear it's good.'

'It had better be,' Stefanie says. 'What happened to your chest?'

'Holy shit, dude, your chest,' Jack says. 'Meg did that?'

'Are you two going to date?' Stefanie says. 'Please say yes, it would be too perfect.'

'Thanks, but it doesn't seem like she's in the market.'

'Don't give up now. You'll work it out.' She dabs at a stain on her dress. 'This is ruined. What a disaster. My PR people aren't texting me back.'

'Are you kidding?' Jack says. 'They're probably out buying second homes right now. Video from tonight is going to have ten million views by tomorrow.' He earns a smile, one of her real ones.

'Who would like to tell me what happened here? I turned my back for ten minutes.'

'Stefanie had this on her,' Jack says. He holds up a small circle of metal, quartered black and red.

'You had no right to look in my bag,' Stefanie says.

'Well, put it somewhere safe next time. It was practically falling out of your bra.'

'Do you see any pockets on this dress?'

'So that's it?' I ask. 'You're the one who told him?'

'That's it. Hail to Sinistro, and all that, I made the deal. I knew you wouldn't understand. Barry certainly didn't.'

'You know, I think I need a minute?' Jack says. 'You two work this out. I gotta make some calls.' His voice actually shakes a little, as bad as the time Potsworth told him his tax shelters were gone. Yanking the patio doors open takes him two tries.

Stefanie flips a lime-green vinyl couch back upright and collapses down on it.

'You'd think he'd be less judgmental after the bees thing,' she says. 'Barry didn't come with you, did he?'

'He thought it might be a little awkward.'

'Don't tell him about this, if you can help it,' she says. 'It was just a strategic alliance. A few favors, then I'd get my throne back, and he'd get his.'

'He can't really be rebuilding his time machine, can he? It's impossible.'

'I think he can. I funded the time stream map – Prion's not cheap, even now. He's going to do the rest.'

'Why were you in my apartment?'

'I was supposed to get that amulet,' she says. 'He said he'd prefer you were taken out of the game.'

'So that's it? You sold us out?'

'Who's "us", idiot? I made a deal, one sovereign ruler to another. And Meg was right about him. He's very civilized when he wants to be.'

'He's a time-traveling psychopath.'

'I know who he is!' She levers herself off the couch and wanders over to the toppled bar. She finds an intact wine bottle and sniffs it. 'He claims he didn't kill Michael Ferris. Even he doesn't know who did that. So why not? I'm hitting forty and CAA is shutting me out. I keep telling them that's still my early twenties in faerie years. I'll probably live to two hundred, but not in this town apparently. Meanwhile Juniper's upped her bounty on me, shadowcats and every damn goblin in the Eastern Marshes have been crossing the bridge. Fuck this whole fucking year.'

'Why didn't you just ask us for help?'

'Again, who's "us"? My useless ex-husband? And don't even mention Cat, she'd laugh in my face. And what would you do? Mope in a library? You used to be a hero.'

'Well, you used to be a magic princess, and look how that turned out.'

Her look darkens, my skin prickles.

'I am still a magic princess. And one day I'll be queen, and I don't care what it takes. If that makes me your enemy, it's fine with me.'

'I don't want to fight you.'

'Well, you and Jack figure it out, then. I'll be waiting.'

Jack is leaning on the railing at the far end of the patio, looking down at the lights and the houses in the hills where he used to live with Stefanie. From this vantage, they look like fairy lights, and the air is as warm as it was on Middlesex Bridge. Maybe LA is the closest she could get to Summerdwell in this world.

'What was that about?' I ask.

'I had to fire the Scrabble guys. How did your talk go?'

'She sold us out to Sinistro. Sorry.'

'Fuck.'

Jack steps back from the railing. He heaves back and then throws his phone off the balcony as far as he can. The moonlight glints off it as it flies, tumbling to land with a tiny splash in the rooftop pool next door. A window lights up, then switches off again.

'Nice shot,' I say.

'That must happen to them all the time.'

'It's like they did it to themselves.'

Jack sits down on the warm concrete of the patio, back resting against the railing. The sliding door opens and Stefanie comes out and slumps down next to him, graceless for once. As tired as I've ever seen her.

'Jack, I really screwed up,' she says.

'Yeah, well. Lots of us did,' he says.

'Barry didn't. He never does. Can you imagine if he knew all this? That's why I had to divorce him.'

'Do you want to come with us?' he says. 'We're investigating stuff. Like we used to.'

'I don't know. Is Cat coming?'

'No,' I say. 'She may or may not be an additional problem in all this.'

'Well, what are you even investigating at this point?'

'Who killed Michael Ferris? Who has the Time Core, if Sinistro doesn't?'

'Can we not talk about it right now?' Stefanie says. 'Just for a minute. God, I just want out of this fuckhell dimension, I don't even belong here. My skin itches all the time and even the sun is wrong.'

'Yeah, this world kinda sucks,' Jack says.

'The Archduke says you have people,' I say.

'Please don't talk about it,' Stefanie says. 'Fuck!'

She yells the word, up into the LA sky, and we all look up as if following the words to their logical destination. Only a few stars are visible, the rest lost in the smog and Hollywood glare, the invisible map of the great Spindrift War being lost, and won.

PART SIX
1992

23

'Alex? The Promenade Trials are almost upon us,' Cat says.

We have a tacit agreement to stay away from one another, but apparently there is urgent business to be transacted while we occupy right fullback and goalie positions in a gym class soccer game. Our teammates are keeping the ball past midfield.

'We just say "prom". But yeah, I guess it's coming up.'

'Stef has found a date, as has Jack. We're in danger of failing.'

'Okay, I don't know if that's how I'd put it.'

'We need a date and also we're meant to have the best night of our lives.' She looks sideways at me, waiting for me to show concern.

'That's what they say.'

'And the punishment if we fail?'

'Well, it's not formalized but traditionally it's lifelong regret?'

She stops to assess this novel form of threat. I don't know what someone like her regrets or doesn't.

'Cat,' I say. 'Are you asking me to the prom?'

This time it's my turn to weigh up an unforeseen hazard. Do I want Cat as my prom date? I have to think pragmatically. Since CLEO began I've been even more of an outsider than before, but that doesn't mean I need to show up to senior prom with the Silent One. But is that so non-linear a move as to defy categorization? It would be a relief to spend the five hours with a person who knows what my actual life looks like.

'Don't worry, I don't necessarily like it any more than you do,' she says.

'All right, then.'

With surprising grace, a boy – Kirk? – on the opposing team liberates the ball from the thicket of flailing limbs, and begins to sprint downfield toward us. We jog into position for our defensive routine.

'You'll have to get a dress,' I say.

'Fine. Any number of soft targets possess these items.'

'Cat . . .'

I run out ahead, then make a dancerly pretense of trying to block the oncoming sportsman, who rightly ignores me.

'That was a joke,' she says as she backpedals toward the goal.

The boy patiently sets up his shot, entertains himself with a little footwork unrelated to any actual threat, then winds up and launches the ball explosively toward the upper left corner of the net, only to see it snatched from the air by Cat who lands, rolls and kicks the ball back downfield.

He can only watch like the audience at a tragedy as the ball soars over the heads of his startled teammates, propelled with such savage backspin that it seems to hover a moment before plunging into the opposing net.

The Promenade Trials have begun.

'Shall I call her parents?'

'Mom, please don't.' The plan was for six o'clock and it's already six-thirty. Cat wasn't in school today. Did she run for it? The requisite corsage lies helpless on the couch cushions, a tangle of lilies and baby's breath and bits of grass. Mom can't decide whether she's sitting in the living room or hiding in the kitchen and keeps changing her mind. I pull at the sleeve of my rented tuxedo and it refuses, again, to get within two inches of my shirt-cuff. Mom hates prom. We both hate prom.

We watch a shiny black limousine whiz down the block, two red-faced boys in tailcoats protruding from the sunroof. A beer bottle smashes in our driveway and they turn the corner onto Grove.

'What if I just call?' Mom says.

'I really don't want you to. And I don't have her number.'

'Isn't she your –'

'She's not my girlfriend.' And she doesn't have a phone. Or an address, parents, or a last name. There's screaming from outside, which could mean Cat has arrived but turns out to be a limo, stretch this time, crammed with girls from my class, in pale-blue and pink crinoline. The driver looks at me and waves, then guns the engine. Tires screech, the girls scream again. The Promenade Trials are at hand.

'Isn't there anyone else you can call? What about that other girl, Stefanie?'

'Mom.'

Another stretch limousine, this one white, noses out past the corner. This one is so elongated it has to go partway into the opposing driveway just to manage the six-point turn that will take it left. I imagine the merriment of the kids inside taking drugs and making out, or whatever else rich popular kids do in giant limos. It crawls down our street and slows to a stop in front of our house like an alien monolith hovering above a Midwestern city. The uniformed driver emerges and opens the door for a small dark-skinned woman who emerges in an emerald dress. She smooths the front of her gown then looks up at the house, nervous for once.

'Cat?' I stumble down the steps.

The gown is silk, form fitting, spangled tastefully with more pearls, delicately draped over a body perfected on its own brutal terms. She has a choker decorated with pearls and she's done her best to cover the scars with long sleeves and foundation. I have to lean forward over her dress to hug her.

'You look beautiful.'

'Thanks. I had to spend the whole afternoon with Stefanie. Did you know there are special stores that are only for rich people?'

'Come in, come in,' Mom sort of screams from the porch.

Cat's smile is a clear imitation of Stefanie's but it serves. She climbs the splintered steps in three-inch heels with perfect ease. Her nail polish is a brilliant emerald. She did not come here to lose.

The pre-prom rituals play out, with Mom serving as prompter for an inadequately rehearsed play. She serves lemonade. It takes several tries to pin the corsage on Cat's dress, thankful for her superhuman pain tolerance. Mom takes our photograph with a disposable camera that she hands to Cat before releasing us to scatter down the steps to the waiting limo. There's a flash of amber lower back as Cat ducks inside before me into a rambling velvet-lined cavern longer than my own living room, strewn with couches and padded ottomans. Cat checks the corners before sitting on the far side. She extracts the camera from her bag and crushes it one-handed.

'Where did that dress come from?' I ask her as we pull away from the curb. The car is so wide I have to raise my voice to be heard.

'It was not my original plan but Stefanie asked me what I was wearing and my answer caused her physical distress. She took me out of class and we got manicures, then went to a lot of different stores where everybody knew her and they loaned me this dress. She hates the choker but that's her problem.'

'Wait, we're not picking her up, are we?' I say. 'Are you guys friends now?'

'No! I think she was practicing being nice to commoners, although she was not successful in that she was a bitch the entire time. But at least she gave us a mild toxin.' She holds up a leather-covered flask from her purse. 'A whiskey with a long name. It's very good.' She takes a swig and slides closer to pass it to me.

It's smoky and awful tasting but in a brand-new adult way. It makes the weirdness of the giant car, the clothes, and Cat herself, make slightly more sense. We're doing a new thing. The vehicle thrums as we pull onto the highway. People in nearby cars glance at us, a few passengers stare.

'Maybe Stefanie's not so bad,' I say. 'I should thank her.'

'We're not supposed to talk to her at the event. She mentioned you especially.'

'Ah.'

'She appears to be taking this very seriously.'

'I'm not sure that's how you win Prom.'

When we pull off the highway, I find the button and the ceiling panel slides away. We stand up and look out at Cambridge passing. Brick buildings, trees, and big houses my family could never afford.

'None of this is how they told us it would be in the Academy,' Cat says. 'In the briefings it was all rubble and ash.'

'You sound a little disappointed.'

'I always wanted to see the Harvard crater. It was glass-bottomed and filled with water and there were mutant fish.'

'I guess I'd be dead in that scenario,' I say.

'Hanover was outside the fireball but the shock wave

would have been lethal in most cases. Only the strong would survive.'

'Okay. Well, bearing that in mind, maybe we can see the evening in a more positive light.'

'We'll see,' she says.

Cambridge flashes by, and Storrow Drive, and the Charles River in the golden light of the setting sun.

'Not everyone hates prom,' I say. 'Maybe it will be the best night of our lives.'

'We'll see.'

Prom happens at the Cambridge Hyatt Hotel, an aging brick and glass ziggurat overlooking the Charles. Guillermo pulls in slowly so we make an entrance. Cat steps out in a combat stance ('Clear!') and I follow. I'm starting to feel nervous. It's not as if I expect to be made prom king, but it would be nice to make it through a milestone of adolescence.

But inside, I forget a little. I've never been in a tuxedo before. Tuxedo-me feels special, festive, and light as a paper doll. I've never been in a hotel like this, just the stubby chlorine-smelling motels we've stayed in on skiing trips. This is like a cathedral. The lobby runs the full height of the building, ringed with balconies and glass elevators. They put something light and sweet-scented in the air. We forget for a moment to be nervous, just stare upward and spin around for a second, listening to our voices echo off the white marble.

'Look at this,' Cat whispers, doing a Ginger Rogers twirl on the slick marble in high heels. Even a few grown-ups turn to watch. She does an elaborate runway walk. 'Heel, toe, heel, toe. Stefanie showed me. She was so pissed when I did it on the first try.'

Signs point us to Ballroom C. The prom's theme, chosen

by a class-wide vote, was 'Golden Age Hollywood', and there's a spotlit red carpet set up in front of doors framed by the cardboard-cutout facade of an old-fashioned movie house. I offer Cat my arm and we walk up the carpet as a hired photographer yells 'Smile!' and takes a flash picture. The voices of an admiring crowd come from a concealed speaker, reaching a climax as we pass through the doors.

Inside, the entranceway is lit so that anyone coming in has to make a grand entrance, whether they want to or not. People turn to look at the glamorous stranger on Alex Beekman's arm. When they start to figure out who it is, the buzz gets louder. The no-talking girl, dressed in a five-thousand-dollar gown, is the kind of drama everyone wants at a prom, I guess.

We hurry to get lost in the crowd. All around the room, boys in tuxedos grin and elbow each other, thrilled in spite of themselves with their boutonnières, gelled hair and grown-up finery. Clusters of girls hover, familiar figures made over into satin dolls with puffy sleeves, hair frizzed up or sprayed down or twisted in brittle up-dos. The daring have gone strapless or low-cut.

Cat leads us through the crowd, toward the giant cardboard letters spelling 'H A N O V E R' like the Hollywood sign. A tall girl going the opposite way bumps her with an elbow, oblivious. Cat turns to face her, and I grip her arm a little harder.

'What happens next?' she says, looking around.

'Next they give us food.'

'Is that all?'

'Then dancing. And then the Prom King and Queen are announced.'

'From what I read, that's usually when the trouble starts.'

Our seats are at a table under one of the fake palm trees,

wedged in among the debate team, triumphant this year, talking about college prospects and afterparties. People I know to talk to, usually, but tonight Cat's aura keeps them at a distance.

'Jack's here,' Cat says.

She points two tables over. Jack is all the way out of his seat, leaning across the table to make a point, his nasal voice carrying halfway across the ballroom. In his tuxedo and crimson cummerbund he looks like a blackjack dealer, although one of his French cuffs is undone, flapping as he gesticulates. A girl in a Ren Faire dress with Pre-Raphaelite curls looks up at him adoringly. She doesn't look seventeen, though. Is Jack dating a college student? Is Jack, in a larger sense, cool?

'Do you know anyone else here?' I say.

'That girl in the ruby necklace. I slapped her once because she was staring at me in the locker room. I don't think we're actual friends, though.'

'I could use some more whiskey.'

She holds our Cokes under the table and dumps in more whiskey. We tap glasses. We aren't the only ones with alcohol. A girl who changed into a miniskirt in the bathroom because her parents wouldn't let her wear it wants everyone to know. People talk about growing up, about the greatest night of our lives.

Cat leans her face close to my ear, bare arm pressed against mine. 'How long can you hold your breath?'

'What?'

'Nothing. I'm not stupid, you know,' Cat says. 'I know you think I'm weird. I know you'd rather be here with that girl Meg, or Stefanie probably.'

'I wouldn't go with Stefanie.'

'Don't lie. She's perfect. She's tall and white and looks like the fake pictures they showed us of happy non-mutated people.'

'I don't even like her,' I say. 'And we have nothing to talk about.'

'What do you and I have to talk about?'

'Well, we're both in CLEO. We both don't like Stefanie. And – I don't know, what do you do when you're not in school?'

'Train, mostly,' she says. 'And I read at the library – horror and sci-fi, mostly. They let you sit all day.'

'I read horror and sci-fi, too,' I say. 'I'm sure Stefanie doesn't.'

'I bet she reads it all the time and doesn't tell anyone,' she says. 'I bet she can't get enough of it.'

'Shit, there she is.'

She's made her entrance and is on a circuit of the room in a strapless pale-blue dress, sleekly tailored and fashionably cut, worlds beyond the puffy, awkwardly fitted local talent. Stefanie looks like what the years will one day make her – a princess and a star. A tall slender boy climbs onto a stage at one end of the hall, to wild cheers. He welcomes us all to Hanover High's Senior Prom 1992, and says a few words, then invites us to party down. This cues the DJ, who gives us Huey Lewis and 'The Power of Love'. The table empties.

'Dance with me,' Cat says. 'You have to. It's the Trials.'

We find a corner on the darkened dance floor under the cool gaze of a gigantic gold Academy Award, and accidentally close to where Stefanie is leaning into her date's broad chest. He's a mortal, a blond red-faced boy aglow with wealth and youthful command. Next year, he will be at Harvard, playing lacrosse and singing in the close harmony group. Stefanie smiles blissfully until she notices us. She wards us off with a panicked little headshake.

'He'd be dead in seconds,' Cat says. 'But he'd beg first.'

'I could take him, too,' I say. 'But we shouldn't.'

'In the Promenade Trials,' she says, 'pain can take many forms.'

'That's actually a good point.'

Depeche Mode starts up and Cat dances in eerie, sexy, snakelike movements. Dance, she seems to say, as if no one were watching, and as if you've never seen anyone dance in a movie or a television program, or seen a television program at all. Dance as if your nerve pathways have been enhanced by a factor of twelve and you don't care that you're in heels because you balance by internal gyroscope. The next song is a slow dance and we do what everyone else is doing, shuffling together in a slow pivot, my cheek against her rough close-cut hair.

'Are you drunk?' she says.

'I might be. Are you? Does alcohol even affect you?'

'Poisons don't affect me,' she says. 'Except when I want them to.' She leans into me again.

Things are weird tonight, I realize. Alcohol and tuxedos change things, and the music of Cyndi Lauper, the air of Ballroom C, grown warm and steamy from so many bodies. Everyone's changed as surely as if they were hit with a zeta beam. I'm dancing with a girl who most people think lives on pine cones, and I can't remember why I thought that might be a bad idea. Who else would I dance with?

A hand touches my arm.

'Sorry,' Jack says. 'But you should probably see this. Hey, Cat.'

On the far side of the ballroom, something is moving through the throng, pushing people back even as they crowd in to see it. A Korean-American couple next to us stops dancing. The girl stands up on a chair to see, steadying herself on the shoulder of her date's powder-blue tuxedo.

'Oh my god,' she says. 'He actually showed up.'

'Can you see anything?' he says.

'Not yet.'

'I'm not looking,' he says. 'I heard his whole face was gone. Just tell me what it's like.'

The crowd parts for an instant and I see what they're all looking at: Chuck Dubek has arrived. He's in a wheelchair, dressed in high dirtbag chic in a bright-white tuxedo, pink bow tie, and gold earring. His long hair hides half of his face. Two of his friends, new ones, trail behind him, along with a girl I don't know, in a short pink sequined dress. He stops every few feet for another student to say hello, lean down to talk in his ear or shake his hand as if he were a wounded veteran coming home. One of Stefanie's friends leans down to kiss him on the cheek.

'You should probably get out of here,' Jack says.

'It's cool. Potsworth says he can't say anything.'

'Potsworth isn't here.'

Whether or not Chuck can talk, I don't want to see him. I want to hide among the cardboard cutouts of Grant and Hepburn and Jimmy Stewart. Then the girl who's with Chuck looks straight at me. She nudges Chuck and points and he spins his chair around to look. He says something to his friends, then starts cutting through the crowd straight toward me, his well-wishers following along. He drives one-handed, the other arm motionless in his lap. It's an expensive chair. I hadn't known he was rich.

'He doesn't look like much. What do you want me to do?' Cat says.

'Don't stay for this. I think he just wants to talk.'

'Okay.' She squeezes my shoulder and vanishes into the crowd like a conjuring trick in reverse.

It's too late to pretend I don't see Chuck as he bears down on me. He's staring at me. The boy in the powder-blue tux stares at me, too, with an alarmed expression. I stare back, puzzled, but it all makes sense when I feel large hands clamp down on my upper arms. I'm lifted then thrown to the floor as 'Baby Got Back' rings out. I can feel the bass coming through the floor. *My homeboys tried to warn me.*

Two teenagers in tuxedos are standing over me, Chuck's friends. I start to speak but one of them raises a foot and plants it hard on my stomach. Around us is a circle of concerned faces trying to decipher the nature of the drama playing out. What would Chuck Dubek have to do with Alex Beekman? Stefanie is holding her hands low, fingers crooked in a spellcasting posture, anxiously waiting to see whether a supernatural brawl will sink her hopes of becoming Prom Queen.

Jack makes eye contact, points a finger like a gun, then quirks an eyebrow.

I shake my head. *Now, are you crazy?*

He shrugs. *Up to you.*

Chuck rolls to a stop in front of me, and holds up his one good hand to silence the crowd. He still has a bully's charisma. His friends pull me to my feet.

Under the greasy hair, the left half of his face is mostly white scar tissue. The eye and ear are gone. I hit him hard.

'Alex,' he says. He's missing a few teeth as well.

'Hi, Chuck. I'm sorry about your accident.'

He leans forward in the chair, shaking the girl's hand off.

'Don't worry, babe. Come here, Alex,' he says. 'Let's talk.'

I step close to him. He waits for me to realize I have to bend down.

'I know it was you,' he says, his breath on my neck.

'I didn't know what it would do.'

'I don't believe you.'

'I'm sorry,' I say. 'I'm so sorry.'

'I told my pastor what really happened. He said I should forgive you. We prayed on it.'

'Thank you.' I start to straighten up but he jerks me back down by my lapel.

'I know that only the Lord can judge. I hope the Holy Spirit guides you where you need to go. I hope it throws you off a cliff.' He releases me. 'Peace be with you,' he says aloud, then spins in place and glides away. The drama concluded, the crowd returns whence it came, to the dance floor and the punchbowl. Stefanie looks back at me once, regal and impassive, then turns her back.

'You okay?' Jack says. 'I thought you'd use the amulet.'

'To fight a guy in a wheelchair?'

'Why not? He deserves it.'

'Were you really going to shoot him?'

'I guess we'll never know. Fuck it, it's over, it's prom night. You okay?'

'Yeah, go party,' I say.

He whacks me on the shoulder. I turn to look for Cat just as, even in the middle of the ballroom, she finds a shadow to emerge from.

'Hi,' she says. 'I saw what happened.'

'I think I lost the Prom Trials. Can we get out of here?'

'I don't know. I had a pretty good time.'

'Was it the best night of your life, though?'

'The Terrorbots stalked the Despair Academy halls by night, and then I slept in the woods. It wasn't that amazing.'

We sidle to the exit, through crowds of drunk and happy teens. Stefanie is in a crowd of girls, tracking us over their shoulder even as she gives a toast. I wave and she turns away.

'We're going to miss Stefanie's big night,' I say. 'She's wanted this for years.'

'I think she'd rather have it without us,' Cat says. 'She'll celebrate with her proper caste.'

'What if she loses?'

'Oh, she shared her plans with me this afternoon,' Cat says. 'We're much better off at a safe distance.'

24

The great white limousine sails down Hanover's wide streets, eases around its corners to slow and come to rest at the embankment by the bridge where we dropped Cat off before.

'Do you want to walk a little?' she says.

'Sure. I can get home from here.'

We climb out and Guillermo nods and tips his cap, then sails off through the damp springtime air and away, leaving us alone. Cat trips her way up the steep slope and I scramble after, slipping on the wet grass and soaking my trousers. At the top are the old railway tracks, a pale barred track here and there overrun by the encroaching grass. Moonlight glints off the rusty metal rails.

'Does anyone ever use this?' I ask.

'No, it's a hundred years old at least. There wasn't even a real town here until they built it.'

She slips her heels off and, barefoot now, walks along one of the rusted rails, balancing easily.

'If you follow it this way, you go all the way into Boston. I used to walk into town to the underground fights, to make money. That's how they caught me, actually.'

'Do you really live out here?'

'Sure. Do you want to see my house?'

We walk a little further down the moonlit forest road to the din of crickets. I feel like the prom's spell has come along with us. Like we're still breathing something lighter than air, and we don't have to be ourselves again, not yet.

'There's a path off to the left. Do you have night vision?'

'Only when I change.'

She takes my hand and pulls me into the denser woods, to a clearing where the pine needles have been swept away. Her place isn't even a cabin, only an abandoned shed built out of corrugated metal, rusted through in places and patched with plywood.

'Come in and we can finish the whiskey,' she says, and squeezes in her beautiful dress through the narrow doorway.

It smells like damp earth inside but it's warm and clean. The tiny room looks like a prospector's cabin with a kerosene lamp, a hatchet, a pantry made up of a milk crate with half a loaf of Wonder Bread, a jar of Nutella and a jug of water inside. There are cinder-block bookshelves on two sides piled with textbooks and old frayed paperbacks and martial arts magazines. A mattress and thermal sleeping bag make a nest in one corner.

There aren't any chairs, so we each stand against a wall, taking little sips from the flask and passing it back and forth.

'I don't have company much,' she says.

'What do you do in winter?'

'I don't notice the cold.'

'Couldn't you go to a juvenile home or foster care?'

'Why would I want to? A bunch of yelling kids. I can't sleep near other people anyway,' she says. 'I like it here. I read, I train. Deer have started coming through.'

'It's nice.'

'You don't have to say that. You live in a normal house with a normal, still-alive family. You don't have to like any of this. Just admit that you're embarrassed that you took me to the prom. The girl who lives in the woods.'

'Cat,' I say, 'you're not –'

'I'm weird! You're weird! An old guy took you to a magic

cave and made you like a Greek god and you're still desperate to convince everyone you're a normal person.'

'It's my secret identity. To protect my loved ones from a world that hates and fears what is different.'

'Fuck your loved ones! Admit you're just scared. I bleed orange and can track fugitives by scent and my brain never stops telling me ways to hurt everyone in the room but at least I can admit it.'

'Well, maybe that's why I like you.'

'Oh,' she says, wrong-footed for once. 'Even though I really do live in the woods?'

'Like Peter Pan and the Lost Boys.'

She laughs at that. 'I'm more like Cinderella right now. I have to give this dress back tomorrow and there's a rip in it. Stefanie's going to scream. Whatever. I liked wearing it.'

'It's perfect.'

'You should come here.'

She smells of the night air and the perfume Stefanie had chosen. I've never kissed anyone except Meg, and this is very different. Cat stays leaning into me for a while, then turns off the lamp.

'You know we can do whatever we want in here,' she says.

'I know.'

She pushes me back against the corrugated metal. We kiss as my jacket tears a little.

'Hey,' she turns around. 'Unzip me.' Even in repose her back is tight and solid with muscle. She turns back, holding the fabulous dress against her chest, then takes a deep breath and lets it fall.

'You look beautiful,' I say, then remember, that was what the jail girl said. But she left and went to Paris.

'Is this okay? I kind of want to. Okay?'

'You know, I've never done anything like this.'

She laughs. 'Um, I think everyone who knows you knows that, Alex. I haven't either.'

'How do we . . . ?'

She puts a hand on my chest.

'I don't like to be touched usually, okay? You can in a bit. I'll start.'

Afterwards, we lie on the mattress holding hands for a bit until she puts her old T-shirt on, and that somehow makes her the old Cat again – Cat from high school and Saturday mornings.

'I can't sleep if you're here,' she says. 'I'll just be in tactical mode all night.'

'Okay.'

I get back into my rented formalwear and she gives me a hug.

I say, 'See you at school, right? Thanks for prom.'

'Yeah. It was nice.'

She whispers it in my ear then squeezes my hand and gives me a shove.

It's a two-mile walk home but it's warmer now, a misty night. I walk along beneath the amber street lights, from darkness to light to dark again. I can hear the thumping beat and the cheers and screams of an afterparty still going strong. It must be two in the morning, at least.

I walk slower and slower as I get near home. It feels like coming home after the Cave again, sorting through memories and trying to fix every momentous detail in place, to secure the joyous feeling that everything has changed irrevocably. Tonight I rode in a limo and went to prom, tonight I lost a fight and went home with a cyborg girl and ruined this mediocre tuxedo forever, and now the Promenade Trials are complete.

25

In the spring of 1992, senior year seems to telescope, weeks growing longer and lazier, eternal as Summerdwell twilight. Stoners and theater kids lounge on the uneven grass of the quadrangle. Senior Skip Day comes, but the four of us in our ankle bracelets stay behind. On Saturday mornings we open the windows to the sound of buzzing insects and the smell of mown grass, and even the National Guard troops crack open their helmets to let in the spring air.

As for us, we savor the drawn-out extended pause before the great changes happen and the future arrives. Kids from affluent suburbs expect a certain kind of future. I'll be going to Wesleyan after all; Jack will be going to Stanford, which is taking him despite his manifest contempt for the admissions process. Stefanie has deferred her admission to Cambridge until she's done a year abroad. Cat has another year of high school to go, and her test scores will probably see her through much better than anyone expects.

The Saturday after prom, we assemble as usual. Cat gives me a warning glance – not a cruel one, but I get the message to shut my mouth and keep my distance, which means I can stop worrying about whether I have two girlfriends or one girlfriend because I've returned to having none at all.

Potsworth announces that Assessment weekend is three weeks away.

'The Metahuman Investigation and Control Agency has taken charge of our little experiment,' Potsworth says. 'I will be there to coach and advise, but ultimately the agency will decide whether you're fit to rejoin society or . . . otherwise.'

Stefanie raises her hand but doesn't wait to be called on.

'What are they going to grade us on?' she says.

'Emotional maturity, control of your powers, positive integration with the community,' he says. 'That shouldn't be hard for our new Prom Queen.'

'So why did we have to write all these stupid essays?' she asks.

'Because if they ask you why you interfered with the mental well-being of your classmates, you might want to have an answer ready, other than "they deserved it".'

'But they did.'

'Then I wish you the very best of luck, my princess.'

On the morning of the appointed day, a chartered bus meets us in the parking lot. We all take rows to ourselves. Jack works his Rubik's cube feverishly, and Stefanie fidgets, tapping long nails on the metal armrest. We pull onto the Massachusetts Turnpike moving west. Cat is the only one of us who seems unbothered. She lounges in the aisle seat opposite me, reading a paperback book about a dragon fighting a different-colored dragon.

I wake to see a sign for Hartford, then sleep again, to wake again at the sound of the wheels striking the gravel surface of a narrow well-kept drive through a dense pine forest that crowds in against the bus. A motorized section of chain-link fence slides aside, then we roll on through neatly maintained grounds until we reach our destination, a concrete building designed in three wide glass-fronted tiers arranged like steps overlooking a wide slow-moving river.

When we emerge sleepily onto the concrete, Potsworth

is waiting with a pair of identically thin gray-suited, gray-haired men.

'Welcome, CLEO students. I congratulate you on your truly adequate performance in the program up to this point. These gentlemen will oversee your assessment for the weekend.'

The two men nod but don't speak.

'What are we being tested on?' Jack says.

'Metrics,' one of them says. 'And attributes.'

Potsworth grins and ushers us inside.

It feels like an expensively kept hotel, furnished with warm red and orange carpets, plate glass and expensive leather furniture. But also a lot of locked doors and, as we're led up to our sixth-floor rooms, Jack nudges me and darts his eyes to the ceiling. Cameras, lots of them.

My bedroom has a queen-sized bed, picture windows and a private bathroom with a bathtub. There are cameras here, too, and although they don't give me a key, I feel childishly grateful for all of it. I've never had a hotel room to myself before, certainly nothing as fancy as this. I sip the coffee they've left me and eat a muffin from a basket, looking out at what proves to be the Hudson River. It's the first nice thing my powers have ever gotten me.

It occurs to me that no one outside the testing has been told where we are. What happens if we fail? If we never come back, would they come find us? I think about smashing the glass and escaping. Could I swim the river? Swim all the way to Paris?

The testing is all in another section of the building.

I sit in a windowless room except for an obviously two-way mirror. I'm getting used to that by now. A fiftyish woman, Japanese by her accent, sits opposite me and reads from the account

I wrote the first day, about my meeting with Michael Ferris and everything that came after, up to the day of my arrest. She reviews it sentence by sentence, stopping here and there to clarify a detail, the exact color of Michael Ferris's 1978 Pontiac Firebird (gold glitter). I wait for them to ask about Megan Price but they don't act like they know about that either.

The medical exam is point by point the same as the day I was arrested, but when it's over, she purses her lips and says, 'We'll need to see Prodigy now.' I wonder when everyone decided that was his name.

The woman betrays no surprise at Prodigy's appearance, only begins the medical exam again, exactly the same. I smirk inwardly when the syringe breaks against Prodigy's skin.

A team of laboratory workers watch me deadlift a thousand pounds, perform handstands and backflips, hold my breath for twenty minutes, stick my arm into liquid nitrogen, molten lead and hydrochloric acid. They daub chemical solutions onto the skin of my forearm. They ask me to hold two clips attached to an electrical generator.

The entire time, no one speaks to me except to issue instructions, and no one steps closer to me than they have to. To them, I'm an unexploded bomb. A person of mass destruction.

A ruddy sunburnt man wheels in a tray laid out with a crossbow, two different pistols and three rifles, each labeled with a Post-It. The whole room puts on ear protectors, then the technician assumes a practiced stance and rapidly fires each of them into my chest. A technician sweeps up the splinters, shells and flattened slugs.

It's getting obvious. They have no idea what they're doing. They don't know what I am, any more than I do. Needles, sledgehammers, high-velocity rounds, all of it's going to break. It's pitifully irrelevant.

The sun is setting fire to the Hudson by the time they've exhausted their hardware and a final team of specialists files in. A woman chants under her breath while she brushes my chest and forehead with a sprig of holly. A man in a powder-blue jumpsuit and shaved head stares at me for a long minute, shakes his head at the doctor, who scribbles something on a notepad. Last is a sixtyish man, five feet tall with a priest's collar and an air of scholarly authority. He reads out long passages in Hebrew and Latin and several other languages and, lastly, the Lord's Prayer. I feel none of it, and they note this down, too.

When I return to being Alex, everyone visibly relaxes. The bomb has left the building.

I'm the first one back to the cafeteria, followed by Stefanie and Jack. Cat comes in last, with a nervous guard trailing her. She has a fading black eye, and the side of his face looks swollen.

'I'm not going to try it again,' she tells him. 'Please go.'

He backs awkwardly away.

Dinner is served: foil-wrapped airplane meals and a choice of soda. I tell them what I went through during the afternoon.

'They found a man of my own country who thought he could test me,' Stefanie says. 'A minor viscount from a minor province. He'll be killed when I come to power.'

'These tests are a joke,' Jack says. 'They did the usual brain scans, tested me on some straight math stuff. Cognitive speed tests, memory tests. If this is what they care about, we've got it made.'

'I think you're all going to die soon,' Cat says. 'You're stupid and you're going to die.'

Jack puts his Diet Coke down.

'I'm not stupid. You think I failed that exam?' Jack says.

She shakes her head, arms folded. 'They make everything nice at first. They give you tests because they know you like taking tests. They let you think you know more than they do.'

'Cat, this is just what high school is. It's fine.'

Cat says, 'None of you knows what high school is, or what adults are. You'll only learn it when they decide they're done with you.'

'Excuse me.'

Potsworth is standing in the doorway. How long has he been there?

'Beekman, may I have a word?'

I follow him to a borrowed office with bookshelves full of medical textbooks, overlooking the front lawn.

'Well, my boy? How are you feeling?' he says.

'Is this part of the test?'

He shakes his head. 'We haven't talked very much, just ourselves. Not since we had our initial meeting. Tell me, are you still in pursuit of that, let's see, Dark Adversary?'

'It's what I promised.'

'But he never explained why, did he?'

'The conversation didn't have a lot of specifics. He told me to save the world. To be good. I promised.'

'And are you? Good?'

'I can't be all that good. I'm in CLEO.'

He leans forward over the desk and looks at me with that same attention I saw when we first met, looking with all the intelligence and analytical power he commands.

'Would you show me the power?' he says.

'Is it required for the test?'

'Let's say that it is.'

I don't know what I should do. I want to show him, I want him to look at Prodigy the way he's looking at me now.

I whisper it. 'Raeclun.' The feeling is always the same, the sense of traveling a huge distance but not. I wonder what he sees.

He steps out from behind the desk and stands close to me, closer than most people dare. I can smell the sweet tobacco on his clothes, and Bay Rum aftershave.

'Well, look at this,' he says. 'Alex, look in the mirror.'

There's a small oval mirror on the wall, displaying the image of a ravishingly handsome stranger wearing my own querulous expression.

'Strength and beauty out of legend,' Potsworth says. 'You don't seem to think much of it.'

'It hasn't done me much good,' I say. 'I haven't lived up to it.'

'You must enjoy it a little. You don't have to lie to me, Alex.'

'Maybe a little.' I blush, remembering the shame and intoxicating joy of brutalizing those kids. 'Sir, can I ask you a question?'

'I'll answer if I can,' he says.

'The other one who was going to be in CLEO, the fifth member . . . was it Megan Price?'

He steeples his hands, gazes at me intently.

'How well do you know that individual, if I may ask?'

'A little. Did they ever find her?'

'Not as far as I know, but I don't know everything,' he says. 'She bested the retrieval team; I'm afraid we underestimated her. You haven't heard from her, have you?'

'No, sir.'

'Would you tell me if you had?'

'Between the two of us?' I say. 'I don't think so.'

'Between the two of us, I'd advise you not to,' he says. 'Now would you tell Ms DiDonato I would like to see her?'

*

It's past midnight but I don't want to go to sleep. Someone taps at my door. I open it expecting Jack, but it's Cat. She silently brushes past me into the room. She looks up to indicate cameras then beckons me to the bathroom and turns on all the faucets. When she leans to whisper in my ear I turn my head to kiss her, but she clamps my head in a hold that feels only temporarily non-lethal.

'Stop it. We need to talk,' she says. 'I snuck out earlier and did some exploring.'

'What if you'd been caught? You could have wrecked our chances for all of this!'

'I didn't take risks. Besides, they weren't watching. Unlike the rest of you, I strategically underperformed on those tests.'

'So what did you find?'

'The complex is much bigger than it looks. Security's very, very tight – high grade MICA operatives and private contractors with specialized weaponry. This isn't some community service program.'

'So? It makes sense they'd have people like that.'

'Do you truly not see how much trouble we're in?' she whispers. Her eyes blaze at me. Afraid.

'You don't think we're going to pass?'

'Nobody's going to pass! There's no passing! They'll take us away and tell everyone we screwed up and got sent back to jail and in reality they'll be dissecting our bodies for anything with useful consumer applications.'

'Cat, they can't do that. There's still due process, or something. And I think the four of us can handle it, if anything goes badly.'

'Jack's slow and fat, and Stefanie's going to break if she has to fight anything more dangerous than a girls' field hockey player.'

'Stefanie seems pretty tough to me.'

'A lot of people seem tough. Then they're in the Agony Maze. You at least might be a survival asset.'

'Might? I don't think anything can stop Prodigy.'

'Wake up, Alex,' she says. 'They just spent all afternoon looking for ways to kill you.'

26

At eight in the morning they knock on my door with my schedule for the day. Breakfast at eight-thirty, and at ten I'm to report to room 35A on the first floor.

The room has a plain-looking door but inside it's an entire boxing gym. Not that I've ever been in one but it's got heavy bags, speed backs, mirrored walls.

The man in the boxing gym is taller than I am, and older, thirty-five maybe. Square-jawed, blandly handsome, thick black hair. In athletic shorts and a loose sleeveless shirt, the muscles of his pale chest and arms are sharply defined, like an anatomy diagram.

He's shadow-boxing in front of a mirror on one side of the room, throwing quick combinations, each jab and uppercut neat and precise.

'Sorry, is this the testing room?'

He stops his workout.

'Jeez, you're just a kid,' he says. 'Come on in. You must be Alex.'

He waves me in. I wait for him to introduce himself or offer his hand. His face, in repose, still seems to smirk.

'You might want to change,' he says.

I look around for a dressing room and he laughs, a pleasant laugh, a man with no worries.

'I mean, change bodies. I've been briefed, kid.'

'Oh. Right.' I say the word and I change.

Prodigy's blue and white jumpsuit feels appropriate for once, like a gymnast's outfit. Unfazed, he tosses me a pair of gloves. Not true boxing gloves, just regular nylon gloves with a little padding.

'Let's go a couple of rounds,' he says. 'Nothing serious.'

There's no boxing ring, just a wide mat colored in red and blue squares. He walks to one corner and puts his fists up in an easy-going, practiced stance.

It's lunacy. An eighteen-wheeler would be a more suitable opponent, but all right. I've done a little shadow boxing but never stood face-to-face with an opponent, one I can't even hit. I square up awkwardly like a cartoon boxer or perhaps a dancing bear. He relaxes and drops his hands.

'How about I show you a couple of moves first?'

'Sure.'

I'm a little relieved. Anything to stop the charade. He puts a hand on my shoulder and turns me into a sideways stance and shows me where to put my feet, then how to put my weight behind a punch, driving it from the hips and legs.

He's a patient teacher, letting me try as many times as I need to get it right. I don't need many tries, though. It feels like Prodigy already knows it, in his muscles and hindbrain. Prodigy was always meant to fight.

He moves on to ducking and sidestepping, calling encouragement as I go. For a little while, I stop thinking of anything but balance and movement.

'You're really picking this up, Alex. Let's try it with an opponent. Try and hit me.'

'Yeah, I don't know about that.'

'Come on, I won't even hit back. Just try a few things I showed you.'

I don't want to disappoint him. I try a few jabs and uppercuts like he showed me. At first I'm tentative, still afraid of hurting him but he's too fast anyway. He ducks and spins aside from every punch.

Abruptly he fakes a jab at me and I flinch in spite of myself. He chuckles and for a moment I see the shadow of Chuck Dubek. What if I just knock him down once? Just to show him who he's dealing with. I press him harder, cutting off avenues of escape, backing him into a corner. It's only a matter of time before I connect.

Then, without warning, he stops dodging, practically leans into my next punch. I'm so surprised I don't even pull my punch and hit him square on the jaw, harder than any mortal man should be hit. His neck should snap, but it holds, unnaturally solid. He barely moves. It's like kicking a pile of leaves and hitting a fire hydrant.

Then I'm lying against the far wall, ears ringing, shoulders salted with glass fragments. A chunk of plaster falls on my head like I'm Wile E. Coyote.

'You're Keystone.'

'Bingo,' he says.

The man transformed by the mysterious theta energy into the unstoppable force and irony-challenged do-gooder that is Keystone. More than anyone else in the world, the person I'm supposed to be.

'I'm Prodigy.'

'Yeah, look, I'm just supposed to see what you're like in a fight.' He sounds a little bored. It's just a day at work.

'That's all? Just a fight?'

'You've never been in a fight.'

Up to now I've been pulling my punches a little. It's ingrained in me. Ordinary flesh isn't made to take the impact of Prodigy's strikes. A tenth part of my strength would be lethal.

He's waiting, his gaze a little amused and a little absent. He's thinking about the rest of his day. Fuck it. I hit him again, left jab, then a right-handed roundhouse to his fat face that he's not quite ready for. Hard as I can.

It knocks him back a step. His cheek reddens. He looks — not frightened, but befuddled.

'Are you absolutely sure you want to do this, kid?'

'You're a really good lab accident. I'm the Champion of the Cave, the Wizard's chosen, a thing of destiny.'

I step in to hit him again but he catches my arm and whirls me into a wall and follows up with a roundhouse punch of his own and the force is beyond reason. I hit the opposite wall and stumble but I don't fall. Can he actually hurt me?

He circles to his right, I circle to my left. We've both had a little training. I have a little reach on him but the fact remains, to hit a person you have to get close enough for them to hit you, too.

I jab at his chin, he jerks out of the way. It's hard to break the habit of pulling my punches. I jab again and he slaps it aside, hard, and with my fist out of line he steps forward, a blur, and then I'm flattened against the far wall, ears ringing. He didn't pull that one. I bet that, like me, he's used to overpowering anybody he comes up against. I wonder what else he has. I wonder what's inside him fueling all that power and whether he could be considered human.

I let him try it again and beat up my forearms, then I snap a roundhouse kick that folds him up, staggers him. I give Potsworth a silent thanks.

Prodigy is coming alive as never before. Fighting is a craft and I'm not a trained fighter but Prodigy seems built to fight. He has an athlete's grace and balance and what feels like muscle memory. Normally, my play would be to bull in and get a hand on him, and let my strength and toughness end the fight. But that means letting him put his full strength on me, and I don't know his limits. I don't even know mine.

I snatch up a hundred-pound barbell and throw it, like I

once threw the basketball at Potsworth. Keystone slaps it aside and it embeds itself in the concrete wall behind him. Plaster dust and mirror shards spray out from the impact. I try to charge in and a left uppercut spins me full circle before my face slaps the floor. His footwork is damned fast but he doesn't try to kick me. A boxer.

I hit out at him in combination, jabs and a roundhouse, and feel the solid smack of altered flesh on flesh, solid meat for once in a world of paper dolls. I'm standing up to Keystone, and why not? What is he, anyway – a gimcrack science project, an accident? I'm a fated king, the Chosen One, and whatever powers me is far, far older than what powers him.

And then we fight for real, the cameras forgotten. We kick, punch, wrestle. Knees and elbows hit flesh at full strength. I wonder what his limits are. I hit him because he may be the one person in the world I can't hurt, the one solid thing in a world of shadows. I hit him just so he'll hit me back, and maybe he hits me for the same reason. *Hurt me if you can.*

At last, though, he decides to end it. He dodges a punch and I stumble. In that moment he pulls back, seems to access something beyond what I've seen. I feel it gathering, see the punch coming. There's a purple flash and crackling like brittle dimensions breaking, and a moment's darkness. I find myself on the floor, nerves tingling, stunned.

The spell is broken. The room is awash in shattered glass, concrete dust, plastic debris.

He sits down beside me, back against the wall. His face shows a bruise, and his costume is torn half away.

'So did I pass?'

'Not up to me,' he says. 'I'll tell them you put up a good fight, though. Even if you're a nerd most of the time.'

'Yup,' I say. 'So can I ask you something?'

'Yeah, I guess.'

'So my body – whatever this is – came from a wizard. He was really clear that it had a purpose, that I was supposed to fight for good and go on a quest, all of that. But you got yours in a lab accident?'

'So?'

'You could just have been a villain. Practically no one could stop you. How did you know to be good?'

'What am I, an asshole?'

When I get back to my room, the first thing I see is a note has been slipped under the door.

BEEKMAN, ALEX

ASSESSMENT IS COMPLETE

5.30 P.M. RESULTS ANNOUNCED. ROOM 6A

27

They left some clothes on the bed for me.

I never expected a costume. Prodigy came with his own already, a white body-hugging one-piece with navy-blue trim. A blue line runs across the chest, to form a circle, a little medallion squiggle in the middle. Ancient symbol of a vanished something-or-other. The cloth is woven very close and fine, and can no more be damaged than Prodigy can.

I realize the costume on the bed is for me. For Alex. I didn't expect one – I'm the second-best body, at most Prodigy's hiding place.

They've given me a simple and precisely tailored bespoke navy suit, a necktie striped with white and a lighter blue, to match Prodigy's colors. I'm a little disappointed.

A technician knocks on my door. The elevator takes me up to 6A. A corner meeting room, with windows at one end. There's a long massive table with eight high-backed chairs and the walls are hung with large Japanese paintings, evidently originals. It has a slightly opulent feel compared to the rest of the building. This is where CLEO will end, one way or another.

The others are already here, wearing their own costumes.

Cat is in a simple sleeveless leotard, midnight-blue, with thin flexible armor plates sewn into the fabric. It leaves her exposed in an intentional way. It reveals the story her body tells, of being stressed beyond all tolerance, broken and then rebuilt. And then again, and again. The longer I look, the more the horror and its survival take on a kind of heraldic beauty.

Stefanie is in a long white slim-cut blazer over a finely wrought silver chain-mail bodice. Hints of forest-green piping, a nod to her royal house, and exquisitely tailored slacks over white leather boots give it a kind of Emma Peel quality. It manages to give her split selves, modern and medieval, princess and warrior, a single home.

Jack's costume is modeled on his original design, the silver and violet uniform of the galactic fleet commander of his greatest future. Except this isn't Jack's ramshackle construction but the true article, if there is such a thing, close-fitting but not quite so murderously exposed. They've given him a silver helmet to go with it, with a retractable smoked-glass visor. He looks ridiculous, not that he notices. The costume's maker saw it, though – that Jack is ridiculous, and that his very ridiculousness is the splendor of him.

My own clothes seem humble by comparison, but I can see a little more of what they are now. Prodigy has his own costume, but this is mine, Alex Beekman's. Prodigy's custodian, his origin-point. It makes a personage of him – not a hero, but a hero-in-waiting.

Potsworth comes in and seats himself at the head of the table, looking small in the high-backed chair.

'Sit down, all of you,' he says. 'Welcome to the final chapter.'

'I thought we were done,' Stefanie says.

'Almost, almost. I'd like to say a few words, first. I hope you're pleased with your uniforms. I designed them myself and, may I say, you look remarkable.'

Cat's eyes narrow. *Kindness is a trick. Always.*

Potsworth steeples his fingers.

'The Metahuman Investigation and Control Agency deems that the four of you have passed your Assessments. The Changing Lives, Expanding Options program is a success.'

I feel dizzy. Everyone's looking around the table, confirming it with each other. *We're fine. We got away with it.*

'Accordingly,' Potsworth continues, 'on Monday they would like you to report to the Metahuman Forces Training Center outside of Louisville, Kentucky, to begin your training as Metahuman Operatives, a position you will serve in for not less than ten years.'

'What?' Stefanie says. 'No. No way.'

'I'm afraid so. The government has no wish to let abilities like yours go to waste.'

'I'm not doing this,' Jack says.

'We don't have a choice,' Cat says.

'There is, however, another option.'

'Research subjects,' Jack says. 'Guinea pigs.'

Potsworth holds up his hands. 'Patience, please. This will require a bit of explanation. As you have no doubt observed, it's no accident that the four of you were attending Hanover High School at the moment of CLEO's inception. I caused this to happen, as I caused many pivotal events in the course of human history. I am nine hundred years old.'

As he speaks Potsworth undergoes a subtle transformation. His voice grows more resonant, his posture more upright. The whole room seems to contract around him as if until now he'd been consciously withholding his own majesty, his own charisma, and now he's letting it take hold.

'When I ruled the thirty-first century,' Potsworth intones, 'the Earth enjoyed a Golden Age until I was dethroned and exiled by selfish, envious inferiors. Immortal, I have traveled the time stream, bent on reconquering my rightful domain.'

'You're joking,' Stefanie says.

'Am I?' He waves a hand theatrically, a conjuror's gesture. Metal clamps spring from each of our chairs to pinion our arms and legs. A gag whips out from the chair behind my neck and clamps over my mouth.

'I've been a slave and a king, a temple priest and a thief. Sultan, emperor, pirate king. I sold fruit on the wide streets of Tenochtitlan and traded slaves in Antioch. Led countless armies and languished in countless prisons. I grew rich beyond dreaming, I acquired servants and agents in all corners of the world, yet always I have failed in my goal.

'Then I found the four of you, wild young talents of the suburbs, dismissed as valueless malcontents. But I see your worth.' He leans in, dropping his voice to a stage whisper. 'Let me teach you, mold you, and I believe that with your help, I can succeed. Join me, and together you can rule the world with me.'

'Your name isn't Potsworth, is it?' Jack says.

'I have many names. You may call me . . . Sinistro.'

My mind is racing. I've heard the name Sinistro before. A shadowy villain who pops up in the news sometimes, foiled in his latest scheme but always escaping at the last moment.

Sinistro stands, looks us over with his old professorial gaze, giving us a last glimpse of Potsworth.

'You have five minutes to decide,' he intones. 'But remember, it's all of you – or none.'

He stands, gives a slight bow. Before he leaves, he gently lifts the amulet from around my neck and places it on the table in front of me, before undoing my gag. He walks from the room.

We look at one another, dumbfounded. The lights of Jack's Thinking Cap are ablaze as he sifts the situation for an angle.

'Well,' Stefanie says. 'What do we make of this?'

'It could be a final test,' I say. 'To find out if we'll turn bad if we get the chance.'

'Alex is right,' Jack says. 'It's the simplest explanation. He's putting us on.'

'No. He's telling the truth,' Cat says. 'He never stood right or smelled right, and now I know why.'

'You can't really believe his story,' I say. 'That he's a time-traveler? That he's immortal? Nobody's immortal.'

'You don't know what's possible,' Stefanie says. 'You don't even know if Prodigy's immortal.'

'So, okay – say he means it,' Jack says. 'I'm not saying I believe it, but supposing it's true – could he get it done? Sinistro's always been middle of the pack, villain-wise. Nobody's odds-on favorite to take the prize. But with us on his team, plus a functioning time machine? I'd give us a shot.'

'You can't seriously be thinking about it,' I say.

'Why not?' Jack says. 'You heard him. MICA's going to force us to work for them. How is Sinistro any worse?'

'He's evil! He's probably murdered thousands of people,' I say. 'He owned slaves, and who knows what else he's done?'

'What country hasn't done all that?' Jack says. 'Don't you read the news? With Russia falling apart, everything in disarray, we'll never get a better chance. We could do this.'

'You're forgetting I already have a throne,' Stefanie says. 'And I bow to no one.'

'Really? Where's your crown, "Princess"? Where's your army?' Jack says. 'I don't see any Summerdwell around here. In fact, I've never even heard of it.'

'Don't flaunt your ignorance.'

'I'm with Jack,' Cat says. 'The people who made this world never gave a shit about me. I would tear it down.'

'It's wrong,' I say. 'Justice is what matters.'

'So what's your plan?' Jack says. 'Do your time for MICA, then what? Go to a second-tier law school, marry the first person who'll sleep with you, get a job. You'll sit up nights thinking how you could have ruled the world. Where's your justice then?'

'No,' I say. 'I swore to save the world.'

'Maybe this is saving it,' Jack says.

'It's nearly time,' Cat says. 'I vote yes.'

'Me too,' Jack says.

'I say no,' Stefanie says. 'And so does Alex.'

The door opens and Potsworth lets himself back in. He's taken his tie off now, and he sports jeweled rings.

'Well?' he says, smiling. 'Have you considered my offer?'

'Sir,' Stefanie says. 'I'm afraid we're going to decline.'

'Thank you for the opportunity,' I add.

'This is unfortunate, I have to say,' Potsworth muses. 'Very unfortunate.'

'I was gonna take it,' Jack says.

'Can we go home now?' Stefanie says. 'I need to talk to my parents about this decision.'

'I'm afraid,' Potsworth says, 'I can't let you leave, knowing what you know.'

'You can't keep us here,' I say. 'We passed and we're not delinquents anymore. That's what CLEO was all about.'

'Oh,' he says, almost sadly, as gas hisses from concealed vents. 'You thought there was a CLEO.'

PART SEVEN

2015

28

'This is Prodigy calling Adept. Over.'

'You don't have to say it like that,' Jack says.

'Fine, then Cat, this is Alex. Say something already. Jack, you're sure this works?'

'She's receiving,' Jack says. 'Maybe she doesn't feel like talking.'

'Do you mind? A little privacy, please.'

'Yeah. Sure. Good luck with your weird thing.' He shuts the bathroom door behind him and it's just me and the subspace communicator and the 2 a.m. quiet of headquarters.

According to the computer, Cat has been on a tear for about two weeks now. She's too professional to leave a proper trail but Jack's computer figured out how to work from negatives. Thefts with a complete absence of evidence; thefts that shouldn't have been possible in the first place. She's been plundering black sites, burglarizing museums and having an annoyingly good time.

Unfortunately, that's about to end.

'Cat? It's Prodigy. Alex. I have to talk to you. Do these things have voicemail? I think I'm in voicemail. All right, I'm just going to talk. I asked Jack to get the subspace communicator upgraded, and he finally did it. He rerouted it through a different dimensional realm this time. He says it's more secure but scarier, whatever that means. He says it's the price you pay for good encryption. Also, it only works from the third-floor bathroom.

'You probably have your own news sources but I don't want any of this to come as a surprise. We were right but also wrong. Yes, Sinistro is trying to reassemble the time machine. Stefanie is working with him, and she got him the time stream map. Jack and I busted her in LA. She's on our side now, maybe? I think she's going through something or other. She said to say hi.

'Thing is, Sinistro is scary but he doesn't actually have the Time Core. He never stole it, somebody else did. So now there are two players in this, both trying to build a time machine. Three players, actually, counting you. More on that in a minute.

'By the way, did you see that video? The one where we crashed Stefanie's party and I violated every condition of my Restricted Status agreement several times over, while facing down an Interpol/ESOC task force? That one. Probably you saw it.

'The good news is, I'm reinstated as a government operative. Costume, name and everything! It's a very delicate arrangement, with a lot of conditions. I managed to make the case that Sinistro is a threat again, and I have more experience fighting him than almost anybody else. Except Jack and Stefanie.

'And you, of course. But you've disappeared, and lately you're starting to scare the shit out of metahuman enforcement. In fact, there is now an enhanced task force assigned to finding you, which is kind of why I called, actually. That was the other condition. The task force is me.

'I'm not going to pretend this isn't awkward. It is. But I'm not the one who ran off with the stated intention of meddling with the time stream. You're welcome to come in from the cold anytime you feel like it.

'My license clears in forty-eight hours but for what it's

worth, a big part of me hopes we don't meet again. I hope wherever you are, I hope you're okay and treating yourself well. I hope you're sleeping indoors. I know you don't feel the weather much, but I hope you're hiding out in a hotel anyway, and getting room service once in a while.

'Anyway, good night, I guess.

'PS: Stefanie didn't say hi. Probably you guessed that.'

'Hi Cat.

'Can I just say how good this feels? Real missions, and I wear the uniform in public. I even had a fan wave at me. Someone remembered!

'Speaking of which, good job on the carnival of iniquity. Are you just robbing banks now? What was the thinking there? And your friends the Order of Nogrith, you know they're fascists, right? You might want to think about the optics.

'Oh, and guess what? Jack says he's closing in on Sinistro. He's tough but we think Barry might be a game-changer. It's actually pretty hard to figure out what Barry's powers are but at least he sounds confident.'

'Hi, Cat. Alex here.

'Good job, okay? Is that what you wanted me to say? Nice one. No one thinks about the Machine Intelligence Coalition anymore. Nth-generation self-evolved Pentium knockoffs. Very old school. So now you have your very own time stream map. I hope you're proud of yourself.

'Jack says that was the easy one, anyway. Good luck getting yourself a fusion plant or a portable black hole or the Seal of Solomon. Jack says he would really like to be left out of whatever this is, by the way.

'And you know, I get it, I really do. Everyone wants a time machine. I'd like one, too. I'd go back and tell myself what the amulet was, and how to use it, and try to get a little more self-insight. I could skip CLEO, spend a lot more time working on that quest, and go to college and be a famous hero and not get disgraced forever, and Michael Ferris would be alive. But I'm not doing it, am I?

'Yes, I know, no one likes a sore loser, but it doesn't look good on my end. My bosses suspect I'm pulling my punches with you. I'm not.

'Good night.'

'Cat, please tell me you didn't think you'd get away with that amateur-hour thing today. A Halloween-store nun costume? I was literally not fooled by that cheap disguise. And what was your exit strategy, a hall of mirrors? By the way, on the internet they're saying throwing stars is "cultural appropriation" now. Do what you want with that one.

'I guess it was nice to see you, even if it was just a "stop right there", "curse you" kind of thing. At least it was a connection. It's a little lonely in these parts. Jack and Barry are back to not talking. They're both still in love with Stefanie, and I leave you to picture how tedious that is. If you were back here we could be watching movies and driving around and complaining about them, and it would be more fun than sitting on the edge of the bathtub talking into a plastic box.

'Maybe it's more fun where you are. Crime is probably more fun, anyway – I never claimed otherwise, I just promised I wouldn't do it. You're lucky you never promised anything like that. I guess you promised all those Prion scientists you would murder them. And then you did.

'I hope this doesn't last too long. Good night for now.

'PS: You should have finished that master's degree! Just my opinion.'

*

'Prodigy calling Adept. Et cetera. You've made your point now. You're at the top of the FBI's Most Wanted Metahumans now, number one, so congratulations on that. I hope that's sufficiently hardcore for you. I hope you like your crimes.

'No word on our mystery foe, by the way. Sinistro's way ahead of all of us. Jack just barely stopped him from hacking the entire Eastern seaboard's power grid, which might have worked. But whatever, maybe you like Sinistro now. Maybe you're best friends! Good luck with that!

'Sorry. I've been pulling double shifts and my ESOC comrades aren't exactly friendly. That, plus insomnia, and some late-night drinking and movies with Jack, which is just him explaining why movie science is wrong.

'Did I ever tell you about that reality show I was on before? I guess I did. Sorry. I hope you're getting these messages. Maybe you don't check them, or you might have had the transmitter removed, which would mean this transmission is only going out to wander the scary alien forest dimension forever.

'Anyway. Good luck in all your endeavors, and see you next time. I promise.'

'Dear Cat,

'Was that a riddle today? Are you the riddle type now? You know how annoying that is, right?

'This whole thing is getting a little old. Tonight's motel is typical of the places they put me up at. It smells of mildew and it's raining like crazy where I am. I can see it puckering the surface of the courtyard swimming pool. I don't know if you can hear it in the background but there's a guy who keeps yelling "Darryl, don't you dare call 911. Don't you dare." I hope I don't have to go out there. It's fucking late already.

'Sounds like Darryl called 911.

'Bye.'

'Dear Cat,

'They're taking me off the case. Understandable, I guess. I guess they figured I wasn't really trying to bring you in. I still have Sinistro and Enemy X to deal with. Fair warning, you may get the Champions after you. At least you'll get another shot at Blackwolf.

'Better that way. I know you never cared about good and evil the way I do. It's not in your story, is it? Evil corporations, trauma and apocalypse and black humor, everything's a gray area. It's a grown-up's world, and I guess punishing crimes looks stupid to you. It looks stupid to me sometimes, too.

'The truth is, villains have a simplifying effect, morally, and without them things get a little bit rudderless. You're left with the larger systemic injustices, and thinking too hard about those is how a lot of people become villains in the first place.

'Anyway, Cat. I hope they don't find you, I really do.

'Do you ever think about how we don't have to do this? Kicking in doors, swinging from ropes, climbing masonry. I know you'll never stop, but it's fun to imagine sometimes. What if you were in an office somewhere doing nothing, taking phone calls, maybe in a school in the Midwest. It's a warm rain outside, wet coats hung by the door. Waiting to get through the week. Out of uniform – bad hair and secret identities forever. I wonder if we'd be friends?

'I'll see you someday, I'm sure. Maybe we'll only be a subspace thing for a while, and that's okay. Voices winding through the caverns of Jack's alarming dimension. Call me sometime. I'm listening.

'Oh, and when they come to get you, I don't care who it is, punish them pretty hard. Give them one for me.'

29

It's starting to get dark early, and Halloween decorations have gone up along the block. In the last temperate days of October, we watch films on the roof deck or in the library when it rains.

Barry's trying to get Jack interested in squash. They've gotten pretty competitive about it, and that usually gives me the house to myself in the late afternoons. So it's unusual to hear the clink of a glass as I'm climbing the stairs. My first thought is Cat, but she doesn't make noises. It could be Jack's cleaning robot getting sloppy. Or he and Barry could be back for an early happy hour.

The visitor isn't any of those people, looking up at me from one of the fat leather armchairs, dressed in autumnal splendor in a brown corduroy suit and a plum paisley scarf.

'Sinistro,' I say.

He looks the same as he did the first time I ever met him, and the last. Muscles like a bull, mind like Machiavelli.

'Hey, kid.'

'Are you here to try and kill me?' My hand goes to the amulet.

'Sit the hell down,' he says. 'Have a drink. My god, you young people are a pain in the ass.'

He swirls a glass of deep-brown fluid at me. I can smell the alcohol from all the way over here. One of his cuffs is unbuttoned. Is he drunk? Sinistro is immune to most known toxins.

He pours himself another, a finger of deep-brown liquor

from a flask, and one for me. He slides it across the coffee table.

'Is that our Scotch?'

'You've never tasted real Scotch. Have some.'

'I'll pass.'

'Suit yourself. And sit down already,' he says.

'I'll stand,' I say. Then it feels too awkward, and I perch on the arm of a couch.

'You know I always liked you, Alex? I don't care what people say, I always thought you were the cool one.'

He sips his whiskey but coughs as it goes down wrong, and goes on coughing. I wait, uncertain of the protocol.

'Can I get you anything?' I say, finally. 'Water?'

'I'm fine,' he says. 'Listen, kid.'

'I'm not a kid. I'm forty years old.'

'Forty years,' he says. 'I celebrated my fortieth on a slow boat down the Valles Marineris, where the water flows like syrup in the Martian gravity, with my golden-eyed bride-to-be at my side. How about you?'

'I took myself to the movies.'

'How nice,' he says.

'It was, thanks.'

'How old do you think I am now?' he says.

'A couple of years younger than when you died.'

'Touché. I suppose CLEO was a mistake. I thought you'd be grateful. I thought you'd have ambition. I suppose I have Generation X to thank.'

'If you're here for revenge . . .'

'If I were here for revenge you'd know it, believe me. Come on, have a damn drink before you die of old age like everyone else I meet.'

He's right about the whiskey. Marzipan and smoke, and a deep soul-enveloping burn.

'Jack and Barry are going to be back soon.'

'They won't,' he says. 'Jack's a real character, by the way. Smartest kid I've ever seen,' he says. 'The way he found you and Cat, all the way back in the Pleistocene. Watch out for that gadget in his head, though.'

'He's a good friend.'

'Trust me, you don't want to know what I know about friendship.' His hands are shaking visibly as he takes another sip.

Is he drunk? Just seeing him is weird enough.

'Are you all right?'

'Seven hundred and sixty years, and they weren't all good ones,' he says.

'You said you were immortal.'

'It certainly seemed like it at the time,' he says. He laughs again, coughs a little. 'Alex, I'm here to make a deal.'

'We don't want anything from you.'

Sinistro goes to the window, and I can tell he's preparing a speech.

'Oh, really! I happen to know you've got no leads. You have no idea who killed Michael Ferris or who has the Time Core now. I can help you find the killer, and the power source. And once you have them, you'll have the Time Core.'

'Why don't you get it yourself?'

'I'm Sinistro! The center of the web. I don't get my hands dirty if I can help it. And I thought I'd give you the chance to put the cuffs on your wizard-killer.'

'What do you want in return?' I say.

He turns and lowers his voice, the way he always does at this point.

'I need your help, Alex. My personal timeline is long but you've seen the end of it. I die on July 3, 1995, and I can't change that. But you could. Get the Time Core for yourself and go back. Fix both of our pasts, erase those mistakes. Beat that whatever-it-was. Get the girl, whichever one you're trying to get at this point. And make sure you and I never meet. Easy enough.'

'Why should I?'

'Why not simple gratitude? No? I can offer more, then. I'll promise to leave your era of history alone. I'll conquer the Earth two hundred years from now – which, from what I hear, is a lot easier. You'll never have to hear my name.'

'If I find the Time Core, I'll destroy it. You know that.'

'Oh, kid,' he shakes his head. 'You don't know yourself. Wait until you're holding it in your hands, knowing you can change your whole life.'

'Suppose I did,' I say. 'What are you offering?'

'To share my knowledge. I know which power sources can run that machine. There are three in all, but only one that's truly vulnerable.'

He extracts paper and a fountain pen from his breast pocket and rapidly writes out two rows of numbers on stationery from the Four Seasons Hotel. GPS coordinates.

'I wouldn't wait around,' he says. 'My sources say they'll get there within forty-eight hours.'

'I'm not agreeing to anything.'

'Say whatever you like. I know you're the type that honors a debt.'

He levers himself out of his chair and smooths his cuffs. I reach out to help him with the stairs but he strides off, no sign of weakness now. I hurry after his broad back as he crosses the entrance hall.

'Before I leave,' he says, stopping at the doorway. 'You should go easy on that girl.'

'What girl?'

'You know the one. In Paris. She's got a thing for you.'

'What? No, she doesn't.'

'She needs your help, Alex,' he says. 'You're the only one who can.'

He starts for the door, and I'm forced to trail after him. 'Wait! Is she okay? How do I help?'

'That Time Core's a get-out-of-jail-free card, and she's in a bind,' he says, ushering himself out. 'You might want to consider it. Or isn't that proper to a king?'

'What did you say?'

But the door shuts in my face, and when I open it, he's nowhere in sight.

'Sinistro? Hello? What did you mean?'

No one's on the street or in the sky above — no time-traveling emperors or anyone else — nothing but the wind blowing yellow pine pollen up and down the sidewalk, whirling it up into the sky.

PART EIGHT

1992

30

'Nice going, guys,' Jack says. 'You really took a stand there.' I can't see his expression because we're manacled to the same cinder-block wall. Cat and Stefanie are on the opposite wall.

They put our assessments to good use. Cat's manacles are twice the bulk of the rest of ours. Stefanie's have a fine metal filigree, silver or iron. I have been gagged again, this time more thoroughly.

'Jack, what is your analysis of our situation?' Cat says.

'He hasn't killed us, so he's got a plan. Brainwashing maybe, or implanted loyalty chips. Maybe he's already done it.'

'A princess chooses death rather than serve another,' Stefanie says.

'I'm not a princess,' Jack says.

'Nothing could possibly be clearer.'

Then we all just look at each other while the fluorescent lights buzz and I breathe loudly in and out through my nose. The room has a circular door like a bank vault, one air vent, and a drain in the middle that no one wants to mention.

Is this the end? I wonder about Jack's timeline, the perfect one where Jack Prime jets off to save the galaxy. Did Jack Prime ever get locked up in a basement? Maybe he did, maybe it built character. I wonder if my prophesied destiny means I have to get out of here fine so I can save the world. Although, when Mr Ferris described it he didn't make it sound like a locked-in certainty. More aspirational.

'I know I'm just a junior,' Cat says, 'but can someone tell

me which parts of this are in a normal graduation and which aren't?'

The door hums, clicks, and opens far enough to admit Sinistro. I can still see Potsworth in him, the same intellect, the same calm authority, but it has a touch more cruelty in it now. Potsworth would never have worn that canary-yellow suit, though. That part is pure Sinistro.

He gazes thoughtfully at each of us.

'You really want to go to college that badly?' he says. 'When I was your age I had conquered a province the size of Brazil. What the hell do these suburbs do to you kids?'

'Stupid man,' Stefanie says. 'If we don't come back, my parents will come looking for us. The rightful King of Summerdwell. He has resources you can't imagine.'

'My dear Princess, they are doing no such thing. I've already informed MICA that your progress in CLEO is unsatisfactory, and that I am extending your period of study indefinitely. You will remain in this private facility until I decide what I am going to do with you.'

'Why don't you just wipe our memories and let us go?' Jack says. 'Stefanie could do it, easy.'

'Ah, but who would wipe hers? You see the dilemma,' Sinistro says. 'I might need to do away with you all together. So what do you say?'

I shake my head emphatically.

Sinistro sighs and throws up his hands. 'But I need all of you. Wholeheartedly. And I don't believe you could make either of your cohorts stay quiet after this.'

His concern seems genuine. I wonder if he really liked me.

'My parents would pay you an honorable ransom,' Stefanie says. 'They have influence in the government.'

'You can't tempt me there. I've plundered the Aztec Empire, and looted the coffers of Byzantium the night it fell. And I have people in every government, the world over.'

'I'll let you live,' Cat says. 'This is your last warning.'

Sinistro smiles at her warmly. 'A brave show, Cat,' he says. 'I'd expect no less. I'll miss you.'

'I'll miss you when you're dead, but only a little,' Cat says. 'It should be in the next half-hour.'

'A half-hour! Really! And how will I meet my untimely demise?' Sinistro says.

'I was thinking about that,' Cat says. 'I wonder what they'll send for me – human or machine, or one of their hybrid creations. I wonder whether I'll know its name.'

'Who do you imagine is coming for you, Cat?' Sinistro says quietly.

'My makers.'

Sinistro looks, for once, touched by uncertainty. 'They can't track you.'

'They can if I let them,' Cat says. 'I reactivated my transponder while the others were asleep. They've had hours to airdrop a team. I would bet at least half of your security personnel have been reclassified.'

'You're bluffing. You'd rather die than let them take you back.'

'I'll die killing them. And you, if I can. That last part will be interesting.'

Sinistro stares into her face, looking for the bluff, but Cat's enhanced muscle control has the side effect of an unbeatable poker face. Then, when Sinistro has only just drawn breath to speak, the world goes dark.

'What's this?' he says. 'Sorcery, perhaps? I'm –'

A muffled grunt of effort in the darkness, then a scream of rage. The lights return to reveal a strange tableau. Sinistro's body is half-turned, spinning away from a violent blow, keys and loose change flying from his pockets. Cat has landed lightly where the momentum of her leap has carried her past him, leaving a trail of blood behind her.

She must have expected the kick would finish him. It certainly would have finished any middle-aged professor of education, but Sinistro is another thing entirely. Torqued sideways, he flows into a spinning kick to Cat's head that fires her into the far wall. She hits it with a sound like ball bearings in a sack.

She lands on her feet, shakes herself, and springs up to grapple with him.

Sinistro is a head taller and a hundred pounds heavier but she swarms up his arm and plants her feet for leverage, then locks Sinistro's shoulder in a ghastly wrong direction. He grunts, knocks her against the wall again, manages to pin her, her back twisted at an impossible angle. He strains, red-faced, his beautiful suit torn at the shoulder. Cat bends her knees, shifts her weight, and then Sinistro is lifted and thrown down, head first, his neck folding under him with a terrible crackle.

Cat crouches, vibrating with indecision, then snatches Sinistro's keychain where it fell. She traces one hand along the wall until she finds the master switch and we're free. I spit out the gag and we wobble over on numbed legs to gaze down at the once and future emperor of the thirty-first century, crumpled in a heap. The walls and floor are spattered with blood but Sinistro doesn't seem to be cut.

'Cat?' Stefanie says. 'You're wounded.'

She's studying her own left hand. The pinky finger is entirely gone, reduced to a stump. The bleeding has already slowed to almost nothing.

'The restraints were too tight.'

'You saved us, and Summerdwell owes you a debt. Remember that.'

'I will,' she says quietly.

Sinistro hasn't moved yet. I look at him, feeling queasy.

'Is he dead?' I say.

'No,' Cat says. 'He seems to be very durable.'

'Kill him,' Stefanie says.

'We don't even know how,' Jack says. 'Let's go.'

'He's right,' Cat says. 'I wasn't bluffing, before. Prion will close on this position within the hour.'

The complex seems deserted; except for a few stragglers they all seem to be above ground. The place is strange, a product of Sinistro's diggings. We pass rooms full of antique weapons, of books, of gold and silver candelabra, until we have to stop for Jack to rest. He bends over, nauseous.

'Say . . . the fucking word, Alex,' he finally manages to say.

And I do. With the change, everything seems to get both brighter and calmer; Prodigy's in his element now.

Cat points to Jack.

'Carry that,' she tells me. 'And the princess, if she needs it.'

Stefanie shakes her head definitively, but Jack just shrugs.

'Sorry,' I say to Jack. I tuck him under one arm like I'm absconding with a store mannequin or a large terrier, and follow the others at a jog. An alarm starts to ring someplace. Faint crackles of gunfire from outside.

Cat scuttles up a flight of stairs, comes back and beckons us on. We find ourselves in the room with the high-backed chairs and Japanese paintings, where the world made at least a little sense. Outside, Sinistro's people seem to be maintaining a perimeter but it's shrinking, meter by meter. I can't see the opposition, just moving shadows.

'Tartarus-class Extraction Team,' Cat says. 'They'll be in the building soon.'

As she speaks, a dark slender form with spindly arms and

legs flows over a low wall and yanks a man down from behind.

'That was Marco,' Cat says. 'He stayed with them.'

'I can't believe they want you this badly,' Stefanie says.

'They love me,' Cat says, distinctly. 'Hundreds of millions of dollars in defense contracts. I'm like nothing they ever made.'

Jack's watching out the window, his head flicking back and forth, up and down.

'I don't think there's any way out,' he says. 'Prion's got air support in place and the perimeter's collapsing. We'll be better off back underground.'

Stefanie walks to the window beside him.

'No,' she says. Her voice sounds oddly indistinct.

'What do you mean, no?' Jack says. 'They'll be here in seconds. We can't fight all of them.'

'What's the date?' she says.

'What? Who cares?'

'June 19th,' I say.

'Yes,' she says. 'What a mistake to make.'

Glass breaks elsewhere in the building. They must be coming in now.

'I'm sorry,' Cat says. 'This was a mistake.'

Cat is in a combat stance, struggling to maintain composure. I've never seen her frightened before, not like this.

'It's all right,' Stefanie says.

Her eyes are aglow with silvery light, and she's smiling a wicked smile I've only seen once before.

'What the fuck are you talking about?' Jack says.

'They should have known. Tonight is Midsummer's Eve,' Stefanie says. 'Tonight, we are all in Summerdwell.'

'Oh no,' Jack says.

*

Stefanie leads us out across the lawn. She walks with her arms up, palms facing out, singing continually under her breath. A desperate battle is playing out around us, Sinistro's mercenaries holding out against the Prion hit team.

As for us, we seem to be enveloped in a bubble of warm air and moonlit calm. The battle reaches us only dimly as we stroll along. I have the impression we are largely in another night entirely, perhaps one that took place centuries ago.

'Ding-dong,' Stefanie sings. 'Fare thee well.'

I keep one hand lightly on Stefanie's shoulder, as she tends to wander.

'This is stupid,' Jack whispers to me. 'The moon is a rock in the sky.'

'She knows that,' I say. 'I don't think it matters.'

'It's science.'

'Don't be such a Capricorn.'

A drone buzzes our lunatic sphere, then veers off into little swoops that seem oddly expressive of merriment.

'Get her to go toward the parking lot,' Cat says. 'We need to be far away before dawn comes.'

'Ding-dong,' sings Stefanie. 'Ding-dong bell.'

Our meandering course through the grounds eventually takes us to the employee parking lot, where Jack has a Cadillac's door unlocked in moments, and the engine purring. It takes longer to coax Stefanie inside. Jack guns the engine and jumps the curb in a short cut, then crashes us through a gate. We fishtail onto the main road and he floors it.

'Did anyone see us?' I ask.

'I spread confusion behind us,' Stefanie says. 'They'll be a while figuring out where they are, and who is who.' Her trance seems to have dissipated.

Cat's gripping her left hand in her right. I'd forgotten all about the injury.

'Jack, look for a hospital,' I say. 'We have to do something for Cat.'

'It's nothing,' she says. 'I'm built to get hurt.'

Jack drives west through the night and into the rainy morning, and slowly the adrenaline fades. The Cadillac is warm, and the seats are wide and soft.

I wake to a damp gray Monday morning. We're the only car parked in an empty lot behind a lonely three-story office building whose white paint is peeling off. Besides that, there is only mist and trees. I dimly remember passing Syracuse last night. We must be a hundred miles beyond it.

Jack is slumped on the steering wheel, with Stefanie beside him, wedged against the door. Cat is curled up tightly in a ball on the floor of the back seat. All still in their costumes of the night before. I let myself out as quietly as I can.

The building is set back from a two-lane road that hasn't been re-paved in a while. I don't know why I feel like walking but I feel strangely buoyant. My old life has been cauterized by the weekend's violence. It's been disintegrating since the moment I got into Michael's car, and now it's gone. Maybe I didn't like it that much in the first place.

A couple of cars hiss past me on the wet street; passengers swivel to stare at the kid in the lovely suit. I keep going until I hit a little pocket of shops and a diner, then turn back.

The others are still asleep, curled like cats in their separate corners.

We find the diner again, old and hung with eclectic local signage. We huddle in a corner, hoping to pass for theater kids, seniors enjoying the tail end of one last cast party.

'None of this is our fault. We're the good guys. We'll go to the government and explain,' I say, once the waitress is gone. 'They'll fix this.'

'Sinistro's got people in the government,' Stefanie says.

'Assuming he survived,' Jack says. 'That Prion team was taking his operation apart.'

'He survived me,' Cat says. 'And the fourteenth century.'

'What do we do, then?' I say.

'We can build a cabin in the woods. There are lots of deer out here,' Cat says. 'The first few winters will be hard.'

'Thank you for your ideas, Cat, but my parents have a place in the Hamptons they never use,' Stefanie says. 'We need clothes first. We look like crazy people.'

'Clothes are in the mall,' Cat says. 'I like the mall.'

Stefanie insists on going in alone rather than suffer through another mall outing with her temporary peer group. She bums a cigarette from a pair of college kids by the mall entrance, flirting as if she weren't in a chain-mail bustier and at war with the most powerful man in the world.

An hour later, she emerges carrying three large shopping bags, one for each of us. She's already dressed in her usual Stanford-bound prep uniform of acid-washed jeans and a tasteful plaid jacket.

The rest of us change in our respective seats, awkward and looking at the ceiling, and emerge remade somewhat in Stef's image. Jack gets a bright-yellow polo shirt, I get a blue Oxford shirt and tan slacks, and a loud plaid blazer that seems to me unbelievably sharp. For Cat, Stef tries for an art school makeover, a baby-doll dress and biker boots, deep purple lipstick, and a lot of bangles.

We get out of the car looking like regular teenage friends – or at worst, a poorly chaperoned debate squad at an away match. It's beginning to sink in for me, that everything is going to be a little weird for a very long time. My world has shrunk to me and a genius and a faerie and a murderous cyborg – and we all live in a car.

We walk around the mall for an hour but then it's still ten in the morning and nobody feels like driving or fighting evil. On a group vote, we go to see an early showing of *Sister Act*.

31

With Princess Stefanie at the wheel, we speed through this strange post-graduation, post-CLEO world. For the first hour every driver that passes looks like a Sinistro plant or a Prion cyborg. But the drivers are just people coming back from vacation in the Hamptons or Cape Cod. The 1-83 is just a place to drive and listen to the radio. The car rocks gently on its cloudlike suspension and Cat has fallen asleep against me. Shutting down to heal, I guess.

No more high school now. No more classes, no more teachers or parents, no more anything except the warm afternoon and the road in front of us and the vast relentless invisible organizations that will hunt us until our last breaths.

A little past three we pull over at a truck stop. I think about calling my mother. Could they trace the call, or is that just a TV thing, and even if I did call, what would I say? *Mom, I'm going to be fleeing an immortal madman for a while. This is just my thing now, okay?*

We spend a little of our meager cash reserves on beef jerky and aspirin (Cat), Gatorade and batteries (Jack), Wheat Thins and cheap sunglasses (me), and 'nothing this store has to offer' (Stefanie).

Cat and I keep watch and wait for our turn to use the bathrooms.

'You okay?' I ask.

'It's not a big deal. I've lost them before.' She holds up her left hand, the stump of a finger healed over clean.

'Does it grow back?'

She shakes her head.

'They have a freezer full of them somewhere.'

A line of eighteen-wheelers roars past, each with its bow wave of warm smoggy air and promise of distant cities.

'What do you think you'll do? Later, I mean, when it's all finished. I was thinking I'll go to college and pursue my quest.'

'Once you and the other two are dead, I'll disappear into the wilderness and emerge occasionally to murder those responsible.'

'Wait, why are we going to be dead?'

'You didn't train for this,' she says. 'They'll catch you. And you'll die.'

'So, either way, neither of us are getting jobs.'

'It's not likely.'

After three more hours on the road, things are getting a little frayed. Jack keeps rerouting us according to some algorithm in his helmet. Stef is barking at him and breaking out from some faerie allergy to the car's metal frame. Cat stares out the window at the sunset, waiting (I assume) for our deaths.

But then we all forget everything when we round the turn on a crumbling parkway and the lights of Manhattan come unexpectedly into view. I've never seen it before, only held it in my mind as the far-off place where grown-up life is, the world of money and apartments and parties and strangers from all over the world.

Suddenly, our freedom seems real and more important than anything else that has happened to us. Even Cat seems impressed. I squeeze her good hand, and she squeezes back.

'That's where I'm going,' Jack says. 'Someday I'm going to own that town.'

And why not? Who, if not Jack?

This is what Meg was running away for, this dizzying freedom, this overflowing excitement. Just us kids, the lights of Manhattan spinning past us, Duran Duran on the radio, on our way to spend the night in a mansion by the sea. And tomorrow just more of it, and more after that. So fast nobody's ever going to catch us.

Jack drives us east into Long Island, to the Hamptons, and the houses get bigger and farther apart. It's ten o'clock by the time we find Stefanie's place by the sea. It's up on a hill, visible only in silhouette, turrets and gingerbread flourishes along the roofline.

Wobbly from the long ride, we follow her up the steps that zigzag up the incline. The wind is higher now, carrying the sound of breakers crashing on the ocean side.

Stefanie mumbles a code word, then pushes the heavy door open and steps across the threshold.

'We'll be safe for a day or two,' she says. 'You can't see the defenses but it's like a fortress. Mom and Dad set up the defenses themselves.'

She sings a trio of notes, and lamps come on, one by one, receding back into the house. The pale wood and high windows give it an airy open quality, so that the sitting rooms and salons rambling away into the shadows look almost like a faerie glade. Here and there, primitive-looking stone and wood statues decorate the place, some small enough to sit above the mantle, some looming up to the ceiling.

'Don't worry, the house won't tell my parents,' Stefanie says. 'We've been friends forever.'

'No one lives here?' I say. It seems impossible that such a beautiful house stands empty all the time.

'I'm not even sure my parents remember it's here. My grandmother had it built as a vacation home when she visited your world. She never thought we'd get stuck here.'

'Got anything to eat?' Jack asks.

'How should I know?' Stefanie says. 'There's a pantry someplace.'

'This place is amazing,' I say. 'Why don't you just live here?'

'It's Earth,' Stefanie says disdainfully. 'I'm not going to live on Earth. I'm going home to chop my sister's head off. You know that.'

I leave them behind and wander through a library, a map room. On the back porch I lean on the wooden railing, looking down at the beach. The wind has died, the waves are slower as they crest and flop onto the beach.

I watch them until Jack yells, 'Dinner!' then follow the clattering of dishes back to the dining room.

To everyone's surprise, Jack has concocted a three-course dinner out of odds and ends in the pantry. It turns out he has four younger brothers and a mom who 'has to lie down a lot'.

'Can we talk about a plan?' Jack says, once we've sat down to eat. 'What happens next?'

'Keep going,' I say. 'We can move pretty fast. Disguise ourselves. Get overseas, travel the world. How's he going to catch us?'

Jack shakes his head.

'I don't like to say it, but he's good. Even after they caught me, I had offshore accounts stashed away. This stuff was buried deep, I worked on it for years, and he rolled it up like it was nothing. I give us a year and a half at best.'

'Stefanie, couldn't you do some magic?'

'Given time, I could change our faces,' she says, 'or find sanctuary in one of the faerie dominions that would still shelter me. But I won't. I'm a princess in exile but I won't be a fugitive.'

That silences the table for a bit.

'We could go to the government, maybe?' I say.

'We're all breaking parole right now,' Jack says. 'And then who knows what story Potsworth will tell them about our escape? He knows how to play the system.'

'So that's it? We're fucking doomed?' I say.

'I think we need to calm down a little,' Stefanie says. 'Stay here and quit freaking out.'

She disappears into the back of the house and returns with three dusty, unlabeled, slightly irregular bottles, still cold from the cellar she found them in.

'If I have to host a slumber party, I may as well do it properly. These were sent over from the royal vineyards. Not dissimilar to a very high-end Pinot, not that you'd know the difference.'

'Aren't your parents saving this?'

'So what? I've been stealing them since I was fifteen. If they're not going to help get my throne back, they at least owe me a drink. I'll send them a few dozen cases when I'm queen.'

We all clink glasses. It tastes like grapefruit and sour peach, but also like mist and the foundation stones of the oldest castle in the kingdom.

We finish the meal and bring two more bottles to another one of the living rooms, this one with a TV, a sunken sitting area and a fireplace big enough that I could walk into it.

Jack flips through news stations to find an aerial view of the metahuman facility on the Hudson. Half of the building has collapsed, and smoke is pouring out. Words scroll by underneath: SABOTAGE AT INDUSTRIAL RESEARCH FACILITY – POUGHKEEPSIE, NY.

'Set it himself,' Jack says. 'Covering his tracks.'

He turns up the volume.

'. . . enhanced juvenile delinquents,' a woman's voice says. 'These are repeat offenders, now at large. Authorities urge you to report any contact with them as federal teams conduct their search for these dangerous metahumans.'

They have photos of all of us, our mugshots from the day we were arrested. Cat is defiant, with a black eye, Stefanie looks shocked and disbelieving. Jack smirks at the photographer. I just look tired and afraid.

'And now we'll go to Dr Sidney Potsworth, an educator specializing in enhanced juvenile offenders.'

And there he is, the kindly concerned Doctor Potsworth, as if he'd never been anyone else.

'I've worked with them, and these are profoundly traumatized, disturbed children. Fixated and delusional to the exclusion of any sense of conventional morality. In my opinion, they are untreatable.'

'That's right! Get scared, motherfuckers!' Jack says.

We all drink to that.

'Okay, enough with Sinistro,' Stefanie says. She shuts the TV off. 'Alex, let me see that amulet already. I want to know what it is.'

I toss it to her and she squints at it through one eye. 'What is it, anyway? Is it old?'

'I don't know. They said it wasn't.'

'They lie. Always. Especially about magic.' She sniffs it, touches her tongue to it. Dips a finger in her wine and rapidly sketches a circular figure around it.

'I can't sense anything,' she says. She holds it against her forehead. 'Raeclun.'

'Hey!' I say.

Nothing happens, but Jack snatches it and tries like before, then tosses it to Cat. 'Raeclun, Raeclun!'

I snatch it back, then change just to be sure.

'That is so fucking cool, you know that?' Jack says. 'Do you ever think about just never changing back?'

'No.'

'Liar,' Jack says.

He's right. I think about it all the time. 'Fine.'

'Think of the advantages. Prodigy projects self-confidence. Fun at parties. Women love him, men want to copy his drink. It probably has a bigger dick.'

'I didn't check.'

'Liar!'

He's right again. Not that it matters, but for purposes of intimacy, Prodigy is provided for on a scale poor Alex Beekman wouldn't dream of.

'What do we do when all this is over?' I say.

'It'll never be done,' Cat says. 'Not until Prion Laboratories is destroyed, and their evil ends forever.'

'Not until I have my rightful throne,' Stefanie says.

'And the Dark Adversary is defeated,' I say.

'And the galaxy is safe,' Jack says. 'We'll do it all – thrones, vengeance, justice.'

We toast again.

I used to know how life would be: high school grades in order, then college, then a job. Now we're in a future I never dreamed of, and everything's changing so fast, I have no way to guess what's coming. I only hope it's something like this.

With the third bottle gone, maybe a fourth, Jack wanders off to find a place to sleep, then Stefanie. Cat lingers long enough to kiss me then punch me in the arm, some semaphore from her private world that doubtless makes sense to her, then retires.

The house has three stories, and all sorts of out-of-the-way guest rooms. I keep discovering more, as if the house is its own kind of magic labyrinth.

The room I end up in has art nouveau wallpaper and

statues, and French windows leading onto a balcony facing the sea, and I change back into Prodigy for a little while. His eyes see more stars.

I wake at six, and in the sunroom I find Stefanie floating in the center of the room in a lotus posture, eyes closed, smiling faintly. Three dusty moons circle her maybe once a minute. One brushes the chandelier every third time it comes around. I want to ask if there's any coffee but it seems awkward, and it's nice to see her so relaxed, a break from her never-ending battle to impress her royal status onto the world. I fall back asleep on the couch next to her.

By the time I wake again, they're all at a thrown-together breakfast, cereal and eggs and whatnot, on the back patio.

'He's a spider,' Cat is saying. 'He has a web, a network. You said it last night, he plays the system.'

'Yeah, it's why we're fucked,' Jack says. 'So what?'

'That's his weakness. He pulls the strings. That means the strings lead back to him. We just have to find one.'

Jack frowns. 'I see it, I see it,' he says. 'But he's kept these things secret for centuries. Tricky to find.'

It's how they get people to join them.

'I think I know how,' I say. 'It's a thing I heard about in jail. We just need to find a sufficiently cool weird party.'

'I've never been to a party,' Cat says.

Jack and I look at each other, then at Stefanie.

Stefanie sighs.

'What kind of party?'

'Underground, I guess. People our age with powers. But, like, cool people and, like, mean . . .' I trail off, the truth being I've been to maybe two non-birthday parties in my life.

'So I get you drunk and I have to take you to a cool party?' Stefanie rolls her eyes. 'Fine, just not in New York. Chicago.'

32

We invent a new game based on which strangers we suspect of trying to kill us, and why.

We watch every car that follows us for more than two minutes, scout every rest stop, every roadside diner. Meta-human Affairs agents are the most obvious type – the boxy, fit Midwesterners who look up with affected casualness as we pass. Prion Labs agents are the ones who pretend not to see us – freelance killers, lean and expensively dressed, impassive behind mirrored sunglasses.

Sinistro's people are the real puzzle. Who would join an ancient secret society devoted to making a century-hopping narcissist ruler of the known world? What exactly is the big draw? We look at lonely teenagers, older men traveling alone, but those are too obvious. What about the woman shepherding four children in the Arby's? In a life with no prospect of advancement, no place for the great mysteries, I might start answering secret society ads, too.

In the end, though, we don't find any spies, secret agents, assassins or cultists. Maybe they're smarter than we thought they were. Maybe they're just not there, and it's all drivers and vacationers and waitstaff who give us an extra look because we're a weird gang of teenagers with an expensive car.

We lose a day on a 200-mile loop designed to throw off invisible pursuit. That night, at a motel outside Cleveland, Stefanie pays for two rooms with faerie-conjured bills, and a feast of fried chicken laid out on the bed in the girls' room. Jack hotwires the second-floor soda machine for us, then the

Galaga game in the lobby. He and I play until late, laughing, breathing the damp chlorine-scented air from the swimming pool.

Afterwards, we lie awake talking about our powers, whether we can beat Sinistro, about Cat and Stefanie and whether they like us. The strange surroundings and late night make it easier to talk, like the normal rules aren't there anymore. Secrets tumble out, rising up into the dark musty air of the room. The loneliness of my father leaving; my fumbling toward ideas about justice. How hard it was for Jack to grow up super-intelligent. Psychiatrists thought he was schizophrenic until he learned to hide what he was. When he goes to sleep, his helmet LEDs slowly wash white then fade, apart from the burst of staticky cyborg dreams, like lightning in a clear night sky.

Stefanie knocks on our door before the sun can rise and her fifty-dollar bills turn back into yellow leaves. The sun is setting when we reach Chicago, but at Stefanie's direction we wait until eleven to arrive at the venue, a 1920s high-rise still with its art deco accents.

'Let's be clear, this isn't about having fun,' Stefanie says. 'We go in, mingle with the crowd, get recruited. Jack, your cover story is what again?'

'MIT sophomore. Physics major, big plans, genius unrecognized. Okay?'

'Alex?'

'Wesleyan. English major, magic amulet, society is bad. Working on a screenplay. I don't get why we can't make up our own backstories,' I protest.

'Because I'm in charge. Cat?'

'Oberlin. Olympic wrestler, just back from a family thing on Capri. I don't know what that is.'

'It's an island. And . . . ?'

'And my stepmom is a bitch.'

'Good. And you are all . . . ?'

'Eighteen years old,' we say together.

'You can greet Jasper if you see him. When you leave, it's "thank thee for thine hospitality". Nothing else. Don't get drunk, don't act like losers, don't accept any gifts. Embarrass me, and we're done forever, got it?'

The elevator has a chandelier in it. Stefanie wears a crimson cocktail dress salvaged from the Hamptons house, while Jack and I wear her father's collegiate-looking blazers, too big for either of us. Cat is still in her leather jacket and skirt look, the only thing she'll accept now.

The doors open directly into a dim, cavernous living room, instantly drenching us with soggy party air infused with pot smoke and bass-heavy hip-hop. High ceilings, tall windows, crown moldings; pocket doors leading off to more drawing rooms, bedroom suites. More Summerdwell wealth.

Until my eyes adjust, the guests are only dimly seen, laughing, shouting over the music, writhing against each other in villainous dances, waving red Solo cups full of who knows what villainous beverage. Gradually, I make out the silhouettes of wild hairdos, helmets, shapes I can't identify.

A tall slender guy, with Stefanie's same cheekbones and bright-blond hair, waves to Stefanie. In a blazer but no shirt, exposing pale skin and lean muscle and a thorn bush of Celtic tattoos, he's handsome at an uncanny, almost hypnotic level, a *bel homme sans merci*.

'That's Jasper,' Stefanie says. 'Do not talk to him. I'll do the formalities. Jack? You're in charge of – these.' She fans a hand at Cat and me.

'Follow,' Jack says. He shoves his way between the backsides of two beefy six-foot fraternity guys in coral and teal polo shirts. Cat slips easily through, I wedge in behind her.

Who are these people? Trust fund kids, dropouts who think their boomer parents sold out, got vampirism and decided to smash the system? Well, who am I to judge?

I remember the traumatized metahuman teens at Hayden, ripped from their lives, on the run, still numb from the shock of uncanny powers stamped into their terrified bodies. Instead, these are rich boys and girls in leather and pearls and skin-tight vinyl, or sequined dresses, or dark blazers, or just the sparkling aura of their own power. There are a lot of plastic implants and metal limbs, some still healing – elective metahumans, back from surgical clinics in the Russian republics and south Asia.

These people were never dragged from their houses like Jack was. At worst, they'd have been shipped off to expensive private schools, just as they might have been sent to luxury rehab. No wonder Stefanie was so angry to be put in a group with us. I would have been, too.

'You'd better think of a screenplay idea in case anybody asks,' Jack says.

A few people glance up at the word 'screenplay'.

I smile and wave at a cute girl with goat horns, just like a guy who knows someone at Paramount would.

We pass through glazed doors to another room of equal size, where Jack spots a folding table crammed with bottles of every color and proportions.

'Drink something,' Jack says. 'You're acting like you've never been to a party.'

He's technically wrong, but most of the parties I attended in high school were movie nights or related to a role-playing game.

'Rum and Coke,' I tell him, the only drink name I can remember. 'So how do we do this?'

'Shh,' Jack says. 'Just give off a vibe. Let them come to you.'

'What if they don't?'

'Buck up, man. You could wipe the floor with most of these wannabes. Rich kids who got a taser implanted in a Bangkok clinic,' Jack says. 'And you literally have two dicks.'

'Huh, I guess I do,' I say.

'They're not coming,' Cat says.

'You need to work on your vibe,' Jack says.

'I think I should talk to a boy. Probably away from you guys.' She snakes away through a gang of witchy sorority girls, somehow touching none of them.

'At least one of us is thinking. We should split up,' Jack says. 'Talk to people! Try not to be such a virgin.'

Wait, is Jack not a virgin? But he's off shouting a question to a pair of witchy girls in tennis skirts, and then the crowd flows between us and he's gone.

I start a slow circuit of the party. The volume of the party is rising. Girls are dancing with each other, guys moving in time behind them. A moment ago I'd fancied myself at least adequately dressed, and now I feel every tug and crease of the ill-fitting jacket.

It's true that evil people look different and, it has to be said, a bit more attractive. Maybe because they chose to be who they are, maybe because they're better at not caring what people think. Even the blatantly misshapen or demi-human among them have a swagger. They all certainly dance better.

I duck through a forest of horns, claws, Plasteel armor, colorful bodysuits over perfect bodies. Tattooed girls in backless dresses arch themselves away from me as I pass.

Cat is in the kitchen listening attentively to a big rosy-cheeked boy in a blazer, Oxford shirt and rep tie, half undone. He puts a metal hand on her shoulder, leans down to say something in her ear.

'Do you like movies?' I shout at a girl passing.

She turns, her snake eyes unreadable, licks the air, turns away.

Am I not conspiracy material, accursed villain? Do you not like movies?

Well, my drink is empty anyway, and I must have walked in a circle because here's the drinks table again. I shouldn't drink so fast but I don't know what else to do at a party if I'm not dancing or talking to anyone.

Stefanie crowds in front of me, trailing her cousin and two tall women.

She leans down to yell at me in passing, 'You might want to give Prodigy a try.'

She might be right. I open a door in search of a bathroom but it's just a girl in black with long faerie ears, sobbing on the edge of a bed. She looks up to glare at me. The next one is a bathroom, tiled in black and white mosaic.

'Raeclun.'

Prodigy's face in the mirror is pointlessly benevolent, like a young doctor in a TV commercial. I squint and sneer, try to give it some shading of menace or malign intent. Isn't this the guy who put three kids in the hospital? But he looks handsome and innocent, as Dorian Gray might have. I give up. I'll just tell people I'm having a good week.

The party is still going at full blast. I edge around a trio of white guys rapping along to 'Cop Killer', grinning at the wickedness of it. I'm surprised to find Prodigy is a little drunk – or is he only thrilled to be at his first party? Either way, I must have lost track of time for a little because then I'm dancing with what might be a dark elf – are those a real thing? She smiles at me, which makes sense, because Prodigy seems like a pretty good dancer. He's just so cool.

'Do you know Sinistro?' I ask her.

'Sure!' She nods happily.

Does she actually think I'm evil? Maybe she can tell I have layers.

'Do you know where I might find him?' The phrasing doesn't sound very evil, but it's too late.

'Tanner might, he's totally connected. With the metal arm!'

'Thanks!' I say.

'Do you want to go somewhere?' she says.

The look she gives Prodigy is vulnerable and hungry, and undeniably attractive. I wonder if she'd ever give Alex that look.

I say, 'I'll see you later,' and hurry away from her hurt and angry face.

A knot of colorful and slightly translucent girls behind me scream with laughter. Through their pellucid shoulder tattoos, I spot a dark figure standing at a window looking out at the city. Her messy black hair spills out over a rather dingy army surplus jacket and jeans. Do people standing by themselves want someone to talk to them? Well, everybody likes Prodigy.

'Hey, do you want company?' I say.

She shrugs but doesn't move.

Okay. 'I like evil. Do you like evil?'

'Alex?'

Her hair is different, she's thinner, and maybe an inch taller, but I still recognize the first girl I ever kissed.

33

What should I do? This is the girl I thought I was in love with. Also, the girl who said she was going to destroy me. And then she disappeared, and an entire year passed. I joined CLEO and met people, and so many things happened. Cat happened.

'Meg. Hi.' Prodigy's voice carries well above the noise of the party.

She looks up from scanning the room, then her eyes catch mine and widen with recognition. Eyes dark and flecked with gold now.

'Alex. Oh my god. Hi.'

'Hi.'

'I didn't know you were going to be here,' she says.

'It was a last-minute thing,' I say, stepping closer out of the crowd.

But she steps back. At a gesture, a flutter of darkness clothes her chest and arms in glossy black armor, shining in the cheap disco lights.

'I heard,' she says. 'About your superhero ROTC program. Junior metahuman enforcement, whatever you call it.'

'CLEO.'

'If you're going to start something, you picked a really stupid place for it.'

Night-black blades curl out from her wrists and nestle in her hands, the edges smooth and sharp. She has better control of it now.

'It's not like that,' I say, keeping my distance.

'What is it like, then, Alex – or is it Prodigy?'

'Okay, yes, first of all, that's what I'm called. Second of all, it's not what you think. I was kind of goofy at first, and then it was nice, then it turned out to be an elaborate plot by a supervillain, and we had to escape.'

Dark eyes watch me for a few seconds, I guess waiting for a punchline.

'Wait, really?' she says.

'Yeah.'

'For a person who just wants to be nice to people, you end up with a lot of problems.'

'It's not funny,' I say. 'We're running for our lives.'

'Yeah, well, samesies,' she says. 'I guess we're not out of the woods, are we?'

'Nope,' I say, raising a glass. 'To mixed blessings.'

We both drink, and watch the crowd for a bit. A man in exquisite black tie, who seems to be a ghost, passes by. Partygoer, or just haunting the building? Should I tell someone? He throws me a wink.

'Good party,' I say. 'I mean, evil.'

'So do you know Jasper?'

'Stef does.'

'Stefanie DiDonato?' she says.

'Yeah.'

'Oh, thank god. I saw her half an hour ago and thought I was having a flashback. Wait, are you two, like, dating?'

'No!' I say. 'When CLEO blew up, we all ran away together. Me and her, and Jack Angler – and remember Cat who didn't talk? She turned out to be a cyborg assassin.'

'Oh my god. High school really never ends.'

'So do you live here now?'

'Sort of,' she says. 'I'm trying to get out. I just need to meet the right contact. Like that guy.'

She points at the round-faced boy Cat was talking to earlier — navy blazer, hair mussed now, shirt open a few buttons. He's navigating the room, holding a red Solo cup carelessly half-crushed in a metal hand. He sways a little, red-faced.

'Who's that?'

'Tanner Black,' she says. 'I talked to him before, I think he's pretty hooked up. That's why a lot of people are here.'

'So these are just wannabe villains?'

'Don't even talk about wannabes, CLEO kid. And yes. You get pretty tired of living in squats. The border's monitored and I just need people who can get me across. And you know? Some of them are pretty cool. The Musgrave Eight has great snacks, and then there's the League Sinister. You know — Sinistro?'

'Oh. Oh right, yeah, he's great.'

'So why are you at the party, anyway?' she asks.

'Alex!'

Jack is edging through the crowd. With his helmet lights flashing, he looks like a toy police car.

'Hey, Alex. Hey, cutie, what's happening?' he says to Meg.

Good grief.

'Hello, Jack. You're looking well,' she says. 'Megan Price. I know I look different.'

Jack recovers well, in fact does a stagey double take.

'It's the jailbird. Do you have any idea how much he talks about you?'

'He's exaggerating,' I say.

'I bet,' she says. 'What's that on your head? Are you a skateboarder now?'

I'm about to explain when thin strong fingers land on Jack's and my shoulders. It's Stefanie.

'Hello, everyone. And if it isn't the fifth Beatle,' she says. 'Hi, Meg. You look thin and weird.'

'Thanks.'

'Meg's on her way to Paris,' I explain.

'I just need to get hooked up with Sinistro's group,' Meg says. 'They're going to fix things.'

'Sorry, what?' I say.

Jack stamps on my foot.

'Sure, we know all about it,' he says. 'Sinistro's totally our guy.'

'Sorry, but I have to borrow this hunk of manhood for a second,' Stefanie says. She squeezes my shoulder.

'Sorry,' I say to Meg. 'Don't leave, okay?'

'I'll be here,' she says.

Stefanie beckons me to follow her to an empty corner.

'That's Meg Price now?' she says. 'Weird, I thought you guys were a thing.'

'What's going on?'

'Cat – you know, your other girlfriend? – is about to be a problem. Fix it, and then we're getting out of here.'

She cocks her head toward the bedroom hallway.

'Why me? Can't you do it?'

She raises one crescent eyebrow.

'Oh, I think you know why.'

The music has been dialed up, signaling a new phase for the party, and the hothouse smell of vinyl-clad teenagers is reaching eye-watering levels. I edge past thrashing lizard-persons in search of my assignment. How large is this place? Small groups and couples have retreated to the bedrooms, and it's beyond awkward looking into them. I soon become locally very unpopular. So it's a mixture of relief and unpleasant jealousy when I find the one where Cat and Tanner Black are furiously making out on the bed.

He's bent over her, at least a foot taller, and none of it is a pleasant image. I knock on the already open door, extremely loudly. Tanner looks up, his metal arm still on Cat's hip.

'Dude, do you mind?' he says, wiping his mouth. His voice is much higher than I expected, with a musically patrician New England accent.

'I think there's been a misunderstanding,' I say. Framed in the doorway, I feel more than usually naked in this leotard. I seem to have made an entrance.

'Oh, shit, is this your girlfriend?' he says, looking at Cat. 'I'm totally sorry.'

He rolls off the bed to stand. He's finding this mildly funny, and maybe it is. In fact, he has a plain likable face and a beery smile.

'Don't worry, I was just about to kill him,' Cat says. 'He used to work at Prion Labs.'

'I said it was an internship,' Tanner says. 'I graduated Northwestern in '90. I've only had this arm for a year. Anyway, why would you –' He stops, eyes darting between us.

'So, yeah, it's getting late,' I venture, but Tanner already has it.

'Son of a bitch,' he says. 'You're Cat. Oh my god, I'm such an idiot. Bro, she does not look fifteen.'

'I'm probably not,' Cat says.

'And you're Prodigy. The whole Eastern Cohort is looking for you people. Sinistro's gonna lose it when I tell him.'

'You sure that's a good idea, Tanner?'

'You're in the wrong place, guy. There are a hundred people out there who'd like to do Sinistro a favor.'

'You know you'll be dead soon?' Cat puts in.

'Cat, could you excuse us?' I say. 'I'm going to negotiate with Tanner here.'

'I can negotiate with people.'

'Why don't you let it be my turn? And tell Stefanie I'll be along soon.'

Cat shrugs and leaves, with not even a backward look for her erstwhile cyborg paramour. If there's any awkwardness to the matter, Tanner doesn't seem to feel it.

'Thanks, bro. She was getting kind of a crazy look, you know?'

'You're going to let us walk out of here.'

'Don't be like that. This doesn't have to be hard, man. Sinistro's a cool guy,' he says. 'This is going to put me on management track for sure.'

'Tanner, you're not even on track to get out of this room.'

'Oh, you don't want to be like that,' he says. At his full height he has four inches on me, and a hundred pounds. On Alex, I mean. He flexes his arm a little bit, just to make sure I've seen it.

'Last chance,' I tell him. 'You've been warned.'

Maybe he's less drunk than I thought. He moves very fast for somebody his size, and his metal-driven punch feels like it could punch through an engine block. It's hard enough to make me take half a step back, anyway. No cheap hydraulics for Sinistro's finest.

He shrugs out of his blazer, grabs something from the breast pocket, then snaps a thin steel baton out to full length, flourishes it in a quick figure eight.

'Don't be stupid,' I say.

'Sorry, kid,' he says, smiling. 'Homage to Sinistro.'

The metal hits my knee and ribs in rapid succession, faster than I can follow it and hard enough to shatter unenhanced bone. It hits my throat sideways hard enough to bend double, then snap back.

But it's still only metal, just like that tinker toy arm, just another gumball-machine augmentation bought with a rich kid's money. I snatch his lapel and hit him open-handed across his likable face once, twice, as hard as I dare. I let him fold insensibly to the ground. Just stunned, I hope. I close the door a little guiltily behind me.

'Where were you?' Meg says.

She's standing where she was. Jack is nowhere to be seen.

'Sorry. I may have had a run-in with your friend Tanner.'

'What's a run-in? Wait, did you fight him?'

'A little. He lost.'

'I need that guy!' she says.

'Don't worry, we're leaving.'

'Now?'

'Meg, come with us.'

'Are you serious?'

'I mean it. We have a car and everything. It'll be fun.'

She looks pained.

'Alex, no. I didn't break out of jail and put two heroes in the ICU just to go on a road trip with Stefanie DiDonato. I'm going to find Sinistro's people and they're going to get me to Canada and then I'm going to see the world.'

'Sinistro's the one who tried to kidnap us. He's crazy! You have no idea what real villains are like.'

'Real villains?' she says. 'Sun-Child and The Decade pulled me off a Greyhound bus. Full-grown men against a teenage girl.'

'My friends aren't like that.'

'You don't even know what you're like.'

'I'm a force for good.'

'God, you're fucked up,' she says.

'At least I'm not trying to join a bunch of villains.'

'You think somebody like Tanner Black is evil? You don't

get to make judgments, you're invulnerable. You don't have to care about anything, if it rains or if a safe falls on you. You're like a rock or, I don't know, a shoe; the world could end and you'd still just bounce around correcting people's grammar. Yes, he's a rich kid, and he had his entire arm cut off just so part of him could be a little like you.'

I'm looking for an answer when a high voice rings out. Not so amiable now.

'Hey!'

It's Tanner, still a little unsteady on his feet, one hand on the shoulder of a distressingly thin girl in black. In fact, it's the crying girl, her mascara still in streaks. The crowd parts for him.

'You know this guy, Blacklight?' he says.

'Who's Blacklight?' I say.

'Me,' Meg says. 'Hi, Tanner.'

'We meet again,' I say.

'This is the guy,' Tanner says to his maybe-girlfriend. 'His friends must still be here.'

'Tanner, this isn't what it looks like,' she says.

I didn't see her get her armor on, but she's in full darkforce mode now, blades out.

'Nice rig,' Tanner says to her. 'You want to stop this guy leaving? I can get you into the League right here, full privileges.'

'Oh, come on,' I say. 'Meg, let's get out of here.'

I reach for her but she raises an arm to ward me off, and then I get a queer sensation on my hand, as if a hot wire is stuck to my palm. I shake it but whatever it is won't come off. When I turn my hand over to see what's in it, it's empty except for the blood pooling there. I stare, stupidly, at the invincible flesh parted cleanly, edges white.

The center of the cut has gone numb but the edges are starting to burn and it's spreading up my arm. I've never been great at pain but this is, I think, something special. I can't even feel my hand now, just a localized cloud of agony.

I look up at Meg. She's looking at one of her blades, and the smear of red on it.

'Alex,' she says.

'Good work, Blacklight,' Tanner says.

I knock him down with my good hand, then stumble off balance.

'Wait!' Meg calls. 'I didn't know!'

I back away from the group, kicking over a drink, shouldering into a yelping partygoer.

Prodigy can't be hurt. He can't.

My vision is blurring. Should I change back? Would I be okay then, or would it be a lot worse? I don't know the rules now. If the darkforce can hurt me, what else can?

Stefanie, Cat and Jack are backed against the elevator doors, surrounded by a polite semicircle of empty space. Nervous partygoers are stealing glances at them. Word has spread, and people are visibly figuring their odds of stopping us.

'You took your time,' Stefanie hisses.

'Sorry.'

'Is that blood on your shirt?' Jack says.

'Yes. I think I'm going to pass out. Can we please get out of here?' I say, leaning on his shoulder with my good hand.

'Elevator's coming.'

Tanner, Jasper and the gaunt lady arrive to confer at the back of the room. Jasper has buckled on a slim sword and patches of silver armor at shoulder and forearm. The three of them keep looking our way. I don't see Meg anywhere.

'Come get us, Jasper,' Stefanie says under her breath. 'Please try it.' Her hands fizz with tiny lightnings. She is, I now realize, quite drunk.

'We can't fight all these people at once,' Jack says.

'What are you waiting for?' Stefanie calls out to the assembled party. 'You want to stop us?'

'Stef!' Jack shushes her.

'I thought we were supposed to be polite,' Cat says.

A man who must weigh three hundred pounds steps from the crowd. Cat leaps, coils and with a ripple of unspooling power, kicks him in the jaw. He sprawls backward, starts trying to sit himself up and keep a hand on his face at the same time. But others are crowding nearer.

'Bitch!' someone yells out.

Stef laughs and raises a hand. An eerie green light streams from between her fingers, throwing her cheekbones into gaunt relief. The crowd reels back from it, seemingly physically stricken. A rotten smell permeates the air.

Jack says, 'Jesus, Stef.'

'You have to teach them respect,' she says.

The room is clearing. The elevator pings behind us, and the wooden doors clatter open.

The night outside is wet and cool. Street lights twinkle in the summer mist as my ears ring from the silence. It's three in the morning, but the office buildings are still lit up and the lights of the Loop stretch away along the lakeside.

'I'm never going to one of these parties again,' Cat says.

'Let me see your hand,' Jack says.

I hold it out. It's not bleeding anymore, but still painful.

He says, 'I thought this was impossible.'

'Meg did it with her darkforce.'

'Yikes.'

He puts the car in gear and sets out for the highway again. Cat and Stef seem like they may be asleep already.

'Where to now?' I ask.

'We get the hell out of here. West, I guess.'

The adrenaline is wearing off and the hum of the car is already making me sleepy, even despite my throbbing hand. I can't help thinking about Meg, and whether we are enemies now. Because when she said she was supposed to fight me, it never occurred to me that I could lose.

34

Stefanie's enchanted leaves last us through Iowa, but sooner or later we know they're going to run out. We do our best not to talk about it. We listen to the radio as the stations change, play word games (Jack had to be excluded), or just watch little towns go by with all that emptiness in between. I watch the gray clouds piling up and up over the cornfields and feel like I'll never get tired of it.

Sinistro wasn't lying. His agents really are everywhere. In a truck stop outside Cedar Rapids, a pale puffy-faced man in a seersucker suit bumps into me, then goes bug-eyed with recognition. Stef makes him go glassy-eyed and walks him back to his patrol car, but it happens again, and again.

After that, we never stop unless we have to. We eat at drive-throughs, sleep parked behind shopping malls two nights out of three. Cat keeps watch at night and sleeps two or three hours during the day. It seems to be all she needs.

We get as far as the Omaha suburbs. We spend the last of the leaves at a convenience store and cruise through the Nebraska suburbs as the fuel gauge ticks down to nothing. Cat breaks us into an empty house. We stretch out on the bare floors to sleep while Cat perches in the unfinished rafters. Looking up at her, I think how like her namesake she is. Then I'm asleep.

In the morning, the light from curtainless windows wakes us.

'I'm not doing this anymore,' Stefanie says, over the last of the trail mix. 'I'm just not.'

'We could all get jobs,' I say.

She makes a rude noise.

'There are plenty of rabbits and birds,' Cat says.

'Does nobody else want to say this?' Jack says. 'We have superpowers. We can just take what we want. Nothing big, a few hundred dollars here and there can get us a long way.'

'I agree,' Cat says.

'Absolutely not,' I say.

'It's for the greater good,' Jack says. 'We won't do any harm. In and out, nobody gets hurt. Everybody's insured.'

'We're not turning villain. Stefanie, help me with this.'

'The laws of this land have no claim on me.'

'But it's immoral.'

'You've done worse, Alex,' Cat says. 'All of us have.'

'We could eat in a restaurant tonight,' Jack says. 'Sleep at a real hotel.'

'Guys, please. I swore a vow. To a wizard!'

'Where's that wizard now? I bet he's not sleeping on the floor. I bet he gets to take showers. We're putting this to a vote. All in favor?'

Everyone but me raises their hand.

'Finally,' Stefanie says.

'Okay, but I'm not using my powers,' I tell them. 'It's forbidden.'

We still have to find somebody to rob. We walk a long two miles along the sandy margins of a sparsely wooded two-lane highway through the July heat, getting swamped in exhaust by each passing truck.

The first sign of life is a gas station anchoring a lonely cluster of shops: a video rental place, a Wendy's, a nail salon and, down at the end, a pawn shop with a sign reading WE BUY GOLD in big red letters.

'That's the one,' Jack says. 'My dad goes to these all the time. They'll have tons of cash on hand.'

'Shouldn't we be doing this at night?' I say.

'They can't stop us,' Stefanie says. 'I'm not waiting around all day.'

We spend the last of our real cash on baseball caps to hide our faces, a screwdriver, duct tape and a few more batteries. I throw in a packet of Sour Patch Kids, hoping this will look like a summer school project and not a teenaged crime spree.

Jack touches my arm. 'Alex, let's hit the head.'

'Listen, Alex,' he says in the cool darkness under the guttering fluorescents. 'We can't screw this up. I need you to use those powers.'

'You know I can't.'

'There's no time to explain,' he hisses across the intervening urinal. 'I'm on a mission to save the galaxy.'

'Jack, are you okay?'

'I should have said this before. My future self told me. Jack Prime. Dude's amazing. I need fifty billion dollars and the Thinking Cap Mark XXII and then I go into space to win the Spindrift War.'

'Why are you telling me this?' I ask.

'Because it's important! I have to get this right.'

'Well, I think you're doing a great job.'

'Shut up! There's only one Jack Prime and an infinite number of Loser Jacks. I'm walking a probabilistic tightrope suspended over an abyss of non-optimal outcomes. So when we rob this fucking store it better go okay.'

'Okay, okay.'

'Just don't say anything to the others. Jack Prime didn't say anything about a princess or a socially challenged murderbot, so I'll probably have to ditch them at some point.'

'I'll try to hold off.'

*

'Stef and I will go in first,' he says, as we huddle around the corner from the entrance. 'She'll handle the staff, I'll sweep the place for valuables and find the safe. Alex and Cat will wait three minutes and follow us in. Act like you don't know us.'

'Cool,' I say.

'Showtime.' The bell tinkles, he and Stefanie disappear inside.

Secretly, I have never thought much of powered criminals at the low end of the scale. The tinpot samurai and minor telekinetic who will go after a grocery store or a strip bar — the ones that real heroes offhandedly sweep up on the way to actual crimes. People with powers should think a little bigger.

Now I see how stressful it is. My heart is racing. I count 180 seconds while flinching at every passing car. Undercover cops have a tell, right? Something with the license plates? I can't remember.

I try to browse the dusty display of watches and jewelry laid out in the window on sun-bleached red velvet. I bet Sinistro never did this. Cat nods to me. She takes my arm like we're teenaged Edwardians visiting a fine shopping emporium.

The warmth from outside dissipates in the air-conditioned cold and the smell of sawdust and old people.

A big white-haired man with a wide sagging face watches me expectantly from behind a thick shield of transparent plastic.

'Help you find anything?' he says.

'No, thanks,' I mumble. I look around for Jack and Stefanie. There was supposed to be a crime in progress by now, but I only see cufflinks and old *Playboy*s.

Still holding Cat's arm, I walk us slowly past shelves of

televisions and samurai swords, replica six-guns, and thick gold watches. I look them over with what I hope is the air of a connoisseur.

Stefanie is at the end of the military memorabilia, wide-eyed, motioning urgently.

'I told you,' Cat whispers to me. 'I told you she would lose it.'

We find Jack kneeling at her feet with an old boom box and a Speak & Spell in front of him, their cases already open. His quick hands are wrapping gaffer tape around a messy pistol-shaped bundle of wires and metal. The front end has a parabolic dish molded from tinfoil.

'You kids need any help?' the old guy calls through the grating. He sounds like a nice guy.

'Just a minute,' Jack calls. He slaps two D batteries into the stock and tapes them in. 'Got it.'

'What is it?' I ask.

'Follow me.'

He fast-walks up the aisle, holding it behind his back, and I trail him.

'Find something?' the guy asks.

'You bet,' and he pulls the pistol.

The man has an instant to panic, then sighs, falls back against the guitars and movie posters, and slumps out of sight.

'What the hell, Jack?'

'It's just sonics. He'll be out ten minutes, tops.'

Cat has no hesitation. She pulls a sword off the wall, jams it into a seam in the tough plastic barrier and starts working it back and forth. The blade snaps. She kicks at the tough plastic.

'I can't get a grip,' she says to me. 'You do it.'

'I can't,' I whisper back. 'I promised.' I glance at the clock.

How long? If we go back to jail, it's all for nothing. I change to Prodigy, who shoves the plastic shield until it cracks, then tears it out. I switch back to Alex as soon as I can. Maybe the Wizard didn't notice.

'Get the register,' Jack says. 'Gotta find that safe.' The beaded curtain rattles and he's gone.

The man looks smaller lying down.

'He's going to wake up any second,' Cat says.

I cuff him with a pair of handcuffs from the counter display.

Stefanie is looking out at the scratched front window.

'Guys? Maybe this was a bad idea.' Her voice has an edge of panic.

'I told you,' Cat says, working on the locked cash register.

'He saw our faces,' Stefanie says. 'We've got no protection, do you realize that?'

'It's going to be okay,' I tell her. 'Jack, how long?' I yell to the back.

'Jack?' I call. 'How long is this going to take? Jack?'

There's a firecracker bang and Jack stumbles backward through the curtain toward us. A man follows him out, younger than the other, and fat, with dark hair and a thin mustache, gripping a shotgun. In the tight space behind the counter it would be impossible to miss.

'That was a warning shot,' he says. 'Dad? Are you okay? What did you do to him?'

He trains the shotgun on me. We're losing a fight with a small family-owned business.

'It's not what it looks like,' I say.

But I can only think, *How am I here? How did being good turn into this?*

'You kids get away from him.' He's fumbling left-handed at the phone on the wall, trying to keep the gun on us.

'Drop flat when I tell you,' Cat says. She's got the broken-off blade of the samurai sword poised in her left hand.

A voice behind us says, 'You kids made a big mistake.'

The older man is on his feet and his eyes are a solid white light. He doesn't look so flabby now.

'Dad?' the younger man says.

Whoever the dad is, his eyes have gone a bright white. They pulse flashbulb-bright, and a shockwave knocks Cat and me to the floor.

He looks down at the two of us with more curiosity than anger.

'Well, I'll be damned,' he says. 'Homage to Sinistro.'

35

'Dad, what's happening?' the man with the shotgun says.

'Quiet, Daniel. I'll explain later.' Light from the old man's eyes gleams off wall-hung trumpets, electric guitars.

His son looks more shocked than we are.

'Who are you?' I ask.

'A Precept of the Sinister Elect. You two kids are a little bit out of your depth.' He digs in his back pocket and brings out a disk, the size and thickness of a stopwatch, the face quartered in red and black enamel. 'They're here, all four. Come get 'em.'

It's all he can say before a tendril of pink light curls around his waist and snaps like a whip to hurl him the length of the store. Stefanie advances down the aisle, letting the strand dissipate like smoke behind her.

'He's fine, sir,' Stefanie says to his son, her voice unnaturally calm and soothing.

The man nods, compliant, either from Stefanie's magic or the shock of whatever family drama we just witnessed. There are more handcuffs. For some reason the store has a whole lot of them.

It's still quiet as we hurry along, back toward the convenience store.

'Three hundred and two dollars? I hope that's worth going to jail for,' Stefanie says.

Her long arms chop the air. She's furious and a bit manic.

We all are. Someone is going to be arriving within the hour. Police or Sinistro's people, or both.

'It's enough to get us out of here,' Jack says. 'Keep your voice down, would you?' He's steering her by her elbow, as if she might bolt at any moment.

'We are never doing that again,' I say. 'Ever.'

'It turned out all right, didn't it?' Jack says. 'He was a bad guy, and we got that communicator.'

'It's still a crime. The son was innocent.'

'What a faker. They were being crafty.'

'That's insane.'

'The criminal mind,' he says. 'Wheels within wheels.'

The stolen cash buys us a full gas can and we start the long exposed walk back to the car. I can almost hear the sirens already but there's nothing to do but hurry along the roadside gravel and hope for the best. We've gotten barely twenty yards when we have to stop again.

Rounding the bend, perhaps fifty yards ahead of us, is a white-haired man mounted on a pure-white horse. He rides on the grass beside the highway, taking his time. He seems to be carrying a flag of some kind.

'Excuse me?' Jack says. 'What the fuck is this now?'

He rides toward us, heedless of the traffic that slows to watch.

'Back to the store,' I say. 'Maybe we can hold him off, whoever he is.'

We retreat, still watching him come to us, steady and unhurried. When the horse shies at an eighteen-wheeler's passing, his carriage stays perfectly erect. What looked like a flag is more like a long banner of green, white and gold.

'No,' says Stefanie. 'Wait.'

*

We stand at the edge of the parking lot and watch him come. He continues at his stately pace, then gives the reins a shake and the horse hops a drainage ditch and surges up the embankment. Behind us, the faces of Wendy's customers are pressed against the glass.

Up close he's just as impressive; a tall man dressed in a white tunic and green leggings, and wearing a short cape. Despite his stark-white hair, he looks no older than his late fifties. The hair is worn long and flows around high cheekbones and a firm chin. There's a scar under one eye and his nose has been broken more than once.

He dismounts, and kneels on the cracked pavement before Stefanie.

'Your Majesty,' he says.

He bows his head and the tips of his long ears poke out through the white mane.

'Who are you to address me so?' she says.

He looks up at her, handsome and grave.

'Long years have passed, but surely you remember Duke Zoriah, your father's oldest friend?'

Stefanie's eyes widen. In spite of fatigue and the shock of the morning, she manages a regal smile.

'Dear Zoriah,' she says, gently. 'Forgive me. Of course it's you. But have the long years muddled your courtesies? I am styled "Your Highness".'

The door to the video store bangs open. Stefanie doesn't appear to notice.

'Stefanie, my forms are correct. Your parents have been dead for two days now.'

'Dead?'

'A device was placed in their car. The vile Queen Juniper has already boasted of it.'

Stefanie's cool features convulse for a moment. One hand gropes for support and grips Jack's shoulder.

'You are Princess Regent now, your Majesty, and Duchess of the Great Undersea, Guardian of the Western Islands, and all other titles and obligations pertaining. Your parents' fortune is yours to command, and the throne is yours by rights. I have come here at risk of my life to pledge fealty to you, the trueborn heir.'

'Oh, Zoriah,' she says as she smiles and blinks away tears. 'We'll take it back, won't we? The Throne of Old Summerdwell shall be mine.'

'Before I die,' he says. 'I swear it.'

'There's a helicopter coming,' Cat says. 'We must prepare to fight.'

But we don't. The helicopter crests the trees and settles on the dead grass, and Guillermo waves and beckons from the pilot's seat. Men, women and children tumble from the shops to watch the true Princess of Summerdwell and her loyal band depart into the cloudless blue.

All through the helicopter ride, Stefanie sits in silent contemplation. When we land in Eppley Airfield we hurry behind her to the waiting limousine, only to have the nameless chauffeur shut it in our faces. Another, smaller one, pulls up in its place.

Stefanie's claim to being a princess never seemed false exactly, just that it only functioned to explain her mannerisms and as a trump card in the high school status game. So it's a shock to meet a whole world of real grown-ups who believe in it, too. By the time we get to her penthouse suite at the Denver Ritz-Carlton, she is already holding court with a dozen hovering mirrors, ovals and octagons showing the faces of matriarchs and patriarchs of the expatriate Summerdwell aristocracy, of all ages and colors. One is a talking badger. I even see Jasper's face among them.

She accepts condolences; conciliates, radiates grace and authority.

'I guess she really is a princess,' Cat says.

'Seems like it.'

'It looks nice. Can I fight her for it?'

'My understanding is not,' I say.

'It happens in books,' Cat says. 'She might try to have us killed, too.'

The other surprise that afternoon is when she adopts Jack as a kind of consigliere. She asks him about investments and advice on points of intrigue and law, and listens respectfully to the answers as if she had never snickered at bullies shouldering him out of the lunch line.

I suppose Stefanie finds it easier than the rest of us to leave high school behind. She always planned to.

It takes Jack only hours to disassemble the disk-shaped communicator he took from Sinistro's operative, and a day of driving around Denver to triangulate the signal properly. Another day to fly to Barstow and drive to the source. I'm perhaps a little surprised that Stefanie accompanies us, but I suppose a Princess of Summerdwell fights her own battles. Sinistro started this one and we're going to finish it.

Two days ago, we woke at dawn on a bare floor, thirsty, having slept in clothes we'd worn for days. Now, under evening stars, we abandon a luxury SUV by the side of the road like a rusty bicycle to walk the last half-mile unobserved along a barely paved access road under a desert moon pared down to a slim crescent.

We've run for a week now – or a year, depending how you

count it – since our powers threw us into our own personal teenage nightmare. Now those powers are what we're counting on against a centuries-old warlord. They fucked our lives up, maybe they can fuck up his.

Stefanie wears a silvered helmet and the finely wrought chain mail that I guess you can buy in Colorado if you know the right people. I'm in a leather jacket we bought at the airport store. Jack and Cat are in T-shirts. The desert cold doesn't seem to bother them at all.

Jack leads us using his makeshift signal tracker, checking the glowing LED display salvaged from a Texas Instruments calculator. He leads us off at right angles to the road, tramping straight through the iron-red rocks and spiny undergrowth, featureless apart from a charred circle from a long-ago campfire.

At last we come to it, a few low concrete walls, edges softened by weather, and a rusted iron plate a few meters square.

'This is it,' Jack whispers.

'There's nothing here,' Cat says. 'It's a trap.'

'I know from nefarious traps,' Jack says. 'This ain't one. It's clever, though. An old Titan missile silo. Nice work.'

The accessway is at the bottom of a sandy dry wash, anciently tagged with a peace sign in orange spray paint. Cat strains at the lock until it gives with a rattle of broken metal on stone.

Jack pulls a flashlight from his belt and points it straight down at a narrow metal spiral staircase. Cat sniffs the air and starts down. I take a last look at the desert stars, remind myself only one thing in the world can kill Prodigy and it's far away, probably trying on scarves and practicing its French.

The rusted metal and weathered concrete end a few flights down, replaced by shiny deck plate, modern fixtures, and air conditioning.

Sinistro's space plane stands upright where the missile would have been, a narrow matte-black cylinder except for the triangular wing and the gentle bulge of the central cabin. It's fueled and ready to go, the autopilot programmed.

It only takes Jack a second to see.

'Bait and switch,' he says. 'He's not here at all. He's up there, somewhere.'

'Absolutely not,' Stefanie says.

'I guess I had it wrong,' Jack says. 'Turns out you can insult Summerdwell royalty and live.'

'Never.'

'He's probably laughing about it right now.'

'Okay! You've made your point,' Stefanie says. 'Make it quick.' She shoulders him aside, flinching at the metal casing.

We descend into the cockpit. I lie flat on my back in a chair padded for acceleration. Next to me, Jack straps himself into the pilot's seat.

'Can you actually fly this?' I ask.

'I've been training on simulators since I was eight,' he says.

In the green light of the instrument panel, his face has undergone its own transformation, as profound as Stefanie's. For a moment, the smart-alecky kid is gone, replaced by Doctor Optimal, future captain and commander of a space fleet.

'Brace yourselves. We're going to the stars.'

He taps a lighted button and there is a rumble and nudge of acceleration, building to a moment of terrible pressure as the hydraulic launcher flings us up and out over the desert. For one terrifying moment we drop, starting to tumble, until the engines kick in, Jack pulls us vertical, and the shadowy desert and the lights of distant towns pinwheel away behind us.

PART NINE

2015

36

After 'Do you know Keystone?' the most annoying question I used to get asked was 'So... can you fly?' No. No, I fucking can't. Either the amulet's makers couldn't pull it off, or they decided to temper its wearer's hubris by leaving them prey to the law of gravity. I used to come and go by GalactiCar whenever possible, to avoid arriving at the crime scene dangling from the ankle of a more gifted metahuman. I've long since lost my metahuman connections, and the GalactiCar's wreckage lies where its last flight ended, on the upper slopes of K2.

As it is, I have just enough pull to get a seat on an Enhanced Operations personnel transport to Seattle that will pass within a few miles of Sinistro's coordinates. The only seating is a pair of narrow benches running along the unadorned interior hull, with nylon straps to hold us in place, me and a dozen or so operatives. A man and woman dressed in stylized versions of the Norwegian flag have seated themselves at the far front. The thing like an ambulatory tree turns out to be the legendary crime-fighter Crossgrain.

I sit across from two men and a woman, each dressed in head-to-toe black body armor, the kind that doesn't come off. Their armor is stenciled with a cartoon scorpion badge. Transhuman squads always pick something like that.

They're tough people. Their reflexes and muscle density are boosted off the charts, 360-degree night vision and two or three extra senses on top of that. They have enhanced hearing, too, and lean together to chatter almost silently in language loaded with metahuman enforcement slang. I can hear enough to know they're making fun of me.

I know why they don't like me. These are the people who wanted to be superheroes. The government has never accepted that we can't be manufactured in a lab. It's a thing that only happens in the wild; the chance convergence of history, desire, despair, wild talents, quirks of physiognomy that ought to kill us and usually does. Then, on very rare occasions, it doesn't and we stagger back from the catastrophe changed, life upended, clothes still smoking from our encounter with the sublime.

Tough as they are, these are the wannabes. They've each had two dozen grindingly painful surgeries and implants, and years of acutely uncomfortable super-soldier drugs, just to become second-rate versions of Cat. I'm an overhyped child star who went into a cave and came out with powers beyond anything they'll ever have. It would piss me off, too.

I stare at them and they stare back for the hour and a half flight to the target in rural Pennsylvania. It's an unassisted airdrop, which is what they do for people who can't fly but can jump out of a plane without dying. I hate falling – and frankly, it terrifies me – but I refuse to give the enhanced ops squad the satisfaction. I throw a sarcastic salute and topple off the loading ramp. Fuck them. They're probably on their way to ruin some poor teenager's life.

The site is a building surrounded by police and emergency vehicles, and a news copter is buzzing back and forth. I'm too late. The disaster has already started.

Whatever it is, it's happening in a wide, stubby concrete building. It might be a warehouse or a manufacturing plant. Nothing unusual about it except the lack of windows, and it's been built miles out of town and out of the way of normal traffic. Up on the helicopter, somebody slaps the cameraman's shoulder and points. Even if I weren't blindingly handsome I would be hard to miss, given I just fell out of a plane in a skin-tight bodysuit.

A white guy in plain clothes next to a police van looks stressed and maybe in charge. He's red-faced and looks a bit worn down by standing all morning near an unknown problem. He frowns to see me walking in out of nowhere. I hold my Metahuman Auxiliary badge up high and in front of me, so I don't take any gratuitous gunfire.

'Can I help you, son?' he says.

'Prodigy. Enhanced Special Ops. I think this one's my problem?'

He looks me up and down. He's probably not comfortable with adding an unknown metahuman to the situation (I don't blame him), added to which Prodigy's skin-tight uniform doesn't hide much of anything. Whatever, only one of us has been to Mars.

'Son, what exactly are you?' he says.

'I'm strong and things don't hurt me.'

'And why's that?'

'I really couldn't say.'

'Fair enough. Well, we got orders to secure a perimeter and wait for backup, and I guess that's you.'

'Do you know what's going on inside?'

'Dunno. It's just a government document warehouse. Most of the workers came out fine but they can't say much, just that it's classified and there's been an intrusion.'

'Do we know how they got in?' I ask. The building looks intact.

'Walked through the walls? Who knows?' He gestures at me and my funny costume. *Your sort of person, not mine.*

'Keep the perimeter,' I say. 'If anything but me comes out, try to make it non-lethal.'

'All due respect, we're just gonna shoot at it,' he says. 'Best of luck.'

I can feel the guns trained on the back of my skull the whole way to the front door. No one trusts any metahuman over a certain power grade, nor should they.

I used to do this all the time. The blank exterior doesn't offer any hint of what's coming, but at least it's not a bank robbery. If they rob a lab or a museum at least there's a plan behind it, some reason for wanting that one specific skeleton. With banks it's always the same – someone needs money. Sad, if you think about it.

The opaque glass front door is locked; I rattle the handle, then yank and the lock snaps. I pull it open. *Shoot me already*. Inside, it's just an ordinary reception area. It could just as easily be a dentist's.

Blue carpet, happy yellow walls, linoleum counter. Safety posters, a community fun board with photos tacked to it. *Please check in at the front desk, no exceptions.*

It's all intact. A few items lie on the floor. A purse, a coffee cup, a pair of sunglasses. People must have dropped them on the way out. A phone on the front desk rings, stops, starts again.

Okay. I used to do this all the time. I poke around behind the reception desk. The room behind it has a few more desks, a clock on the wall, obsolete PCs set up. They've been collecting dust. The whole place gives the curious impression of a stage set. Another door at the back is locked. I pull on it and it doesn't give, then kick at it but it doesn't move. I kick harder. It dents only slightly, which is odd. Doors aren't usually a source of trouble.

It's been disguised as an ordinary, hollow core door – but obviously, it isn't. I kick it a few more times. The sound of an alarm trickles out from deep in the building's interior. I finally get it deformed enough so there's a gap I can get my fingers into and I yank it out. It's three inches thick. A secure facility, then, and the designers had somebody like me in mind. Not to keep me out, but at least to slow me down.

The space beyond looks entirely different than the outer room. A bare concrete hall, five feet wide and ten feet long, and another door at the far end. When I step inside there's a deafening clang behind me. A door has dropped from a recessed slot, as thick as the previous one. The space is cold and almost silent, except for the alarm.

I feel a tickle of panic. I'm not exactly claustrophobic but I've always been afraid of the possibility of being buried. In theory, I could always work my way out, but it would be deeply unsettling. Then, the rhythmic pulse and thwack and hiss. *They're pumping the air out*, is my first thought, and I inhale by reflex. The pressure isn't changing, so it takes me a while to figure it out. *Not poison. Inert gas.*

It would kill an ordinary person, even most metahumans. Whoever the intruder is, if they came in this way, they didn't damage anything. An inside job, or they hacked the locks. Thinking, as I go to work on the door, who this intruder could be.

Cat, probably. There's no better, cleaner infiltrator. A standard Prion team might succeed but they'd leave a mess. Meg's a possibility – gone rogue again? In truth, the most likely candidate is Sinistro himself. Not the one I met, but a later edition. Or maybe earlier, maybe on some entirely different adventure. Everybody needs a good power source at some point in their life.

Kick, kick. Beyond is a workroom, windowless. Centrifuges, a drill press, a kiln, refrigerators, a lot of glassware. A materials lab. Jack would know, I wouldn't. A Bunsen burner has been left on. Nothing looks touched.

Another door down the end. It opens at my touch, to reveal an ordinary-looking room, but without furniture. Now what?

Another door slams shut behind me, and then it seems like the room is rising, but no, the walls are retracting to reveal another space behind them. I brace for whatever it's going to dish out.

The walls are crammed with a spiky confusion of objects. Crosses, crucifixes. Nazar charms against the evil eye. A board studded with colorful gems, another with dried plants. The smell of burnt sage wafts in, driven by a tiny fan. Scarabs, odd little faces carved of jade, bone, exotic wood. The floor is dense with runes and magic circles. 'Keep out' written in Latin, Aramaic, Greek, six other scripts I can't read.

A layered defense. If stone and argon don't faze you, maybe you're an astral projection or a vampire or one of ten other kinds of dead guy.

It doesn't bother Prodigy, however. Another door kicked in.

Beyond is a reference library, sealed and silent. Anthropology texts, medical reference, art history, political history, atlases, scattershot poetry. All of it well-used. Which makes sense, because I know what this is now.

I've heard about it, but never knew where it was, or if it in fact existed. Officially, it's the Federal Anomalous Items Repository, colloquially the 'Curiosity Shop'. Items recovered out of UFO crashes, deep caves, ocean depths, laboratory incidents. Weapons wielded by dimensional intruders. Stones that distort light around them, or buzz, or tell you lies about the future. The endpoints of stories, usually with bad endings. Things just too dangerous to leave lying around – and too potentially valuable to throw into the sun.

I turn the knob on the last door. It gives a quiet click, then opens without any resistance at all.

The room beyond is unadorned, just rows of glass-fronted gray shelves and filing cabinets. But the contents are like a museum out of dreams. The shelves hold strange and beautiful objects: tiny statues, wooden idols, carved gemstones, each tagged and labeled. A depressing row of mummified hands, fingers. Locks of hair. A stone image of a human-like frog, whose wide mouth exhales smoke or fog in a continuous stream. Some objects give off an inexplicable hostility, others seduce, begging to be touched. A row of mirrors I instinctively avert my eyes from.

A second room is focused on unfamiliar technologies. A needle-sleek rifle, a row of helmets, some fitted for human skulls and some not. Orbs and belts. Blackened fragments that must be crash debris. A third room of profane and sacred books. There's a room of bones, an alcove of teeth.

It's all so bewildering to the eye, for a second I miss the person standing in a doorway watching me.

It's no one I recognize. A knight in chrome armor. I'm so startled, when he punches me in the face I fall right over. I try to stand and he knocks me down again, so hard I bounce a little on the concrete floor. It's not a medieval thing, this is powered armor. I can hear the cooling fans running inside it.

'Who are you?'

Whoever ordered this armor has opted for the skull-face design, and their sword is embossed with flames, the edge a streak of white-hot light. I'm getting beaten up by the cover of a heavy metal album.

I throw a punch and they block it, hydraulics straining, then convert the momentum into a sideways cut that judders off diamond-hard skin, tearing the fabric of my costume.

Nope. I hit the skull face and the figure reels backward.

They shake their head to clear it – there's a person in there, for sure. I keep hitting, driving them backward from room to room. The knight dodges, cuts and thrusts, until the sword shatters on my skin.

'Who are you?' I say. 'Just tell me.'

Silence. He comes at me unarmed now, glittering and relentless, and throws a decent brown-belt-level roundhouse kick. I don't even bother to block it. There's a human being underneath that armor, and even armored bodies can only stand so much punishment. Another hit to the face, a third, and the knight goes down.

'Where's your boss?' I ask.

The reply is an obstinate stare from silvered-over eye sockets. A few rooms away, glass breaks. A second intruder.

'Stay down,' I tell them, and set off toward the sound.

Is it Sinistro? Is it Meg? It's not going to matter. I have skin like titanium, fists like cinder blocks, and a grip like Satan dragging down the damned. Sooner or later, they'll go down like Skullhead did. I kick in the door.

He doesn't even bother turning around. My first thought is, *Sinistro's really let himself go*. But no, it's not even him. Just a regular twentieth-century guy, and the silver leotard is no more flattering than it ever was.

'Jack?' I say.

'One sec,' Jack says. He pulls open the drawer of a filing cabinet, peers inside. He slams it shut and opens another.

'Dude, what the fuck?' I say.

'One goddamn second.'

He looks up, finally. He has a metal helmet and goofy-looking goggles like an old-style carnie daredevil. A small metal briefcase lies open beside him.

'Yeah. I was gonna text,' Jack says. He keeps on opening drawers, shakes his head at the result.

'Jack? What is this? Who's that guy in the armor?'

'Yeah, sorry about him. Part of his deal,' he says. He scans one of the shelves.

'Ha! There you are, you little bastard.' He plucks a lavender jewel the size of a golf ball from the shelf and tosses it in the briefcase where it lands heavily.

'Jack,' I say, 'this looks kind of like, well, you know. Crime.'

'The lab workers got out okay, right? And they weren't using the power gem. It could run the west coast for a decade, and they never even knew what it was. Ethically, I have a hard time seeing the stakes.'

'This seems like a thing we could have talked about.'

'Look at all this great stuff they have lying around. It's crazy,' he says. 'I bet they'll never miss it.'

He jimmies open a metal box half full of jewelry. He scoops a few loose diamonds into a plastic bag.

'That's a crime,' I say. 'But I guess you know that.'

He holds it up to the light and nods.

'Not even fake. You should take a few for yourself. You're pretty broke, I happen to know.'

'How long were you planning this?'

'A while. Years.' He waggles the little bag at me. 'Come on, take it. Untraceable. Consequence-free. You sure?'

'Don't be ridiculous.'

Outside, the police chief's bullhorn is barking but I can't make out the words.

Jack hears it, too. 'Guess they're getting impatient. I better do the getaway part.'

He spreads a circular sheet of stiff white fabric on the floor, the size of a manhole. He presses a button on his belt and the edges light up while the rest of it darkens to gray, then a deep black. He tosses the briefcase onto it, but instead of landing, it drops silently through.

'Portable hole. Cool, right? The Hong Kong investors are going to go crazy for it,' he says.

'Jack, I'm sorry, but you see how this has to go.'

'I really don't.'

'I can't believe you're making me do this.'

I snatch a handful of his jumpsuit and, gently as I can, I lift him with both hands and pin him against the wall behind him.

'We've done this before,' I tell him. 'You lose. Always.'

He sighs. 'Everyone thinks I'm stupid.'

I'm calculating how hard I can hit him without hurting him too much when I feel a cool pressure under my jaw, then a burning feeling. He's holding something to my neck.

'You know what that is?' he says.

'It hurts.'

'Remember Sinistro's darkforce blade? That showed up here, too. Figured it would come in handy.' He shifts his grip a little and I feel it, just a little cut in the skin. But he's right over the vein.

'What do you want, Jack?'

'Change. Be Alex.'

'I can't do that.'

'I'm right on top of the jugular here. It's checkmate, Alex. Say the word.'

I whisper the word.

Jack is too heavy to lift now. He lands on his feet. Now we're just two forty-year-old men facing each other, neither one in great shape. He's still got the knife – metal, edged with a sliver of black like chipped glass.

'Where did you get that?' I say.

'Where do you think?'

He shifts the knife to his left hand, then squares up. I put my hands up but he's as fast as ever. He punches me in the nose, then the stomach. I can't believe how much it hurts. For a moment I can't see at all, and I'm bent over, holding my face. *I'll have to get my nose fixed again.*

I feel his hand close over the amulet. He pulls and it feels like he's yanking my heart out. The chain snaps and it's gone, out of arm's reach. He kicks me in the stomach.

'I can't believe you didn't see this coming, but then you were never that complicated. The funny part is, you don't even care about it that much yourself. Except you want a dead magic-user to like you – I guess because your dad left. Or Meg, or whoever. I don't even know.'

'Okay! You can stop now. Why are you doing any of this? Is it still about the galaxy?'

'You'll find out. Oh hey, happy birthday. Forty-one, right?'

He's right. After using Rick Tower's birthday for years (I made him a Gemini), I'd totally forgotten the real one.

'Thanks. What did you get me?'

'Ever wonder about your first marriage?' he says. He watches my face for understanding. 'Six months with Cat in the Pleistocene. Remember that? I would have showed up early but, you know, it went like I thought. Yeah, you're welcome.'

'That was an accident. You missed the arrival point.'

'It's so insulting to me that you believed that part.'

He almost goes to kick me again, but stops. His face is red from exertion or emotion.

'You killed Michael Ferris,' I say.

'Nobody wanted that,' he says. 'But for the record, it wasn't me.'

'Then who was it?'

Instead of answering, Jack just points to something over my left shoulder. I turn just in time to be staggered by an open-handed blow from the knight's armored hand. In future, I'll leave this part to Prodigy. If there is a future.

'Here you go, Chuck. A deal's a deal.' Jack tosses the amulet to the silvered knight.

'See you, champ,' the knight says, but of course I know the voice now.

The armor must be all that's holding Chuck Dubek up. Exoskeleton, neural interface.

He holds the amulet up for me to see, then loops it around his own neck. He folds his arms, steps backward, and drops through the hole.

'Look, I have to go,' Jack says, with what might be an apologetic note in his voice.

'Stay and fight, you cowards,' I say, but I can barely form the words.

'Nah.'

'At least tell me what your plan is.'

He laughs softly, an echo of the villainous cackle he used to do.

'Ten years ago, I might have fallen for that,' he says. 'Your backup's hitting local airspace in four and a half minutes, so excuse me if I don't wait around. Besides, you already know the plan. I'm going to finish this time machine, and I'm going to take over the world.'

He sits and scoots awkwardly to the edge of the hole, like a kid afraid of the diving board, and drops through.

'Fuck you!' I throw my communicator down after him.

'Asshole!' is the last thing I hear.

After a few seconds, something is tossed up out of the hole. It hits me in the chest and I catch it by reflex.

The disk turns solid again. There's a pop and the smell of burnt plastic. I'm alone, a man with no superpowers . . . and a bag of three medium-sized diamonds.

The shelves around me are full of things people probably

want. Relics of empire, ancient magic (if anybody knew how to use any of it), like a glass spider, and a thing like a three-dimensional Moebius strip, and the shattered sword of Chuck Dubek.

I weigh it in my hands, heavy as memory, sharp as regret.

37

Jack is gone and my powers are gone and I'd rather not see Barry or any of the rest of them. I've started sleeping at my regular apartment again. Professor Tower's leave of absence will be up in another month and I'm starting to think I may as well go back to being him. Maybe he's kind of my default state anyway – who I'd have been if Prodigy never showed up.

At some point in all this, I stopped thinking about money. I decided, without admitting it, that I was going to go into financial freefall and not care. I'd spend money on the next thing, and then the next, until I found Mr Ferris's killer. Now the adventure's petered out, and I just want an ending. Paris is as good a place as any.

I stay in the best hotel I can afford, Hotel Raphael near the Champs-Élysées. It's more than I can afford, actually. But hey, I'm finally going to Paris.

I land at noon, fall asleep in the taxi from the airport, and wake to sunshine, traffic circles, zooming through busy afternoon streets. At the hotel I give myself up to the expensive luxury I've bought. The valet chooses not to notice my fading black eye, and I tip him extra for it. I set my weekend bag on the thick carpet and steal an hour's nap on the wide canopied bed.

Meg's business card is ragged and smudged but the number there is still readable.

'*Oui, allô?* Karen Cena.'

'Meg, hi. It's Alex Beekman. I'm in town and I thought I'd give you a call.'

'You're here? In Paris?'

'For a few days. I'm here for a conference. I wondered if you wanted to get a drink this evening.'

A few beats of silence before she replies.

'Sure. What neighborhood are you in?'

I've never heard of it. She names a bar.

I have a long drowsy bath in a marble tub, then spend forty-five minutes fussing with shirts and ties. I wind up in jeans, T-shirt, and the jacket from the old navy-blue suit I bought for academic job interviews eleven years ago, back when Rick Tower was forever.

I can't believe I've never been to this city. I walk most of the way to meet her through the narrow streets, the circular plazas and wide boulevards bulldozed into existence in the nineteenth century. Every street is lined with the five-story town houses with their gabled, slate-shingled roofs, the view that tells you you're in Paris. It's dazzling.

Meg has picked a crowded after-work bar with modern amber lighting and squared-off leather sofas. It's crammed with rich young French guys whose clothes fit effortlessly.

She waves to me from a table near the street. She's in a dark wasp-waisted blazer and gray skirt, her devil-chic intact. It's starting to show in her face that she's not thirty anymore. In mine, too.

I sit across from her, suddenly aware that we're comparative strangers, that I've spoken to her twice in the last fifteen years. It only felt more often because she'd always been there in the back of my mind.

'So . . . Paris,' I say. 'We finally both got here.'

'You're here for a conference? Are you seeing the city at all?'

'Some.'

'How come you're here?' she says. 'I thought Restricted types couldn't travel.'

'I lost the amulet, so it doesn't really matter.'

'I know,' she says. 'Sorry. At least you're friends with Stefanie again.'

'Well, old friends and all that.'

'You know, I don't know if she has real friends? Did you know everyone at Hanover hated her, and she had absolutely no idea. She was only Prom Queen because they were all terrified of her.'

We both smile, Meg with pointed teeth.

'Sinistro came to see me just before,' I say. 'His younger self.'

'He did?' She looks up, focusing for the first time on the conversation. 'Why? What did he say?'

'It was weird. We didn't fight at all. He seemed really unwell, or drunk maybe. He said I should help you.'

'Oh my god, I told him to quit with that,' she says. 'I guess it's always nice when your ex still thinks of you.'

'Wait, you guys were an item? I thought you just worked together.'

'Oh, on and off. You know how he is.'

'I guess so.'

'Alex, you're not really here for a conference, are you?'

'No.'

She takes a deep breath.

'Please tell me you're not trying to find Sinistro. Because he and I don't talk anymore.'

'It's not that! Jesus. I don't want to fight him anymore. I don't want to fight anybody. If you want to know, the whole thing was Jack all along. He was building the time machine this entire time. He and Chuck Dubek beat the shit out of me and took my amulet.'

'Jesus. Okay,' she gulps down the last third of a glass of

wine, 'this stuff isn't doing anything. Why can't I get a real drink in this town?'

Paris isn't a city for cocktails but we find a brick-lined faux-Irish bar crowded with expats. They give us a funny look – a metahuman woman and a guy with a broken nose – but serve us a very expensive whiskey. She pays for that one, and the next.

'Sindo Pasha,' she says.

'No!'

'It's his real name, I swear. You didn't think it was "Sinistro", did you?'

'Don't ask me, I thought it was Potsworth. He had these glasses and this loveable old teacher vibe.'

She laughs, finally. 'Oh no. I cannot picture this.'

'The whole time he was planning to lock us up for experiments I still thought I was his favorite. I guess, with people like him, everyone thinks they are.'

'That is horribly true,' she says.

We clink glasses.

'I'm lonely,' she says. 'Paris sucks.'

'Come back to my hotel.'

She shoves me hard but we both manage to stay on our bar stools.

'It's really stupid that you didn't come with me after jail.'

'I had that whole adventure I was doing. I had a destiny.'

'Oh god, the nineties were so stupid. You should have just come. It was really tough here.'

'You cut my hand open. And you said you were my nemesis.'

'I'm not saying I didn't have issues, but you could have argued with me, at least. You could have ignored the whole thing. But you loved it.'

'Well, I'm here now.'

'You think that matters?' she says. 'I waited for you. I waited and you didn't come. You had your chance. You chose your wizard and your friends who talk trash behind your back. You can't just show up when you're forty and act like it's cool. Why didn't you come when I needed you?'

Her voice has risen. The bartender looks up, but she waves him away.

A loud party of guys in sweatsuits pushes past behind us.

'I was a kid,' I say, when they're gone. 'They said I had a destiny. What kid wouldn't do what a wizard says?'

'Me. I wouldn't.'

'Oh, bullshit.' I may be the one shouting now.

'I stuck a strange gem to my forehead and internalized an animate solid darkness so I could tell wizards and parents and whoever else to fuck off. I've done a lot worse than that since, so don't tell me what I'd do.'

'What about the twenty-five years thing, then? Did you ever find a way out of that?'

'I tried for years, every kind of ritual or exorcism. This gem is powerful as hell. There's no undoing it.'

'How long now?'

'Six weeks. I don't know what's going to happen. I mean, I work for Interpol. That's not exactly in the terms of the bargain.'

'I broke my vow, too. Lots of times. Nothing ever happened.'

'Yeah, well, this thing isn't your kindly old wizard. It's going to come back and demand its due.'

'There must be a way out. I'll help you.'

'You don't even have powers.'

'The time machine. It could take one of us back to stop it all from happening.'

'No, we wouldn't. You know why? Because I'd go right back and make the same decision again. I'm sick of getting judged by people like you who got their powers the nice, socially acceptable way.'

The bar's gone quiet, and I have to keep my voice down.

'I would have done it, too,' I said. 'I would have vowed anything if it meant being special somehow. Why do you think I followed him into the woods? He could have done anything. He could have had my soul if he'd asked for it.'

She leans her shoulder against me. It must be two in the morning now, late for a work night.

'I didn't ask you to come here,' she says.

'I know. I did it on my own.'

She looks out at the empty Paris street.

'So how far is your hotel?'

38

Undersea domes, mountaintop hideaways, dead volcanoes, houses on the moon. Tracking a villain to their lair is usually a pain in the ass, but this one's not hard to find. 'Dubek, Charles' is in the phone book. He never even left Hanover.

I'm just plain Rick Tower now. I sleep at my old apartment, rent a car with my driver's license, dress in his shabby jeans and tweed jacket. The address isn't what I expected – in fact, it's not far from where Stefanie once lived. The cheapest house here must be worth over a million.

I park on the street, right in front of the house, an enormous white neoclassical mansion surrounded by a hedge eight feet high. A Bentley in the driveway is fitted for wheelchair access. I walk through a gap in the hedge and up a brick pathway to the front porch. No point in crawling in through an air duct. I have things to say. The two-toned doorbell rings deep inside the house.

I wait two, three minutes, listening to the rich suburban silence. I'll stay here as long as it takes, although it smells like rain. But I have nowhere to be.

Without warning, the door opens and here he is, in a padded chair that hovers, unsupported, three feet off the ground. He's aged well, but kept the long hair; he's a little thinner, wearing a T-shirt over a still-muscular torso. The hair hides one eye, the other glares at me.

'What?' he says.

I was planning on a speech but it doesn't seem appropriate. We're like two actors meeting after the play has closed.

'Can I come in?' I say, at last.

'What is this about, Beekman?' he says. He leans to look past me for an ambush.

'It's just me, I swear. You know I don't have any powers now. I just want to talk. It's not an ambush.'

'Better not be, you little bitch,' he says, in the venomous tone I remember at the trial. But he reverses the hovering chair a few feet to let me pass.

It's dark inside and the air conditioning is cranked to maximum. I expected clothes on the floor, game consoles, bachelor squalor. Instead, we're in a neat, almost matronly parlor with solid wood furniture and shelves lined with knick-knacks. A studio portrait shows the Family Dubek: mustached, dark, solidly built Charles Dubek, Sr. Chuck must get the blond hair from his mom, who smiles warmly in her azure business suit, curly blonde hair in ringlets. She rests a hand on Chuck's shoulder, in a Green Bay Packers shirt. He must have been eleven. He's already got his mullet in place.

'Nice place,' I say.

'It was my parents' house.'

'Are they home?'

'Dad died five years back. Mom went two weeks ago.'

He smirks at a point scored, spins and drives off, and I trail him to a living room with an overstuffed sofa and armchairs in matching floral prints, and a model ship over the fireplace mantle.

He stops by the fireplace and looks at me again. I sit on the edge of an armchair.

'Don't beg,' he says.

'I'm not here for that,' I say. 'I just want to explain. About what happened. Before.'

'I don't care. Whatever, it worked out. Dad never would

have given me that armor. He went nuts trying to put me back together.'

'He was an inventor?'

'He was a Prion exec. How do you think we got this house?'

A panel on the side of his chair slides back and he extracts a can of Miller Lite and pops it open. He doesn't offer me one.

He takes a sip, and sighs. 'I heard your story at the trial.'

'I just want to say, I shouldn't have taken the amulet. I knew it was wrong. And when you came up to me in the parking lot, and the power happened ... at first, I didn't know what it was going to do, that's true. But then I did know, and I did it all anyway. It was wrong, and I wish I could take it back, but I never, ever can. I'm sorry.'

'Chris is dead,' Chuck says. 'He killed himself.'

'Oh. Shit.'

'What do you want from me? I can't help you. I'm not in Jack's thing anymore.'

'Did you kill Michael Ferris?' I ask. I hadn't even planned on it. 'I'm not going to the cops. I just want to know.'

He nods.

'Yeah. It was an accident, like Jack said. I broke in, he went for me. Jack didn't say how strong he'd be – not strong like you, but still scary as hell, and pissed. I hit him too hard, he went flying. I was just trying to do the job. Shouldna happened, though.'

He's looking away. All I can see of his face is scars.

'Okay,' I say. 'Okay. I just wanted to know. Thanks.'

'Look, I got things to do,' he says. 'Mom's dead and there's a fuckload of work. You know the way out.'

He spins and glides away, deeper into the house. Did I just lose again?

Outside, the first drops of rain are speckling the brick

pathway, coming on fast. Down in the street, a kid riding his bike in circles gives up and sprints off, pedaling hard.

I'm halfway down the path when I feel the sharp blow between my shoulder blades.

I spin, panicked. Did he stab me? Shoot me? But it's neither. It's just a piece of cheap jewelry on a broken chain. I look back at the house but the blank windows give no sign.

I stuff it in my back pocket. I'd better hurry, I'm about to get soaked.

PART TEN
1992

39

The would-be emperor of the world lives in a castle in the sky, circling the Earth at seven kilometers per second. It grows in the front viewport from a point of light to a gray pebble.

The Western Hemisphere below is ablaze with towns, cities, parking lots, baseball fields. From up here, the distance we traveled in the car looks tiny, like we barely traveled at all. But we did, all the way from Hanover, Massachusetts, to a space station in low Earth orbit. It feels even farther. I can hardly remember what life was like before.

'Can we hurry?' Stefanie says. She looks pale and gaunt. 'I hate this.'

I hate zero gravity, too, but it's worse for her. Her kind wasn't meant to be near this much metal, wasn't meant to leave the Earth at all, for a place where there's no midsummer, no golden afternoon. Does Summerdwell even have an outer space? I would ask but it would probably make things worse.

The radio fizzes, then a computerized voice speaks. 'Cleared for docking. Switch to autopilot, please.'

'Done. Homage to Sinistro,' Jack says, and signs off, hitting the switches crisply, as if he does this every day.

The station's shape becomes clear, a disk like a great crab, claws spread the width of a football field. More details appear as we get closer: antennae and engine nozzles and tiny lit windows.

'What exactly is the goal here?' I ask. 'Hitting him isn't going to make him leave us alone.'

'It does when I do it,' Cat says.

'I want him to know we can get to him, even here,' Jack says. 'We're not the easy pickings he thinks we are.'

The fortress grows and grows, until its crab-jaws open to admit us to the docking bay. Automatic jets pulse to ease into the docking chamber. The doors slide shut again, the windows fog up as air fills the docking bay, then the spacecraft settles heavily onto the deck.

'God, this is ugly,' Stefanie says. 'Looks like a space bordello.'

She's right. Sinistro's tastes stopped evolving somewhere around the time of Louis XV. He can't seem to resist putting mirrors and little gold flourishes on the otherwise utilitarian interior.

'He can't be far,' Cat says. 'I can smell him.'

'We all smell things,' Stefanie says. 'Stop being creepy.'

More corridors. Does he really live here by himself? Perhaps he built it with a dozen or so underlings in mind. It would, I must admit, have been nice to live in a space station, looking down at a world we could dominate as we pleased. Actually, it would have been really cool. Well, vows are vows.

The doors on the far wall slide aside to reveal a long salon, strewn with opulent Louis XV chairs and sofas. Spotlit in the center is Sinistro. He's in full dress now, wearing a white and gold robe with an enormously high collar, and a staff of office. For some reason the combination of cheap spectacle and otherworldly charisma actually works. I can believe, maybe for the first time, that he ruled the thirty-first century.

'Come in, come in, my students,' he says. 'I'm afraid we didn't part on the most pleasant terms.'

We step in, warily keeping our distance.

'Sinistro,' Stefanie says. 'Your harassment will stop at once. This is your only warning.'

'Also, you're trying to take over the world,' I add. 'So that's the other thing.'

'I formally refuse both requests,' Sinistro says. 'I presume you'd like to settle the matter by combat?'

'I beat you single-handed before,' Cat says. 'You could have been dead if I'd wanted.'

He spreads his hands, unruffled.

'Oh, I admit it, that round went to you,' he says. 'You fooled my medical staff as to your capabilities. I won't be surprised again. And I've come armed.'

He flourishes the staff, and colored lights play up and down its length.

'Are you ready?' Cat says.

'First, let me make one final offer. If even one of you will join me, the rest can return to Earth free and unharmed, on condition that they never reveal my secrets.'

'We already told you no,' I say.

'I'll fulfill your dreams, any one of you. Stefanie, the army that will conquer the Earth for me can just as easily march on the gates of Summerdwell.'

She shakes her head. 'The throne of Summerdwell is not yours to give me.'

'You want vengeance, Cat? No one does it like I do. The fate of Carthage will look like mild sanctions.'

Cat shakes her head.

'Alex? Any chance?' Sinistro says.

'You know the answer.'

'Jack, then,' Sinistro says. 'You're the last. It's the rational choice.'

The lights on Jack's helmet have been flashing faster and faster this whole time, navigating the maze of the future through pure logic.

'Never,' Jack says.

'Very well,' Sinistro says. 'I suppose we all know what comes next.'

'Bring it on,' I say, already plummeting through the trapdoor that has opened beneath my feet.

This time, the cell is a metal alcove only a little bit larger than a telephone booth, with metal bars running horizontally across the open side. Past that, I can't see anything but a bare metal corridor. No air vents, no locks or hinges.

Is this a joke? The bars are easily two inches thick, but I have only to touch one and the familiar shock feels like it runs all the way up my arm to the base of my neck.

'Meg?'

'That's not my name,' she says.

She steps into view in front of the bars, posing in nervous defiance. I can't even describe what she's wearing. It's breathtaking in a way, a kind of lingerie, but very complex and strappy. I don't know whether it's leather or vinyl, or what's holding it up. It must require a lot of darkforce – or at least double-sided tape.

'Okay, "Blacklight".'

'This is embarrassing,' she says.

'I'm embarrassing? You look ridiculous.'

'I don't care. Nobody asked you here.'

'I told you. He tried to kidnap us,' I say.

'Well, you and your stupid friends probably did something.'

'We can all hear you,' Jack says. He must be a few meters down the hall.

'Well, stop listening!' I snap. 'Meg, stop with this. It just isn't you.'

'It's Blacklight, and what do you know? You barely know me. You don't even know which body is yours.'

'Who knows you, then – Sinistro? Are you like boyfriend and girlfriend now?'

'None of your business,' she says, arms crossed.

'Well, it's gross if you are. He's a thousand years old.'

'It's different if he's immortal.'

'He's still a teacher,' I say.

'I'm not a student! You sound like an idiot.'

'Guys, this is excruciating,' Stefanie says.

'Shut up, Stef,' Meg says. 'No one likes you. And I'm so done with this. He can do it himself.'

'You'll never get away with it,' I call out to her retreating footsteps. 'Sorry I'm not cool and evil like you!'

'Fuck off,' she yells. A metal door slams.

'Well, bye.'

I can hear her faintly, yelling for Sinistro.

'Nice work, Prodigy,' Jack says. 'You played it just right.'

'Thanks.'

I try the bars, and they bend like jumbo licorice. I feel bad about the teacher remark, but this is my nemesis. No quarter, no mercy.

40

To see one person unleash their superpower might be unsettling or awe-inspiring. Six powers fighting in a confined space almost instantaneously swamps the senses. I can barely follow it. I just register it when Jack goes down twitching, and I see Stefanie's slashing pink energy bolts shattering against black glass. Then Sinistro bulls into me and it's all lost.

It's the second-hardest fight of my life thus far. Sinistro is very nearly as strong as I am and either knows a lot of kung fu, or else invented it himself in ancient China. I punch air, then my legs are whisked out from under me.

I feel the bite of his ring against my chin as he shoves my head into the floor. I smell his breath and aftershave, hear him grunt as I squeeze his biceps. These are the moments when I envy the ones who can fight at a genteel remove, trading psychic blasts or wind powers or novelty arrows. Everything I do, I have to do by hand, up close and intimate.

It's a frenzied, suffocating interval that goes on and on until we both hear that synthetic voice say a single word spoken over the loudspeaker.

'*Sixty.*'

All at once the pressure is gone and Sinistro is off and running, like a kid playing freeze tag racing for home.

I don't understand until the voice says, '*Fifty-nine.*'

We're alone in the momentary quiet. Meg is gone, Stefanie still panting with the effort of the fight. Cat is disengaging herself from a glob of adhesive the size of a bean-bag chair.

Jack appears, tottering on stiff legs, the Thinking Cap in temporary command of his motor functions.

We all look at one other, momentarily dumbfounded.

Sinistro is in retreat, his fortress doomed. It's the end of the quest.

The airlock launches our spacecraft on a puff of escaping atmosphere. We drift a moment, while Jack scratches out orbital equations with a stubby pencil, then a silent flash fills the viewport. The dying station illuminates our features, blank with exhaustion, numbness, relief, confusion. For a moment our lives tumble, as weightless as our bodies. We could go in any direction, land anywhere, become anything.

But the gravity of our pasts and the destinies ahead of us will pull us back eventually. Jack gooses the engine and tips our trajectory into a slowly decaying orbit that in a few hours will bring our cherry-red space plane screeching out of the sky to land in a reckless sidewise skid on the National Mall.

Traffic noise all but ceases. The cockpit door hums, then hisses open, a staircase unfolds. A battered yet charismatic teenaged princess steps into view. A lucky reporter, knowing a career-making moment when she sees it, thrusts a microphone toward her.

Stefanie leans forward with nascent superstar poise and speaks the first words any of us have said since we left the space station.

'You can call us the Newcomers,' she says, and then four unforgettable years pass.

Of course, Sinistro isn't defeated. We fight him in deserts and Arctic tundra, in caverns below the Earth and on the high seas. Often, he has Meg by his side, or else one of a rotating cast of sidekicks, all capable, all powered, all brunettes.

We score a lot of real wins that, in my opinion, have been unjustly forgotten. The Return of Margaret Hook-hands? The short terrifying reign of Robo-Sinistro? The brief confusing reign of Clever Jill, Jack's cross-time analogue? Does no one appreciate these things? But people like the Champions always have bigger powers, bigger crises. And of course Keystone, that handsome bastard, can fly.

Occasionally, we go off on our own, one to bring a Prion executive to justice, another to battle Queen Juniper's pet dragon. Jack has mysterious errands, presumably required of him by his future self, and I have my own interests, largely academic research into the nature of my power, and Meg's.

But we always come back to the Newcomers Mansion, and there are parties and so many, many good days and nights. At one time or another I tell each of them that I love them, and even if it's a drunk thing that they've forgotten in the morning, I still remember the fumbled attempt to give them the utmost I have to give.

Three years, ten months and twelve days later, we meet him for the last time. The real battle. It's in outer space again, infiltrating the latest of Sinistro's orbiting strongholds.

We've got our own ride this time, the GalactiCar that twists and weaves through automated defenses with Jack at the controls, reflexes enhanced past human limits by the Thinking Cap VII. I step through the breached airlock to draw fire while Cat wordlessly peels off to recon the tunnels, slipping from one camera's blind spot to the next.

'My sorcery perceives no hostile minds,' Stefanie says, coolly stepping over the airlock's bent metal frame. She's in silver scale mail detailed in green, hair tucked into a silver helmet.

'Ditto cybernetics,' Jack says from the aperture, a little disappointed.

He just wants to try out his hand-held flame-thrower. We told him not to bring it but I guess the heart wants what it wants.

Cat drops soundlessly from an air duct. 'Control room's on the top deck. Empty. You'll want to see this.'

We hurry, through polished metal corridors, up the broad translucent steps of a spiral staircase, to emerge in Sinistro's latest command center, wraparound windows giving a view of the tilted Earth, his longed-for dominion.

'Ho-lee shit,' Jack says. 'He's gone and left us the keys to the kingdom.'

He's not talking about the space station's command center, but the thing parked in the middle of it. It's the Time Cycle, a single-seater, built in iconic thirtieth-century style, an upright art nouveau whorl, placing the seated pilot just beneath the *pièce de résistance*, the spherical Time Core suspended above their head. We've seen it a dozen times but always as a fading image and occupied by Sinistro, laughing in our faces as he makes another escape, vaulting to elsewhen.

We've never been alone with it. A gold sphere with five spherical gems placed evenly around its equator, half sunk in its uncannily smooth, clean surface. It's so glossy and reflective it looks like a drop of liquid gold that will lose its shape in the next second.

Jack runs his hands across the curved edge of the control panel.

'Damn good workmanship,' he says.

'Don't touch it,' Stefanie says.

'I'm not going to do anything.'

'We need to destroy it,' I say. 'Now, while we have the chance.'

'Wait,' Cat says.

'What do you mean, wait?'

'She's right,' Jack says. 'Let's think about this.'

'I'll bring it right back,' Cat says.

'What do you mean, you?'

'Prion Laboratories is expanding,' Cat says. 'I can't destroy them fast enough. I'll never get my vengeance. But I could go back.'

'We have more important things to think about,' Jack says.

'Do I have to remind you what they did?' Cat says. 'My friends, dead. Years I spent under fluorescent lights eating vat-grown protein. Picking at surgical scars and waiting for my next trip to the proving grounds.' A knife in her fingers keeps appearing and vanishing again. It looks a trifle neurotic.

'I grant you it's bad,' Jack says. 'But it's nothing – the Spindrift War will wipe out dozens of civilized worlds. I must take command, however I can, as early as I can.'

'Jack. You can't still be talking about that stuff from when you were a kid,' Stefanie says. 'It's infantile. What aliens? What war? Why would they put a kid in charge?'

'It's all in letters. Alex, you understand, right?'

'Well, um, nothing's exactly proven, right?' I say. 'I mean, it's not impossible, sure. Potentially.'

'You think Prion Labs is going to stop with Earth?' Cat asks. 'They'll take Mars and then expand and expand until nothing else is left anywhere. The future is corporate.'

'Yet Summerdwell is eternal,' Stefanie says, cool and even. 'I demand this time machine in the name of the Golden Throne and Crystal Scepter.'

'Who cares? We're not your subjects,' Jack says.

'That can change.'

'Why should we help you? You always think you're better than us,' Cat says. 'I'm not letting you use the time machine. I don't even know if we're friends. I don't know if I want to be.'

Cat's nine remaining fingers are flexing in the air, nostrils dilating. Somewhere inside, combat routines must be spinning up.

'I have good news for you, then,' Stefanie says. 'Because we're not friends. You're a weirdo and a murderer. And you slept with Alex, which is disgusting.'

Jack gives a huff of bemused surprise at that one. Apparently, a few bits of data escaped his notice.

'Keep talking, Stef,' Cat says. 'I killed my best friend in the arena, and she was worth ten of you.'

Stefanie raises only a finger, and Cat's voice vanishes into the smallest possible croak. Her knife clangs to the metal deck.

'Cat. Oh honey, I'm sorry. You see, all you have is your little fists, whereas I have my mind.' Stefanie's eyes cloud over and begin to glow. In moments she'll take command of the situation. The only thing to do is to take it for myself.

'RAECL—'

'Nope.' The barrel of Jack's gun is inches from my face, in the fast-draw conjuring trick I've seen before, just never from the front end. 'Not another syllable. The stun setting is a work in progress, so don't buy yourself any nerve damage.'

'Come on, Jack. Crap.' I put my hands up.

'Not a word,' he says. 'You either, Stef. I gamed all of this out five minutes ago. I know every move every one of you makes in this situation.'

'Then you should know it's "Princess Stefanie". Say it. Or should I make you do it myself?'

'Try it, Princess. Go on and tamper with my brain's motor-control center. Because I built another one, especially to take over if that happened, and you won't like what I've told it to do.'

'Can we just –'

'The funny thing is, Alexander Beekman,' Stefanie says,

cutting me off, 'that no one even knows why you're here. What would you do with all that power once you'd put Sinistro down? Beat up more stoner kids? Enough with the "it's a secret" crap. Who the hell are you?'

'I told you, I'm here to save the world.'

'Really.'

'It's true! That wizard gave me the task, or maybe I was destined for it, or both. Either way, the prophecy tells us the darkness is coming and only I can save us.'

Even paralyzed, Cat manages to look incredulous.

'What darkness?' Stefanie says. 'You never explain. An eclipse? A power failure, maybe?'

'It's metaphorical.'

'Well, it sounds racist.'

'I didn't write the prophecy. I didn't ask to be chosen.'

'Begged would be more like it,' Jack says. 'How do you stop this darkness?'

'It's non-specific, you know that.'

'Who fed you this nonsense?' Stefanie says.

'Michael Ferris.'

'Ew,' she says. 'The perv.'

'It wasn't like that.'

'I never thought I'd hear a dumber origin story than Jack's,' Stefanie says.

'The amulet works, doesn't it?' I say. 'Explain that, why don't you?'

'Jack, since you know how this all ends, why don't you just tell us?' Stefanie says. 'Quickly. While I still feel the slightest respect for any of you.'

A faint jolt passes through the floor, its vibration registered in the soles of our feet. There can't be any doubt what it means. It's the impact of a spaceship reaching the docking bay.

'Of all the low-probability scenarios,' Jack says.

'It's him. Let's destroy this thing, quickly,' I say.

'Don't you dare!' Cat says. Stefanie has let go of her.

'Can we all just be a team?' I say. 'He's coming.'

The automatic door huffs open and Sinistro himself stands in the doorway, in an armored space suit enameled a splendid Easter-egg pink. It opens like a clamshell and he steps out, dressed as for a formal dinner. The knot in his tie is gentlemanly perfection.

'Unexpected guests,' Sinistro says. 'How pleasant.'

'Don't move, or the time machine gets it,' I say.

'You wouldn't,' he says.

'Of course I would.'

'Destroy the machine that could grant you your dreams? I wonder if even you can do it, Alex. It's academic, since your teammates certainly won't permit you. You think I don't hear what happens on my own space station?'

'We'll just beat you and settle it after.'

Sinistro looks at each of us for a long moment, bemused.

'I wonder if you will,' he says.

He takes off his beautifully tailored jacket, folds it carefully, and begins.

It's not our most glorious battle; the argument has thrown us off, and we keep getting in each other's way. He's as fast and tough as ever, though – fierce and regal – and he's got a new fighting stance I don't recognize, and new toys. He's invented a sound cannon that puts Stefanie out of the fight, and disables Jack with a blow to the temple while he's still trying to create a counter-resonance.

I catch him by the throat and pin him one-handed against a wall, savage as the night of the school dance. He crouches, suddenly heavy as a dump truck, twists my wrist with a devilish strength, and I'm left holding only a torn shirt. Cat dives for him, but he catches her easily by the collar and swings her into a bulkhead door frame. She cries out at the frightening impact, the only time I've ever heard it. Standing over her, he fires a tranquilizer from a wrist holster.

'Tailored venom,' he says. 'She'll be out for a while. It's just you and me.'

I've never fought him alone. He bows slightly. Panting, stripped to the waist, showing his hairy chest and the genetically perfect build that goes (I would guess) with ruling the Earth in the thirtieth century.

'This is stupid,' I say. 'I'll just keep coming. I always do.'

'Did I ever tell you about the time I spent in northern India?'

'I don't think you did,' I say, circling.

He moves with me, in no hurry.

'This would have been the early sixteenth century. Two years back, perhaps, I went to spend a decade there. Very interesting fighting techniques. Good with knife work.'

He holds up a short-bladed knife, ornately decorated and etched, evidently concealed until now.

'So?' I say.

He advances in a deliberate fashion, body angled sideways, knife in the trailing hand. He makes a cut at me and reflexively I step backward.

'What's the matter? It's only a knife,' Sinistro says.

He feints at my eyes, and again I jerk back. I just don't like having that thing waved at me.

'Of course, that's not why I went to India. They were also masters of many crafts. Pottery and weaving, for instance.'

'Very educational.'

'It was, actually. They have another specialty, though.'

He lunges for real this time, slicing backhand, and I'm

done with this. I put up a forearm that instantly goes numb, followed by a blinding pain. Blood spatters the floor.

'Gem-cutting.'

He lets me have another look at the knife. It's a beautiful but functional piece of work, now slicked with bright-red blood. Near the point, a half-inch of the edge isn't metal at all, I see. It's a dark, reflective material, sharp as cut glass. Just a sliver of the darkforce gem.

'Her parting gift,' he says. 'I can kill you now, and I'm honestly not sure why I shouldn't.'

'You won't,' Stefanie says. Shaking, fighting the sonic effects, she brandishes a spectral spear, the tip green glass with smoke trapped inside. She holds it two-handed, angled not at Sinistro but the Time Core itself. She's ready to sacrifice the prize.

'Don't do it,' Sinistro whispers.

'Drop the knife,' she says. 'I should have done this long ago.'

'You don't know what you're doing,' he says. 'There's none like it in all of Continuity.'

How many centuries has it been since Sinistro's voice shook with panic? He takes a step toward her, then another.

'Last chance, Sinistro.'

'Please. You stupid child,' he says, voice trembling.

His fingers shift on the knife and I lunge for him, too late to stop him, only able to crowd his arm a little bit as he throws. I'll never know his real aim, or if I spoiled it, but the knife lodges in Stefanie's biceps. She huffs out air but doesn't hesitate even a fraction. The emerald spear plunges into the fragile, ineffably complex sphere of the Time Core.

I guess, correctly, that we'll be arguing about all of this forever.

The air around the Core deforms, as if a mighty shockwave were imploding around it. I run and pull Stefanie away before it emits an awful white light, then a stinging explosion. Sinistro hasn't moved, and it takes him full in the face.

When I can see again, he's on his back and the control room is a ruin of smoke and flashing red lights. White star-shaped cracks in the glass grow larger until they obscure the stars and the Earth. There is a shriek of ruptured pipes, and a seam in the wall begins to work itself open. Something structural broke in the fight. Warping, unbalanced, the spinning space station is beginning to tear itself apart.

I can't think of anything but getting out of here, dragging Jack and Cat behind me as Stefanie stumbles on ahead, retracing our steps. I don't think to look back. I wonder if Prodigy can withstand hard vacuum, the burn of reentry and the colossal impact. Keystone did once, but he's Keystone. The space station shudders again. We crowd into the space plane. I slap the lock to disengage us, and then we float free.

We have a great view of the burning space station as its orbit begins to decay; soon it will sink into the upper atmosphere to heat up, burn, and then vaporize.

Homage to Sinistro.

41

It should have meant something good. Victory over evil, freedom from Sinistro's undying enmity. But in the months after Sinistro's death, nothing seems to go right. Jack sulks in his lab most of the time. Cat goes missing for days at a time. Stefanie arranges to take classes at Harvard, working toward a degree. She makes new friends, some powered, some just rich, and they go up to New York almost every weekend. As usual, I'm the last one to realize what's happening.

One morning, she wanders in, sleepy, cigarette smoke on her clothes. Still a teenage witch at twenty-one, awake all night and still a little hyped, snaky hairdo a little dented after a long night's partying and an early morning's teleportation back to Cambridge. I'm up early, having breakfast in the lounge. She pulls herself together on seeing me, and props herself against a wall.

'Elite's offering me a modeling contract,' she says with strained unconcern. 'I kind of think I'm going to do it. I kind of think I'm moving to Los Angeles.'

When she says it, it's so obvious I'm embarrassed not to have seen it before. She's leaving the team.

'Yeah. I mean, congratulations.'

'Thanks. It's the right next step for what I want to do in my life,' she adds. Rehearsed.

'Did you tell Jack?'

She nods.

'He's going, too. Palo Alto. It's all starting to happen for him.' She blows at a stray hair, still golden.

'Are you guys seeing each other?' This has been in the air for a while, I might as well ask.

'A little. I don't want to talk about it.'

'So will I see you?'

'Oh, I'll be around. Definitely.'

'Okay. Good.'

She gives me an awkward big-sister hug and goes off to bed. I sit and watch the big screen. Crises have bloomed on the global map: sentient goo, zombies, and the first swarm incursion from the bee dimension. One by one, they fade and disappear and are gone. Other people are going to take care of it, and maybe none of these things ever actually ends the world. Maybe it all just works out. There used to be a talking mouse with lots of warnings, but he's stopped coming around.

Stefanie moves from Cambridge down to New York. I even see her once with her friends, happy drunk girls on high heels, giggling as they stumble over cobblestones in the Meatpacking District. They're the skinny girls at parties who are always a little cold, hunched over on the sidewalk smoking, all wanting the world, just like Stefanie or Jack or any of us.

Four years in the Newcomers have left me more or less the same person. I chase product endorsements, eventually acquire a government license to fight crime. Cat does, too, and we even team up a few times before she wanders overseas.

I try to avoid seeing Stefanie's face on magazines in the supermarket. One day, I read the news of Jack's dramatic arrival in Silicon Valley in 1996, perfectly timed for the digital revolution and the Great Internet Bubble. It turns out he's exactly the right brand of self-mythologizing eccentric that culture loves. He drives a street-sanitized version of his amphibious flying car to work, his business card reads 'Gadgeteer', and if his high-profile battles with federal regulators slow his ascent, they burnish his reputation.

He has a stint at Yahoo, then AltaVista. Then Microsoft, which ends with the notorious 'Bill Gates is a dumb motherfucker' press conference. He founds his own company, loses it, starts another.

Two years after the Newcomers end, Stefanie starts to be famous. Her fragile beauty precisely suited to the heroin-chic trend, she leverages her modeling career into a few small character roles in film, then a lead role, a nuanced and startlingly vulnerable turn as the title character in an adaptation of *Daisy Miller*. I'm embarrassed to say I never expected her to actually be talented.

She and Jack get married in 1996 before a mix of Hollywood up-and-comers, Silicon Valley personalities, and a scattering of exiled Summerdwell aristocrats. As Jack's best man, I hold the frighteningly expensive ring, while Jack recites his vows in flawless High Summerdwellian. He is named a Grand Duke for the occasion. The press unkindly names them 'the Princess and the Frog' but I have never seen Stefanie look happier, before or since.

It's a busy night but I manage to catch Jack's eye once, a private nod to say we are still a little bit ourselves, still on some level the scared CLEO kids on their first bathroom break. Cat and I dance, gawk at the famous guests, and raise a glass to their future and ours; to all the futures at once.

The first and only Newcomers reunion happens by accident, in a crowded hallway of the George R. Brown Convention Center in Houston. Stefanie, I know, is keynoting. I didn't bother to go through the rest of the speaker list.

It's the second day, and the afternoon sessions are over. The corridors are flooded with journalists, lobbyists, congressional staffers, the odd scientist, and the occasional bright costume. It starts when Stefanie and Jack bump into each other. They've been divorced less than a year and haven't quite figured out the ground rules. They stop and chat awkwardly by a cluster of empty folding tables.

They're both in costume, each with their own reasons for keeping this part of their image current. Stefanie is in the finest faerie chain mail and a silvered domino mask. Jack is in a silver shirt and purple pants, with the heavy matte-steel plasma pistol on his belt, and the Thinking Cap VII running a new piece of tech – a ruby gem pulsing weakly on a thick plastic headband. He's making a point to Stefanie, touches her arm. She laughs. I start to move on, but she sees me and waves me over.

At that instant, Cat comes into view over his shoulder, angling through the conference-goers. She's wearing the black leather catsuit. Already a controversial figure, it's the last of her legitimate public appearances before going permanently underground.

'Hey, guys.' Her voice is a shade deeper than I remembered. She says it brightly, a good imitation of casual.

I think she must have missed us. Her situational awareness is too good for this encounter to be an accident.

'Mom says hi,' Jack says, to no one in particular.

I remember meeting her at the wedding, a surprisingly kind person, bewildered at her son's ascent to fame.

'How's Barry?' I ask Stefanie.

I've read they're engaged. She looks straight ahead, like she's mind-controlling someone in the middle distance.

'He's good.'

Long silence. So this is what happens to people, I guess.

'How's California?'

'Fine. Great. Really busy.'

'Jack, you okay?' Cat says. 'You look like crap.'

'Yeah, fuck you, too,' he says, but not angrily. 'I'm in crunch mode. Closing the B-round on the force field start-up. It's gonna be big.'

'Alex? Still being a good boy for the Feds?'

'Cat, people are watching,' Stefanie says. 'Press.'

A publicity type from the conference spots us and gets us to pose for a photo. Then Jack gets a call, a man asks Stefanie for an autograph, and Cat slips away. I see her a moment before she disappears, walking stiffly and fast. Easy as that, they're gone for another six years.

The picture is online that evening. I'm doing a practiced PR smile. Stefanie looks amazing, obviously. Cat's blurred out – she must have been wearing a device that does it.

Back in the hotel room, it's bourbon on ice and movies until dawn. First *Ronin* comes on and then *The Big Chill*, the one about histrionic middle-aged baby boomers obsessed with holding on to their youthful dreams. Their generation told ours to hold on to those dreams when we grew up, or else our hearts would die. But maybe our hearts or dreams or souls weren't that delicate or important in the first place. In any case, there isn't going to be another Newcomers reunion anytime soon.

42

1998, sometime. I am in a hexagonal chamber, the walls and floor made of an amber-like substance that flowed and hardened around me while I was unconscious. I have no idea where I am, but that's not uncommon nowadays.

An archway forms in one wall and Jack strides through it. His silver suit is bunched and wrinkled, as if he's slept in it a few nights running. My new teammates and I glare at him. Blame his childhood, blame the job market, blame Gen X, but Jack is evil now.

'Well, well, well,' he says. He hasn't slept in days, it looks like.

'Hey,' I say.

'Look how the mighty have fallen.'

'Are you done?'

'Just getting started. Don't bother trying to escape. Or do try, actually. There is no escape.'

'You'll never get away with this.'

'Yeah, yeah. So who are your friends here?'

'That's Atomika to my right.'

'I will defy you to the last,' Atomika says. She tosses her chestnut mane, heaves her great muscles against the amber stone.

'And that's Gandalf,' I say.

'Seriously?' Jack says.

'He's the Wizard of the West.'

'It's ironic,' Gandalf says.

In truth, Gandalf is a twenty-year-old with an unfortunate

facial tattoo but he has real talent. They're four years younger than me but it feels like a lot more.

'Well, kids,' Jack says. 'Alex and I go way back. Don't we?'

'Call me Prodigy,' I say. I haven't done real names with the other two. 'Jack, what are you doing?'

'What I should have been doing all along,' Jack says. 'The world's never going to give me the respect and position I deserve, so I'm taking it.'

'It's just not going to work. You'll get in trouble.'

Jack laughs – a pretty good, if rehearsed, villain laugh.

'Even now, world leaders are reading my surrender terms. They're out of options. China's always the big holdout, but once I've got the West and Russia they'll crack soon enough. I'll be the ruler of this little world, and then finally things are going to get interesting.'

'What "things", villain?' Atomika says.

Sometime after 1990, they stopped teaching kids irony.

'The Earth is sad and backward, and I'm going to change all of that. Flying cars, and we're going to the moon, and we'll get floating cities within a decade. Galactic citizenship in thirty years. This is the future everyone wants! They'll all realize, once it's happening.'

'Never!' says Atomika.

'And the transmitter?' I say. 'You'll contact the aliens?'

'Damn right,' he says. 'We'll join the galactic union and I'll settle the Spindrift War.'

'Did you ever find any proof that was real?' I say. 'The Spindrift War? The future?'

'I'll find it, Chosen One,' he says. Then he asks the others, 'Did you ever get any proof of that? Did he even tell you his origin?'

'He's a great hero,' Atomika says.

'Thank you.'

'You obviously haven't shared a bathroom with him,' Jack says. 'You have no idea what kind of poser you're dealing with.'

'Jack!'

'We know all, evil one,' Gandalf says.

We're interrupted by a roaring sound elsewhere in the complex, followed by a thunderous buzzing. Jack excuses himself.

'It sounded kind of cool about the flying cars, though,' Gandalf says.

'Careful what you say, sorcerer,' Atomika says.

'Okay, whatever. What is it with you and this Doctor Optimal guy?' he stage-whispers to me.

'We went to high school together.'

Jack returns, glancing once behind him.

'So what was that noise?' I say.

'Nothing much.'

'It wasn't the Quantum Swarm, was it? They don't sound happy.'

'People need to calm the fuck down about that,' he says. 'It's a temporary arrangement.'

'Traitor.'

'There are going to be long-term benefits you're not seeing right now. But you know, why do I even talk to you people?'

'Jack, what is happening? This isn't you.'

'Don't act like you know me,' he says. 'We worked together for four years, and that's it. God, what a clown you turned out to be. Jumping around for sponsorships and government money.'

'Jack –'

'I really bought into your bullshit. I thought you were something. What a waste.'

'Come on, Jack.'

'Forget it. I've got things to attend to. Have fun in extra-dimensional bee jail. See you next millennium.'

When he leaves, the buzzing returns, louder.

Gandalf quietly begins the song that will turn him to mist-form.

Jack loses that one, and the next, and the next. He tries weather control and nanotech, robots and submarines, all to no effect. He spends New Year's Eve of 1999 planning to seize power in the chaos that never arrives. He drops me in liquid nitrogen, suffocates me in sand, bathes me in acid. We start to drift apart. We fight other people.

It's around this time, I have my first inkling that it isn't all going to work out exactly as planned – either for me or for Jack. He doesn't conquer the world. Mr Ferris doesn't come back. I fight Meg a few times, but it doesn't really go anywhere.

I turn thirty in Red Hook and some forgotten friend of the moment stops me from throwing the amulet into the East River.

I ran into Meg a few times in the late nineties. Never on purpose, but I was working a lot – and as we both did enhanced crime in America around that time we probably fought at least once or twice. Or maybe it was destiny, I don't know. I'd show up to a jewel heist, or escort an armored car, and she'd be there. I'd circle the block a few times until she was done, or she'd just walk away mid-heist, like she'd remembered a phone call she had to make. Maybe I'd lob an empty car at her retreating form, just for show. Neither of us wanted to start something we didn't know how to stop. It would happen one day, that was all.

Then, one day, she stopped operating in the US. A few months later, MICA tagged her as a political actor, a rogue power. She was spotted hunting snipers in wartime Sarajevo and disabling Russian armor in the Second Chechen War. She went from Blacklight to Harridan to La Bruja.

They never caught her. But if surveillance data could be relied upon, she did indeed wear amazing scarves.

The very last time we met was in 2004 in Prague. It was a cold winter and the global war on terror (GWOT to the true believers) was in full swing, on both the powered and unpowered fronts. This was in the brief misguided phase when I thought I'd be better off in regular government operations. I was part of a sting operation to draw out an elusive network of posthumans. My professional reputation was at a low point, marred by on-duty drinking, unstable moods, unprompted violence and a tendency to go off-mission – like James Bond if he were realistically bad at his job.

It was Chicago all over again, a party in a gargantuan Soviet-era apartment complex. We were meant to blend in, confirm enemy presence, pick up likely targets. My buddy in CIA intelligence tried for hours to find a disguise that would let Prodigy mingle with the cigarette-smoking anarchist-cum-musician types, but short of putting a hood on him he's just a radiant demigod. It was his idea to send me in as Alex in a scratchy wool suit, bent wire eyeglasses and a copy of Gramsci sticking out of one pocket, a socialist intellectual slumming it in the demi-monde.

I knocked on the metal door and ducked out of the winter air into the hothouse darkness hammered by east German techno. A woman in dark lipstick handed me a brown drink in a plastic cup. I sniffed and downed it, sweet and fiery. She gave me another. A tall, shaggy man pushed past me, with the distinctive hopalong gait of an East German knock-off super-soldier. They made hundreds of them, now stranded in post-Soviet Europe.

I sent a little text back to my handler. I probably should have followed him but I let the smell of cheap tobacco and booze and sweat of strangers carry me away for a while. I felt safe in the crowd, human for once. My phone buzzed once in a while, probably looking for the situational update I was supposed to be giving every ten minutes, and I ignored it. The drinks, the pounding noise, the pressure of the crowd drove the thoughts out in a pleasant way. I wondered pointlessly if the Wizard had any particular hatred of Eastern European gangsters, and if he'd appreciate my taking care of them. It didn't seem to matter. The Wizard's concerns had been taking a back seat for quite a while.

Toward one in the morning, Meg made her entrance in full warpaint. The darkforce coiled around her arms like living tattoos, and pinned her hair in an elaborate up-do. She was at the height of her underground notoriety, a nineties Carlos the Jackal in a white leather jacket, dark red lipstick, and fishnets. She was also peaking on the CIA's metahuman targets of opportunity lists – fair game, and a prestige target at that, if I could pull it off.

She passed by me close enough to see the new scars. Her gaze tracked right over me, just another tweedy silhouette and besides, it was years since she'd seen my natural face. But when I got within a few feet she stopped short, newly wary. She might have forgotten me but the dark gem hadn't. It must have warned her. She was still a fugitive and I was, however erratically, an agent of the law.

Also, her destiny.

I let her spot me first. Hands up where she could see them.

'Alex, no,' she said. 'Not now.'

'You need to get out of here,' I yelled at her.

'Why?' she said. Her feet planted.

'Come on,' I said, 'we need to go.' She looked more annoyed than threatened. What was her drunk arch-enemy talking about?

'What the fuck, Alex?'

'I'm not here to fight –'

There was a shattering boom as something hard hit the hollow metal door behind me. Men were shouting commands at each other. They were coming in. I stripped off my amulet and shoved it into her hand, then took her arm and pulled her away, deeper into the building.

A fire door led us to a fluorescent-lit hallway slanting through the apartment complex. At the sound of a distant bullhorn we ran, kicking through drifts of food-wrappers and bits of newspaper. Spiky bright graffiti splattered the walls. She pulled me into a stairwell and we climbed, ran, climbed again, the air growing wintry. Another flight took us to the roof. I bent over gasping in the stark wintry air. Alex wasn't running much in those days.

When we could both speak again she pushed the amulet back at me. 'I don't want this.'

'Thanks.'

'Who was that at the party?'

'CIA, Interpol M, and whatever local types,' I said.

'Aren't you with them?'

'Fuck those guys. I barely know them.'

'Well, thanks, I guess,' she says. 'How are you?'

'You know me. Same old shoe.'

It was a strange night. The spires of Prague were lit up in the distance, the sky was clear and the air burningly cold. The pair of us, tiny under the huge field of stars. How had I forgotten this? That she'd sold her soul, I'd sold my face and my future. That neither of us had anything more now than we had in the jail.

We were both shivering. I put an arm around her and she leaned against me, heart still going from the run. I don't know how much time passed.

'This is crazy,' she said at last.

'Yeah,' I said. 'Fuck, I'm lost.'

She yanked me closer. I kissed her and she met me, open-mouthed, our bodies pressed together. She slid her hand up under my shirt. The gem in her forehead flashed, perhaps in irritation but we stayed there, locked together, for long minutes.

A thunderous shock rattled the complex, followed by a roar of shouting.

'They're fighting back,' she said into my ear.

'Good for them.'

'I need to help. My boyfriend is probably down there.'

'That's okay,' I said, by reflex.

'Sorry.'

'There's fifteen guys – regular military in body armor – plus three metahuman elements attached. Two metas now.'

'Thanks.'

'Will I see you?'

'Someday. That's what they told us, isn't it?'

She kissed me and left, down the stairs. I tossed my phone over the edge of the building into a snowbank. In a few minutes I changed to Prodigy, just to keep out the cold, then waited twenty minutes more before going down again.

Another failed operation meant the end of government work for me. Six months after that the lawsuit came, then life as Rick Tower, and what did all the prophecies in the whole world matter then?

*

Where exactly did I lose the thread? Somewhere in the long archipelago of early-noughties apartments? The place in Allston where Johnny Atomic got laid, constantly, or the group home in Silverlake for those four months I thought I was an actor? Or those ten months in Odessa hunting down a bandit tribe called Broken Toys, remnants of Soviet human augmentation programs?

It was a relief to be back in the United States, in New York, fighting Jack again, but it didn't last long.

Our final battle was perhaps the closest he ever got to a win. The plan was to break into the Department of Metahuman Affairs itself and steal its classified records: all the weaknesses, real identities and dirty secrets of every hero they tracked. He would blackmail every hero in the world, and we would be helpless before him.

The battle rages through Washington DC. In the end, he bails out as the GalactiCopter pinwheels out over the National Mall, boxes of classified documents spraying from a gap in the hull.

The National Guard closes in but a few crucial documents go missing, and one of them is mine. The story of my rampage through the Hanover High School becomes national news and although I can't be tried for it, I am deemed an embarrassment to the metahuman strategic command.

Having a government license gives people like me a lot of extra privileges, especially when it comes to civil litigation. Those were gone now. And so I came to stand exposed, defenseless, before my most ancient foe.

43

It starts one morning with an official-looking envelope delivered to my government-subsidized penthouse, just off Union Square in Manhattan. I open it at my ease in the expectation of a check or perhaps another formal declaration of gratitude. I read it, then reread. In elaborately phrased legal language, it tells me that the Dubek, Boucher and Collins families are bringing a civil suit against me under the complicated set of statutes regarding damages incurred by the use of 'supernormal powers' exercised by 'persons of mass destruction'. All these years, they were only waiting quietly for their chance at me, and now they have it.

The only good news is that the government is anxious to avoid further scandal around employing an unstable metahuman asset. The Department of Metahuman Affairs finds Amit for me, a dark, handsome wiry young gun only a few years older than I am. We confer over coffee in his high-windowed Tribeca office, overlooking the park.

'I thought this was all over,' I tell him. 'Case closed. Records sealed.'

'Civil laws around juvenile metahuman assault are just as hair-trigger as in criminal law, and frankly there isn't much doubt over the facts of the case,' he says. 'But these families don't know what they're getting into. Odds are they'll fold before we ever get to trial.'

'Great.'

'Sit tight and don't talk to the press. I'll be in touch.'

The press gets wind of it anyway. A flurry of articles,

nothing front page. Then a big-name op-ed in the *Times* detonates, television news picks it up, and my phone starts ringing. My girlfriend wants to see other people. I hire a publicist.

The next week, Amit calls to inform me we're going to trial. My publicist quits.

That first morning of the trial, I arrive early at the New York County Courthouse to walk past a gauntlet of press. A cold wind pins my new and expensive suit against me. In spite of the cold, a small band of protestors hold signs reading 'THANK YOU PRODIGY' and 'PRODIGY FOREVER'. A larger contingent flourishes 'JUSTICE FOR DUBEK' and 'HOLD METAS ACCOUNTABLE'. An older man in a parka has a 'FREE DOCTOR OPTIMAL' sign. He keeps his distance.

The plaintiffs arrive second. Chuck takes a long slow ride up the handicapped ramp. Chris climbs the steps on his cane, making a show of it. Jared's hair has been cut short to display the purple caterpillar scar running halfway around his skull.

The courtroom looks small. No reinforced concrete, no force field, just a low-ceilinged chamber with a desk, a podium, a jury box, and wooden benches seating sixty or seventy people. Sound pings hard off the wood-paneled walls. It's packed with press and curious members of the public, and my mother who has made the trip. I look in vain for friends or teammates. *Et tu, Atomika?*

The lawyer for the plaintiffs is a man named Abilene, fiftyish, white-haired and doughy, sloppily dressed in a gray suit. Amit is neatly tailored, hair slicked back. He nods to me and smiles, and I smile back. This is a fight, and I don't lose fights.

Judge Grosvenor, a hale man of nearly seventy with

beautiful silver hair, brings us to order and the room hushes for the opening statements. Abilene argues without much flair that my alleged actions fulfill the legal standards for aggravated metahuman assault. Amit's defense tells a more nuanced story, of how young Alex Beekman was collateral damage resulting from the actions of a sinister and capricious sorcerer, one Michael Ferris. It's not the tale of valor I'm used to, but Amit knows what he's doing. I'm still the hero of my own story and everyone else's, too.

Now Abilene starts to show his teeth. Alex Beekman, he explains, was a troubled loner who preyed upon three innocent chums. He produces a smiling yearbook photo of the three boys, mischievous but good-hearted kids, and contrasts it with my brooding expression.

'Who is this troubled loner?' Abilene asks. 'And what is he capable of? I have obtained previously redacted CCTV footage from the night in question.'

A large TV monitor is wheeled into the court. It shows a soundless medium-long shot of what could easily be interpreted as four kids horsing around in the parking lot. *We were almost the same height. Why do I remember staring up into his face?*

My younger self clutches the object hanging around his neck. There is a scribble of static and Prodigy appears. Now we see three children and an adult, then an explosion of terrifying, motiveless violence. Prodigy's disarmingly handsome face has always been an asset, but here it looks unsettling. His smile flashes out of the muddy black-and-white security footage, as I cut off Boucher's escape route and run him down. The video lasts four long minutes. The courtroom listens in rigid silence, then explodes into angry murmuring.

Grosvenor gavels for silence, and Abilene continues with photographs of the victims' wounds taken at the ER, and testimony from the admitting physicians. Amit has little to say in return.

The second day is no better. Chris identifies me, pointing with a shaking hand to where I sit in the courtroom. He recounts his long journey through post-traumatic alcoholism. Chuck talks about finding Jesus at the Episcopalian Church, of which he is now a deacon. A psychologist testifies at length about the traumatic shock of superhuman encounters.

Finally, Amit gets his turn. All three plaintiffs admit they had disciplinary records, yes, but it's mere adolescent mischief next to the terrors we've seen on the security footage. He moves on to the shadowy figure of Michael Ferris. Who was he? Bachelor's in English from Boston College. Teaching evaluations were uniformly positive, then his sudden disappearance. It feels thin – and worse, disloyal to Mr Ferris. Surely he deserves better.

Amit reads aloud the account of the cave incident I wrote for Dr Potsworth. A magic cave that disappeared, a missing wizard, a lonely child. He calls his own psychologist to the stand, who declares it to be *the delusions of a vulnerable, traumatized, emotionally stunted child*. The jury looks unmoved, and why shouldn't they? A sad story is not an excuse.

That night in his office, I give Amit my ultimatum: put me on the witness stand. Let me tell my side, the story of a good man and a hero fated to save us all. Haven't they cheered for me? Haven't I proved my worth? Should I be condemned for a single mistake?

Amit allows it but looks skeptical, but he doesn't know me. He certainly doesn't know Prodigy. We don't lose fights.

The courtroom looks very different when viewed from the witness stand. Down at the table with Amit, it felt like an intimate little stage. From up here, it's a cavernous theater.

Where am I supposed to look? Spectators? Jury? Back wall? Stefanie would know. She would have them eating out of her hand, but of course she would never wind up here. She'd pay whatever it took and never feel it.

The room quiets. The prosecuting lawyer approaches with an apologetic expression, as if even he feels bad for what is about to happen.

'For the record, you are Alexander Beekman?'

'Yes.'

'Or would you prefer to be addressed as Prodigy?'

'Beekman's fine.'

'Mr Beekman,' he says. 'Did you carry out the violent actions we have seen and heard described in this courtroom?'

It's not the question I'd hoped to start with, and I shift in the chair as if there were a way of physically evading it.

'Technically, Prodigy did.'

Chuck glares, one-eyed, across the length of the chamber. Amit looks at the floor.

'But you are Prodigy?'

'Philosophically, that's a bit of a poser.' Pause for laughter. None comes.

'You are responsible for his actions.'

'...'

'Please speak into the microphone.'

'I didn't –' I lean in closer, which produces a burst of feedback. At least I have everyone's attention. 'I didn't know what it would do.'

'But having seen the initial results, you continued in your actions.'

'It was a very stressful moment.' I look to Amit, who only grips the edge of the defendant's table like a man having second thoughts after boarding a roller-coaster.

'You're a monster,' a woman yells from the crowd.

The gavel bangs.

'That's a loaded word,' I fire back. 'I'm here to save the world.'

More gavel.

'Mr Beekman – if I have your full attention – let's review. You were endowed with your metahuman abilities in April of 1991. Yes?'

'A wizard gave them to me. After school. In a cave.'

'For what purpose?'

'To do good. Fight evil. To save the world.'

'And your actions on the night in question, would you call them good? World-saving?'

'No, but –' I say.

'But what, Mr Beekman?'

The three of them, the victims, watch me carefully, savoring the moment before their lawyer delivers the killing blow. For a moment, I see them as they were.

'It's just that they started it,' I say quietly, scarcely in range of the microphone. Why not – in these, the waning seconds of my career – say a few things?

'Excuse me?'

'They started it. The three of them. They were bullies. They made people's lives miserable and scary because they thought it was fun. That's who they were.'

'So,' Abilene begins, shouting over the crowd to quiet them. 'So if I'm clear, in return you used your powers to inflict irreparable harm on them?'

'Yes.'

'And would you say you feel remorse? Are you sorry about what you did?'

Amit nods furiously, almost vibrating with the effort to evoke a correct response. Sometimes it's not hard to know the right thing to do.

'Well,' I say. 'Not as sorry as they are.'

The courtroom has become a less orderly place than it was. Shouting, jeering. I don't know if Amit has anything else planned but I suspect it doesn't matter much now.

The bailiff plucks at my sleeve and I shake him off. I'm not inclined to leave. In fact, I'm just getting started.

He takes a firmer grasp on my arm and then all I can think of is Chuck's hands on me. I'd like to tell him to stop, but why even bother? After all, all I need is a word.

The reaction in the courtroom I can only describe as seismic, a wave of shock and fear. The podium splinters in my grip. The bailiff's grip is a feather now. I wave and send him cartwheeling. Police are firing and their bullets are like puffs of air. My smile, as recorded by a brave courtroom artist, is a rictus for the ages.

If I were a villain, they'd know what to expect. I'd want the money, or the state capital named after me. But when a hero goes off-script, no one knows what the rules are. Even I don't know. I only know you can get sick of being the good one, the rule-follower, so sick you want to smash the world.

'Mr Beekman?' Judge Grosvenor is the only one here who still has his composure. When he speaks, his voice is a bit shaky, but not unkind. 'Would you please the court by resuming your more customary guise?'

I look back at the cowering mass of spectators, lawyers, reporters. I savor it just a moment longer, then I say the word again. I won't be saying it again for a long while.

The three families are awarded their damages in full. A slow news week puts me on front pages across the country, the public face of the mid-nineties panic about powered juveniles, the literal super-predator.

Stefanie issues a press release: 'I stand by our dear friend and will do everything to support him as this difficult situation is resolved.' I receive a postcard from Bangladesh, in Cat's upward-looping handwriting, that reads 'Fuck 'em all.'

At a press conference the next day, someone takes the photograph of Chuck with one eye peering through greasy hair, a stoner Odin in a Nirvana shirt. It will become one of the iconic photos of the nineties. Shepard Fairey's version sells widely on posters, mugs and silk-screened T-shirts. I still wear mine.

44

Secret Origins of Rick Tower. Scene: the back of a tiki bar in Fort Lauderdale, because I can't show my face anywhere in Massachusetts. I am met by a solid-looking man from the government, late thirties, pink from the sun, in a Hawaiian shirt and wraparound sunglasses. He doesn't bother showing ID.

'Not a lot of people get this kinda deal, chief,' he says over a beer.

I'm having Long Island Iced Teas. It's five o'clock somewhere, and the end of my career everywhere.

'I know.'

'You understand we're making a one-time exception.'

'I get it.'

'Good.' He lays a stack of forms down on the colorful place mats. 'I've marked the relevant places. Press down hard.'

'Thanks.' I start signing where marked, not bothering to read the fine print. It's starting to sink in, I'm a criminal again.

'Do you have a name in mind?' he asks.

I don't, which is how I get to be Rick Tower for the next ten years. I don't even think to put 'Richard'.

'What about photos?'

'Later. After the surgery.'

He pays for the drinks.

Along with a new nose I get a BA in Communications from Fordham, a driver's license, passport, Social Security number, a fictional childhood in Connecticut. It would have been poetic justice for Chuck if they'd botched my surgery, but no luck there. My new features have a handsome delicacy that I enjoy.

I learn to be Rick Tower. Rick Tower stands straighter, pitches his voice higher, reads a room before he speaks.

He has few friends, likes Italian new wave cinema, and doesn't mind losing at pool. He has a fun thirty-fifth birthday party, at least the first half. He gets a PhD in English Literature at Fordham.

He attracts the sort of women who are drawn to the sense of something missing, the polite handsome man with something kept out of sight. They think they can solve the riddle and find the treasure, but they never do, and his relationships all dovetail into the same downward spiral of 'what are you thinking?' and 'where are you right now?' Although, for heaven's sake, I'm out here in plain view. I was on the cover of *Time*; put the pieces together. I'm only forty, and my disguise isn't even that clever. Even if they did get it, I'm not interested in anyone without a secret of their own. Somewhere in my middle thirties, I figured out it's better if I go with strangers, or no one at all.

I'm allowed to keep the amulet, in case the government needs to reactivate me for emergencies, but they never do. Prodigy, whatever he is, sits idle in his alternate dimension or mental crawlspace. In his own way, Alex Beekman does, too, preserved in aspic while Rick Tower begins his long autumnal thirties, en route to middle age.

PART ELEVEN

2015

45

'Team Karma'. 'The Residuals'. 'The Prodigal Sons'. Thinking of a new team name at the last minute is hard, especially for such an important mission. Cat, Barry and I have run out of ideas, and we're not even halfway through the four-hour car ride to the target area, a vacation house Stefanie and Jack bought early in their marriage. Barry suggested it – a favorite of Stefanie's, left empty most of the year.

There isn't much else to talk about. Barry and Cat were barely introduced the last time, and they're not exactly natural allies. I'm glad she's here, though. She turned up six hours after I gave her the news over subspace, which means I guess she was listening after all.

I told them both the basic story. The fight with Stefanie, Meg, Sinistro's sudden appearance, then fighting with Jack and losing the amulet. I barely mention the Paris trip but I'm sure they sensed something weird going on there, given that Barry's a detective and Cat's a walking polygraph.

We have no idea how long it will take Jack to repair the Time Core. We only know that if he thinks he can do it, he probably can.

We pile into the car, bound for something between a final battle, a class reunion and an intervention. Cat wears her sleeveless catsuit, zipped to the chin. Barry's in a blue jacket with brass buttons and a crimson cape, which might have looked like a costume, but he wears it so naturally it doesn't have the temerity to look anything other than princely. I wear a rough recreation of my original costume, with a dark blazer and tie, to preserve the dignity of the occasion.

When Prodigy arrives, of course, it will be in his timeless white spandex. It's not exactly the first time Jack and I have come to blows. Jack in Tibet, Jack in an unmarked warehouse in Macau, Jack's Fortress of Evil, Stronghold of Malice, Bastion of I've Lost Count of How Many Bastions and How Are We Fucking Forty Now?

'The Latecomers,' Barry says from the driver's seat.

'Too obvious,' I say. Not everyone has a gift for this. 'Temporal Remediation Committee.'

'Too dorky,' Cat says. 'Backlash.'

'Not bad.'

Making up names is one way of passing the time, while no one brings up the obvious fact that, even if we win, we'll have to decide what to do with the time machine itself. Michael Ferris, dead on the floor, all his secrets lost forever. What if I can take the machine for myself? Surely, he'd want me to go back. After all, he was building one of his own.

Thirty miles to go. Barry pulls in at a roadside bar outside Stockbridge to wait for sundown. Seated in a corner, Cat glares back at the locals while Barry gets us an armful of four-dollar whiskeys.

'Cocktail Hour Crusade,' Barry says.

'The Jackhammers,' I say.

'Justice for Dubek.'

'For fuck's sake, Cat, that's not even a name.'

In the end, we go with Minor Threat.

The sun is just at the horizon when Barry slows down in front of a wrought-iron gate deep in the rarefied woodsy Connecticut suburbs. No houses on either side, not for miles.

Barry sighs. 'I've only been here once before,' he says. 'We mostly left it alone. Obvious reasons.'

We keep driving and pull onto a sandy shoulder a half-mile past the entrance, then hike back as the sun through the trees touches the horizon. The evening's growing chilly. Barry brought a tweed overcoat and Cat brought whatever's in her bloodstream. I didn't bring anything but Prodigy.

When we get back to the gate, Cat doesn't even bother picking the lock, just rips it off the post.

'What's he thinking?' she says. 'You can get these at Home Depot.'

'I don't think it's a lair per se,' I say.

'Not even cameras,' she says. 'If Jack's here, he doesn't know we're coming. Or else he's fucking with us. Per se.'

I can just see the slanted roof from here, gables and chimneys standing up against the darkening sky and the first stars. It's another quarter of a mile uphill through the wooded grounds until we come out under the brighter sky, standing at the edge of a cleared space of immaculate lawns and neat hedges.

In the center is an enormous house, vaguely Georgian in style, three stories high, slate-gray. It looks quite new, one of the overinflated houses of the present-day rich, boxy with mismatched turrets. It's the ugliest lair Jack has ever had. The one shaped like a skull was better – and it wasn't even that good a likeness.

It's dark except for a single small third-floor window, a warm little square in the dark. We hang back among the trees. It's a clean cool night, and the moon overhead is waxing and nearly full.

'Nothing,' Cat says, giving the grounds a practiced glance.

'What does one normally do?' Barry says. 'Do you think we'll have to fight him? Physically?'

'I'm going to fight him,' Cat says.

'Is he terribly dangerous?'

'He usually has robots at this point,' I say. 'Or gun turrets, or lava. I guess he really thinks we can't find him.'

Barry frowns up at the house. 'It does leave one a bit wrong-footed.'

'You can handle yourself in a fight, can't you?' Cat says.

Barry shrugs. 'One hopes.'

Cat huffs at that and starts off across the lawn to the unlit house, black against the darkening sky, and she trots up the brick steps to the front door.

'Wait, wait, wait. You're going to ring the doorbell?' I call, too late.

'You think he doesn't know we're here?' she says, pressing the button. It gives a cute triple chime.

The windows show nothing but darkness. Barry tries the door. It isn't even locked.

The foyer is furnished in what might be called 'high-end hunting lodge' – fur rugs, flagstones, antler chandeliers, an enormous hearth. There are big solid chests of dark wood, nautical prints and memorabilia, no doubt bought by the lot in estate sales.

Cat cocks her head, listening or smelling, or whatever her other senses are. She puts a finger to her lips. We creep around the ground floor like nervous prospective home-buyers. The fireplace hasn't been used and the kitchen's empty. We climb the wooden stairs, where crooked hallways sprout multiple bedroom suites. I'm not used to rich people's houses, and quickly lose my way among rooms with striped wallpaper, four-poster beds, a decorator's faux New England quaintness.

A trap door lets us onto the roof. The three of us look out at the empty night where a chill wind is blowing across the winter-bare forest.

'It must be nice in the summer,' I say.

'This appears to have been a bust,' Barry says.

'Jack is a diabolical mastermind, after all. He probably saw this coming.'

'We should probably get going. It's a long drive, unless we want to spend the night here.' He kicks at the trap door. 'Do you suppose there's any wine in the cellar?'

Cat and I exchange a look.

'Barry?' I say.

'Yes?'

'When were you going to tell us there was a basement?'

'Ah! I see the significance. Obvious, really.'

The wooden stairs to the basement go down one flight, but then the style changes, a metal spiral staircase that takes us down two more stories. We're down as deep as the house is tall. There are bright lights beyond, and machinery, and conversation.

46

It's an enormous space, far bigger than it needs to be. Most of it is empty, save for a circle of work lights standing out from a Sargasso Sea of takeout containers, shipping boxes and bubble wrap and styrofoam.

There's a makeshift laboratory under the lights. Tables laid out with tools and racks of computers, and whiteboards covered in scrawled calculations to the edges. These are the most recognizable parts – the rest of it is a classic Doctor Optimal miscellany, a Rube Goldberg arrangement of machinery, computers, toys, musical instruments and what seems to be the front half of a motorcycle, all connected via a precarious chain of power strips to a framework holding the power gem I watched him steal.

The real masterwork is in the center: a circular scaffolding that rises gracefully above the forest of humming knick-knacks. At the top of the circle is the Time Core. It has been hammered back into its approximate shape, the cracks in its ruptured surface filled in with a silver metal.

Jack is up on a stepladder with his back to us, fiddling with one of five industrial robot arms arranged around the central sphere. Each carries a different tool – a laser welder, a canister that jets white vapor, and one of his tiny parabolic speakers. The other two end in claws gripping incongruous items: a metal staff topped with an obsidian sphere, and what might be a statue of a fish.

Stefanie looks up from the paperback she's reading, feet

up on a cheap folding chair. She stands and chucks away her cigarette.

'Well,' she says, 'you were right and I was wrong.'

Jack spares us only a quick glance.

'Take care of it,' he says. 'The schedule's tight but I can hack this together and it should work.'

She nods, and I don't know why but I get the strong sense they've slept together recently. I glance at Barry, who is gripping a gleaming, three-foot-long sword that cannot possibly have been on his person a moment ago. He stares back as if to say, *What? How much sense do your powers make?*

'It's over, Jack,' I say. 'Just step away from the machine and we'll figure this out.'

'Sorry,' Stef says. 'It's already figured out. You can stay and watch if you like.'

She doesn't flinch when a matte-black metal dart hits a hard, unseen surface a few inches from her left eye. There's a staticky pop and a strobed after-image of a translucent dome surrounding the two of them and their machinery. The dart tinkles away into the darkness.

'I hope that was a joke,' Stefanie says.

'It was,' Cat says. 'I'll be inside soon enough.'

'Don't be petty, just because throwing things isn't a power,' Stefanie says. 'Admit it, you all want a time machine. Your lives are as fucked up as mine, with your sad little jobs and your losing battles. I'm just the one who's going to fix mine.'

Jack has hopped off the ladder now and he looks us over, through the invisible field. The new Thinking Cap is flaring every few seconds.

'Hey, guys,' he says. 'Hey, Alex, sorry about before.'

'You should be. I thought we were friends.'

'You know, I actually did, too,' he says. 'And it was a fun

game for a while; you'd show up and we'd fight and I'd lose. I didn't really mind so much. Most of the time, I let you. But I think a friend would realize I was actually trying to do something important. I needed that day to come. I needed the Earth. Just for a little while.'

'But what about Jack Prime? What about your whole quest?'

'The aliens were scheduled to come on January 12, 2005, around 1 a.m. on a beach in Malibu. I waited all night for them, and when the sun came up, it was the worst moment of my life. That's when I really lost. If I'd had a real friend, I could have told them about it. But you're not a real friend, Alex. You only want to be friends when you're winning, and that's not much of a friend.'

'That's not true!'

I punch the force field. It sizzles and flashes but doesn't give way.

'Do that all you want,' he says. 'That's exactly why I built it. Welcome to losing.'

He walks back to his console. The robot arms start to perform a mechanical dance, the laser firing intermittently down at the metal sphere, and the wand leaves a looping trail in the air as the staff emits a wavering melody in a voice like a distant soprano's. As the arms move, they touch the five different gems in sequence, faster and faster. The sphere glows white, then shades to purple.

'Shit!' Jack viciously hits a button, and the arms slow to a halt. 'Stef, one of the spells is wandering again – with the Greek name?'

'Turn it off!' she says. 'Excuse me.' Stefanie climbs the ladder and unclasps the staff from the robot's hand. She seems to be giving it a talking to.

'Is this how it normally goes?' Barry says.

'No,' I say. 'There's normally a weakness.'

'We can't give up,' Cat says. 'The field's transparent to energy. Does anyone have a laser?'

'I don't even have pockets,' I say. 'What about a sonic attack? A hypnotic chant?'

'Stefanie's will is indomitable, if you hadn't noticed,' Barry says. 'How can she be helping him? Or even trust him? It doesn't make sense.'

'You're right. It doesn't.' I walk back to the force field's edge. 'Jack? Stef? I have a question.'

'Shoot,' Jack says, bent over a robot's access panel.

'The machine only takes one person, so which one of you is going back? Stef, do you really trust Jack to go back and spend years undermining the Summerdwell regime for you? Jack, is Stef really going to help Doctor Optimal conquer the world?'

'Jack is not stupid,' Stefanie says. 'Nor am I.'

'Fuck the timeline,' Jack says. 'Fuck the galaxy. Fuck Jack Prime. Stef's going. I'm staying here.'

He shuts the access panel and hits the button and the robot arms begin their weaving motion, more smoothly this time. The Time Core begins to glow with a soft white light, silhouetting the two of them. She takes his hand in hers, and kisses it.

'I will shortly be journeying back to the year 1990,' Stefanie says. 'I will arrive at my own sixteenth birthday party and announce myself. I'll be a fairy godmother of sorts to my younger self. Together we will take action, and by our combined might Queen Juniper will be destroyed. Young Stefanie will rule Summerdwell for the 1990s and long after that.'

'That makes no sense,' I say. 'Do I have to point out the temporal paradoxes involved?'

'Time is one thing here and quite another in Summerdwell,' Stefanie says. 'Especially for the one on the throne.'

'You actually think Jack is going to just let you climb into a working time machine and vanish?' I say. 'He's a diabolical mastermind. I should know.'

'Oh, go fuck yourself,' Jack says. 'I'm mastermind enough to figure out that the optimal timeline is probably impossible to achieve, and it wasn't even that optimal. Not when I got to marry Stefanie. Jack Prime never got that. Not even him.'

'Steffie, I don't understand,' Barry says. 'How long has this been going on?' He sheds a tear, but not pathetically, just like a poignant noble soul. Even getting dumped looks good on him.

'Only a few weeks,' she says.

'Are you in love with him?'

'Quite.'

'But don't you love me?' he says.

'Of course I did. You were my prince, darling. But I was never quite your princess. Maybe that will change, in the past.'

'I hate to cut this moment short,' Jack says, 'but the time machine is just about ready to go.'

The robotic arms' twisting and striking has slowed, and now the motion stops all together. The Time Core is whole and unmarred.

'So that's it?' I say.

'We win,' Jack says. 'You lose.'

'I'm so terribly sorry,' Barry says, 'but you don't.'

He raises his sword with an elegant flourish. The silver flashes and flares as he wheels round, gathering momentum, and brings it squarely down on the side of the delicate, invisible dome of the force field.

The unseen membrane spits and fizzes into view as the sorcerous blade strikes and penetrates by a few inches. Barry shifts his grip, then levers it in further. The field is fully visible now, jittering, flashing nearly opaque through red, orange, blue.

He twists the blade, snarling with the effort, and at last something in the swirl of Jack's machinery snaps with a squeal and a concussive boom. The field snaps entirely out of existence, leaving only a smell like burnt caramel.

The Time Core is getting brighter by the second. In moments it will reach full activation. There is that instant of stillness that comes when five people, each with their own profound grudge against the past, realize there is nothing standing between them and a fully functioning time machine.

47

We all agreed, way back, that a time machine is too powerful for anyone to have access to. There's too much of a temptation, too much risk of accidental or intentional harm to people or whole civilizations. No one respects that more than I do.

But there's one right in front of me and one of us is about to use it. Why not me? The most principled, the most steadfast, the best intentioned. The one who humbly bowed out when society told him to. Who meekly submitted, let them carve his face up, and hid for decades. The one who swore an oath and never forgot.

Except then I forgot everything when Chuck Dubek grabbed my arm. Sometimes that happens.

Can I do it, though? I'm starting in last place, not counting Barry who looks out of the running. Jack is the closest, Cat's the fastest, and Stefanie's already in motion. On the other hand, I have only forty feet to run and I'm just under 300 pounds of super-hardened, bewitchingly handsome flesh and bone. I run a one-minute mile, bench a semi; spells break on me; plasma won't burn me. Knives and bullets are like puffs of air. And maybe it's even true, after all this time, that I don't lose.

Cat moves first, just like always, airborne from a standing start, Prion Labs engineering going strong in its thirty-eighth year, but Jack's still the fastest draw in Silicon Valley. It only takes him one, two shots to clip her, a third to knock her to the concrete floor. He coolly checks on the time field and tweaks a dial. He could be through the field and gone, but evidently the Frog Prince will see his princess to her throne.

Stefanie's the second nearest, but I guess she doesn't trust Jack to cover her exit because she pivots into the air, hair adrift on a phantasmal breeze, and slings spun-sugar lines of force like a whip at my running form. I catch her smiling, as she used to. I jag to one side and it shatters concrete. On the second try she doesn't miss. It staggers me, but shatters into pink sparks.

Get in my way if you want, Princess, see what it gets you. See what it got Chuck Dubek.

'Forget them! Get to the machine!' Jack shouts.

He fires a round straight at my face. It's blindingly bright and actually stings a little. I have to stop a moment to shake it off, enough time for Cat to catch me around the waist, lift me off the floor and throw me hard to the ground. It doesn't hurt me, of course. I've seen her do this too many times, and guess right about where the follow-up is coming. I catch her ankle, squeeze hard, swing her into the floor. She doesn't make a sound.

Stefanie is singing a brief doleful verse and places one hand on the floor, fingers spread. The curse flows outward, staining and liquefying the concrete beneath it. I know the smell of her darkest magic, the necromantic underside to her sparkles and flower petals. When we were teenagers, she'd be sick for days after trying it. I nerve myself, leap, and clear it by inches. The smell is rotten.

Stefanie's terrifying, but she's only as fast as an athlete her age. I shoulder past her and now there's only Jack, silhouetted against the white-gold disk of the time field. He's holding the knife edged with dark gemstone, spins it nervously in his fingers, licks his lips. He shakes his head at me, circuitry strobing on his temples. *Stop, don't make me do this.*

Jack's not a fighter, though, and doesn't think much about acceptable risk. Cat would know I decided forty feet back that I was going to get cut and hope for the best. I run, ducking, arms out, hoping to catch his arm or just knock him aside. At this point I'm just an object in motion, and I have too much fucking momentum to do anything else. He sidesteps, graceful as a matador. The knife flashes out; I flail an arm trying to get in its way. I can feel the cut happen on the side of my neck.

My outstretched hand hits the time field and flashes out to cover my body. I can see, as through a shimmering gold curtain, the world beginning to slow down. Barry is kneeling, propped up by his sword; Stefanie is still in mid-flight, lips curled in a last, furious curse. Cat's body is twisting, following through from a motion I didn't see her make. Jack is sprawled forward after his swing, but his head is up and clocking my motion, cognitive hardware still racing up and down the decision trees in search of the winning scenario. Each outlined in gold fire, slowing down. All my old friends, all hating me together, forever. And me, selfish to the last.

Above me, the Time Core shines brighter and brighter, five jewels connecting to form a five-sided figure hovering overhead. Then I'm reeled backward through time, back to the year of the amulet, of the cave, back to high school, back to a time when all our worst mistakes were still ahead of us. Only now, perhaps they aren't.

48

The most expensive place you could eat in Hanover used to be a French restaurant named Michelle's. I arrive in the alleyway next to it. It's night-time on a summer evening. This must be the destination Stefanie chose for her entrance into the past.

Stefanie would be steadying her breathing, checking hair and make-up, getting into character for her grand entrance into her younger self's life. As it is, I'm clutching at my neck, feeling for the cut, trying to remember where the jugular is and whether there's any chance you can hold the blood in. After a few seconds, it's clear I'm not dying. Jack didn't hit the vein. I go back to being Alex; Prodigy doesn't belong in this world yet.

From the sidewalk, the restaurant is a warm, candle-lit space. The teenaged Stefanie is celebrating her sixteenth birthday inside. That must be her parents on either side of her, tall and slender and proud; uncles, aunts and cousins around the table. Everybody shushes everyone as the white-frosted cake comes out, its sixteen candles alight. She blows them all out.

She is as poised and beautiful as I remember, but the arrogance that used to terrify me looks poignant now, here at the very beginning of the story that will make her so hard and strange and such a power in the world. She unwraps a diamond bracelet and gasps, claps her hands over her mouth. She's smiling as if the promise of her future is a joy so great it is almost more than she can bear.

I leave before she can notice the middle-aged man loitering ominously outside her birthday party.

A copy of the *Boston Globe* gives the day as September 27, 1990 – a Thursday. It's 10 p.m. by the post office clock. There's no hurry now. I'm twenty-five years early for anywhere I'll ever have to be.

Old Hanover looks smaller and less intimidating. Was this place really the center of my universe? Main Street is lined with the little craft shops long since vanished in my time. The high school is still standing. The four of us will be in school tomorrow, with our powers, our secrets, our boundless potential intact. The future is ours to lose, and we will lose it.

I breathe the fragrant air of a bygone late summer evening and wander sidewalks sparkling clean in the moonlight, past houses bought by migrant aerospace engineers drawn here by overblown Department of Defense budgets. All that money flowing out of a Cold War dream-logic makes the town itself feel like a dream. The clean beautiful houses have an unreal quality. Unreal houses, unreal schools. Unreal, like a planetary radar array, like a suburban fairy princess, or a bigger genius boy, like little girl super-soldiers underground. Like me, a middle-aged man from the future.

As I move away from downtown, the houses get smaller and smaller. It's past midnight when I reach the yellow two-story colonial with the tiny yard in front with its one tree and neglected tire swing. Pine needles have silted up the roof, where they'll stay until my mother climbs the rickety ladder from the garage and clears them off.

We never locked the doors in those days. I stand in the foyer where we hung our coats and kicked off our shoes, sniffing the air, after-dinner smells, and the perfume of mom's scented candles. I'd forgotten the map on the wall, torn at one corner, the panoramic photo of Roman ruins.

I climb the stairs, mindful of how easily sound travels in our flimsy house. The fact that it's Stefanie's birthday means Alex went into the Cave of Wonders just three days ago. He's gone to bed with the amulet clutched to his chest, knowing himself sacred to a pure and thankless cause. This is as true a king as I'll ever be.

You're the real Prodigy, I want to tell him. *You'll do great things, I promise you.* I want to tell him everything, every mistake, every stupid wrong turn.

But I know, too, that he's made of the same stuff as I am. He'll keep faith for less than a year after tonight, and cripple three kids. He'll make all the mistakes I made, or else come up with new ones. Giving him more advantages won't change who he is.

Think of the others. Stefanie will be home by now, writing in her diary or memorizing the names and titles of nobility who will one day owe her fealty. Cat must be lying awake in her makeshift bed in the woods, reading a Tom Clancy novel, or perhaps prizefighting under the lights in a Back Bay warehouse. Jack is probably up late chatting on a hacker bulletin board, still thinking he's got the Feds beaten, boasting and dropping the hints that will lead them right to his door.

Not kings or queens, not any of us. Just ill-made stewards of a crooked timeline. I steal a flashlight from the drawer in the kitchen, and an envelope. I write 'To Shirley', slip the three diamonds inside, and leave it in the mailbox. *Bye, Mom. Have a good future.*

There's no sign of any momentous occasion, just a quiet suburban street under a bright moon, and a strip of forest.

It's all gone, in my time. Hanover's real estate values skyrocketed in 2002, and most of the houses in my neighborhood were sold to plastic surgeons and patent lawyers who tore down the cheap 1940s homes to build lofty overinflated mansions. Then in 2008, the adjacent forestland sold for millions and became a housing development called Greenwich Farms.

When it changed, I came back every few weeks to watch what happened. They rooted out the trees and boulders, and bulldozers scraped the ground flat. They cleared the boulders put there forty thousand years ago by the Ice Age glaciers that swept down to cover the hills, forests and the cabin I shared with Cat. With the trees gone, owls swooped to catch displaced mice and chipmunks. In a few months, the first wooden frames began to appear along neatly laid-out streets. No one ever reported finding anything unusual in the ground – not a single statue or throne or burnt-out torch.

But we're back in 1990 now, and there's still a dark and airy silence under the pines. I kick the pine needles aside and find the grating set flush with the dirt. The iron rungs set in the shaft are beginning to rust but are still strong, though the torches have all gone out.

The passageway floor slopes easily downhill past all the carvings, statues, the tombs, all the window dressing for our great event. Now that I'm paying attention, I can marvel at how elaborate this all was.

The beam of the flashlight picks up places where the stone is settling, crumbling. Only three nights after my visit, a few statues have lost their features entirely. The whole complex gives the impression of accelerated decay, as if relaxing back into the dirt, bereft of its sustaining enchantment. The flashlight catches a little spark of tarnished gold on the throne steps. A cufflink, cool to the touch. I run my thumb over the embossed Firebird.

When I find the throne room, the details have crumbled

but the great stone seat and the vaulted ceiling retain their majesty. It's been three days since I left, surely the all-knowing Wizard stuck around? Usually for one of my triumphs there's a cheering crowd, sometimes confetti, at least a mayor or local chief, or whatever the relevant aliens have. All is quiet. No lights, no fanfare, no welcoming committee. No wizard.

'Mr Ferris? Are you here?'

I pan the flashlight here and there, in case he's lurking ominously in the shadows.

'Mr Ferris? Wizard? It's Alex. Grown-up Alex. I've come back from the future. I have so much to tell you.'

I listen but only hear echoes and the distant sound of running water.

'I have questions.'

Is he really not anywhere? Crouched behind the throne? Clinging bat-like to the ceiling? Hovering, invisible?

Come on out, you old rascal. Don't you at least want to know how you died?

There are more passages leading out of this place. Maybe he's back there somewhere?

I follow the sound of running water down one of the passages, sloping gently downwards. Carved walls give way to natural stone. The air becomes chill and damp, and the sound builds to a roar until the passage lets out onto the rocky shore of an underground river, wide and swift and cold.

It looks ancient, so old it could be a remnant of the nameless river Cat and I lived beside in our little house during the Pleistocene. I imagine the river digging its way deeper into the New England bedrock as the cliffs closed over it, but always it was here. There's even a little pile of stones, like the cairn I built for Prodigy's old costume. We had a little goodbye ceremony, drank some of the terrible beer we brewed, and laughed and sang eighties pop songs. As Prodigy I belted 'Take on Me' into the primeval wilderness. Not counting any Neanderthal chieftains out there, we were rulers of the world. Kings.

Maybe I should be a king now, why not? No Wizard to stop me. A man with the might of Hercules and the beauty of Adonis, armed with a knowledge of the future – what couldn't I accomplish? I could be what Jack wanted to be. I could rule this land, easy as picking a shiny quarter off the sidewalk.

Prodigy the First, strong and wise. In some ways it's the logical endgame. Why fight crimes piecemeal if I can take over and rule it all? Was that what the Wizard was hinting at all along? Except what gave me, Prodigy, the moral authority to go around deciding who to punch? I had all the power but I never earned it, never suffered for it. I was never strapped to an operating table like Cat, or doomed like Jack to fight all my life to reach an impossible standard, against infinite odds.

I never had a right to it. I knew it from the first day.

The amulet feels as thin as ever, the little scrap of metal that ruled my life for decades. I could throw it away right now, out over the black water, and let it be gone forever from my life.

I can only picture it being washed away by the river's powerful current, tumbling downstream toward the cold Atlantic, where it comes to rest, waiting for its rightful inheritor who would one day claim it, years or centuries from now. A true king or queen, wise and pure and unforgiving.

I slip the chain back around my neck, like I always have before. There's a nagging sense that maybe there's something good left to do; or else I just don't have the balls to chuck it. I can always throw it away tomorrow.

*

It's still night outside when I emerge. I sit down on the curb in the moonlight and close my eyes. It's too much, all at once. What will I do tomorrow, in 1990? Buy stocks? I'll need money first. I'll need clothes, I need to get a job. I don't even have a place to sleep.

I look up at the sound of a worn sneaker-tread scraping asphalt.

'Hey, dummy.' Jack is standing, backlit by a time portal that looks into a brightly lit room.

It's my Jack, the one I left behind in 2015. He's not in uniform now, just baggy corduroys and a T-shirt.

I stand up too fast. I'm so tired I almost fall into him. I get my fists up anyway. Time to fight.

'Raeclun.'

'Calm down,' Jack says. 'I came to take you back. That's all.'

'Really? Are you lying?'

He sighs. 'I'm not lying. Ten seconds left. Move your ass.'

I hesitate one more second. I could still stay here and try to fix things. Tell Young Alex to wait for the right moment. Warn Jack about the Feds. Tell Stefanie to stay straight and keep her grades up, and help Cat to fit in better. Beyond that, we'd never meet, never be friends, pass each other in the halls without a second glance.

What then? Alex might turn out a better hero. Or maybe Jack's right, and he'd wind up a sad mediocrity. Cat will still be Cat, and that will never change. Maybe Jack will never need to turn villain. Stefanie will keep to her clique and never be friends with weirdos like us. Maybe it will be better, but I think we'll still be us, still make mistakes. At forty, we'll just have a different bunch of regrets.

Jack knows all of this, much better than I do. The Thinking Cap must have run a hundred thousand variant timelines. He's seen it.

'Would you come on, already? I'm using an eighth of the world's plutonium here,' he says. 'Plus, I got snacks.'

Where else am I to go? I step into the time field. Just as it takes hold, I hear a noise behind me like an ancient devil clearing his throat, the unmistakable roar of a Pontiac Firebird's V8 engine, then the screech as it peels out and takes off for good.

49

The time field sputters and dies, a fading sun behind us. In its dying light I see Jack, and the old laboratory. A few of the machines are humming now, pipes and tubes in evil jukebox curves. It smells like he's been living here a while.

He switches on the light. He looks pale and tired. His forty-year-old face is leaner, the incipient jowls less in evidence. Enormous whiteboards stand at odd angles, covered in angry-looking equations.

We don't move.

'Prodigy,' he says. 'Welcome back.'

'Doctor Optimal,' I say. 'How long has it been, in this timeline?'

'It took a week. The math was easier this time.'

'Six hours for me,' I say.

'I know that.'

Neither of us moves. He doesn't have anything in his hands, but that doesn't mean he's not armed. This whole place could be booby-trapped. He could be a robot.

'Is it different?' he asks, at last.

'What?'

'The present. Did you change anything? Do I look different?'

'You look like somebody punched you in the face a week ago,' I say. 'Why did you bring me back? You could have left me there. One less obstacle to your evil plans.'

'Couldn't have you rampaging through the past, manipulating the timeline to your own fatuous ends. And it's only twenty-five years. In the end you'd still be here, only now you'd be sixty-six.'

'Gross.'

'Yeah. Better to loop it,' he says. 'So, I'm making omelets. In the kitchen.'

When did I eat last? My eyes flick to the darkness beyond the laboratory door, then back to him.

'Okay. You go first.'

The house all looks the same. Same framed photos, same headlines. Same history, as far as I can tell. Even smells the same.

In the kitchen, Jack rattles around in the pantry and dumps a carton of eggs, vegetables. A bottle of white wine from the wine fridge I'd forgotten we bought. He pours two glasses, then gets back to breaking eggs and chopping things up.

'Are we going to fight?' he says. 'Because I don't have my stuff with me.'

'I don't know yet.'

'Have a seat already. Have some wine.' He points to a bar stool at the counter.

Was that always there? It looks suspiciously modern.

'I'll stand.'

'You think it's a trap?'

'I know what you can do with a chair.'

'What exactly are you imagining?'

'Well, something objectionable.' I sit, anyway. 'What happened to your eye?'

'Cat tagged me right at the end of things. Didn't even apologize,' he says. 'You like peppers in it, right?'

'I'm not hungry. Is anybody else here?'

'Stefanie went back west. Barry got a room at the Charles. He was crying the whole way back. That was a long fucking drive.' He starts whisking the eggs.

'Where's Cat?'

'She took off like always,' he says, not looking up.

He starts dumping everything in a pan. It sizzles and smells amazing.

'She just left after all that? What about the battle?'

'After you left, it all kind of petered out. The three of us were mostly just pissed at you. Cat says she's going to train up some of these teens the government goes after. Form a new team and then set some shit on fire. She says she's going to call you. Someday.'

'What about Sinistro?'

'Who knows? The time stream's not exactly virgin snow anymore, he's probably got a shot at getting back in it. Have some of this wine at least, now that I opened it. It's late, I gotta crash soon.'

'So where are you staying?' I ask.

'In my room,' he answers over his shoulder.

'You can't live here. I live here.'

'So what?'

'You can't live here, you betrayed us. You are banished from Newcomers Mansion! Henceforth!'

'Dude, it's really late.'

He plops half the omelet on a plate. It smells good. I give in and try the wine. It's chilled and apple-tinged and incredibly good. He starts in on his omelet.

'You really don't want half of this?' he says. 'I'm not eating all of it.'

'What's in it?'

'Cheese, tomato, peppers. Other stuff.'

'What stuff?'

'Just eat it. Look, I'm eating it. Yum, yum. Totally not evil science.'

'Fine.' I gingerly take a forkful.

'Ha! I win again,' he says.

It's good late-night food, salty, oily. Jack really does know how to cook. We eat silently at opposite ends of the kitchen island. The silence stretches on. I'm trying to remember all the things we're fighting about now.

'You kicked me in the stomach,' I say.

'It was a weird day. And you're scary as shit. And I gave you like fifty thousand dollars in diamonds. I hope you kept it.'

'It went to a good cause.'

'Weenie.'

'Don't change the subject.'

'Stefanie's pregnant,' he says. He looks at me, waiting for a reaction, a challenge or approval.

'You're kidding.'

'She says it's a girl.'

'Oh my god. That's great,' I say. 'Are you getting married again?'

I can see he's trying not to show how happy he is.

'I don't know. We're doing long-distance for a while. A lot went down while we were rebuilding that time machine.'

'Congratulations,' I say. I don't know what else there is to say, so I clink glasses with him.

'Thanks.'

'So you were really going to make her queen? If you could?'

'Still am, maybe. Next time she goes up against Juniper, she's going to have an evil genius backing her.'

'But wait, what about the timeline? How are you going to be Jack Prime and lead the galactic armada?'

'You know, maybe I don't have to do everything just to get those aliens' attention. They can come talk to me if they want. Or else they can solve their own problems for once in the history of their dumbass cosmic civilization,' he says. 'I told you before. She's the one.'

'Wow. Congratulations. I mean it. This is unbelievable.'

'Thanks,' he says. 'Cat said you got with Meg finally. Speaking of unbelievable. What's happening with that?'

'I don't know. I like her. We might be doomed to destroy each other,' I say.

'Yeesh. Sounds hot, though,' he says. 'Maybe we're not so different, you and I.'

'We're totally different.'

'Fine. I still live here, though.'

'Fine. So do I,' I say. 'Is there any more wine?'

'Plenty.' He pours me another glass.

'So, you want to tell me about your evil plans, or anything?'

'Yeah. I do.'

50

Six weeks later, in the darkened lobby of the Banque Nationale in Paris, a shadowy figure threads a ribbon of darkforce through a hole in the main vault door. A stack of gold ingots is accumulating on the floor beside her. I drop the long two floors from the skylight to land, almost gracefully, on the marble floor.

'Hi, Meg,' I say.

Meg steps into the light. She's in the old costume. Her profile in moonlight looks more gargoylish than last time, as if the changes are accelerating in her as the clock winds down.

'You took your time. You've been in town for two days already. The gem told me.'

'It would have been easier if you just called. I spent a lot of time with a police scanner and a French phrase book.'

'Well, you found me,' she says. 'Good job.'

The darkforce swirls in strands around her body. The amulet thrums against my chest in response. *You know what needs to happen.*

'What are you doing?' I ask.

'Blacklight is having her last fling. It's been twenty-five years. If I'm going to lose these powers, I'm going to put them to good use first.'

'What happened to Karen Cena?'

'She's taking a leave of absence. Personal business.'

'Rick Tower is, too.' My petition for reinstatement is under review, as is my tenure application, but at this point, I don't even know if I'm Alex Beekman, or Rick Tower or Prodigy – or some new as-yet-unnamed individual.

'How much time is left?' I say.

'With the time difference, I have until about five this morning to destroy you or face whatever the consequences are.'

A scorpion-tail darkforce tendril flicks out in an exploratory stab. I step to one side and it cracks a tile.

'I'm here to help.'

'There's only one way you can help.'

I duck the knife edge of a limb of darkforce, thick as a tree trunk, and watch it spray chips from a marble column. I dive-roll, come up with a brass stanchion from a velvet divider. We fence a few moments, the metal singing, before she snatches it and tosses it into the shadows.

'You should get out of here,' she says.

'Didn't you always wonder who would win?'

'Not really. You never put up much of a fight.'

A black baseball bat flows smoothly into her right hand. It fans the air and I backpedal out of range. She swings again and I lunge, hoping to close the distance first. She's ready, grip high on the bat's handle, cocked for a fast swing that buzzes past my nose.

I spin into a fancy backhanded strike that she catches on the bat's handle, then she brings it back into line with a fluid swoop. She's trained since we last fought.

Kung fu, maybe, with sword techniques mixed in?

Slick moves, but fighting is second nature to Prodigy. I fake a punch and she checks her swing just enough that I can grab the bat. The darkforce writhes in my grip, as mutable as thought, and now I'm holding a viper poised to strike at my jugular. I yank it forward by the neck and it dissolves into vapor.

Blue and white lights flicker across the lobby, refracted

through the glass revolving door. Shouts in unintelligible French filter through.

She looks over my shoulder and straight into a spotlight. They're on the roof. Blinded, she throws up a shield just in time to meet a knockout punch. The shield holds, its glassy surface starred with white fracture lines. She turns and runs for the rear exit, scattering darkforce spikes across the floor behind her. I follow carefully as flashlights paint the walls.

In the Avenue Marceau I spin in place until a two-tone whistle sounds from above. There she is, seated atop the bank's neoclassical facade, silhouetted against the pallid urban sky.

'Keep up,' she calls.

One leap takes me high enough to grab the cornice, and I swing myself easily onto the roof. It's broad and flat, and Paris rings us like an arena crowd.

We circle. She's got a whip of darkforce raised high, floating on the air, quivering. It strikes, slapping the tarry surface where I just stood.

A chop of the hand shatters the darkforce whip, and I reach for her wrist, but she's off sliding down a darkforce ramp to the next roof. I leap after her, then a darkforce fist to the face spins me around and I fall to my knees. She thinks it's finished but I spring at her. She squeaks and throws up a darkforce grating that I strain at until it breaks.

I can hear a helicopter buzzing overhead but I don't dare take my eyes off of her. She stares back, panting, a thin blade held en garde. My hands are numb from the pain and I've been cut in half a dozen places. She's got a nasty scrape up one leg; the blood's trickling into her boot.

The first one to break concentration is going to lose this thing.

'This sucks,' I say.

'You can quit anytime.'

'Wait,' I say. 'What if we get a drink?'

The sirens are getting louder again.

'Okay,' she says. 'But just one.'

We buy stupid tourist sweatshirts and hats, then try the first stupid tourist bar we see. It's serving cheap shots for the American crowd, and then it turns out to be more than one drink, and then it's more than one bar. Then there's a taxi ride, and a hotel elevator.

Sometime afterwards, Meg is lying face down on the bare fitted sheet of the bed in another expensive hotel room.

The top sheet and comforter are on the floor. Bits of Blacklight's costume are on the floor, too, leather boots sprawled. Everything smells of her cigarettes and the powdery scent she wears.

I sit next to her on the bed, my bare back against her shoulder. I still don't know what to call myself, but for once I feel like I'm in the right place.

She props herself on her elbows.

'This is a nice room,' she says.

'It's Jack's money.'

'How long are you staying?'

'A couple of days, maybe. I could stay longer. If you want.'

I feel her shrug against me.

'I guess it doesn't matter,' she says. 'Given everything.'

'Of course it does.'

I want to touch her shoulder but she pulls away.

'It's just a fling,' she says. 'You're not going to live here.'

I don't say anything because I can't imagine living anywhere. I'm certainly not supposed to be in France.

'Sorry.'

'It's fine. Sinistro never moved here, either. Boys are like that.'

'Maybe you should go, then.'

She heaves herself off the pillow, finds a T-shirt and a pair of boxers and walks to the high windows. We're on the top floor. The waxing moon is high and small and radiant. We can lean out and see the steeply tilted slate roof on either side, and the mazy Paris streets.

'Are you going?' I say.

'Don't sulk,' she says. 'It's a witches' moon.'

'So?'

'Did I tell you I can fly?'

She puts one foot on the low windowsill.

'With the darkforce?' I say.

'I've been working on it. Just recently, since the power's gotten stronger. Come on, I bet I can take us both. Let's try it.'

'You can't be serious.'

'I'm not going to drop you. You've been a superhero for twenty-five years and you never even flew. Just admit you want to.'

She steps up on the sill, puts one foot out and tests the air, then gingerly steps out into the night air where she floats easily, borne up by a thin dusky cloud of force.

'This isn't going to solve anything,' I say.

'Forget about us for a second. Let's fly.'

I take her hand. She tugs at me and I come away from the floor, drifting. My legs churn for balance for a second, before I relax and realize how easy it is. We rise through the air together.

'It's working,' she says, grinning wildly. She loosens her grip, gradually, but I'm still floating alongside her, borne up over the rooftops.

Five stories up, the night air is cool and clean. It's past two in the morning and the Avenue Kléber is quiet and empty below us. We drift along, a little bit faster, down a side street to the broad, floodlit corridor of the Champs-Élysées. One of a pair of late-wandering revelers looks up, laughs and points us out to her friend.

'I think this is against the law,' I say.

'Oh, who cares?' she says. 'It's probably our last night. Let's see Paris.'

She's right. As we speed up and race east and southward toward the river, it gets harder to process being confused or heartsick. We pass over the Grand Palais and the witches' moon is splashing in the Seine, chasing after us. Past the Île de la Cité and then north over Le Marais. Below us people are coming out of late-night clubs, getting into cabs. Crowds in rooftop bars spot us and wave. Everybody seems thrilled, like we're making their night.

We rise, past hotel windows, up and up, our pale forms reflected in a glass-fronted office building. I glimpse a man in an untidy suit at his desk, working either late or early, then we're up above even the highest buildings.

A police helicopter turns and banks, trying to follow us, but it's much too slow. We go higher still, and faster.

The flat trail of the Seine is ridged with silver-white; the Eiffel Tower's ironwork is lit blue and red. The pale disks of the city's seven traffic circles gleam. Far off to our left there's a cluster of dark figures flying, silhouetted against the lit streets below. Paris looks beautiful and ancient and infinitely tired. We turn north, fly over housing blocks and suburban street lights and supermarkets. I look back to see Sacré-Coeur shining, pale and vigilant, on the heights of Montmartre. Goodbye city, goodbye everything.

We drop low to skim over fields and forests. Meg whoops as we brush the treetops, side by side. Rain spatters over us, the wind dries us again. Higher now, over dark realms of forest divided by the luminous threads of highways.

Faster and faster. The forests beneath us are formless and dark and old. Patches of mist collect in the hollows. It feels like we could go all the way to London, all the way to the North Pole, or the stars. Like Peter Pan. I think of Cat and her house in the woods and smile, and Meg smiles back.

'Where are we going?' I yell.

'Who cares? Look at the moon now. Isn't it amazing?'

She's right. I've never seen it so broad and clear, gushing light, robed in clouds, gray and white in seas and continents. Venus is out now, and Mars, and the stars are bright and singing as we skim along, swooping and diving. We plunge into the clouds again, thicker this time, duck under into the rain. It's so ridiculous I haven't done this before, just to fly. I carried that weight for so long.

'I can't believe I almost missed this,' I say.

'I'm sorry I lied.'

'It's okay. Wait, what part was the lie?'

'The one about not dropping you.'

I yelp and clap my hand to the amulet as gravity sucks me under.

I really do hate falling. Apart from the indignity, it shows up my core weakness. Prodigy's only really useful when the solution is to apply absurd amounts of force to a nearby solid object. Meg's face is lost in the dark, and the wind of my falling rises from a whisper to a roar in my ears. I kick and thrash for a second, then just give up.

I've fallen this far before but never, not to make excuses, in such a state of emotional vulnerability.

The moon overhead dissolves into the cloud cover, and the night-gray fields below are becoming ominously real, before I even remember what the word is, and say it. The impact is a shock but there's no pain, and only the briefest disorientation. I'm spread-eagled, embedded in the wet ground, smelling hay, manure, raw earth.

'Get up,' Meg says.

'I thought we were having a nice evening. Together.'

'Poor unhappy Alex,' she says. 'Put up your fists.'

I lever myself out of the shallow crater and square up to her. She flourishes a black fencing foil. Her eyes are bright and the darkforce is at its peak, its hour come round at last.

I circle, pawing for a wrist, but she keeps her distance. She's got all the reach she needs to keep me at bay and pick me to pieces. But then, I only need to get past her guard once, and she'll be as helpless as Chuck Dubek ever was.

I really do feel like winning now.

I swat the foil aside, crowding her, but my fists hit nothing but hastily formed shields. The bat is back and knocks me sprawling, but I pop back up. My forearms feel like one solid bruise, and I may have busted a finger. Breathing hurts, like what they tell me a broken rib feels like – but I wouldn't know, would I? Prodigy's ribs don't break, not until now.

It hurts but there's a grim satisfaction in knowing Prodigy's getting his pretty hair mussed, finally. For once, he's not a vanity project, not a trophy or a fancy sports car to be taken out and shown off and put away. He's taking his lumps, like the rest of us.

She brings back the foil and I snap it, ignoring the searing shock to my hands. I actually think I can win this. In the intimacy of the fight, any trace of weakness will come out eventually, and it's obvious Meg can't do this forever. The darkforce's supply of baseball bats, chainsaws and cartoon boxing-gloves is limitless, but the woman wielding them is only human. This pace is exhausting her forty-year-old body.

She knows it, too. She's getting reckless, like a boxer fading in the final rounds, but keeps swinging for that knockout.

The whip has grown thorns now. It re-forms each time I break it, thrashing, hydra-headed, kicking up earth and grass each time it misses.

It snakes out again and I reach out to bat away the tip, and it grows a three-cornered spike that juts right through the back of my hand. Shit. The pain hits all, and for a moment I literally can't think of anything else.

Then I see a flash and stop thinking entirely.

'Look who's awake,' Meg says. The purple gem is humming, enjoying the moment.

'Wait, did I lose? Seriously?'

'One of us had to.'

'Yeah, but . . .'

My ears are ringing, my face is numb, missing what must be a few minutes of memory. Flat on my back in a field in France, and I've probably ruined another nose. There's a collar of pure darkforce around my neck, lined with needles pointed inward. I can feel the pulse of my heartbeat against them.

Meg stands over me, looking pretty thrashed herself. Her darkforce armor is gleaming, though, and her eyes shine with their own light.

I fucking lost, and the foundation of my universe is skewed.

I mean, I lose lots of things: court cases, odd socks, my bearings. I've been tricked, trapped, wrong-footed, but I don't lose fights – not a stand-up fight like this one, toe to toe, the fight of my life. I still can't believe it.

'What now?' I ask.

'First of all, I believe this is now mine.' She lifts the amulet from my neck.

'Hey!'

'Tough luck, loser,' she says, and contemplates her prize. 'It's thin. I could snap it in two.'

In her long fingers it does look flimsy, like a cheap bit of tin. It looks like the cheap souvenir it always was.

She could do it, and a part of me feels a perverse relief in it. She'd be doing what I couldn't. Why not be rid of Prodigy, that fatuous do-gooder I turn into? What did I even make out of Prodigy? A lie from the start, a false hero, and all those fine promises in rags.

'Do your worst, villain.'

'Not so fast,' she says. 'I'm gloating. Get up, would you? Or at least on your knees.'

'Come on.'

'I bet you did it for Jack. What did he use to say at times like this? You know, when you were all tied up, the doomsday machine counting down? You heard it often enough.'

'Well,' I say. 'He'd start with a rant about a world that never respected him. That's about ten minutes. And he'd do the gloating about how he'd finally beaten me.'

'You're my oldest enemy and you are beaten. You went down like a used rag. You should have seen it.'

'Okay, okay.'

'What else?' she says.

'Well, he'd start to digress, getting into Ayn Rand books, and what's wrong with the Trilateral Commission.'

'We can skip that bit.'

'Oh, and then how he was going to conquer the world, obviously.'

'Got it. So now the world can at last be mine. Except I don't actually want to run it, that seems like a hassle, I just want to enjoy the good parts.'

'This isn't how Jack does it at all.'

'You know, I used to think Mr Ferris should have chosen

me, but now I think he was probably right to pick a rule-following nerd like you. I would have hated it. I don't even think I got a bad bargain. I thought this whole time I made a pact with the devil. My whole body looked like a curse. I didn't understand it until now. They saw me. I just didn't want to stay home anymore. I told them I wanted to be free and that's what they wanted for me anyway.'

She stops, rain pattering down around us.

'I'm glad you got what you wanted,' I say, softly. I'm done with the sarcasm. 'Break it, if it'll do you or the gem-thing any good.'

She looks down at the soft metal disk, turns it over in her hands for a while.

'Nah. You asked for it in the first place, and he gave it to you and it's yours. Take it,' she says, and just in that moment her voice isn't quite her own. There's a ripple of thunder in it, a long-remembered power discharged, an ancient pact made or undone. She tosses it back to me.

'Thanks. I guess?'

'Figure it out later. Come on, tough guy. Let's go home.'

She takes my hand, and we lift from the ground. It's true, we've been up late, just like the night she left me in the cell, pierced with joy and regret. I felt like a fool then and didn't sleep for a moment. Like those late nights staying up with Jack on our stupid patrols, trudging along the frozen sidewalks of Hanover till three in the morning. Like those very first nights after Michael Ferris gave me the amulet, and I felt so full with the joy of my new purpose I couldn't sleep. I thought I'd burst at any moment. I didn't even know what it was, back then, only a poorly defined adventure in a nameless cause.

We fly upward through the clouds, toward the fading moon in its last hour, higher and higher. From up here I can see everything; the faint path of the Milky Way, all but gone, and all the way across the English Channel to Dover. I can see that invisible thread leading back to home, and high school, running out last. I can even see Prodigy for what he is, an ill-made knight standing his long vigil in the darkness. Dawn is breaking in the east and, up ahead, the lights of Paris.

Acknowledgements

First and foremost, thanks to my agent Luke Janklow and to Rowland White, editor at Penguin Random House UK, for their talent and perseverance in bringing this book to print in its absolute best form.

Fight Me was written over almost a decade, and had the benefit of many readers and editors, including:

Libby Boland
meriko borogove
The Center for Fiction
The Corporation of Yaddo
Claire Dippel
Riana Dixon
Lara Ewen
Carrie Frye
Judith Grossman
Lev Grossman
Shan Morley Jones
Tanya Kalmanovitch
Jenifer Leigh
Catherine McCarthy
Barbara McClay
Puloma Mukherjee
Clare Parker
Helly Schtevie
Alanna Schubach
Sean Stewart
Ashley Strosnider
Greg Travis

He just wanted a decent book to read ...

Not too much to ask, is it? It was in 1935 when Allen Lane, Managing Director of Bodley Head Publishers, stood on a platform at Exeter railway station looking for something good to read on his journey back to London. His choice was limited to popular magazines and poor-quality paperbacks – the same choice faced every day by the vast majority of readers, few of whom could afford hardbacks. Lane's disappointment and subsequent anger at the range of books generally available led him to found a company – and change the world.

'We believed in the existence in this country of a vast reading public for intelligent books at a low price, and staked everything on it'
Sir Allen Lane, 1902–1970, founder of Penguin Books

The quality paperback had arrived – and not just in bookshops. Lane was adamant that his Penguins should appear in chain stores and tobacconists, and should cost no more than a packet of cigarettes.

Reading habits (and cigarette prices) have changed since 1935, but Penguin still believes in publishing the best books for everybody to enjoy. We still believe that good design costs no more than bad design, and we still believe that quality books published passionately and responsibly make the world a better place.

So wherever you see the little bird – whether it's on a piece of prize-winning literary fiction or a celebrity autobiography, political tour de force or historical masterpiece, a serial-killer thriller, reference book, world classic or a piece of pure escapism – you can bet that it represents the very best that the genre has to offer.

Whatever you like to read – trust Penguin.

read more
www.penguin.co.uk